'Confirms Catherine Kirw[...] [...]
Irish crime fiction. Her deviously plotted mystery,
filled with vivid characters, distinctive dialogue and
a detailed and loving portrait of the "real capital of
Ireland" is captivating' *Irish Independent*

'*Cruel Deeds* has a vividly drawn sense of place, an
amused eye for character, class and all manner of
Corkishness and, above all, in Finn a winning, vital
lead character; her vibrant energy and good humour
animates and drives the action at break-neck pace.
Hugely enjoyable' *Irish Times*

'With intricate plotting, relatable characters, and a
thrilling story, *Cruel Deeds* has all the ingredients needed
for a page turning read' Patricia Gibney

'Atmospheric and intriguing with a brilliantly
relatable heroine and an explosive, gripping
conclusion, nothing in *Cruel Deeds* is
quite as it seems' Sam Blake

'A pacy tale that sweeps the reader along through
the murky waters of the legal world in this layered,
Leeside thriller' Siobhán MacDonald

'Pacy, gripping and atmospheric, with a brilliant
Cork setting, *Cruel Deeds* is a cracking read!'
Andrea Carter

'Chock full of secrets and with a compelling plot, *Cruel
Deeds* will keep you glued to the pages!' Lesley Kara

Catherine Kirwan grew up on a farm in the parish of Fews, County Waterford. She studied law at UCC and lives in Cork where she works as a solicitor.

PREVIOUSLY BY CATHERINE KIRWAN
Darkest Truth

CATHERINE KIRWAN

CRUEL DEEDS

HACHETTE
BOOKS
IRELAND

First published in Ireland in 2022 by HACHETTE BOOKS IRELAND
First published in paperback in 2023

1

Cataloguing in Publication Data is available from the British Library

ISBN 9781529381412

Typeset in Bembo Book MT Std by Bookends Publishing Services, Dublin.
Printed and bound in Great Britain by Clays Ltd, Elcograf S.p.A.

Hachette Books Ireland policy is to use papers that are natural, renewable
and recyclable products and made from wood grown in sustainable forests.
The logging and manufacturing processes are expected to conform to the
environmental regulations of the country of origin.

Hachette Books Ireland
8 Castlecourt Centre
Castleknock
Dublin 15, Ireland

A division of Hachette UK Ltd
Carmelite House, 50 Victoria Embankment, London EC4Y 0DZ

www.hachettebooksireland.ie

For Marcia and Neil

In the end, you were left with no choice.

It had to be then.

It had to be there.

And it worked out for the best. You knew that when you heard her car stop so close to where you were hiding. The clunk of the locks when she pressed the key fob. The jangle of keys when she tripped past without seeing you.

When you were sure that you were the only one listening.

The only one watching.

She called out your name.

Impatient when she got no reply. Abrasive.

In her final seconds, giving you the strength you needed; the certainty that what you were doing was right.

She pushed the door open fully and walked towards the light. Candlelight. Warm. Cosy.

You congratulated yourself on that little touch, afterwards.

But the instant her toe crossed the threshold, you were all action. Every cell and sinew focused on the task in hand. Silently, you moved behind her. Matched her step for step.

Your quarry.

Your prey.

And you raised your arms high above her head.

Double grip.

And no scream escaped her. No cry.

Only an involuntary exhalation of breath.

Her dying.

Later, they called it a frenzied attack, and that bothered you because it was so far from the truth.

Because you'd planned it down to the last detail.

Because as soon as it was done, you stopped.

Stood.

Took the bundle of baby wipes from your pocket and rubbed the biological evidence from your face and the cheap hooded rain jacket and the waterproof trousers and the rubber boots and the latex gloves. All brand new. All disposable. Then you cleaned the sharpened claw-hammer, and put it and the soiled baby wipes into the black plastic bag and stepped backwards out the door.

You checked carefully for footprints and any other traces you might have left.

There were none.

1

YOU WON'T SEE IT ON A STREET SIGN, BUT US locals know. You have to look down when you're walking in Cork. Look down or fall victim to the traps this city lays for the unwary. The errant paving slab. The drain cover gone rogue. The vomit. And, sometimes, the blood, a vivid, ruby trail when freshly shed, fading as it dries, melding with the caked-in grime on Patrick Street's pink footpaths, laid in a fit of long-vanished boom-time optimism and, by the look of them after three days without rain, never cleaned since.

I was waiting for Davy Keenan by the front door of Brown Thomas. Looking down. Trying to resist the urge to pace. Definitely not calling. Even though he was late. Ten minutes late. Then twelve minutes. Then fifteen. Then I raised my gaze and glimpsed him at last, all six foot two of him, sauntering in my direction. Sandy hair and beard. Powder-blue, soft-cotton T-shirt. Old jeans. Scuffed brown suede shoes. I felt like I often feel when I see him. Like the sun's come out and I might burn.

'Sorry, sorry,' he said. 'But I'm here now, right? Half-looking forward to it in a weird way.'

I sensed something in him that hadn't been there when he'd left my house that morning – a kind of nervousness, or it could have been excitement – and I badly wanted to ask why he was late. But I pride myself on not being needy. So I told myself that the why of it didn't matter and flashed him my second-best smile.

'You're going to love her,' I said.

He smiled too, a neat pretty one, and tucked a few strands of my long black hair behind my ears, and wrapped his right arm around my shoulders: I'm five foot eight, so we're a snug fit. We walked on in silence, settling into a familiar rhythm as we cleared the city centre. Hugging the river most of the way, we kept walking; and I thought about how often it went like this between us – the raised heart rate, the nearly conflict, the unasked question, the almost resolution: the benign version of a destructive pattern I'd known long before we'd met that I was doing my best to change. Only it turned out my best wasn't up to the job most of the time.

After a while Davy said, 'It's always farther than you think.'

2

DOLLY PARTON'S TWO PREVIOUS VISITS TO CORK hadn't gone to plan. On the first, in a venue normally reserved for equestrian events, a lighting rig had collapsed during sound-checking and the gig had to be cancelled at the last minute. The second time, she'd made landfall in the middle of a deluge. And, as it was a Saturday, a lot of the audience had been drinking since lunchtime. Let's just say that there was an edge.

Third time lucky? It looked like it. A good-humoured after-work crowd on the balmiest of Thursdays. Dolly emerged to the sound of the Marquee roar and the night took flight, the audience word-perfect on most of the songs; quiet for 'Coat of Many Colours', when she sat alone at the front of the stage and sang to the sweaty throng gathered at her feet like we were family round the fire in her Smoky Mountain cabin. Tears in my eyes, I looked up at Davy, standing right next to me. He pulled me closer.

'You big eejit,' he said. Then he kissed me.

Later, on the walk back to his place, we were doing that thing where we weren't talking but communicating all the same. He was letting me know that I was okay and I was wondering how come he was so sure. And I didn't know how it had happened but there I was – a woman with soap opera standard messy origins – in an actual relationship, with Davy.

Who used to be my client back when he was having recurring legal troubles related to his cocaine addiction: a couple of low-grade possession charges, a drunken and a careless driving, a bundle of unpaid parking fines. Later, after he'd got sober and retrained, I'd checked the lease on his gym for him and he became my personal trainer and my 'just good friend' for several years. Later still, this – something I hadn't admitted to myself I'd wanted for a long time, until a night last November when he'd come round to my house for dinner and stayed till morning. More than seven months ago. Barely six if you counted the multiple breaks we went through, the short periods of adjustment – hissy fits, if you prefer – instigated by me, as I tried, and tried again to get used to having him share my life.

But there had been no breaks since way back in February – nearly five months that felt like longer – a magical time, apart from the occasional arguments and misunderstandings that I told myself were normal for any couple. I had to make a conscious effort not to link how we were with each other with our past, with his, and with mine.

Because otherwise, I'd find myself wondering how smart being with him was for me. How safe. Taken into care at the age of four on the grounds of neglect, I was fostered by the people who became my forever parents – my real ones, as far as I'm concerned – while my birth mother kept on drinking. She gave up often but was never able to stay sober, however much she wanted to. After her death Mam and Dad were able to adopt me. Birth father unknown so his consent wasn't needed; no maternal relatives scrabbling to take me on either.

I was nine when my birth mother died. Old enough to be taken to her funeral. Young enough to think that it was all my fault. In the years that followed, I locked her – the memories and the pain and, I suppose, the love – in a strong box deep inside me.

Then, decades later, I ended up falling for Davy. I don't know what that is, but don't tell me it's a coincidence. What goes around, comes around, as they say. And yet, in real life, he and I seemed to work. We didn't swamp each other or cling on too tightly. We ebbed and flowed. We gave each other space.

Beside us, cars crawled towards the roundabout. It was easy to distinguish the blissed-out country fans who'd been to the gig from the unfortunates caught in the traffic. Up ahead, in the front seats of a Mark 1 silver Audi TT, a couple embraced passionately, a woman in the driving seat, the dark-haired passenger's elbow around her neck, pulling her ever closer to him. I recognised the car, as belonging to Mandy Breslin, Finance and Trusts partner at MLC, the law firm where I work. There'd been a recall of those cars to have a rear spoiler fitted, after they'd been found to be unstable at high speeds on the autobahn. Most people had opted for the spoiler. She hadn't. She'd said that she liked the TT the way it was.

I glanced at Davy but he was typing something on his phone. As we passed by, I waved, but Mandy didn't reciprocate. And her face, when she saw me, was a picture.

Understandable. I didn't know who the dark-haired man was. But he wasn't her husband.

3

THE MORNING AFTER THE CONCERT, COMING UP to 10.15, I was chewing on a biro in my cramped and pathologically untidy office, trying to work out the most diplomatic way of telling a client that he would be a fool to reject a defence offer of €21,000 in a case worth €15,000, and that hell would freeze over before any judge would give him the €50,000 he thought he deserved, when Mandy slid in and clicked the door shut behind her. Slim and athletic, she was in her mid-forties but looked younger usually. Today, the thick dark blonde hair and barely-there make-up were perfect as ever but no amount of concealer could disguise the black circles under her eyes. And I could have sworn she was wearing the same teal linen sleeveless shift she'd had on at work yesterday. Either that, or it was a duplicate and whoever did her ironing had gone too easy on the starch.

She hadn't spoken since she came in and I was fighting the urge to fill the void with some inanity about how great Dolly had been, when it dawned on me that Mandy probably wasn't at the gig.

She broke the silence. 'Last night,' she whispered.

'Look,' I said. 'It's your own business. I …'

Before I knew it, she was standing over me, my side of the desk.

'As I was saying, before I was interrupted,' she said. 'Last night, whatever you think you saw, you saw nothing. Get that?'

'Sure. Like I said …'

'Say it.'

'I … I saw nothing?'

'Say it again.'

'Hey, I saw absolutely nothing. Not a thing,' I said. 'Honestly, Mandy, I'm like the grave. I haven't told a soul.' Not even Davy, I might have added, except I don't talk about him at the office.

Mandy stepped back from the desk, and there it was again – the same expression I'd seen on her face last night. Understandable, I'd thought at the time. Only now I didn't understand at all. She turned and left without another word, and I sat back in my chair and puffed out a breath and tried to analyse what the fuck had just happened. Surely she believed me when I said I'd say nothing?

But, if she believed me, why did she look so scared?

THREE MONTHS LATER

4

SUMMER LINGERED UNTIL MID-SEPTEMBER. THE
first wet Monday morning, it vanished. The college students
were back and quite a few of the little treasures have cars so my
previously serene walk to work was fuggy and loud. Add to that
the chill that cut through my light mac, and that I'd forgotten
my umbrella, and I was feeling distinctly autumnal by the time
I got to 17–19 MacSwiney Street, the three restored Georgian
townhouses occupied by McGrath Lynch Cleary, the mainly
commercial law practice where I've worked for fifteen years or
more. MLC has seven partners, sixteen solicitors, and don't ask
me how many trainees, legal execs and support staff in total,
because I'm not sure anyone knows that from week to week,
apart from Marian in Wages.

And Gabriel, obviously. That's Gabriel McGrath, the firm's
founder and managing partner. He's the person who, for reasons
best known to himself, took me on back in the day. I had no
legal contacts, applied to every firm in Cork for a traineeship.
Didn't even get an interview until the call came from MLC. I
never understood why, but Gabriel must have seen something
in me he liked. Out of the four trainees taken on that year, I was
the least connected and the most grateful.

Which probably explains why I'm the only one of the four still working for the firm. I don't do much of the corporate stuff. We found out fast that that wasn't where my talents, or my interests, lay. Think legal dogsbody and you're closer to the mark. Or general operative. Essentially, all the low-paying knobbly miscellaneous work that crops up in a big firm like ours that nobody else wants to do. As for me, I like problem-solving, I like variety and I *really* like being able to pay my bills, so the work I get to do suits me as well as anything would.

Except when Dermot Lyons starts complaining at partners' meetings about my fee-earnings. Though even he was looking at me marginally more favourably after my recent investigatory work on a murder case led to the exposure of a serial sex offender and a slew of civil actions for damages, some of which had ended up coming the way of the firm.

But no matter how much money I brought in, I would never be quite right for MLC. I didn't try to be. I slipped into the office, did my job, and slipped back out again, and binned the bowling night and the barbecue and the mulled wine and the mince pie invitations as fast as they hit my Inbox.

'Whatever happens, Finn,' my assistant Tina Daly was saying, between slurps of a giant caffeine and milk-based hot drink and bites of her regular morning Danish, 'stay here. Gabriel's back from his long weekend in Nice and he's like a bear.'

She was standing in the open doorway and I was on my knees in front of my desk. With a groan, I shunted two tall stacks of files aside and reached along the wall for the main switch of the ancient electric storage heater. The public areas of MLC are luxurious and beautifully conserved. By the time you get to the attic where my office is, it's the servants' quarters. Even if I managed to turn it on successfully, it wouldn't start to spit out heat until the next morning. I moved the dial first to a conservative three and then to a more realistic five and looked up at Tina. She was twenty-eight, nine years younger than me, and the most glamourous fat person – her words, not mine – in Cork. Her nails always polished and never chipped, her red curls styled and glossy, her skin springy and glowing a golden tan whatever the season. She worked downstairs in a shared office with some of the other secretaries but came up to me first thing every morning to plan the day ahead.

'Any idea what's up with him?'

'No,' Tina said.

I waited. If she didn't know, she definitely had a theory. As well as being super-smart generally, she was better versed in the politics of this place than I could ever be.

'Though it might have something to do with the fact that Mandy Breslin hasn't come into work yet this morning and that there are two clients of hers that nobody knows anything about waiting for her in reception. And that she's not answering her mobile.'

It was 9.45. Mandy was normally in by seven, eight if she was having a lie-in. Her husband Ed gave the kids their breakfast and took them to school. It was no secret that Mandy was the high-flyer in the family, that she was the one who paid for the school fees and the lavish holidays in California and Dubai. I hadn't heard where they'd gone this year. I hadn't been seeking out her company after 'the incident'. No, it was more than that. The prickles of unease up the back of my neck told me that I'd been avoiding her in the three months since June.

And that I'd been wrong to.

•

My desk phone rang.

'Uh-oh,' Tina said. 'Don't answer it.'

I reached my hand up and grabbed the phone. Before I could put my ear to the receiver, I heard Gabriel's voice.

'Finola? Finola?'

He's the only one who calls me by my full name.

'*Shit!*' I mouthed at Tina.

'Told you,' she mouthed back.

Gabriel was still talking.

'Why Mandy arranges an appointment with clients and doesn't put it in her diary or tell her secretary and doesn't show up to meet them is beyond me. And why I'm supposed to deal with it, why everyone runs to me, that's another mystery. Find out what they want, will you please? See if you can move the matter on in some way.'

I raced through the post, delegated as much as I could to Tina and made my way downstairs to the client waiting room off reception. A glass door led off the landing into a large rectangular room with a dozen burgundy studded leather armchairs, four small end-tables, one in each corner, a Ballygowan water dispenser and, in the middle, a low glass and chrome coffee table with the *Irish Examiner*, *The Irish Times* and the *Financial Times* and a stack of MLC promotional brochures. The *Examiner* looked like someone had leafed through it roughly and thrown it back down unread. I went next door to talk to Dervla, receptionist and fount of all knowledge, with the firm since its foundation by Gabriel. Instead, I found a slim blonde woman in a crisp white shirt.

'May I help you?' she asked.

In her early twenties, she spoke with a slight accent.

'I'm looking for Dervla.'

'Sorry, I don't know who that is.'

'The woman who usually works here?'

'Ah. No. I don't know her. I'm Katja Majewska. First day. Temping.'

I leaned across the desk and shook her hand.

'How's it going, Katja? I'm Finn Fitzpatrick, one of the solicitors. 'I'm looking for two clients who came in to see Mandy Breslin, one of the partners.'

'Yes, I asked them to wait in the other room.'

'They're gone.'

'They didn't tell me. I didn't see them leave.'

'Did you get their names?'

'Only one, the older one. McInerney.'

'First name?'

'Sorry. The phone was going crazy and—'

'Don't worry about it. Can you remember what he looked like?'

'Not really. He was old. Fifty, maybe sixty.'

'And the other one?'

'A lot younger. Twenty-two, twenty-three?'

'Hair?'

'Yes.'

'I mean, what colour?'

'Oh I see! It was black. Or dark brown. Cut short at the sides and longer on top. And he was tall, not too tall though. Really strong. Wearing a white T-shirt and a black Jack Wills hoodie. Black denim jeans and boots.'

She laughed.

'You see now why I wasn't looking at Mr McInerney. His friend was ...'

'Good-looking, by the sound of it.'

'For sure.'

'Did he say anything?'

'No, just the old guy talked. Gave his name, said that he was here to see Mandy Breslin and that she'd know what it was about. But Mandy wasn't in and her secretary said she had no appointment in her diary. She didn't know who McInerney was but she said she'd check. Then Gabriel rang down and told me to offer them a cup of coffee. But McInerney said he didn't want coffee, he only wanted to see Mandy. He said he'd wait as long as it took.'

'Was he from Cork?'

'Let me think,' Katja said. 'Irish, definitely. Maybe from Cork. But he didn't have a strong Cork accent.'

•

Behind me, the door to the reception area opened. Ed, Mandy's husband, walked in. About Mandy's age but baggier, he had on a navy Musto sailing jacket over an ancient sun- and salt-weathered pink polo shirt, rumpled chinos and docksider shoes. His face was the colour of parchment.

'Where's Dervla?' he asked.

'Off. Is Mandy with you?'

He shook his head slowly.

'Ed, is everything okay?'

'She didn't come home last night.'

I kept my expression as neutral as I could in the circumstances.

'I went to the garda station in Blackrock this morning,' Ed went on. 'But they said she's not missing long enough for them to do anything. They said I had to give her time. That it was too soon to … I took the kids to school and I didn't know what else to do, so I came here. I know she's not in the office. I was talking to Kathleen earlier. I don't know. I just thought …'

Katja came out from behind her desk and handed him a paper cup filled with water. He gulped it back in one swallow. Then his phone rang. He answered it.

'Ed Wallace.'

He said a few terse 'yeses' and a 'no' and an 'I'll be there as soon as I can'.

'That was the guards,' he said. 'They wanted to know where I was, if I was at home. When I said I wasn't, they asked me if I could come to Coughlan's Quay garda station straightaway. That's not a good sign, is it?'

'It probably means that they're taking it seriously, that they want to get all the essential details from you. It's nothing to worry about,' I said.

But Ed was right. It wasn't a good sign at all.

5

IF SOMETHING BAD HAD HAPPENED TO MANDY,
whether she was still having an affair or not, the man standing in
front of me was the default prime suspect. If he'd been a client
of mine, I'd have told him to lose the pink top before he went
to Coughlan's Quay. But he wasn't my client. Besides, it was
ridiculously ghoulish of me to jump to conclusions – in this job,
you're always thinking 'worst-case scenario'. I reminded myself
that, wherever she was, there was no reason yet to think that
Mandy was anything other than fine. Caught up in something.
Unavoidably detained. Probably, and unfortunately for Ed, with
the other man I'd seen her with in June. But fine.

Ed, on the other hand, looked anything but.

'I'll go along with you to the station if you want,' I said.

'There's no need. I ...'

He seemed to forget what he was about to say and stared at
me, wide-eyed.

'I'll get my coat,' I said.

•

I ran the five flights to my office, pausing on the way to let Tina know what was happening. On the way down, I rapped lightly on Gabriel's door.

'Come,' he said.

Gabriel's office was on the first floor, next to the boardroom and only marginally less palatial. He had a seating area in front of one of the sash windows (original glass and wood, fully working lead weights) with two high-backed wing chairs facing each other, chat-show style. His desk, at the far side of the room, was a heavy carved leather-topped partner's desk never sullied by anything more than the single file Gabriel was working on at the time, a pen and a barrister's notebook (unlined). A side table held a computer keyboard and two monitors. In one corner, two padded hangers – one for his exquisitely tailored suit jacket (always dark blue or dark grey pinstripe, the weight varying according to the season), the other for his coat – hung from a mahogany coat stand. Unusually, today both hangers were empty. Gabriel's coat lay strewn across the back of his swivel chair and he, still in his suit jacket, was standing by the window. Though it was well after 10 a.m., his computer didn't look like it had been switched on.

'Em, Gabriel, Ed is downstairs. Mandy didn't come home last night apparently. He got a call while he was here to go to Coughlan's Quay immediately.'

'Good God,' Gabriel said. 'Is he on his own?'

'Yes.'

'You should go with him. Mandy would like that. Unless …'

He'd had the same bad thought I'd had. He pushed it away, like I had.

'You should definitely go with him,' he said.

'I will.'

'And those two clients of Mandy's?'

'Gone. By the way, did you know there's a temp on reception?'

'Of course I did,' he snapped.

Then he turned away from me and gazed out the window.

'Please go,' he said.

I backed out of the room. Tina had been right. Gabriel *was* like a bear.

6

ED'S CAR WAS A METALLIC BLUE VOLVO 4 X 4 estate, the passenger seat buried under a pile of sports clothes and equipment. I helped him move the stuff into the back and sat in beside him.

'The kids are into their activities by the look of it.'

'They take after Mandy so they're every bit as good as you'd expect.'

'It's just the two girls you have?'

'Yup, Ava and Ruth,' he said. 'Hockey all winter, and tennis and sailing all summer. I'm kept going, driving them here, there and everywhere. I don't know how they'll cope if …'

I realised he had something specific in mind, something that hadn't occurred to me until that second. A swirling started in my belly.

'Is there anyone you'd like me to call? A friend or relative?'

'No,' Ed said. 'I don't want to worry anybody. Not unless I have to.'

'But Mandy's family, you told them she was missing? You checked to see if she was with them?'

'I didn't tell anyone except the guards. I rang the office at a quarter past eight. When she wasn't answering her mobile or at work, I knew there was something seriously wrong. Mandy would never take a day off unless it'd been scheduled six months in advance. She loves her job. Or did. She's not been herself lately.'

'Not herself?'

'She's been a bit down.'

'I'm sorry, I …'

'You weren't to know. She hid it well.'

'She's the last person you'd ever imagine would … but do you think—'

I stopped, thought better of the question I was going to ask.

'I can't let myself go there,' Ed said. 'But it's a possibility.'

7

ED FOLLOWED ME UP THE STEPS TO THE GARDA
station. Boats haven't docked at Coughlan's Quay for a century
or more. The river still flows here but it's culverted, hidden and
quiet, except when it isn't. At ground level, where in times past
cargo was loaded and unloaded, there's a car park, the arches
open but with cast-iron vertical bars blocking access from the
street. The people who work here use the back gate. The front
door, where we were headed, is used mainly by solicitors and
members of the public, though there are fewer of those than in
most garda stations. Coughlan's Quay is the headquarters of the
regional detective branch.

At the public office, I gave Ed's name and my own, and we sat
on two of the dusty plastic chairs. His right heel off the floor,
he jiggled his knee up and down repeatedly. I tried to read the
yellowed curling notices sellotaped to the wall but they might as
well have been in Japanese. All I could think of was the children
– teenagers – Ava and Ruth. I didn't know them well but I'd met
them several times with Mandy over the years, in the office and
around town. They were at school now, Ed had said, oblivious
to the storm that might be coming their way. Then I thought
of the man I'd seen Mandy with, and whether I should say

something about him to Ed, or to the guards. I'd promised her I'd tell no one. But promise or no promise, every minute would count in a missing persons investigation, wouldn't it?

It would. If that was what we were still dealing with here.

•

As the minutes passed without anyone coming to get us, Ed grew more and more agitated.

'This is not good,' he said. 'This is not good.'

'I know someone who works here,' I said. 'I'll send her a text.'

Detective Garda Sadie O'Riordan had been my best friend since our first week studying law together at UCC. She'd go through fire for me and I would return the favour. The fact that we hadn't been getting on as well as usual over the last few months didn't matter. I started typing a message but before I could press 'Send', the door to the left of the public office hatch opened and Sadie came out. She was pale and wiry with unbrushed hair cut in a bob. She was wearing her permanently tatty, jeans-based work outfit. She wasn't surprised to see me – I'd given my name to the guard on the desk – but she didn't look pleased.

'Sorry for keeping you waiting, Ed. We're ready for you now.'

'Hi Finn,' she added, without looking at me. She started to usher Ed through the door she had come through in a way that made it clear I wasn't invited. When Ed realised I wasn't behind him, he turned.

'Finn? Are you coming?'

'Sure,' I said. 'If you want me.'

I got up from my seat but Sadie held up a palm to stop me. 'Could I just clarify your role here today, Finn?'

'Friend,' I said. 'I work with Ed's wife, Mandy.'

'Is that right?' Sadie asked.

I resisted the urge to say something sarcastic. She had to have known that Mandy worked at MLC.

'It's more a family than friend situation,' Sadie said. 'We won't be long.'

'Okay,' Ed said.

He took his car keys out of his pocket and handed them to me.

'Will you put a parking disc on the car?' he asked.

Sadie raised her eyebrows, threw me a glance, darted her head around the door and spoke quickly to another plain-clothes officer who was waiting inside.

'I think it's better if you hold onto the keys yourself, Ed. And there's no need to worry about parking fines. We'll move your car into the station car park. Finn, you don't mind showing Detective Fogarty where it is, do you?'

Ed took the keys back from me and passed them to Detective Fogarty. I went outside with him. He pulled on a pair of latex gloves as he went down the steps.

'It's the blue Volvo over there,' I said.

He nodded, pointed the key fob in the direction of the car and moved briskly towards it. He was fast for a man who looked fond of a breakfast roll.

•

Strolling around to the rear of the station, I ambled into the corner shop and took my time getting a paper cup out of the dispenser. I took even more time choosing whether I wanted a nasty machine coffee or a slightly less nasty tea. Then I snagged a seat on a high stool at the greasy counter inside the window and worked my way through the reading material provided, the weekly freesheet, the *Cork Independent*.

Twenty-five minutes later, I heard the electric gates swing open. An unmarked garda car emerged at a sedate pace, Sadie driving, Fogarty in the passenger seat. In the back, perched in the middle like his parents were taking him out for a Sunday spin, sat Ed. I watched the orange indicator light blinking slowly as the car moseyed south and out of sight.

8

BACK AT THE OFFICE, GABRIEL WAS IN A CLIENT
meeting so I went straight to my room and shuffled the papers
on my desk for a while, Ed's words going around in my head.

She's not been herself lately.

You weren't to know.

But I'd known something was wrong and I'd side-stepped
it, thought it was nothing to do with me. What Mandy did in
her private life *wasn't* anything to do with me. We were work
colleagues, nothing more. Yet I couldn't help thinking that
there was something I could have done all the same; and that,
whatever I could have done, I'd left it too late for Mandy. And
for her kids.

I pushed away the document I wasn't reading and stared out
the window at the slate rooftops, shiny black from the rain. I felt
myself sinking into the dark place.

Suicide was something I already knew too much about. I'd
been sixteen when I found out that that was how my birth
mother had died. Older than that when I heard that the birth
sister – half-sister – I'd never met had gone the same way. Finding
out about her had made me want to know more about where I'd
come from. In theory, I still wanted that knowledge. In practice,
I'd done nothing about it.

Shutting my eyes on the world, I took a breath and another one, making it longer on the out-breath.

Managing myself.

By myself.

●

After a time, hearing a tread on the attic stairs outside, I turned my face towards the door, expecting to see Tina. Instead, Gabriel walked in and, his expression grim, sat on the only chair not stacked high with files. Tina's chair, usually.

'I haven't been up here in a good while,' he said. 'I see it's tidy as ever.'

'I know where everything is,' I said.

'I doubt that very much.'

I do most of my work on screen. But when I have to think properly, I need paper, reams of it, and the feel of a pen in my hand. I said none of that to Gabriel. In the long silence, he sighed.

Then he asked, 'Is there any news on Mandy?'

'No,' I said. 'But it's not looking good. Ed told me she's been … That her mood lately has been …'

'Oh.'

'The guards drove him home, I think. I saw them leaving. He had his car with him but—'

'Dear Lord.'

'It's desperate altogether,' I said.

'Those unfortunate children.'

'Yes.'

'And the Law Society investigators,' Gabriel said.

'What?'

'Mandatory firm inspection in case of suicide by a solicitor.'

He'd said the word out loud.

'Poor Mandy,' I said eventually.

'Mandatory *major* inspection,' Gabriel continued, like he hadn't heard me.

'But Mandy was, *is*,' I said. 'Mandy *is* a brilliant solicitor. I mean, even if she did … die like you just said, the Law Society wouldn't find anything wrong with her files, would they?'

'It shouldn't be a problem,' Gabriel said.

'But you think it might be,' I said.

'I don't know. Let's pray to God she's okay.'

I hoped that he meant we should pray for Mandy rather than the firm, but the little dip my heart took told me I might be wrong.

'Anyway,' he said, rising quickly from his chair. 'Keep me in the loop.'

He was gone before I had a chance to ask what loop he was talking about. Then I remembered that he knew I was friends with Sadie. As a detective in Coughlan's Quay, she'd be in whatever loop was going. I took out my phone and looked at it for a moment and put it away again. My desk phone rang.

'What did Gabriel want?' Tina asked. It didn't occur to me to ask how she knew he'd been up to see me – I take it for granted she knows everything.

'Nothing much,' I said. 'He had no news on Mandy, I mean.'

'Right,' Tina said.

'We'll just have to wait, see what the guards turn up.'

'Right,' Tina said again.

'So that's it for now.'

'Em.'

'Tina, has something happened?'

'No. Nothing. Well, maybe.'

'What?'

'Finn, it's on breakingnews.ie that a woman's body has been found in Cork. Miles from anywhere Mandy would be, though. It's not her. It couldn't be.'

I brought up the website on my desktop. There it was, like Tina had said:

> The body of a woman in her forties has been found in a house in the
> Glasheen area of Cork city. Gardaí are treating the circumstances
> as suspicious.

The media code for suicide or natural death was, 'foul play is not suspected'. If the dead woman did turn out to be Mandy, she hadn't killed herself. She'd been murdered. I grabbed my phone and express-typed: *Is it her?*

Eight minutes later, Sadie rang me back.

'You didn't hear it from me, but it'll be on the lunchtime news. Identity established. It's her. It's Mandy.'

9

CORK IS SMALL. WHEN TRAGEDY STRIKES, IT'S smaller. Long before the official pronouncement, and without a word from me, everyone knew. Below me, I could hear doors opening and closing, and rapid footsteps and stage whispers and raised voices and sobs. The 'OMG's and 'RIP's were piling up on Facebook and Twitter but I stayed in my attic room, alone and still and thinking. Thinking about what I'd seen three months ago on the night of the Dolly Parton concert. Reassessing it in light of what I knew now. Trying to bring to mind the dark-haired mystery man's face. Failing.

Mandy's own Facebook profile gave no clues. She had fourteen friends, no profile picture and no posts. On Instagram, she followed a lot of people but posted nothing about herself. It looked like she was on social media to monitor what her children were seeing, and for no other reason. And now she was dead and they were left without a mother.

Sadie had rung off before I'd had a chance to tell her what I knew about Mandy's marriage. Tell I'd have to, either Sadie, or one of her colleagues at Coughlan's Quay. I'd have to make a formal statement too. I didn't want to break my promise to Mandy. But I would.

Not here, though. I wouldn't say it to anyone in the firm.

They'd find out about her affair – of course they would, there's no privacy in a murder case. But they wouldn't find out from me.

•

I went downstairs. Tina was in the tea-room with her arm around Kathleen, Mandy's PA. In her late fifties, her light brown hair in a low maintenance shoulder-length style, Kathleen was a stalwart – a quiet, solid presence, someone who got on with everyone and did her work impeccably. Her hands over her eyes, she was crying softly.

'*How's she doing?*' I mouthed.

'*Bad*,' Tina mouthed back.

'Have a sip of the tea, Kathleen,' Tina said.

'The sugar,' Kathleen managed to reply. 'I can't.'

'Oh no! I thought it might help with the shock,' Tina said. 'Unless anyone has brandy?'

'Gabriel might,' I said. 'Or Dermot?'

'I'll go check,' Tina said. 'Will you …?'

I nodded. After Tina was gone, I tipped the sugared milky tea down the sink and made a fresh mug, leaving it black.

'You remembered,' Kathleen said.

I smiled. Back when I was a trainee, my desk was little more than a shelf beside the photocopier in a second-floor office shared by Kathleen and some of the other secretaries. Kathleen's desk had been nearest to mine. She answered all my questions, no matter how stupid. In return, I plied her with regular cups of tea.

'This is horrific,' I said.

'If it was an accident, it'd be bad enough,' Kathleen said. 'But murder. Who on earth would want to murder Mandy?'

10

'YOU'RE TALKING ABOUT ME RUNNING A PARALLEL investigation,' I said.

'In a way, yes,' Dermot Lyons said. 'In another way, no.'

We were in Gabriel's office. Lyons was sitting opposite me in the other wingback chair. Gabriel had wheeled over his swivel chair to sit beside him. The contrast between the two of them couldn't have been greater: Gabriel lean, precise, rigorous, hard-working; Lyons, bursting out of his expensive shirt, a red-faced, glad-handing old-school-tie golf and rugby bore, a rainmaker who brought in lucrative work, though he never did much of it himself, with all the right connections to old money Cork. Mandy had been a blend of both of them. She'd made partner soon after I joined MLC as a trainee. And she was the person everyone had tipped to take over from Gabriel as managing partner. Her death would always have been a massive blow to the firm, but the particular circumstances meant that the loss was especially problematic.

'You'd have a different focus,' Gabriel said. 'The "whodunnit" aspect, for want of a better word, is none of our concern – it's a garda matter. What we have in mind is completely different. Like I was saying earlier, there's bound to be an inspection by the Law Society. We need to know what, if anything, we're facing.'

It's hard to overstate the terrorising effect the words 'Law Society inspection' have on solicitors, even – perhaps especially – über-organised perfectionists like Gabriel. Despite the fact that, most of the time, and for most firms, the gruelling administrative ordeal passes without serious consequences, the fear is final-exam-and-no-revision-done real.

'You're talking about me going through Mandy's files, her computer, emails, client accounts, that kind of thing.'

'Exactly,' Gabriel said. 'You've done this kind of work before, not quite like this, admittedly, but I've no doubt you'll manage.'

'With a lot less drama this time, hopefully,' Dermot Lyons said.

He was talking about the sexual offences and murder case involving Oscar-winning film director Jeremy Gill that I'd helped solve the previous winter. At the time, Lyons had done everything he could to stymie my investigation.

Ignoring him, I addressed Gabriel: 'Tell me honestly, do you expect me to find anything?'

'No,' Gabriel said. 'No, I don't.'

'But you still want me to do it.'

'Yes.'

'And you don't see any contradiction between those two positions?'

Lyons interjected, 'Fail to prepare, prepare to fail.'

'Is this *really* where our priorities are at this time, Gabriel? Mandy Breslin, a woman I've worked with for fifteen years, you for far longer than that, is dead. Murdered. It's a time to mourn her, surely? To help the family she's left behind?'

'Of course, Finola, of course,' Gabriel said. 'All that. Help in every way we can. Send a floral wreath. Close the office for the funeral. Organise a guard of honour.'

'No guard of honour,' Lyons said. 'No weeping and gnashing of teeth till we know what's what.'

'Well, yes, I see what you mean, Dermot,' Gabriel said. 'Though I might have put it a little differently. Finola, unfortunately the fact is that the Law Society – their investigators – will be in by the end of the week. In the unlikely event that Mandy's murder had anything to do with her work here, we need to know about it. Otherwise, this dreadful and tragic affair could bring the entire firm crashing down around our ears.'

'The Law Society investigators aren't the only ones who'll be interested,' I said. 'You do realise that the guards might seek access? They'll want all her emails and financial records. They'll start with her personal life – but they're bound to show up here with a warrant and a court order at some stage. Legal professional privilege *can* be lifted in the event of illegality.'

'All the more reason to get moving,' Lyons said.

I didn't like what he was saying. I didn't like any of this. But he was right.

11

I POPPED INTO TINA'S OFFICE AND UPDATED HER
on what Gabriel and Dermot Lyons had asked of me.

'Sounds riveting,' she said.

'These things are sent to try us.'

'What happened with those clients of Mandy's, by the way?'

'Left the building before I got downstairs. It's strange. All
I know about them is one of their surnames: McInerney. And
there's a temp on reception. It's a real pity, because if Dervla had
been there, she might've recognised them. Is she on holiday?'

'Hardly. She's only back from Portugal two or three weeks
ago.'

I looked around.

'Where's Kathleen?'

'Gone home. She was in a bad way, the poor thing. Why do
you ask?'

'I was hoping she might have Mandy's computer password.'

'Sure you can get it from Pauline, can't you?'

•

Firm regulations required each staff member to hand-write their password on a piece of paper and place it in a sealed envelope. The envelopes were stored in a locked box in the safe – Gabriel held one key to the box, while Pauline Doyle, the office IT manager, held the other, though she didn't know the safe combination – to be opened only in case of emergency. No one had envisaged that the first time the arrangement would need to be used would be because a partner had been murdered.

Even without her password, all Mandy's client files would have been accessible to me via the case management system held on the firm's secure server and to which all the staff terminals were connected. In theory, once I pinpointed Mandy's files, I could have sat in my own office and read them on my own computer. Or I could have gone old school and read the paper versions that were stored in the central filing system downstairs. But Gabriel had decreed that, for as long as my investigation lasted, I should put as much of my own work as I could on hold, and move into Mandy's office.

'This is your primary task,' he had said. 'I know we can rely on you.'

'All I can do is investigate. In the unlikely event that Mandy did something unethical or illegal, there's nothing I can do to change that.'

'Obviously not,' Lyons had said dismissively.

But Gabriel had said nothing. And I reckoned I'd never seen him as worried.

12

MANDY'S OFFICE WAS UNLOCKED – I KNEW THAT
because I'd turned the brass doorknob – but I hesitated before
going in, ran my fingers over the name-plate that I'd passed so
often and barely noticed before, 'MANDY BRESLIN' etched in
white lettering on a stick-on black plastic rectangle. The door
was old, original to the building. It had outlived Mandy and the
previous occupants, whoever they had been. I tipped my right
shoulder to the heavy cream-painted wood and stood as it fell
open.

Framed education and training certificates interspersed with
several pieces of contemporary Irish art – including a good-
sized and presumably pricey Donald Teskey seascape – hung
on plaster-coloured walls. A desk, smooth to the touch that I
reckoned was made of cherry-wood, sat cleanly in the middle
of the large space, a low-backed chair in paler wood – elegant,
simple – in front of it, a couple more of them stacked in a
corner. I imagined Mandy walking around the room, deep in
thought, reaching up her slim hand to select a law book from
one of the shelves, the volumes neatly ordered by subject. She'd
know exactly which one she wanted and exactly where it was
because everything here was perfect, down to the tasteful black-

and-white studio double portrait of her lovely daughters, a few centimetres to the right of her keyboard.

It felt wrong to sit in her chair – black leather, high-backed, ergonomic-looking – so I moved it to one side and put one of the others in its place. Settled, I slid open the drawers of Mandy Breslin's desk one by one. There was nothing in them about her lover; about who he was or how long they'd been together. The drawers held no secrets of any kind.

Unless you counted the tupperware box half-filled with fruit gums and jelly beans and mini red Bounty bars.

'Mandy, you dark horse,' I said.

Or the silver-framed wedding photograph of her and Ed stowed face-down underneath.

13

THE FIRM'S IT MANAGER, PAULINE DOYLE AND I
spent the rest of the afternoon putting a shape on the task ahead.
We ranked and ordered the files Mandy had been working on
based on the time she'd spent on each. So that I could work
independently of the case management system, we opened a
new set of folders on the desktop and pulled copies of each file in
alphabetical order into them. Then we compiled an alphabetical
list of all Mandy's clients and files into a new Word document.
The name McInerney appeared nowhere. Whoever the man
who had called to see her this morning was, he wasn't an existing
client, of Mandy's or of anyone else at MLC.

•

'It's a quarter past seven,' Pauline said. 'I'm going to have to go.
My babysitter won't wait any longer. Call me if you need me.
Anytime.'

I grimaced.

'Seriously,' she said. 'Do.'

'Thanks.'

She stood by the door and pushed her glasses up her nose, and
buttoned her suit jacket.

'It's a rotten job they have you doing. Like you're digging Mandy's grave for them or something.'

'Digging it deeper.'

'Hmm,' Pauline said. 'You staying on for a while?'

'No, I've had enough for one day,' I said. 'Hang on for me there and I'll be down the stairs with you.'

I didn't want to be alone in Mandy's room as night fell.

14

I LIVE A TEN-MINUTE WALK FROM WORK BUT I wasn't going home. Not yet. As I was walking down South Main Street, I saw the 216, the bus that goes through Glasheen, taking on passengers. On impulse, I hopped on, handed my €2.40 to the driver and edged into a seat down the back.

I wouldn't have walked or driven by − I wouldn't have wanted anyone to see me, Sadie in particular, though I had every intention of asking her about the case next time I spoke to her. Which needed to be tonight. I had information, potentially of considerable value to the garda investigation, that I was obliged to disclose to her. I had to make a proper start on my own investigation too. And I wanted to have a mental picture of the murder scene before I did any of that.

The exact address hadn't been released but I reckoned I might see something if I rubber-necked out the window as the bus passed along Glasheen Road. I didn't know what difference it would make to me. I just knew I had to get some sense of the place where Mandy had drawn her last breath. For now, I was assuming that she'd died where her body had been located, the same side of the river but a very different suburb to her home in Blackrock. Glasheen had spread and filled in organically as the city grew. As a result, there were any number of side roads and small estates off the main road. The housing stock went from grand to grotty, with student accommodation and other rentals mixed in among a mainly older demographic, and younger families occupying a few new builds and fresh renovations.

The bus laboured up Sharman Crawford Street and climbed higher via a succession of squeezed turn-offs until eventually the road widened and started a westward descent. The sky was darkening into twilight. My phone told me that sunset was due shortly. But there had been no sun that day.

Stopped at the traffic lights at Dorgan's Road, I glimpsed the telltale neon yellow of high-vis jackets up ahead. We took off again and I moved to a seat on the right side of the bus. Two uniforms were stationed at a barrier blocking the narrow entrance roadway to Alysson Villas, a cul-de-sac of houses I vaguely knew, the same way I vaguely knew everywhere else around here. Behind the barrier were garda cars and crime-scene tape and the Garda Technical Bureau van. I couldn't see any of them, but I knew they were there. I had been wrong, I realised. Knowing where Mandy had died was no help. Her murder was just as shocking and incomprehensible to me as it had been when I'd first heard about it.

•

I got off the bus at the next stop and cut through Glasheen Park onto Magazine Road, using the walk as an opportunity to return one of the seven missed calls I'd got from my mother.

'I'm okay,' I said instead of hello when she answered.

'I know you are,' came the reply. 'But it's dreadful news.'

'Dire,' I said.

'I can't believe it.'

'No one can.'

'Did I ever meet her?'

'I don't think so.'

'Where are you now?'

'Walking home.'

'You should take a taxi. It's not safe for you to be on your own. Your father said you should move back in with us for a while.'

My mother was the family worrier-in-chief. It was a sign of how unprecedented the situation was that Dad was joining in too.

'I promise I'll be really careful. Tell Dad, will you please? I'll call you tomorrow.'

It had started to rain by the time I reached Lennox's. I joined the queue and listened to and scrolled through the rest of my messages, texting, *Thanks, talk soon* responses to the myriad 'isn't it awful's and 'are-you-okay's sent by friends and colleagues from other law firms.

It was only after I'd paid for my chips and was heading down Barrack Street, my umbrella buffeted by the breeze and the scent of vinegar in my nostrils, that I registered that Davy hadn't called me all day.

15

LEAVING THE LIGHT OFF, I FILLED A GLASS OF MILK
and emptied the chips onto a plate. Then, I took a seat at the
table and gazed north over the darkening city.

The kitchen–living room is on the top floor; my bedroom
and en suite bathroom on the middle; the ground floor has a
study, a small spare bedroom, and a shower, loo and laundry
room with an entrance hall opening onto a tiny garden with
a high stone wall and a grey wooden door. Beyond that is the
narrow lane that leads to Barrack Street. The restricted size of
the site dictated the footprint of the house I was able to build at a
time when the Irish banks were giving out home loans like Rice
Krispie buns at a child's birthday party, but it needn't have been
a round tower. For that, you can blame my childhood obsession
with Rapunzel. My tower is brighter than hers, though. The top
floor is made of glass, and a perforated steel balcony encircles the
exterior. In summer, I can fold back the south-west-facing doors
behind the dining table to let in the evening air and the last of
the sun. Now, rain beat against the windows and wind blew wild
rivulets in every direction, and I tried not to think about Davy.
With Mandy dead, it felt wrong to be feeling sorry for myself,
just because I'd gone twelve hours without hearing from him.

Or had it been longer than that? He hadn't stayed Sunday
night, though he usually did. Some early work thing on Monday,
he'd said. That's how he'd said it, too. Casually. Non-specifically.
I hadn't noticed anything off at the time.

Now that I thought about it though, I hadn't seen him since
late Sunday morning. Hadn't had any kind of message from him
since early Sunday afternoon. And on the day that one of my
workmates was found murdered, which he had to have heard
about by now, he hadn't made any kind of contact with me. Not
even once.

But then I hadn't phoned or texted him either, had I? What
did that say about the kind of relationship we had? Maybe he
was at home thinking the same thing as me, worrying about
why, when this awful thing happened, telling him hadn't been
my top priority.

And maybe he wasn't.

•

I took the plate and scraped the uneaten chips into the compost
bin – ordinarily, I'd consider it a crying shame not to finish every
last delicious morsel. I grabbed my phone from the kitchen
worktop and checked Davy's social media. He didn't do personal
profiles but his gym had the usual Facebook and Instagram. The
Facebook page had a post: 'Reminder! All Davy PT cancelled
Monday', and detailed alternative arrangements for his fitness
classes. The reminder was some comfort. Whatever he was
doing seemed pre-planned. It might have been a meeting with
his accountant or the bank. Though he'd usually talk to me about
that kind of thing; said he valued my advice.

But if his absence had nothing to do with his business, what was he up to?

•

I could imagine plenty of things the old Davy might have been doing, none of them good. I'd known him when he was like that. The fake confidence. The I'm-clean-now lies that the judge might have believed the first time but that I didn't. Not really. After one of his court appearances, I gave him a card for the rehab facility in Tabor Lodge and urged him to seek help.

It took a while but he did it. He came to me and I helped with getting him a place – made some calls, nothing major. He'd reached that stage all by himself. When I saw him just before he went in, the thing I remember is the desperation, the longing he had to be done with it all. He'd told me he was finished. Never going back down that spiral. And, in more than five years, he hadn't.

But what if he'd slipped and hadn't wanted – or felt able – to tell me? What if that explained why he'd been distant with me over the last while?

Distant was the wrong word. When we were together, mostly it felt the same as it had, though he was more quiet more often. Taciturn.

When we were apart, he was busier. Less available. Only a little.

Barely noticeable.

Until now.

•

I hated thinking like this about him, about who he used to be. I heard enough of it from Sadie, my closest friend right through since we were deeply uncool freshers. We'd both graduated with BCL degrees but, while I slogged through the Law Society entrance exams, she went into the guards and got into the detective branch as soon as she possibly could. She was still a detective garda; hadn't gone up the ranks, even though she'd come under pressure from some of the higher-ups to apply for promotion.

Davy was the reason a sort of unacknowledged coolness had developed between us. I'd guessed that's how it would be. It was the reason I'd held off telling her about him at the start.

I wasn't wrong.

I told her finally the Saturday before Christmas, when we met for a late lunch in the Long Valley. The relationship with Davy was still pretty new but I hadn't wanted to lie about why I wasn't going to be at her house as planned on New Year's Eve.

The pub was packed but we'd managed to get one of the small round tables in the snug. I stood at the side opening and raised my eyebrows at Peadar behind the bar at the far end. He weaved a passage towards me, past other staff pulling pints and filling fragrant lemon-and-clove hot whiskeys, the length of the polished wooden counter. I ordered a pot of Barry's for two and a white cheddar-and-egg salad for Sadie – her favourite sandwich in the world. For myself, I went with a toasted special on brown. I'd been overdoing it on the spiced beef since the start of December – they only serve it seasonally in the Valley though it's available year round other places in the city.

I'd waited till Sadie's mouth was full, and spoke fast, eyes down. As I dotted English mustard on my toastie I said I'd met someone and that I was cooking dinner for him and me on New Year's Eve. I said that his name was Davy Keenan. No more.

But she remembered him. She'd seen me representing him at the courthouse in Anglesea Street when he'd been my client.

'Jesus Christ, Finn,' she said.

She took a second bite of her sandwich.

'Not a ringing endorsement, so?'

She took a sip of tea. Then another one.

'I'll admit he's had issues,' I said. 'But "had" is the operative word. Past tense.'

'We all have issues,' Sadie said. 'He's got more than his fair share. Probably a lot more than you know about.'

'I know about him. He used to be my client, remember?'

'Yeah. How does that work? Surely there's some kind of a no client-shagging clause in the legal code of ethics?'

'Course,' I said. 'Except when they're really good-looking.'

'Interesting response,' Sadie said. 'Evasive.'

'Stop fucking interrogating me,' I said.

'Defensive now,' Sadie said. 'And still no answer.'

'I'm not breaching any code,' I said. 'He's my *ex*-client. And my friend. I know him. He's clean. He's a health freak, for fuck's sake.'

'You sure about that?'

'I'm sure.'

'And it doesn't bother you that he spent years hoovering up cocaine like there was no tomorrow? Consorting with criminals?'

'It bothers me. It'd really bother me if he was still doing it. Which he isn't.'

'Dealing,' Sadie continued.

'He was only ever done for possession.'

'That's all he was caught for, you mean. He was *known*. Well-known. There are loads of Friday-night cokehead gobshites out there. Davy wasn't like that. He was way beyond it.'

'"Known to the gardaí". Now there's a handy catch-all. If there'd been evidence of dealing, presumably he'd have been charged?'

She eagle-eyed me.

'Are you *really* that naive, Finn?'

It was a good question.

I didn't answer it.

After a while I said, 'He's good for me. He cares about me. I care about him.'

'You should keep away from him. He'll let you down. He'll drag you—'

'I'm hearing you loud and clear, detective. Now, can we not talk about this anymore today please?'

'We can not talk about this all you like. Until the day we *have* to talk about it.'

'What's that supposed to mean? What day?'

'I don't know,' Sadie said. 'But when it happens, you most certainly will.'

TUESDAY

TUESDAY

16

I WOKE AT 5.20 A.M. TO THE PING OF A PHONE
message.

> *Bad news about Mandy. Heard about it too late to call. Hope you
> OK. Talk later xx*

I sat up in bed and thought about ringing him, but lay down
again and reread the message. On the plus side, Davy was alive
and, based on the composition of the text, he seemed to be sober.
Against that, he'd made contact at a time when he could bank on
me not being awake. For some reason, he didn't want to talk to
me and I hadn't a clue why.

I had a choice. I could compose a long text asking him how he
was and where he was, and saying I was worried about him and
that I'd like to meet up with him as soon as possible.

Or not.

•

In the end, I went with 'not', though the decision took time, and
a series of distracted *vinyasa* sequences on my yoga mat, followed

by a cold shower. Luckily, I wasn't likely to be seeing anything except the inside of Mandy's office for the day so I didn't need to make much of an effort with dressing. I rubbed in a minimum of tinted moisturiser and dragged on a black cotton long-sleeved T-shirt and an old grey pinstripe trouser suit and trainers, and scraped my hair into a ponytail. I considered going up to the kitchen and making porridge with milk and black coffee – my regular breakfast. Instead, I sat on the stairs and checked my phone. No new messages.

But Mandy's death was all over the news sites. Along with appeals for anyone with information to contact Coughlan's Quay garda station. I had information – the man I'd seen her with after the Dolly Parton concert. I wondered if Ed knew about him. Probably did. Mightn't say anything, though. I checked rip.ie: no results found. Too soon for funeral arrangements. The post-mortem examination would delay things. And the shock. I sent Ed a message ending in: *Let me know if I can do anything to help*. Then I texted Sadie: *Call me. Have something for you re Mandy B. Might be important (very) to investigation*. I should've told her last night as I'd planned. But I'd been too caught up in thoughts of Davy and the wrinkles in our relationship. While a woman I'd worked with for fifteen years lay dead.

I badly needed to cop myself on.

●

My phone rang. It was Sadie.

'I'm fairly sure Mandy was having an affair,' I said.

'Go on.'

'Yeah. I saw her the night of the Dolly Parton gig in June. She was with a guy. He was wearing the face off her in a car down by the roundabout just before the National Sculpture Factory. Next day she told me to keep schtum about it.'

'Unsurprisingly.'

'Agreed,' I said. 'But there was something off. She looked terrified, and the terror seemed to be about something more than the fear of getting caught. But I don't know.' I added, 'You're the only person I've told.'

'Are you prepared to make a statement? Assist us in making up a photofit of the man you saw with her?'

'Sure. Yes. Of course. I don't know if I'd recognise him though. It happened fast. I mainly noticed the hair colour. That it wasn't Ed. Ed's fair. The guy in the car was dark.'

She told me I might know more than I realised. She said she'd get back to me about my statement. And that she'd been tied up so far with the crime scene and the surrounding houses and streets. Also, as the incident had happened at the weekend, they'd been concentrating on what Mandy had done on the day of her death and the day before it. They'd spoken to close family. None of them had mentioned an affair. She said they'd be moving onto her neighbours in Blackrock today and to Mandy's co-workers after that. She said she didn't yet know who'd be coming into the firm to do the MLC interviews yet – it might or might not be her.

Then Sadie said, 'Tell me everything you noticed about Mandy in the weeks preceding her death. Disputes with colleagues. Unusual meetings. Behaviour changes. Money worries. Even if you think it's not relevant, tell me. Any investigation is as much about ruling suspects out as ruling them in.'

In response, I told her the truth.

Which was easy.

Because I didn't know anything.

•

I walked to work on streets that weren't as frantic as they would be later. A mist hung over the river as I crossed the South Gate Bridge. The tide was low and, on the weir, a heron watched.

I swung by Gusto and picked up a large Americano and a custard tartlet. It was going on for 8 a.m., as I was climbing the steps to the front door, that it hit me afresh that Mandy wouldn't be doing this ever again. It hit me even more strongly how little I'd known her. All those years sharing a workplace and we'd never even had lunch together, apart from being in the tea room at the same time occasionally, while she nibbled a Ryvita with zero per cent fat cream cheese, simultaneously rattling off instructions for her secretary into a voice recorder. Ed had said that she'd been feeling down over recent months, but the last time I'd seen her, she looked the same as ever, in a sleeveless black dress with arms so toned and sinewy they made Michelle Obama's look flabby. When had that been? Four, five days ago? Had anyone apart from Ed noticed that she'd not been herself? Was Ed telling the truth or was he lying? Had there been any change in her work practices? Those were the kinds of questions I'd have to keep in mind for my report. Doing something felt better than doing nothing. Mandy had been murdered. Like countless other women, she was dead by association; dead by random act; dead just because. Whoever she had been in life, now she was a statistic.

And that was wrong.

17

RECEPTION WAS EMPTY. I STOOD FOR A MOMENT in the eerie quiet, recalling Mandy's clients from yesterday, the clients nobody had known – McInerney and the younger man in the Jack Wills hoodie. I hadn't remembered to mention them when I'd been talking to Sadie but I'd tell her later. By then, I might know more. Had it been mere coincidence that they'd come to the office on the day Mandy's body was found? Maybe. They might have been first-timers she'd spoken to over the weekend and given an appointment to, not knowing that she wouldn't be here.

It was such bad luck that the usual receptionist had been off work – if the clients had been to see Mandy before, Dervla would have met them. Still, if she was back today, I could talk to her. Then I remembered the CCTV that covered the area around the main entrance and the hallway as far as reception, viewable live on a split screen by the receptionist on duty, provided she was looking. If I could access the footage for yesterday, Dervla would be able to get a look at McInerney and his companion after all. I'd talk to Pauline Doyle about it later.

•

By noon, I'd gone through enough of Mandy's files to establish beyond doubt that she was a better solicitor than I'd ever be; better organised; more detail-driven; always engaged. The paper files were double punched, every page lined up regimentally. I had an impression of absolute certainty, of a world without grey areas. The digital files were more awkward to read – I had to click in and out of documents rather than flick pages – but just as pristine. I was comparing the paper with the digital, checking on the basics that the Law Society would look at first: anti-money laundering compliance, client identity documents, costs. But when there's serious misconduct in our profession, most of the time it's about money, so that's what I was looking at mainly. Thus far, the only remarkable thing was Mandy's efficiency. I had been through barely five per cent of her files but already I had the feeling that Gabriel and the rest of the partners could sleep easily; that whatever the reason she'd died was, it had nothing to do with her work at MLC.

None of that came as a surprise. Mandy had always struck me as a Type A, top-of-the-class achiever. In her job as Finance and Trusts partner, she acted for some of Cork's wealthiest people, arranging on- and off-shore structures and shelters to ensure that the 'haves' she represented stayed that way. I was far from being an expert in the area, but none of what she was doing looked illegal. It was how the world worked. Her client list read like a social column report of the attendees at a €5k-a-table charity ball. Noblesse obliged generously for all kinds of worthy causes – provided they weren't being obliged to pay too much nasty old tax.

●

Tina popped in for a chat around 12.15.

'How's it all going?' she asked.

'Slowly,' I said. 'Like rolling a boulder uphill.'

'I'm sure Kathleen wouldn't mind if you phoned her. She knows this stuff inside out.'

'I'd prefer not to bother her for the moment. Any idea how she's doing?'

'Completely distraught.'

'No wonder.'

'Coming back tomorrow, she says. Though I told her to stay off another day. The place won't collapse without her.'

'She should take as much time as she needs,' I said.

'Yeah,' Tina said. 'She's probably worried about her job though. She's not getting any younger. And with Mandy gone, some of her clients might move to other firms.'

'That's true,' I said. 'Though Gabriel didn't say a word to me about any of that.'

But I was sure he'd thought of it.

18

AT 12.30, PAULINE DOYLE DROPPED ME IN A
memory stick with the security camera footage copied onto it.

'8.30 a.m. to 10 a.m.,' she said. 'Three cameras. Three video clips.'

'Have you looked at them? Do they show anything?'

'I have too many other things to be at,' she said. 'Gabriel has me like a headless chicken reviewing all our tech and data policies, checking backups – you name it – in anticipation of the inspection.'

'He's not come near me this morning,' I said. 'Do we know yet when the Law Society are arriving?'

'No,' Pauline said. 'Or if they ever will be. He's being a bit over-the-top, I think. I don't know what's wrong. I've never seen him like this. Though I suppose it's not every day that one of your partners gets murdered.'

'True,' I said. 'By the way, is Dervla back on reception? I've been in solitary confinement here most of the morning so I haven't seen her.'

'She's back. I've not been talking to her. Been a tad busy.'

I laughed. 'Just a tad, by the sounds of it,' I said.

•

After Pauline had left the room, I slotted the memory stick into Mandy's desktop and started to watch. Straightaway I realised that, as well as providing a record of the two men, it would also show my work colleagues' unguarded morning habits – who was early; who was late; who bounded up the steps; and who made it look like this was the last place they wanted to be. The cameras covered the front door, a partial view of the entrance hallway and reception itself, but not the client waiting room. The purpose of the CCTV was straightforward security rather than anything more sinister. Occasionally in the past, thieves had tried to gain access to the building, seeking out unattended handbags and phones or other portable technology. Occasionally, too, clients became aggressive, though, given the firm profile, that wasn't as much of a problem in MLC as it might have been in other offices. Employees had a card, while everyone else rang the bell, spoke their business to the communication box on the wall and got buzzed in or otherwise.

I checked through the three clips and selected the one for the front-door camera, figuring that if I could isolate the time that the two clients arrived, I could fast forward easily through the irrelevant portions in the interior clips to get a better look at them. I sped on until I saw a glum-looking me get to the door at 8.50 – I was almost sure the men hadn't come before then – then slowed the clip to real-time speed. The stream of people entering peaked around 8.55 with some holding the door open for others and a few stopping to chat – Tina one of those, unsurprisingly – before going inside. I didn't see Gabriel at all but that was because the video only started at 8.30 a.m. He would have been in long before that. Kathleen wasn't there either, presumably for the same reason, not suspecting that Mandy wouldn't be at work with the dawn that day as usual. The postman came at 9.05 followed by a yawning Dermot Lyons, looking like he'd spent too long at the nineteenth hole. Then there was a lull. While other mornings were often busy, very few clients wanted appointments this early on a Monday. Finally, at 9.20 a.m., I saw two men at the door. I sat up in my seat.

Going by Katja's description, this was them.

They walked up the steps together, the older one slightly in front. Katja had said that he was fifty or sixty, but I put him at sixty to seventy. He wore a light-coloured, suit type jacket and a pale open-necked shirt. He wasn't wearing a coat, which surprised me, as yesterday had been coolish, but maybe he'd driven and left his car nearby. As he reached the door, he turned back towards the younger one, who was in a black hoodie with 'Jack Wills' in block capitals on the front, just as Katja had described him. The older man was small, white and thin; the younger man was tall and well-built, possibly mixed race, with dark hair. They had a short discussion in the course of which the man who had called himself McInerney seemed to get more and more animated, though I could no longer see his face. The younger one patted him a few times on the upper arm and shoulder, in what looked like an attempt to calm or comfort him. It seemed to work. Then he reached across the older man and pressed the buzzer. A few seconds later, they went in.

I rewound and tried to work out the dynamic between them. There was a familiarity in how the younger man dealt with the older one. Whoever they were, they knew each other well.

Next, I clicked straight into the reception video and fast-forwarded to 9.21. Things played out much as Katja had said, McInerney doing most of the talking, Jack Wills saying nothing. As the video was silent, I couldn't hear what was being said. Nor could I, due to the angle of the camera, see their faces. Nevertheless, based on the hand gestures, it was reasonable to describe McInerney's mood as increasingly irate as he stood by the reception desk, and reacted to being told that Mandy wasn't available and that nobody else was expecting him either.

The hallway clip didn't show them leaving reception and going into the waiting room – there was a blind spot there, though that's where they'd gone, according to Katja – but I rewound and caught them walking into the building at 9.20 and out again at 9.48. Then I reopened the front door video and saw them moving quickly down the steps and out of sight.

They had spent less than half an hour in MLC, most of that apparently unattended in the client waiting room. But why had they come? More importantly, perhaps – why had they left in such a hurry, and without a word to anyone?

19

I OPENED A FILE FOR THE VIDEO CLIPS ON Mandy's desktop and sent them to myself as well. Then I took screenshots of the two men, and saved them to Mandy's desktop and to my phone, so that I had something on hand to show to Dervla and Kathleen. If they weren't able to identify the two men, I could circulate the photographs to everyone in the office. I'd decide later if that was a good idea or not. I didn't want to create unnecessary panic. Or gossip. My instinct was that the investigation into Mandy's murder would come down to a two-horse race between Ed and the dark-haired man I'd seen her with in the TT, and that McInerney and Jack Wills were unlikely to have anything to do with it. Coming to her workplace and making an overt connection between her and them seemed like bizarre behaviour for people who'd just committed murder. On the other hand, maybe attention-seeking was part of their modus operandi? I reminded myself again to tell Sadie about them. And that it wasn't within my area of expertise or my job description to say what a murderer might or might not do.

But my job *was* to review Mandy's workload. For better or worse, the two Monday-morning visitors were part of that so, as far as I was concerned, I had to make every effort to find them.

Besides, a manhunt was a hell of a lot more interesting than reading Mandy's brain-numbingly dull files. And, if I was doing something active, my mind was less likely to drift off down side alleys into thoughts of Mandy's bereft children or, even more likely, of Davy and the question of how much longer I'd be able to stop myself from replying to his 5.20 a.m. text message. The longer I left it, I reasoned, the calmer I'd be.

My stomach growled. I assigned myself one final easy task before I went to lunch.

•

Gabriel McGrath wasn't a man given to loitering. As a rule, he moved purposefully from duty to duty with barely a pause for breath. But when I went to find Dervla at reception, he was there before me, the second time in two days that I'd found him – and there was no other way to put it – hanging around doing nothing in particular. He had a furtive look about him and said nothing when I entered reception.

Dervla was seated at her desk. Married to a teacher, she had three children she rarely mentioned, though Tina had told me that all of them had gone to university on high points courses. Discreet, dependable and highly intelligent, Dervla had always worked full-time. Her official role was receptionist but everyone knew that she acted as Gabriel's intelligence operative, monitoring post and telephone calls, feeding back information on staff productivity and suspect behaviour. She wasn't the office manager and had no allocated HR role but, if she wasn't keen on a new staff member, they didn't last.

'May I help you, Finn?'

Dervla's tone was haughty.

'I hope so,' I said. 'I wonder if you could take a look at these photographs?'

Gabriel and Dervla exchanged glances.

'What kind of photographs?' Gabriel asked.

'Of Mandy's clients from yesterday,' I said. 'I checked the CCTV.'

'Oh yes,' Gabriel said, and it might have been relief that I heard in his voice but I wasn't sure.

'Give them here,' Dervla said.

'Scroll right,' I said and passed my phone to her.

After a few moments, she looked at me.

'I don't think so. I can't be a hundred per cent, but I don't think they've been in before.'

She passed the phone to Gabriel. He swiped back and forth impatiently.

'No. No. I wouldn't get bogged down with them if I were you. Concentrate on the files.'

'They'll be back,' Dervla said. 'Or they'll phone. I'll let you know when they do.'

'The older one was called McInerney,' I said.

'So I hear,' Dervla said. 'The name means nothing to me.'

She looked at Gabriel again and he looked at her. Then he looked at me and I looked at the two of them. I left the room and trudged down the steps to the street.

I was starting to realise that there was nothing easy about any of this.

20

I LOVE SUMMER IN CORK – THE SHORT NIGHTS,
the endless days. I hate autumn, when the dark draws in and
the mists descend, and a bitter nostalgia for what's soon to be
lost taints every breeze. The only advantage to this season of
disappointment is that the crowds thin out in the English Market,
making negotiating the narrow aisles less of a chore. They're
still there, the mindlessly strolling, rain-jacketed knapsack-
carriers, clogging the passageway between the olive stall and the
Alternative Bread Company, but they're fewer, circumventable
and, crucially, far less likely to be wasting precious lunch-eating
space in the Farmgate café with leisurely coffee-drinking and
guidebook-reading. All the same, I climbed the wooden stairs
with trepidation. It was well after 2 p.m. and the rush of locals
had probably passed, but you could never tell with tourists. I'd
be lucky to secure a single high seat at the ledge overlooking the
fountain, though a table would suit my purposes better.

Thankfully, the place was manageably busy rather than
heaving. I gave in my order at the counter and Rebecca directed
me to a two-top by the wall. I put my coat over the other chair
and prayed I wouldn't run into anyone I knew. When it's quiet,
the vaulted arch of the roof and the dreamy haze of the light

give this beautiful place the atmosphere of a cathedral. People have been known to write poetry here.

I took out my notebook and tried to think.

·

By the time my lunch came – egg sandwich on brown, caramel square, peppermint tea – I'd decided that, whatever Gabriel had said, McInerney and Jack Wills were key. I didn't know what they were key to, but I knew that I needed to find out who they were. After that, I needed to find where they were. I wouldn't send around the photos of them to everyone by email – not yet – but I'd talk to the people in the office who were close to Mandy. Doing that would also give me the opportunity to indirectly raise the issue of the man I'd seen in the car with Mandy. I'd have to talk to Ed about him far more directly. When Sadie called me back to arrange my statement, I planned to trade my information on the TT guy and on what I'd found out about McInerney and Jack Wills for information from her on the crime scene and what they'd found there.

And on the post-mortem. The updated news reports on my phone were saying only that Mandy had died from a head injury, nothing about the kind of injury, or whether or not a weapon had been used. I sent Ed a message, asking if I could call out to see him later in the day. Then I devoured my food and returned to the office.

21

AFTER PRINTING OUT EXTRA COPIES OF THE
McInerney photographs, I commandeered a small meeting room
and spent the afternoon interviewing Mandy's team: an associate,
two junior solicitors, a trainee solicitor and three secretarial staff.
Mandy's PA, Kathleen, was still out on compassionate leave – I'd
have to talk to her separately on her return. I didn't know when
the gardaí would show up here wanting to do pretty much the
same thing I was doing. I didn't think it mattered. They had
their role. I had mine.

•

I prefaced each interview with a statement: 'As you know, I've
been appointed by Gabriel and the other partners to carry out a
review of Mandy's work. I hope I can rely on your cooperation.'

'Absolutely', 'sure', 'of course', 'no problem', the replies
came, one after another. But little else of any real worth did:
Mandy had been a great boss, tough but fair; no one had seen the
two men before; and no one gave any hint of knowing anything
about a love affair. Interestingly, however, none of them had
noticed any deterioration in Mandy, in her mood or in her work.

She hadn't seemed worried about anything; she hadn't seemed depressed.

Maybe she'd been putting on a front? Or maybe Ed had been lying when he'd implied initially that she'd seemed low enough to take her own life? Because she hadn't done that. She'd been brutally murdered by a person or persons unknown.

Though if she was being threatened by someone – by the man in the TT, say – that *could* fit with what Ed said about her mood in the months before she died. So maybe he wasn't lying.

But maybe her team were? Reluctant, perhaps, to acknowledge that she'd been in trouble and that they'd ignored the signs?

•

The last interviewee was Hugo Woulfe, Mandy's trainee. I didn't get a chance to utter my opening statement because he spoke first.

'You're wasting your time,' he said. 'If you're trying to pin something on Mandy, you'll never find it.'

I put down my pen and studied him. Early twenties. Tall. Short dark brown hair. Very muscular. And very handsome.

'What sport do you play?' I asked. Mandy's chosen ones always played something to a high level: the sporting discipline varied, it was the competitive instinct she was after.

'I swim,' he said.

'You're used to the early mornings, so?'

He shrugged a response but said nothing. I leaned across the table towards him.

'I'm not looking to pin anything on Mandy,' I said softly. 'Mandy's the victim.'

'Even if you were,' Woulfe said, 'you couldn't.'

'Is that because there's nothing to find?'

Without missing a beat he replied, 'Of course.'

'And no,' he added. 'I haven't seen those two before. Plus I wouldn't have thought they'd fit her regular client profile.'

'Why do you say that?'

'They don't look wealthy enough,' he said.

I picked up the photographs again. Woulfe was right. Whoever they were, they didn't look rich. They didn't look poor either. They looked ordinary.

'What work did you do for Mandy?'

'Drafting, mostly.'

'Trusts?'

'Yes.'

'Any other kind of work?'

'No,' he said. 'That's the only work she did.'

'How was she in the weeks before she died?'

'Great.'

'Not worried about anything?'

'She didn't worry. She could handle anything or anyone.'

'Except her murderer, obviously,' I said.

He coloured. 'I didn't mean—'

Interrupting him, I asked, 'What were your duties?'

'Drafting, like I said. And when she'd take instructions from clients, I'd usually sit in, take notes.'

'Usually?'

'Sometimes she'd want Kathleen to do it. Occasionally she'd see people on her own.'

'And after a meeting?'

'We'd talk through what was needed. Then she'd tell me what she wanted and when. Which was always yesterday.'

He laughed. Then he teared up.

'Sounds like you were close,' I said.

'We were,' he said. 'She was amazing.' After a pause he added, 'Are we done?'

'Almost,' I said. 'There's just one more thing. Did you know much about her private life?'

'You're talking about her family?'

'Apart from her family,' I said.

'You're not suggesting she was having an affair?'

I hadn't. But he had. The only one of Mandy's team to do so. And though he realised immediately that he'd made a mistake, he didn't give a millimetre on what he'd said, held eye contact too long for it to be anything other than an act of sheer willpower. I waited for him to say something else but he didn't. In the end, I broke the silence.

'Was she?'

'I couldn't see it,' Hugo Woulfe said. 'I mean, where would she get the time?'

'Honestly? In my experience, people make time.'

He glowered at me and left the room.

●

After that, I returned to Mandy's office, sat at her desk and shut down her computer. I gathered my rough notes and the photographs into a buff-coloured folder. I put the folder and a barrister's notebook in my briefcase. Then I left.

I told no one that I was going or where I was headed.

22

AN ENDURING GREYNESS HAD SETTLED OVER THE
city. As I walked, I remembered that long-ago June night I'd
spent near here at the Dolly concert at the Marquee with Davy.
He'd been late that evening, I recalled, and I hadn't asked him
why. The same way I hadn't yet asked him what he'd been doing
since Sunday. The same way I'd been ignoring how he'd been
with me over the last three months – the blowing hot and cold;
the unexplained absences. With Davy, periods of unavailability
were nothing new, though this one was the longest. Previously,
he'd volunteered information about his absences. This last while,
he'd left it to me to ask. And I never did.

I couldn't pinpoint when the change in him had started, because
most of the time we'd seemed as good together as we'd always
been. We fit. We wouldn't have before he got sober. We both
knew that. I wouldn't have gone near him and, more to the point,
except professionally, he wouldn't have come within ten miles of
me, though he'd had a lot of previous girlfriends. A few long-term
relationships. Co-dependent, he said they were. Unhealthy. Until
we got together, on his counsellor's advice, he'd avoided any kind
of serious relationship for years. I knew that, even though I rarely
asked him anything straight out about the time before us.

Nothing personal.

Nothing about his addiction.

I left it to him to tell me stuff. And he *did* tell. A lot.

I truly believed he'd tell me everything in time.

Everything important.

I didn't need to go all Spanish Inquisition on him.

•

On summer evenings, this part of Blackrock has the feel of an imagined Italy about it. It's no accident. The Marina, a long, raised, tree-lined riverside promenade built on reclaimed land sometime during the 1800s, was named by the city councillors after a similar construction near Palermo in Sicily, a place that few, if any of them, could ever have had any hope of visiting. Which probably tells you everything you need to know about Cork people.

But it was cold now and the tide was coming in fast. A keen wind blew up the river from the outer harbour, whipping the water into rough peaks. I headed up Castle Road to Mandy's former home. The house, an early nineteenth-century gentleman's dwelling with dark plaster and an aubergine-painted door, was on the slope below the castle. A climbing rose had scattered white petals on the slate path. The curtains were drawn on all the front-facing windows. No sound came from inside. I rang the bell.

Seconds later, my phone pinged. It was a message from Ed: *Is that u Finn?*

I replied: *Yes.*

Ed opened the door. He was wearing the same ancient pink

polo shirt he'd had on the previous day. He looked like he hadn't slept.

'Sorry about the MI5 capers,' he said. 'We're pretending we're not home. We've had so many visitors calling. And journalists. We're completely exhausted.'

'I'm sorry, Ed, maybe I shouldn't have come.'

'You're okay,' he said. 'You're the last person I spoke to before it all turned to shit.'

He pressed his right hand to his mouth and burst out crying.

'If this is too much for you,' I said, 'I can come back another time. But we do need to talk at some point.'

'I'm glad you're here,' he said.

He turned in the direction of the back of the house, gesturing for me to follow. I felt my way after him. With the thick drapes and no lights switched on, it was hard to see. I fancied that the place smelled of money and privilege. Though it might have been the beeswax furniture polish. Ahead of me, Ed stopped.

'We'll go into the kitchen,' he said.

•

It was one of those new extensions familiar from television property makeover programmes but rarely as impeccably presented in real life. We stepped from the 1810s into the twenty-first century; from darkness into light. The entire rear wall was glass, south-facing, with massive sliding doors. Roof lights illuminated the space, decorated in muted shades of white, offset by limed hardwood furnishings, pale stone floors, brightly coloured rugs and, to the side, a huge tan aged-leather sofa laden with cushions. There was no television. The room felt warm. It felt like a sanctuary – Ed's or Mandy's, I wondered.

'When she was at home, this was her place,' Ed said. 'She loved cooking, you know. Baking especially. You wouldn't think it of her. But she always said there was nothing wrong with a home-made treat. I ended up eating most of her produce, mind you.'

He patted his non-existent potbelly. I wasn't sure I bought the tradwife version of Mandy he was peddling, but I didn't know.

'Where are the girls?' I asked.

'Upstairs,' Ed said. 'I told them you were coming. They'll be down to say hello in a while, I imagine.'

'How are they?'

He put his hand to his mouth again and his eyes welled with tears.

'Devastated,' he said.

•

He sat at the table. There was an empty wine glass in front of him.

'Do you want a drink?'

'I'm fine,' I said. 'I just wanted to touch base with you. Talk through a few things.'

'Talk away,' Ed said. 'The guards have been here a few times. They're not long gone, actually. Terribly nicey-nice. None of them saying what they're all thinking.'

He paused.

'That I'm *suspecto numero uno*. It's always the husband, isn't it?'

I made no response. He had it right.

Except, in this case, there was the added complication of his deceased wife's lover.

'I didn't kill Mandy,' Ed said. 'Of course I didn't kill her. I mean, I would say that, wouldn't I – but you saw me yesterday morning, you know—'

'Tell me about the weekend,' I said.

'Normal enough. Ish. Friday, she got home … I'm not sure when. I wasn't here, I was in Crosshaven until about 7 p.m.'

He grimaced. 'Had to see a man about a boat. It seemed important then. Yeah. It's absolutely fucking irrelevant now, obviously. Anyway, when I got back around half past, she was out running, but she'd been home – her car was here. She got back around eight. Made pasta. After we ate, we all sat together in the drawing room – the girls, typical teens, not talking to us, headphones on, streaming on their own screens – but they went upstairs about ten. Mandy and I half-watched *The Late Late Show* for a while and she went to bed before half past. I switched over to Graham Norton after. I'd had a few glasses of wine. Conked out. Woke up around 1 a.m. She was asleep when I went up. Next morning when I woke, she'd gone into work. Came home around 3 p.m. Quiet. Not in great form. I asked her was she okay. She bit my head off, so I didn't ask her again.'

'Did she often work on a Saturday?'

'It was more sometimes than often. She'd been trying to cut down, to be here for the girls at the weekends. Took stuff home. Rarely went into the actual office at weekends anymore. But last weekend, I think, I … I … I definitely had the feeling she was worried about work, but—'

'And what happened Saturday night?'

'Well, in fact, as regards Mandy, I don't actually know. I popped down to the local around 6 p.m. For just the one. But I got waylaid. By the time I got back – I was home by ten – she was gone to bed. She'd left a dinner for me on the worktop, so I nuked it. Then I drank a few glasses of water, took a couple of paracetamol and went to bed. Still had a fucking dog of a hangover, mind you. That bloody craft beer is supposed to be good for you but it kills my stomach.'

'And Sunday?'

'I stayed in all day. Glued to the sofa. She left the house at 5 or 5.30 p.m. and went for a walk – up past the castle, and along by the water towards Mahon, was her usual route. She must have come back, I'm not sure when, and taken the car. I'm nearly sure she didn't come in, though. She'd been out earlier in the day as well to the big Tesco and M&S food in Douglas to do the weekly shop – it took her a few hours; not sure how long. Arrived home laden down as usual. Which has been quite handy the way things went. We haven't even had to go out for milk. Not that it matters. *Jesus.*'

He put his head in his hands.

'Did the gardaí tell you what time she died?'

I heard him let out a breath. Then he looked up at me and started talking again.

'Sunday night. Sometime before midnight. I was here. Ava too. Ruth was at a sleepover at her friend Bronagh Galvin's house down the road. Came back here early Monday to get ready for school.'

'I was up in bed when she was dying,' he went on. 'Not asleep. I keep thinking that if I'd only reported her to the guards, told them that she was missing on Sunday night, that they could have found her before … They might have saved her if I'd … But I didn't.'

'She was an adult,' I said. 'They probably wouldn't have acted all that fast. You weren't to know. Especially if …'

'If what?'

'If it wasn't her first time staying out all night.'

Ed didn't try to conceal his annoyance.

'That's an odd thing for you to say.'

'I suppose it is,' I said.

I waited. Then Ed spoke again, his voice higher. Cutting.

'Was there some particular reason you came? Apart obviously from wanting to offer your *kind* condolences to your dead colleague's husband and children?'

He stopped himself from saying more but I had the strong feeling that he could have, and that he had done exactly that, and often, right here in this room. The 'domestic bliss' picture he'd attempted to paint started to fade. Instead, 'unhappy differences' – the standard phrase lawyers use in separations and divorces, to cover everything from blazing rows to antagonistic silence – came to mind.

'Actually, there was,' I said.

I took the photos out of my briefcase and passed them across the table.

'These men came to the office yesterday morning looking for Mandy. The older one said his name was McInerney. But they had no appointment. She had no client called McInerney. No one in the office has either. I just wondered …'

Ed looked confused, then clarity dawned.

'You think these two might have something to do with Mandy's murder,' he said.

'Quite possibly,' I said.

If her husband didn't do it.

Or her lover.

He nodded, then picked up the photographs and scrutinised them.

'McInerney, you said?'

'The older one, yes.'

'Not the most common Cork name,' Ed said.

'They mightn't be from Cork.'

'I've never seen either of them before. And I don't know any McInerneys.'

'Okay,' I said. 'Thanks.'

'Have you told the guards about this?'

'Not yet,' I said. 'But I will.'

'The thing is,' I added, 'I've had to tell them something else too. I'm sorry … I don't know how to put this. I assumed they would have said something to you by now?'

He shook his head.

After a pause he said, 'Whatever it is, just say it.'

I didn't know why the gardaí hadn't questioned him yet about the affair. And Sadie hadn't told me not to say it to him. She might have assumed that, as I hadn't told anyone before I said it to her this morning, I'd keep on keeping quiet about it. She hadn't known I planned to visit Ed though. But it was too late to row back now. I took a breath and ploughed on.

'Back in June I saw Mandy with a dark-haired man. I didn't get a look at his face. But they seemed, well … I had a feeling they were more than friends.'

Ed's face hardened.

'Why are you telling me this?'

Because I wanted to know if you knew about him.

And who he is.

'I'm not sure,' I said.

Without a word, he got up and went to the fridge. He sloshed white wine into his glass, slugged back some of it, refilled the glass to the brim and returned to the table.

'I can't tempt you?' he asked, an artificial lightness in his voice.

I shook my head. He took another drink and put down the glass. Then he took in a deep breath through his mouth and let it out slowly.

'I had an idea there was someone else. I never said it to her. But I knew.'

'Is that the reason you didn't call the guards or call around Mandy's family and friends on Sunday night and Monday morning?'

He nodded.

'And it *wasn't* Mandy's first time staying out all night?'

He took another sip of wine.

'Last Sunday night,' Ed said. 'I assumed Mandy was with him.'

'How long had the relationship been going on?'

'A while. A good while. More than a year. Maybe two.'

'Is that what you meant when you said that she hadn't been herself for a while, that she'd been feeling down?'

'It was partly the ... affair. I had the feeling that she was unhappy. At first, I saw it as a positive sign. I thought she might be about to end it with him. But she had a lot on her mind last weekend. I told you that already. After she went missing, I wondered if I'd got it wrong, if she might harm herself.'

'We know now that didn't happen,' I said. 'But you said before you thought her low mood was about work. Do you think now it was related to her extra-marital relationship?'

'It could've been either or both. I still think mainly it was work. Gut feeling.'

'Was she having problems with someone on her team? With Hugo her trainee maybe?'

'If she was, she didn't say,' Ed said.

'Or might she have been having a disagreement with one of the other partners – Dermot Lyons, perhaps, or Gabriel?'

'I don't know. Maybe. All I know is, she went to work on Saturday. Unless …'

'Unless this time, she didn't.'

'She rarely bothered to lie. She'd just say she was going out, or that she was going for a walk. I learned not to ask questions. I knew she wouldn't give me an answer. On Saturday, I took her at her word when she said she was going to work. But she might have been with him.'

'Will you tell me his name?'

'I didn't want to know it. I hoped that if we never mentioned him or the affair that she'd tire of him, that she'd come back to us. I was wrong. If I'd said something, she mightn't, wouldn't, be dead now.'

'You're asking me to believe that you don't know the other man's name?'

'I don't know it. Honestly I don't. Scout's honour.'

'But you think he killed her?'

'It's the only possibility I can think of.'

'And you didn't consider saying that to the guards?'

'I thought about it and decided against. I wanted to leave it till after the funeral. To allow her to go to her grave in peace, before they start ripping her reputation to shreds. It probably comes across as foolish.'

●

It didn't seem foolish. It seemed strange. It *was* strange. Most people in Ed's position would have wanted to find their wife's murderer.

Most people would have been out for blood.

23

I WAS FAIRLY SURE THAT NEITHER OF THE GIRLS
had heard my conversation with Ed but they'd come into the
kitchen so soon after, I couldn't be certain. They showed no signs
of anything other than the deepest grief – their faces red and
blotchy, their eyes swollen from crying; both swaddled in night-
clothes, fluffy dressing-gowns and furry slippers, like more childish
versions of their usual selves. Ava, the elder, was sixteen and was
the image of Mandy. Ruth, two years younger, looked like Ed.

'I'm sorry about your mum,' I said.

I didn't say that I knew how they felt. I didn't know. Not
really. Not quite like this. But I knew something – I knew
enough to keep it simple.

'I'm so sad for both of you,' I said.

'You bought us ice cream once,' Ava said.

'Did I?'

'We were at the Opera House with Mum. We were very small.
Do you remember, Ruth?'

'I don't know,' Ruth said.

'Mum had bought us popcorn, but you said it was illegal for
children to go to the theatre without ice cream. You bought us
tubs of Ben & Jerry's.'

'That was you?' Ruth asked.

'I don't remember the ice cream,' I said. 'What did Mandy say about it?'

'She laughed,' Ava said. 'She said it was okay. Later, anytime we went to a show, I'd remind her of it.'

'*We* would,' Ruth said.

'It became a tradition,' Ava said. 'I don't think I'll ever go to the Opera House again.'

'Me neither,' Ruth said. 'Not for a long time.'

'Not ever,' Ava said. 'Thanks for coming but …'

She ran from the kitchen, followed speedily by Ruth. They thumped upstairs and a door slammed.

Ed called after them, 'I'll be up in a minute.'

'I'll go,' I said.

'Yes,' Ed said. 'Before you do, can I ask you something?'

'Sure.'

'Do you think I need a solicitor?'

'You need two,' I said. 'There's no immediate rush with the first one – I'm sure you're well aware that you'll need someone to process Mandy's estate?'

'I presumed MLC would handle that side of things?'

'In theory the firm could, but it's complicated. I think you're better off getting someone independent – a solicitor or an accountant, preferably both – to represent your interests in relation to the termination of Mandy's partnership, the terms of severance and so on. I can give you a few names but, like I said, there's no urgency with regard to any of that.'

I paused. 'You need a criminal lawyer too. You shouldn't talk to the guards again, however informally, without obtaining specialist legal advice. Getting a solicitor doesn't mean you're admitting guilt. It's nothing like that. It's a sensible precaution, that's all.'

'Can you recommend someone?'

'There are several very good criminal solicitors in Cork and I'd be happy to use any of them if I were you. On balance, though, and taking everything into account, I'd go for Conleth Young – I'm texting you his name and contact details now. You should call him soon.'

'Not before the funeral,' Ed said.

'You should call him today,' I said. 'Though I do understand why you wouldn't feel like calling him before then. Do you know yet when it will be?'

'Probably Saturday,' Ed said. 'Noon most likely. The parish church. No funeral-home viewing. No wake. Mass and burial in St Michael's. Then to Maryborough. After that …'

He stopped.

'After that, there's no escaping from it. Me and the girls are on our own.'

24

THE WIND HAD DROPPED AND THE TEMPERATURE was almost pleasant. I needed to decompress. I walked down the hill into Blackrock Village, then crossed the paved plaza, where the farmers' market is held on Sundays, to the water's edge. Being in Mandy's house had been harder than I'd expected. Still, though there was no getting used to what had happened to her, I knew I'd move on from it. Those I'd just been with – Ed, Ava and Ruth – had had their lives changed irrevocably and beyond measure. From now on, so much of what they would do and who they would become would be defined by this event. But if Ed proved to be innocent, it would be marginally less difficult for the girls. For that reason more than anything else, I wanted him to be not guilty. I hoped he was. Time would tell.

He was definitely a suspect – his admission that he knew about Mandy's affair only confirmed it. He had been quick to proffer an alibi, but it wasn't the strongest I'd heard. He had protested his innocence too. I'd have been quicker to believe him if I hadn't been left with the sense that he was lying about some of what he'd said to me, and maybe about most of it. For one thing, how realistic was it that, after an alleged two-year affair, he'd never said anything at all to Mandy about it? And, even if that part was true, how likely was it that he didn't know the identity of her lover and seemed to have made no effort to find out? At the same time, it was hard for me to see him as a murderer.

It was 8.45 p.m. Time to go home. I checked my phone. Two missed calls from Sadie. I sent her a message: *Ring me if you're free.* I also had a missed call and two texts from my mother. I typed a quick response to her, saying I'd call in the morning.

But there was nothing from Davy – nothing since his 5.20 a.m. text message. I was going to *have* to text him back. My default option, that in these situations it was best to let the dust settle, had started to feel more and more like cowardice.

●

The phone rang. It was Sadie.

'You home?' she asked.

'On the way. I'm in Blackrock at the moment. The corner by the Natural Foods bakery.'

'I'm just finished for the day. Finally. You got your car with you?'

'I was going to call a cab.'

'I'm not far away,' Sadie said. 'Pick you up?'

'Affirmative,' I said. 'What's your ETA?'

'Any minute now.'

25

THERE'S A LOT TO BE SAID FOR THE SUBURB OF
Douglas – and the locals tend to say it. Frequently. The two
shopping malls and the old village centre mean that your every
conceivable need can be met on your doorstep. There's no reason
for you to leave Douglas at any time. Unless you want to.

Sadie parked in a tow zone on the main street just up from
KC's, and I dashed in to get her food. We sat in the car with the
windows down while Sadie ate and I didn't. I told her that I
didn't feel like take-out two nights in a row. I didn't tell her that
I'd dumped most of last night's because I was obsessing about
Davy. Since the argument in the Long Valley before Christmas,
he was a topic we tended to avoid.

Scratch that. He was a topic *I* tended to avoid. She mentioned
him often. Too often for my liking. I accepted that her concern
was genuine and well-meant. But I didn't agree with it.

The end result of the whole thing was that Sadie and I had been
seeing less of each other in person in recent months and that our
relationship had become more phone-based. Before Davy, Sadie
and I used to meet at a minimum most Sunday afternoons, while
her husband Jack watched other men struggle for control of a
ball, the size or shape of which didn't appear to matter to him.
Now, we had occasional snatched lunches. Double-dating – me

and Davy and Sadie and Jack – was never going to be happening, in this or any other universe.

•

'What are you doing out here?' Sadie asked.

'Visiting Ed and the girls,' I said.

'O-kay,' Sadie said.

'And asking about these two.'

I handed her the photographs.

'Keep them,' I said. 'I can print more.'

'Who are they?'

'I don't know yet. The older one said his name was McInerney. The younger one didn't give a name. They showed up at the office yesterday morning first thing, looking for Mandy – then disappeared, without warning, leaving no contact details. And I checked. She has no client called McInerney; no one in the office does. After I found out what happened, this just seems …'

'Odd,' Sadie said.

'Yeah,' I said. 'Though it could be innocuous. Potential new clients, who felt neglected and lost patience, decided to move on. Wouldn't be the first time it's happened.'

'Anything else you want to tell me?'

'I asked Ed if he recognised them.'

'Did he?'

'No.'

'What did he say? Did he repeat the thing about Mandy feeling down?'

'He did. He said he thought it was about work, that he was nearly sure it was, but—'

'But what?'

'Well, you see, I told Ed that I knew Mandy was having an affair.'

'Ah Finn, what did you do that for?'

'I thought you'd have asked him about it already. I don't know why you didn't.'

'Operational reasons,' Sadie said.

'Which means what?'

'Which means my boss was of the view that, strategically, we should wait a little longer before confronting Ed with that information.'

'Why?'

'My question exactly. I disagreed with the eejit, but it wasn't my decision.'

'I'm always telling you, you need to apply for promotion. You'd be *way* better at being an eejit.'

Sadie laughed. 'The trouble with me going for promotion is that I'm already in my ideal job.'

'In other words, you like driving around the place far too much.'

'I do. Preferably at the top speed my advanced driver training permits me to manage effortlessly, with zero risk to the general public.'

'I beg to—'

'There's also the fact that I don't need the migraines and the trolley loads of paperwork that'd come with a promotion to DS or inspector. I joined the guards so's to *not* have an office job. And sergeant is the worst job going, by the way. Heart attack territory.'

'I still think you should go for it,' I said.

'We'll see.'

She went on, 'What did Ed say when you mentioned the affair? Did he admit he knew about it?'

'You'd have to ask him that yourself,' I said.

'I'll take that as a "yes".'

'Take it as you'll have to ask him that yourself,' I said.

'Okay, okay,' Sadie said.

'Ed told me ye think she was killed Sunday night,' I said.

'That's right.'

'Head injury?'

'Yeah.'

'What caused it?'

'A hammer, we think – though no murder weapon was found at the scene or anywhere in the vicinity. Five or six blows to the back of her head. The skull was in bits.'

'Jesus!' I said. 'And do you know anything about the house she was found in?'

'Alysson Villas. Number 3.'

'Who lives there?'

'No one. It's semi-derelict. Vacant for many years after the previous occupier died. We've had no joy finding the current owner.'

I made a mental note to do a title search as soon as I got into the office the next morning.

'What's the crime scene like?'

'A big fucking mess. The Bureau have taken samples but the place is littered with DNA and bodily fluids of all kinds, most nothing to do with the murder. Loads of empty cans and bottles. The house was used as a drinking and drug-taking den by kids from the locality.'

'What about her phone?'

'With her body – and clean as a whistle. Looks like she drove from Blackrock to the house where she was killed. No "come round to Alysson Villas, so's I can murder you" messages anyway. There may be deleted ones. We're checking. But—'

'Sounds like it's going to be a tough solve,' I said.

'Possibly,' Sadie said. 'Possibly less so, now that we know about the affair.'

'Oh?'

'I can't say anymore,' she said. 'I've said too much already.'

'Come on,' I said. 'You know I won't – *can't* – tell anyone.'

'No,' Sadie said.

'I've told you about the affair,' I said. 'That has to be worth something.'

'It is,' Sadie said. 'It's helpful. But … I don't think …'

I watched her wrestling with whether it would be more advantageous having me inside the investigatory tent than outside. Eventually she spoke again.

'This is in the strictest confidence,' she said. 'We're waiting for the swab results. But initial tests revealed that Mandy had sexual intercourse with someone in the hours before she died.'

26

WHILE SADIE WAS GETTING PETROL, I TYPED A
message to Davy:

Didn't get a chance to text till now.

Not true.

Exhausting day.

Not exhausting enough to prevent me asking you what's going
on.

Hope you're well?

I'm not sure what I'm hoping for anymore. He replied
immediately:

No worries. Take care of yourself. Early start. Talk tomorrow x.

•

Sadie got back into the car.

'You okay?'

'Grand,' I said. 'Tired. You won't forget about getting me in for a look at the house?'

'I won't,' she said. 'But we'll have to do it discreetly. And only if you stop fucking pestering me about it.'

•

At home, I went straight to bed. I tossed and turned and no sleep came. There was something wrong between me and Davy. I knew it, and I didn't have the guts to face up to it.

No, it wasn't about guts. I didn't have the tools. I was frozen, caught in a holding pattern. I should never have got into a relationship with him. I had been wrong all along when I told Sadie he was good for me.

And now? I didn't know what he was doing. At the same time, I knew all too well. I was in love with an addict, a trader in lies, who would hurt me and keep on hurting me. Just like my birth mother had – the stranger I'd lived with till I was saved by Mam and Dad. When they adopted me, they'd delivered me from that kind of life. Permanently.

I was the fool who'd willingly, with eyes wide open, ventured into the life again. Now, I was paying the price for my recklessness.

And I had a feeling this was only the down payment.

WEDNESDAY

WEDNESDAY

27

IT FELT LIKE I'D ONLY JUST DROPPED OFF TO SLEEP
when, at 6.45 a.m., my phone pinged with a message from Sadie:
*If you want to have a look at that place you were so interested in last
night, be at the top of Barrack Street in TWO MINS!!!*

I grabbed what clothes I could and ran to meet her.

•

We were signed in by the uniformed guard on watch at the front.

Sadie nodded in my direction.

'Witness,' she said.

Then we went round to the back door.

'Touch nothing,' Sadie said.

'Aren't the Technical Bureau people gone?'

'They are. But it's still an officially designated crime scene.'

'I feel a bit sick,' I said.

'Look around you, Finn. Look at all these houses. People's
lives have ended in most of them, you can be sure. But very
few – probably none – have had their lives taken from them. So,
yeah, feel sick. If you stop feeling sick, that's the time to start
worrying … That said,' she added after a pause, 'please don't
puke.'

28

SADIE UNDID THE PADLOCK AND SLICED THROUGH
the tape with a pocket knife.

'Is that allowed?' I asked.

'I want to get a few more photos,' she said. 'Well, I don't
really, but that's why I said I had to come back. I always do. To
think my way in; get a sense of the place when it's quiet. I'll
reseal the door when we're leaving.'

She went in and I followed. We were in a small back porch,
plumbed for a washing machine, but empty apart from a grim
heap of soiled toilet paper in a corner.

'Jesus,' I said. 'What was Mandy doing in a place like this?'

'That's only the start of it.'

A door to the left opened into a downstairs WC. The stench
made my eyes water. Mercifully a piece of broken plywood had
been placed across the toilet bowl.

'You do *not* want to see what's underneath there,' Sadie said.

•

The kitchen was narrow but would have been bright enough
if the only window hadn't been filthy. There was a cluster of
burnt-out nightlights – I counted ten – on the draining board,

beside the clogged and squalid tea-brown sink that had once been shiny stainless steel.

'Odd place to illuminate,' I said. 'Or was someone tidying up?'

'I thought the same. We've taken samples from the area and we took a few of the nightlights away to test for DNA – no fingerprints on any of them – but they may be unrelated to the murder. Dozens of people have been through this place, even in the last few months. We haven't yet managed to find anyone who admits they were here Sunday night. But why come here when there are parties you can crash in other houses? And the kids who frequent this house are younger. Still in school. They seem to favour Fridays and Saturdays for their gatherings.'

'So no one saw anything?'

'There are five houses in the immediate vicinity. Four in Alysson Villas, apart from this one, and the big house, "Alysson", down the end, behind the high walls. These houses were built on a part of its garden during the 1930s. Unfortunately, over the last twenty years, Alysson Villas, just like much of the rest of this area, has been colonised by UCC students and it's party central around here from now till May. College term was starting on Monday so this Sunday night gone, all the neighbours were in a state of extreme inebriation, with dance music being played at ear-splitting volume. They're all saying they saw and heard nothing.'

'Any garda noise complaint reports on the night? Common enough around here.'

'Nothing has shown up yet but it's a fair point. Worth looking into.'

'No owner occupiers?'

'The big house, yes. But not really. The old man who lives there has been in hospital for the last few weeks. Dr Seamus Keyes. Retired GP. I went to see him. I don't think he'll be coming home.'

'He might know something about the owners of this house?'

'He might – except he's not well enough to talk to us at present.'

'Does he have a family?'

'Daughter in England – Polly. Vague on the phone but coming home next week, so there's a chance she'll be better in person. Our hope at first was the carers. He had teams of them coming and going at various times every day. But not on the night of the murder or for several weeks prior sadly, because—'

'He was in hospital.'

'Exactly.'

'There's a chance one of the students – one of the ones who lives around here or one of the party-attending visitors – might come through for us. We've been doing house-to-house on repeat – it's worthwhile because we've been getting a different pot-luck set of randomers every time we call to each of the houses – and we've put out an appeal. There's a hope that someone might remember something, especially once the thickos realise that we're not remotely interested in the stashes of weed and pills under their pillows. Or one of the carers for the old guy, Dr Keyes, in the big house might have seen someone at the house during the months before the murder. It's quiet here out of term-time. Any atypical activity would stand out. It's a long shot, but it's worth checking it out.'

'You think it was planned?'

'It *could* have been opportunistic. Grab a hammer and beat her over the head. But, like you said yourself, what was she doing here in the first place?'

'Is there any CCTV?' I asked.

'Here? No. On Glasheen Road, at the bus stop, yes. But no view of this turn-off. We've made a public appeal for dashcam footage, but realistically …'

•

Sadie walked ahead of me down the narrow black and terracotta quarry-tiled hall, and turned right into an empty space that had probably originally been used as a dining room. An opening that had once been graced by double doors – though they had long since been removed or stolen – led into a sitting room, where a destroyed sofa was splayed in front of the ash-piled fireplace.

'Cosy,' I said.

'We evidence-bagged the cushions but they're so stained, the lads might as well be searching haystacks for needles.'

I walked to the window. The view onto the road was obscured by overgrown fuchsia and Escallonia hedging. You could do anything you wanted in here and no one would ever know.

'Is this where she died?'

'No.'

She went through another door, to the front hallway, and pointed at a collection of smeared wine-coloured puddles of varying sizes on the tiles inside the front door. I understood then why we'd come in the back way.

'That's where her head ended up. She was attacked from behind with a hammer to the back of her skull. Hit the deck, broke her nose in the fall. Bled heavily from there and from the multiple head wounds directly onto the floor surface.'

Sadie pointed at the walls.

'There's blood and tissue spatter on the wallpaper on both sides, from the weapon being brought up and down repeatedly – at least five times. Some minor spatter on the outside of the front door. It looks like it was opened inwards when she was assaulted and pulled partly closed, presumably by the murderer, as he was leaving. Her shoe was caught so he couldn't close it fully. Or leaving it open might have been deliberate on his part.'

Being here was what I'd wanted. Now I couldn't think why. I said nothing. Asked no questions. Stared at the gouts of blood and brain. Tried to make meaning out of the scene.

•

Sadie handed me a thin buff cardboard folder.

'Colour printouts. For your eyes only. And you didn't get them from me.'

I leafed through the sheets of photographs, worse than anything I could have imagined, of Mandy's corpse.

Of her skull, cracked like a broken egg; of her shiny hair, matted and ruined. The right leg, bent like a figure four against the left, stretched straight and full-length, the toe of her left Stella McCartney trainer pointed against the door jamb. Her arms limp by her side – she hadn't even had time to try to save herself. Her bloodied bag – an Orla Kiely stem pattern backpack that I'd never seen her with at work – askew from her right shoulder.

'Did she suffer?' I asked.

'I'm sure she did,' Sadie said. 'But not for long. It was quick.'

'She was wearing sports clothes. Ed said she'd been out for a walk. Looks like she didn't change after. In a hurry to get here, possibly? Had she just arrived when it happened?'

'It looks that way, but there's no way to know. Not yet, anyway.'

'You said she'd had sex with someone that day?'

'Yes,' Sadie said.

'Not here?'

'We found several used condoms here in the house. We're testing them. But Mandy didn't use one on Sunday – like I told you before, we recovered traces of semen from her. No results yet.'

'Any sign of sexual violence?'

'No, it doesn't look like she was raped.'

'I take it you haven't asked Ed yet if he and she …?'

'No. If he's guilty, we wouldn't want to fuck up our chances of a conviction by risking inculpatory admissions without legal advice and without a caution being administered. But we've taken voluntary DNA samples from him and the kids – for elimination purposes.'

'Ed told me she was out of the house a couple of times on Sunday, so she could have met the other man either of those times,' I said.

'Or it could have happened in this place.'

'You were in Mandy's house,' I said. 'I worked with her. I couldn't see her doing anything in this dump.'

'But she was here all the same, Finn. The longer I'm in this job, the weirder I think … no, the weirder I *know* people can be if they think no one is watching.'

'She couldn't have had sex here. She had to have been brought here for some reason afterwards. Either by the same man or by someone else.'

'Maybe,' Sadie said.

'What if she was being blackmailed?' I asked.

'It's a possibility. That's why we checked her phone. It's clear of any dodgy messages, even deleted ones. We weren't able to track her exact location, only the approximate one. She had location services switched off.'

'Adultery 101,' I said.

'Other than here, she seems to have been nowhere unusual. Just Cork city southside.'

'She probably had a second, affair-only phone. A burner,' I said.

'Probably.'

'And?'

'Presumably it's been turned off by now and dumped,' Sadie said.

'Maybe if you tracked all the phones that were active around here last night? And find the ones that aren't active anymore?'

'And then what?'

'I don't know,' I said.

'I don't know either. We *will* be looking into all that. It's going to take a long time but we might get some kind of a result eventually.'

'You don't sound very hopeful.'

'Not about that. I can't help thinking that either the murderer was very lucky with the night he chose, given all the phone activity around here and the multiple mixed DNA profiles in this house – or else he knew exactly what he was doing.'

'He?' I asked.

'I'm saying "he" out of habit. Ninety-nine times out of a hundred, if a woman dies, it's a man who killed her.'

'Is that an actual statistic?'

'You know what I mean,' Sadie said. 'It's most likely to have been a male assailant. It took considerable strength to batter her head like that. But the murder weapon probably isn't heavy in itself. In theory, I suppose it could have been a woman.'

'Was there anything else in the bag apart from her phone?'

'Very little. Her wallet. A sweatshirt. A bottle of water. No make-up or the usual rubbish you'd get in a handbag. She didn't use it much, I'd say.'

'So you think nothing was taken?'

'Hard to know. Those things weren't taken obviously. But the affair phone, the burner, if she had one, could've been removed. We're examining the bag to see if there's any DNA transfer. Those tests are complex, mind you, so the results will take time.'

'Sounds like there's going to be no progress for a while?'

'Well, the DNA on the vaginal swabs and the semen won't take as long.'

'Oh. When will you have them back?'

'Next week. They say probably late Tuesday or early Wednesday. Whatever they show – Ed's DNA or someone else's – it's a good solid place to start.'

•

I stepped out of the hallway and back into the front room. Then I made for the rear exit.

'Where do you think you're going?'

'Sorry, but I need fresh air,' I said. 'Then I have to go to work.'

'All in good time. Right now, you're coming with me.'

29

I GRABBED A LARGE AMERICANO FROM THREE
Fools on the Grand Parade, and made it into the office a little
after 8.55 a.m. I met Gabriel on the stairs.

'We've heard from the Law Society,' he said. 'By the way,
how are you? You're looking a bit peaky.'

My eyes were bloodshot. I hadn't any make-up on. I hadn't
showered. I was wearing yesterday's clothes. I'd just made
a dawn visit to the scene of a horrific murder. Followed by a
trip to Coughlan's Quay garda station, where I'd had to write
up and sign a formal statement about the man I'd seen Mandy
with, and spend enough time not being able to describe him
beyond what I'd told Sadie repeatedly already – that he was
dark-haired, strong, probably Caucasian – for her to finally
decide that engaging any further in a photofit process wasn't
worth the bother.

In the circumstances, 'peaky' was a compliment.

'Some kind of bug,' I said. 'On the mend already.'

'Good,' Gabriel said. 'Anyway, we've managed to put them
off for a few weeks.'

'Sorry, who?'

'The Law Society. They've agreed to postpone the full

inspection, provided we give them an interim report immediately on how Mandy's workload is being managed, and provided we can assure them that we've found no red flags. Now. What can you tell me?'

'In terms of her work, so far, there's nothing there that shouldn't be. Her team is working away on her files. I spoke to them yesterday. They're good. From what I can see, everything's in hand.'

'Anything else?'

'Look, Gabriel, I know you told me not to bother following up on McInerney and Jack Wills—'

'Who?'

'The two clients from Monday. I called the second guy Jack because ...'

Gabriel bristled. 'Forget about them,' he said.

'I think they could be important,' I said.

'I disagree. The *files* are important. The clients this firm *actually* has, rather than two ill-mannered ne'er-do-wells who didn't even leave a mobile phone number. Didn't Dervla tell you that she'll let you know the moment they call again? And if they don't, what of it? Did it ever occur to you that Mandy's murder might have put them off instructing MLC? Did it? And they won't be the only ones, I can tell you. We're facing an existential crisis here. It's not the time for any of your Agatha Christie tendencies.'

'You sound like Dermot,' I said.

'He's no diplomat but he has a good head on his shoulders. And I have to say he's been spot on about all this from the beginning – credit where it's due. About the risk to the firm, and so on and so forth.'

I was too tired to get into an argument about Dermot Lyons. 'Fair enough,' I said, to get Gabriel to move on.

'Right,' Gabriel said. '*Ad idem* at last.'

'Is Kathleen back?'

'Yes. *Very* upset. It's probably too soon for her to return but it might do her good, you never know. And I can't say we don't need her. It's all hands on deck for the foreseeable.'

'Speaking of which,' I said. 'I'd better—'

'Agreed,' Gabriel said. 'Does 5 p.m. sound alright?'

'What?'

'For you to have completed the interim report, naturally.'

'Gabriel, in all fairness, how can I write a report and simultaneously review all Mandy's files? If you want me to do both, I'll need more time. If you want it by five you'll have to pick one or the other.'

'Time is the very thing we don't have, Finola. It's not rocket science. It's an interim document. Clearly you have to prioritise that, and you can return to the files afterwards. But I must have that report done and gone off to the Law Society today, and that's all there is to it.'

30

WHATEVER GABRIEL HAD SAID, I REMAINED
convinced that McInerney and Jack Wills had a connection to
Mandy's murder. I couldn't understand why Gabriel didn't see
that. Or why he didn't want to. They hadn't simply decided that
MLC wasn't the law firm for them. On the CCTV, McInerney
had seemed far too engaged to just walk away. The temp Katja
had said that he'd wanted to see Mandy. That he'd been insistent.
Yet the two men had left the office in a rush *before* there'd been
any news about her death. There were too many unanswered
questions. All the same, I knew I had to let my search for them
drift into the background for now. I had other work to do.

Including my continuing search for the name of Mandy's
lover. I'd promised Sadie that the moment I had any news on
him, I'd tell her. If he turned out to be a client of MLC, I'd have
to find a way of doing so that didn't breach the Day-One-of-
Law-School rule that, not only are we solicitors not allowed to
divulge the private business of a client, we're not even allowed
to divulge the fact that they *are* a client without their express
permission. My Plan A way around that was to make a direct
approach to him – in broad daylight, with plenty of witnesses to
our meeting – and advise him to go to the guards and disclose his

identity. If that didn't work, I'd have to come up with a Plan B. Which was why I really hoped Plan A worked.

Or that the guards got there before me. On the way to Coughlan's Quay, Sadie had told me that they would be re-interviewing family and close friends early today, with specific queries about the dark-haired man. Then they were moving on to Mandy's Blackrock neighbours, who might be more forthcoming than the family about who they'd seen her with and what they'd seen them doing. After that, tomorrow probably, they'd be focusing on MLC and Mandy's work colleagues.

At 9.10 a.m., in Mandy's office, a delegation – made up of Tina, Pauline Doyle from IT and Kathleen Rowson, Mandy's PA – came to see me.

'We heard about the report deadline,' Tina said.

'I'll help in any way I can,' Kathleen said. In the two days since Mandy had been found, she'd aged ten years and looked like she'd lost at least ten pounds in weight.

'Are you okay?' I asked.

'Mandy was my friend,' she said. 'She loved working here. Apart from the time she took off after the … sorry … after lovely Ava and Ruth – Ruth is my godchild, you know – were born, she never took a day's sick leave. She had no time for wimps. If she was here now, she'd be telling us to get the finger out. She'd want us to go on. I want to go on. What else is there?'

Any reply I might make felt inadequate. After a short pause, I turned to Tina. 'What's happening with my regular work? Anything I need to deal with?'

'I'm basically deferring everyone and everything to next week when I presume things might be some way half back to normal.'

'In as far as they can be,' I said.

'It's all going okay so far,' Tina said. 'Any problems, I'll let you know. But by this afternoon I expect to be pretty well on top of things at that end, so …'

'Great,' I said.

'I have zero time right now,' Pauline said. 'But call me if you've any questions, especially any *specific* questions – I'm more likely to be able to answer if you know what you want, or if you're in the ballpark at least.'

If we were on telly, this would have been the moment where I'd have clapped my hands together and said, 'Go team!', or, 'Sounds like a plan'. I didn't.

'Okay,' I said. 'I, em …'

'Need more coffee?' Tina asked.

'Oh yes,' I said.

31

HAVING KATHLEEN AS MY GUIDE MADE GETTING
a proper handle on Mandy's caseload seem much more attainable.
She took me through Mandy's methods and procedures and,
most importantly for the Law Society investigators, how she
kept track of monies out and monies in. By noon I'd dictated a
clumsy overview that I asked Tina to type up. It was nowhere
near what Gabriel wanted but, as I always say, if you want to end
up with a good document, you have to start with a bad one.

Which reminded me that I hadn't checked any of Mandy's
'My Documents' folders yet. I'd do that later. And I hadn't yet
asked Kathleen the questions I'd asked the rest of Mandy's team.
I did so now.

'I thought she might have had something on her mind,'
Kathleen said. 'The awful thing is, I didn't say anything to her.'

'None of the rest of the team noticed anything.'

'I'm not surprised. It wasn't anything you could point to, a
vague feeling only.'

'How were things at home?'

'Fine, as far as I know.'

'You sure about that?'

'I am, but ... Why? Did you hear something?'

The story of the dark-haired man was out now. The guards knew. It was only a matter of time before everyone did. I *could* ask Kathleen. But she was just back from compassionate leave. It seemed like too much, too soon.

'Nobody said anything really,' I said. 'But Hugo Woulfe was super-defensive about her. What's he like?'

'Good worker. Going places. He adored Mandy, hero-worshipped her. But to be honest, he's a bit intense. Young for his age.'

'And how did Mandy feel about him?'

'She was fond of him. Is "fond" the right word? Took a special interest in him, that would be more accurate. More than any of her previous trainees.'

'How did that manifest itself?'

'She spent quite a bit of time with him. Private chats in her room. Giving him pep talks, I suppose.'

'Is that what she said was going on?'

'Well, she didn't really say anything. And I didn't ask her. What are *you* saying?'

Sidestepping quickly, I asked about the McInerney man.

'She never had a client of that name,' Kathleen said.

'No one at MLC did,' I said. 'Any idea who they were?'

'They?'

'McInerney and the guy with him.'

'Oh, that's right. My head is …'

'McInerney was the older man, apparently. There was a younger man too. I've been calling him Jack Wills.'

Kathleen looked at me blankly.

'He was wearing a Jack Wills hoodie.'

'I'm sorry,' Kathleen said. 'I have no idea what that means.'

'It's a clothing brand. I'm sure you can buy it in Cork. I don't know where, though.'

'Right,' Kathleen said. 'Do you think he bought the hoodie around here?'

'Maybe. But we don't know where he's from. He might be from somewhere else.'

'True,' she said.

I handed her my phone with the photographs open on it. She took her time. Then she said, 'I've never seen them before.'

'I'll have a look at the Jack Wills website,' I said. 'If it's a new product, there might be some point having a word with whoever stocks the brand in Cork. If it's last season's or before, there seems very little point.'

Kathleen looked at the photograph again. 'It doesn't look new to me,' she said. 'But I can't be sure. I'm more of a Marks and Spencer woman. Per Una's got quite trendy lately, you know.'

I laughed. The work had helped. She was more like her old self – unfailingly good-humoured and diligent, despite what I knew had been a tough decade, caring for two elderly and infirm parents in their final illnesses. Now she lived alone in the home she'd grown up in, north of the city. That Mandy's death had been yet another terrible blow was written all over her face. Mandy could often be tough with other people in the firm, but never with her. They were close. Despite a good attempt at a smile, Kathleen looked crushed, exhausted.

'We might never find out who those two were,' I said.

'Or we might,' she said. 'They might come back sometime.'

'That's what Dervla said too,' I said. I leaned forward in my chair. 'C'mere, is it just me or is Dervla a bit off at the moment?'

'I think we're all a bit off,' Kathleen said. 'But I know what you mean. I *did* notice this morning. She couldn't have been nicer, but it's like she had something else on her mind all the time she was talking to me.'

'And she wasn't at work on Monday,' I said.

'Oh, please. You can't seriously think Dervla had anything to do with the murder?'

'I don't. Of course I don't.'

But I wasn't half as sure as I said. I wasn't sure about anything anymore.

32

AT 1.30 P.M., I WAS ABOUT TO KNOCK ON
Gabriel's door when Dervla swept past me on her way out.

I went in. Gabriel was at his desk.

'Why are you here?' he asked.

'The report,' I said. 'You want it for 5 p.m. This is a copy of
the first rough draft.'

'Oh yes,' he said. 'Are you happy with it?'

'As happy as I can be.'

'That's fine, then.'

'Don't you want to read it?'

'I've no mind for it right this very minute,' Gabriel said. 'I've
got a headache. This week has been …' He paused. He seemed
weary. Vacant.

'Gabriel, is everything okay?'

'Yes,' he said. 'But, you know …' He straightened, cleared his
throat. 'I'll read the report in due course. Email them to say it's
on the way by recorded delivery. As soon as it's done, send it out.
They want it by close of business tomorrow.'

'Do you want your name to go on the letter?'

'No,' Gabriel said. 'No. It's your report – it should be your
name.'

'Okay,' I said. 'But I don't understand why you don't want to read it.'

'Finola, it's just provisional. Interim. Provided we don't tell them any barefaced lies and we couch what we're saying with plenty of caveats – which I take it you have …?'

'Yes.'

He went on, 'Then what matters is that we're seen to cooperate. Now you need to get back to work. If there's a smoking gun anywhere in Mandy's work connecting this office with a murder, you need to find it.'

I'd known Gabriel McGrath for fifteen years but I felt like I didn't know the man sitting in front of me. And, I didn't know why, but I was starting to feel like I'd been shafted.

33

I'D DROPPED A PRINTOUT OF MY WORKING DRAFT
of the report in an envelope on Kathleen's desk before going
down to see Gabriel. She was waiting for me when I got back up
to Mandy's office.

'I've had a quick run-through. Have a read of that and I'll
bring you a coffee. Now, what about something to eat?'

'I'm okay. Tina's bringing me back a sandwich from the
market.'

'Great. Make sure you eat it.'

'Em, have you actually met me? Of *course* I'll eat it.'

She laughed and handed me the document, now decorated
with green highlighter marks and yellow Post-its.

•

By now, I knew a lot more about how the various trusts
operated, and was making substantial progress. After Kathleen
returned, we worked steadily until 3 p.m. – when Hugo
Woulfe appeared at the door, saying that he'd been sent to ask
if Kathleen was free to rejoin the rest of the Finance and Trusts

team for the remainder of the afternoon, and that she was badly needed there. I felt confident enough to let her go. She stood and looked around.

'I've spent so much time in this room with Mandy over the years,' she said. 'But I won't come back, I think. Not unless you ... of course, I mean don't hesitate if there's anything ...'

'I'll be fine,' I said.

'I know you will,' Kathleen said. She smiled. 'Finn would be a great addition to the F and T gang,' she added, looking at Hugo.

'Thanks, but no thanks,' I said.

Kathleen laughed.

'Are you ready to go?' Hugo asked her, ignoring my response.

She turned to me. '*He's very upset*,' she mouthed. 'Think about it, Finn,' she said aloud. 'Don't say no yet.'

•

I would – and I'd keep on saying no. Bad and all as the old-time merchant princes must surely have been in many ways, at least they had a sense of civic pride. Admittedly, much of the old money had gone on church-building, paving the benefactors' way to heaven. But not all of it. The Crawford brewing fortune had funded the municipal gallery and the College of Art that still bore the family's name. These days, from what I could see, a lot of business profits were funnelled via elaborate legal scaffolding into holding companies in places like the British Virgin Islands and Turks and Caicos. That was what Mandy had been doing, and I didn't like it. Apart from any qualms I might have, the work was boring and repetitive. Once I drilled down into it, I saw that she was providing much the same massively expensive and highly specialised suite of services, over and over and over again, and to a relatively small portfolio of clients.

With the willing assistance of Hugo Woulfe. Who, according to Kathleen, had 'adored' Mandy. That was the impression I had too when I'd interviewed him. He'd denied strenuously that Mandy had been having an affair. Was that because *he* had been her lover? Was his deep sadness at Mandy's death normal? Or was it a sign that their relationship was more than professional? I knew that he was approaching full qualification as a solicitor. Though he was still a month or two away from receiving his parchment, the word around the office was that Mandy had offered him a permanent job in her department, and that he'd accepted. He'd started as a trainee two-and-a-half years ago. That fit with Ed's alleged timeline for the affair too. And now Kathleen had told me that Mandy had a 'special interest' in Hugo and that she'd spent a lot of time alone with him in her office.

•

I checked the emails between them. They were in touch numerous times per day while he was based at the firm but not, it seemed, while he was absent for a couple of longish stretches at the Law School in Blackhall Place in Dublin. Mandy's emails to him were often brusque, occasionally jokey and usually demanding. Mostly, they were familiar. But, apart from one or two comments of the 'have-a-nice-weekend' kind, they were all about work.

It stood to reason that they would have been smart enough to keep personal stuff off email. Mandy almost certainly had an affair phone for all communication outside work. During office hours, all she had to do was make an internal phone call and ask him to call up for a private 'pep talk', as Kathleen put it. The trouble was that, however I looked at it, I couldn't see Mandy risking a predatory liaison with a junior employee. It would amount to gross professional misconduct.

And yet, if that's what she was up to, it would explain for once and for all her look of terror, both on the night of the Dolly concert and the next day, when she'd come to see me in my office. The same explanation could apply to a sexual relationship with a client, though that would have been significantly less problematic.

Both scenarios seemed equally unlikely to me.

But Ed had said that Mandy's lover was someone she'd met through work. And she *had* been seeing another man. I knew that to be true because I'd seen her with him. If I hadn't, I mightn't have believed Ed, when he said that she'd been cheating for so long. One relationship was hard work. Two? I couldn't imagine how she did it, sleeping in the same bed as Ed and with another man on the side. Yet what she'd been doing was common, so common that judges in family law cases barely remarked on it. Clients with straying spouses got upset often when I told them that our family law system was a mostly 'no fault' one. That adultery was considered a normal reason for marriage breakdown; that, on its own, it wouldn't earn them any extra credit – or their partners extra punishment – from the court.

A lot of the time, marriages continued, during and after infidelity. Spouses knew and chose not to know. They hung on. The way Ed had told me he had. He'd told me as well that he didn't know the identity of Mandy's lover. The more I thought about that, the less I believed it.

•

As I clicked out of the emails, it came to me that Kathleen *must* know the identity of the other man. Maybe she'd even been dropping hints about Hugo, with her pointed comments about how upset he was?

I spent a short time kicking myself that I'd wasted so much time wondering about Mandy's lover and hadn't, out of respect for her feelings, asked the person most likely to know everything. I stopped when I realised that it didn't matter. My morning visit to the murder scene had been enough to convince me that this case was not going to be solved by me, but as a result of the efforts of Sadie and her colleagues once they got the DNA tests back from the Forensic Science Lab. Even if Mandy had originally met the other man via MLC, in all likelihood her death would prove to have little to do with her work here; and what Gabriel had derisively labelled my 'Agatha Christie tendencies' would not be required.

I returned to the document. The sooner I finished, the sooner I could get back to my attic room and my regular job.

34

AT 4.35 P.M. KATHLEEN RANG TO ASK IF I NEEDED her for anything else. I told her that I didn't and, at my insistence, she went home. Her official hours were 8 a.m. to 4 p.m., allowing her to avoid peak traffic times and fitting well with what had been Mandy's early-morning schedule, though she would normally have been in the office at least an hour before Kathleen. Except of course this past Monday morning when Mandy hadn't come to work at all.

After Kathleen had gone, while waiting for Tina to bring me up a printed and bound copy of the latest draft of the report, I examined Mandy's 'My Documents' folders.

There was a CV, well out-of-date, but still surprising. I'd had her down as an MLC lifer. She must have thought of leaving at one point. Maybe everyone does. The rest of the documents looked personal. Phone and utility company account numbers. PDFs of her marriage certificates, and birth certificates for her, for the two girls and for Ed – Edmond David Florence Lyons Wallace. I wondered if he was related to Dermot Lyons. There had been a lot of intermarriage in the old Cork merchant families. The Wallaces had owned half the city at one time. But their fortunes had declined. Now, Ed messed about doing not very much. Nominally, he was a yacht broker. In reality, he was a house husband on light duties. I knew that Mandy employed a cleaner and a gardener – I'd heard her talking to them on the phone many times over the years. Ed must have had a lot of time on his hands.

I clicked into a Word document entitled 'Policies'. At the top were the name and contact details of Mandy's financial consultant. I noted it down but there wasn't a chance he'd talk to me without Ed's written authority. Under the name was a single-spaced list of company names, letters and numbers, and short explanatory notes beside each: 'Home, fire and buildings'; 'Life 1'; 'For girls'; 'Pension 1'; 'Pension 2' – and so on, for almost a page.

A second Word document, 'Shares', listed her share-holdings together with the date of acquisition. There were some Irish bank shares, now worthless or close to it, along with a good spread of other shares/holdings/stocks that a Google search told me, when added together, made for an extremely valuable haul. Insider trading might have been an issue if they'd been related to clients of hers but, apart from Apple, none of the companies had Cork links. Also, none of the shares had been purchased any more recently than two years before Mandy's death.

The next Word document was a shorter list of personal bank account numbers. Apart from one savings account, the accounts were jointly held with Ed, and all were for banks in Cork. No balances were listed, presumably because they went up and down but, from what I'd seen thus far, I was willing to bet that they were healthy.

After that came a PDF of the MLC partnership agreement. I scrolled through it. In the event of Mandy's death, a policy paid out a fixed sum of €500,000 to her beneficiaries. Next, there was a PDF of Mandy's will. Fourteen years old, made shortly after Ruth's birth. Leaving everything to Ed. Appointing him sole guardian of the children and trustee of the proceeds of a Zurich savings policy intended for their education. No value was given for the trust, but I didn't doubt that it was substantial. Both girls attended private schools. Mandy wasn't someone who was likely to skimp.

Had Ed died before her, the girls would have inherited everything, with Mandy's sister Debbie and her brother Jonathan appointed as joint trustees and guardians, the children to reside mainly, if possible, with Debbie. In the current circumstances, that alternative option didn't arise.

•

There was nothing more. I checked the Recycling Bin but it was empty. I sat back in my chair and did a mental tot. A house worth at least a million that Ed would inherit by survivorship. A €500,000 payout from the partnership. A shedload of stocks, and pension and life policies. Numerous joint bank accounts. With Mandy dead, Ed was independently, and seriously, rich.

Even if he hadn't known about the affair, he had a motive for murder.

35

AT 5.10 P.M., BLEARY-EYED, I READ THROUGH THE
final version of the interim report. It would have to do. Even if
there was something to find, or more to say, my brain was too
dead to make sense of it. I ran down the stairs and handed Dervla
the report.

'Can you send this by registered post please?' I asked.

Dervla took the envelope and held it at the corner tip, as if it
was contaminated. She said nothing. I stood open-mouthed for
a moment. Then I said, 'If you're too busy, I could ask someone
else?'

Again, she made no reply. Astonished, I went up to Tina's
office. I stood at the door and said, 'Would you mind checking
with Dervla about sending the report to Law Soc or can you do
it for her maybe, please, because I—'

'Sure, no problem. But first you need to see this,' Tina said.
She, Pauline Doyle and three other women were gathered around
her computer terminal. They moved aside. They'd been reading
a story on the RTÉ news website:

Gardaí in Dublin are appealing for assistance from the public in
tracing the whereabouts of Jerry McInerney and Dean McInerney-

Reid, a grandfather and grandson from Cardiff on a visit to Ireland, who have made no contact with family since last Tuesday.

The surname would have been enough. The photographs confirmed it.

'That's them,' I said. 'The two men who were in here asking for Mandy.'

36

I WENT BACK UP TO MANDY'S OFFICE AND DID
what I should have done on Monday afternoon – circulated
an email to everyone in the firm with photographs of the
McInerneys, saying that if anyone recognised them or had any
relevant information, no matter how trivial, they should contact
me immediately. I didn't consult with Gabriel in advance. I didn't
think he'd stop me but I couldn't take the chance that he'd try to
stall again, even if he was going to have to finally admit that the
McInerneys' visit to the office might be related to Mandy's death.

I sent a separate internal mail to Dervla, asking for the contact
details for Katja, the temp who'd been in on Monday, or the
temp agency's contact details. The way Dervla had been acting,
I didn't expect a speedy response, and she had probably gone
home by this time anyway.

After that, I rang Kathleen on her mobile. She picked up
immediately. 'Finn, what's up?'

'I'm sorry to bother you at home,' I said, 'but …'

'Say no more. I'll come back in straightaway.'

'It's not about work, though it is in a way. Em, I've got two
things to ask you. The first is, well … awkward.' I paused.

'Finn, just ask me, for heaven's sake, whatever it is.'

'It's about Mandy and Ed. Their marriage. You see, I think

Mandy was having an affair. And I'm wondering if you knew who he was?'

She responded immediately and forcefully. 'Not a chance,' she said.

'You won't tell me his name?'

'I won't tell you because he doesn't exist. Mandy would never do that to Ed or the two girls. Never in a million years. Now, what's your second question?'

'I think you're wrong. She—'

'I don't want to fall out with you, Finn, but I won't tolerate you spreading muck like that about Mandy.'

'Please Kathleen, tell me, was there something going on between Mandy and Hugo Woulfe? It's his reaction to her death that makes me wonder. And they spent time together alone.'

There was silence for a time at the other end of the line. Eventually, she spoke again in a small, shocked, little-girl voice. 'That's not something I'm prepared to contemplate.'

Which wasn't quite the same as 'no'. I decided on a tactical retreat for now. I could renew my enquiries with her at another time. 'O-kay. So … my second question is: have you seen the news?'

'No. I've had enough news this week to last me a lifetime. Is it to do with Mandy?'

'It's the two men from Monday morning, the ones who came to the office.'

'The photos you showed me?'

'They've been identified. Jerry McInerney and Dean McInerney-Reid, from Cardiff. A grandfather and grandson. But the strange thing is that they're missing.'

'Good Lord. How dreadful.'

'The reason I'm phoning is ... You didn't meet them, did you?'

'No, I didn't,' Kathleen said. 'I *told* you.'

'You see, that's what I'm wondering about,' I said. 'Why didn't you go down to them, to ask them who they were, or what they were doing? Reschedule their appointment?'

'I was in Gabriel's office when the call came,' Kathleen said.

'What call?'

'From that temp on reception.'

'And why were you there?'

'Well, Mandy was late and I was telling him – he was questioning me, actually there was a touch of the Gestapo, the way he went on – about where I thought she was and what efforts I'd made to find her. I didn't want to say too much at the time, but Ed had been onto me earlier on asking the same questions and I knew, well, I knew it was serious, or at any rate that Ed thought it was serious. Though I was hopeful and I told Ed that; I told Gabriel too. I expected her to walk in the door any minute. I still do, to be honest. That's why being in her room with you was so hard, why I was so glad to get back to my own desk, though it'll never be the same, but—'

'You said the call came from the temp, Katja?'

'Yes. Saying there were two men downstairs looking for Mandy. I said I'd never heard of any McInerney and that they must be new; and that I'd go down and talk to them, or else I'd ask one of the solicitors on the Finance and Trusts team to go down. We were very busy – I think I said that it was the worst day Mandy could have picked to be late, as she had so much on. When I think of it now, how little any of it matters ...'

'What did Gabriel say?'

'He said not to worry, that he'd get someone to sort it. He

rang the temp again while I was there and told her to offer them a cup of coffee. Then he said that I should get back to my own work. I can't remember if he mentioned you. He might have. But it was definitely after I left that he asked you to go down and see them, because the only phone call I remember him making was the one about the coffee.'

'Did he say anything about going down to see them himself?'

'No. Nothing.'

'Could he have gone downstairs?'

'It's possible, I suppose, but it doesn't seem very likely, does it?'

'I agree,' I said. 'But nothing about this week seems likely.'

'Nightmare,' Kathleen said. 'Every rotten bit of it.' She sounded weary.

'Can you remember anything else? Anything at all?'

'I'm sorry, Finn,' Kathleen said. 'I can't.'

'Thanks. Try to get a good rest tonight,' I said. 'See you tomorrow.'

I ended the call and sat back in the chair. Apart from establishing that Kathleen was adamant that she'd known nothing of Mandy's love affair, I'd learned nothing of great significance from the conversation. Gabriel had asked me to go down and talk to the McInerneys. I'd been aware of that since Monday, though I hadn't known the circumstances.

Now that I did know – that he'd waited an unknown length of time before he'd rung and asked me to meet them, instead of asking Mandy's PA who'd been standing right in front of him, and whose job it was to deal with Mandy's clients – I thought that the circumstances were, to say the very least, curious.

37

I DIDN'T HAVE TO PHONE SADIE. SHE PHONED ME.

'I know,' I said by way of greeting. 'The McInerneys. I mean, what the fuck?'

'What the fuck is right,' she said. 'It's a separate case for now – missing persons. The family in Wales reported it to the lads in Dublin.'

'And what have they done about it?'

'Not a whole pile up to now, I imagine. Bear in mind that as a general rule, adults are *allowed* to disappear off the face of the earth if they want to.'

'But there's got to be a link between the McInerney disappearances and the murder.'

'Or else it's some almighty coincidence.'

'What have you heard about them?' I asked.

'Not much,' Sadie said. 'They flew from Cardiff to Cork on Sunday morning.'

'That puts them in the city during the time Mandy was murdered.'

'It does. They booked a room in Jury's Inn for two nights. Paid in advance. Didn't take their planned return flight to Cardiff on Tuesday morning. Mobile phone coverage indicates that they went to Dublin instead. The last record of them was in Clondalkin.'

'So *that's* why it's the Dublin guards,' I said.

'And those fuckers up there won't give it away too easily,' Sadie said. 'Not now there's a possible murder connection.'

'They'll have to though, won't they?' I asked. 'It's a Cork case, like.'

'Maybe. It depends. The McInerneys might end up being part of another operation.'

'What does that mean?'

'It means I don't fucking know what's going to happen with the McInerney case. We only found out they disappeared literally, like, five minutes ago. Okay, maybe slightly more than five. Hey, any news yet on who Mandy's mystery lover might be?'

'Nothing worth talking about yet. I'm on it, though. You didn't hear anything?'

'Not about the lover, anyway, no. Listen, I've got to go.'

'Any news about anything else?' I asked.

But she'd rung off.

I analysed the implications of what Sadie had said. If the possible McInerney link to Mandy's murder piqued the interest of the guards in Dublin or the Criminal Assets Bureau, MLC could expect an invasion of hard-bodied, steely-eyed clones armed with search warrants and court orders for the removal and preservation of files and computers. The PR damage to the firm would be irreparable. Dermot Lyons would be apoplectic. It was no comfort to me that it was what I'd predicted might happen ultimately, though the McInerneys' disappearance would likely increase the pain considerably. Our only chance of avoiding total carnage was that it might take a while for the gardaí to definitively connect the McInerneys to Mandy's murder. Meanwhile the investigation would continue along traditional lines. Despite his alibi, Ed still retained his position as joint prime suspect, along with the mystery lover. With a bit of luck, the murder might be solved quickly, and the McInerneys might simply show up again.

I needed to talk to Gabriel. I rang his office but, to my surprise, he'd left for the evening although it wasn't yet 7 p.m. I tried his mobile but got no answer. I didn't bother with voicemail. He'd see the missed call and get back to me. If he didn't, it would be astonishing. Like permitting my report to go to the Law Society without reading it. He'd seemed almost dazed earlier. Or had that been a pretence? A deliberate ploy to get me to take on all the responsibility? But why do that?

Unless he needed a fall guy.

Someone disposable.

Someone like me.

38

I THOUGHT IT THROUGH. HOWEVER PARANOID I felt, I couldn't bring myself to believe that Gabriel would deliberately set out to damage me. His distraction had to have been genuine; his concern about the future of the firm had certainly been real. Indisputably, also, he had never treated me anything but decently. At the same time, I had a feeling that he knew more about Mandy's death – or about her life – than he was saying, and that he'd asked me to carry out an investigation without telling me the full story. In a more positive interpretation, that might have been because he'd thought that it wasn't relevant to the regulatory investigation. Or that for some reason I was better off not knowing.

I decided that, for the present, I was panicking unduly. I reminded myself too that I'd done nothing wrong. I'd prepared a report – an interim one, as Gabriel had been at such pains to point out – on what I'd found in Mandy's files. There was nothing that shouldn't have been there, they were so neat and tidy that even her junk and trash folders had been empty. She'd been completely on top of her caseload. Ed's theory that she'd been worried about work didn't hold water.

Yet the McInerneys had shown up here on Monday morning, looking for her. And now they were missing. That meant one of two things. Either their sudden appearance and equally sudden disappearance were connected to Mandy's work here at MLC; or they were connected to Mandy's private life rather than to her work. There was a third possibility – the almighty coincidence, as Sadie had called it – that I chose to dismiss. I was still left with a choice between two unknowns, two big piles of zeroes. In desperation, I googled, 'Jerry McInerney missing Ireland'. The Irish news outlets carried no updates. But Cardiff's *Western Mail* had a fresh post that provided more information. Under a photograph of a woman standing in front of a bottle-green painted front door, the article read:

Fears are growing for the safety of Canton grandfather and grandson, Jerry McInerney and Dean McInerney-Reid. Dean's mother, Charlene told the *Western Mail*: 'The last I heard was when Dean texted me – which was strange because he normally used WhatsApp – and he said they were in Dublin. What they were doing there, I don't know. I texted him back to ask but got no reply. I don't understand it. They were only supposed to go to Cork, and they ended up going to Dublin.'

But police in Dublin say that there have been no sightings of the two men. Dean's mother has had no contact from him since the last poignant message he sent her. 'My son told me that he was with my father,' Charlene McInerney said yesterday at her home in Llangollen Street. 'He said they'd phone me after lunch. But they never did. It's not like either of them. If anyone saw anything, anything at all, please tell the police.' Ms McInerney broke down. 'I never wanted them to go to Ireland in the first place. And now look what's happened.'

The news story was little help. The McInerneys came to Cork on Sunday and to this building, to MLC, on Monday. They left again quickly and went to Dublin sometime after that. There had to be a link with Mandy's murder, but the idea that they were the perpetrators who'd come here to divert attention from their crime and then skipped town didn't sit well with me.

Could they have seen something they shouldn't have? Come into the office to check on Mandy and, when she wasn't there, realised that they were in danger too and decided to lay low for a while? It was possible, though the only ones who could progress that theory were the true murderer and the putative witnesses, the McInerneys, who were nowhere to be found. I could make no sense of any of it and the more I thought about it, the more plausible Sadie's almighty coincidence theory was starting to look.

It struck me then that, up to this point, I'd been trying to extract evidence – breadcrumbs – from the information I had available to me that might point towards a solution. And that, after all of my work, I'd found precisely nothing.

But what if I started viewing the case differently? What if I stopped analysing what was there, and started thinking about what wasn't?

39

ON THE NANO NAGLE FOOTBRIDGE, FIVE OR SIX
people clumped together excitedly, staring and pointing into the
water below, some taking photos and filming on their phones.
One of the river's resident otters was out for an early-evening
swim. I joined the others on the bridge, watching, fascinated,
as he twisted and changed direction effortlessly. Above him, the
sun had completed its descent and St Fin Barre's Cathedral was
carved in grey relief against the saffron sky. The otter dove and
reemerged to gasps of wonder, a fish squirming helplessly in his
jaws. Then he swam to the stone steps from Sullivan's Quay,
found a comfortable perch above the waterline and demolished
his supper bite by bite.

On a whim, I went back the way I came. The streets were busy
and the air had an extraordinary heightened clarity. In the tree-
lined park off the Grand Parade, I walked past benches occupied
for the most part by those of my fellow citizens who spend their
days in the pursuit and consumption of alcohol and drugs. For
a fleeting moment, as their shouts and laughter echoed off the
high stone walls, I envied them their freedom.

Immediately, I felt ashamed. I knew well how shallow such
apparent freedom was. The people in the park had lost families,
children, friends – the chance of a normal life – to addiction.

But alcohol wasn't the only scourge. Hadn't been for a while. Over the past five years, it had been hard to miss the tightening chokehold that heroin had taken on the city. The begging. The dealing. The discarded paraphernalia. The heartbreaking sight of pale, dazed, nodding young men and women in their late teens and twenties. For all I knew, Cork's drug problem was no worse than in other places of the same size, but the deterioration seemed especially visible here because it was so compact.

I left the park and headed for the Coal Quay on the north of the island. When I reached the quay wall, all other considerations left me and I was lost for a while. Because one January night, the birth sister I'd come to know only after her death had walked here, down these same cold stone steps, and gone with the swollen winter river.

From minute to minute, the day was fading slowly. The street lamps had yet to come on but car headlights, yellow as cats' eyes, raked the gathering twilight.

•

On the way home, I rang Sadie.

'I forgot to ask you something. How was Mandy found so soon?' I asked. 'She might have lain there in that house for days.'

'We would've found her,' Sadie said. 'She was easily traceable – car parked outside. Her phone was in her rucksack, and turned on. The reason we got to her that fast was because a couple of the students next door heard it ringing over and over again when they were on their way to college. They took a look. Which they had no problem whatsoever doing, given that the front door was open.'

'How did you manage to keep the students out of the media?'

'By frightening the living shite out of them. I don't expect the embargo to last too much longer. Not the two themselves – the poor lambs are traumatised. But family, friends – someone will say something soon.'

'So either the killer messed up or …'

'Or what?'

'Or he wanted the body found quickly,' I said.

'And why might that be?' Sadie asked.

'Maybe he loved her and didn't want her lying in that dump too long.'

'Maybe he wanted to show off his handiwork,' Sadie said.

'Or he just might have been incompetent.'

'Or the opposite – supremely confident that he'd left no trace of himself behind.'

'Do you have any sense of him?' I asked.

'Not yet. If only we knew the identity of the lover. We'll get him. *Someone* knows who he is. The omertà won't last much longer.' She went silent.

'Is there something else you want to tell me?' I asked.

She sighed. 'There's nothing. I was just thinking about the McInerneys again, and where that element of the investigation might go. Which, frankly, could be anywhere or nowhere. Like I said before, adults vanish and reappear all the time.'

•

After Sadie rang off, I saw that I had a missed call from Gabriel. I got straight back to him and, following our telephone conversation, returned to the office.

I'd had an idea.

40

EARLIER, I'D HALF-PROMISED MY PARENTS THAT I'D
call up to see them after work but, before I left the office again, I
rang from the landline to let them know that I wouldn't make it.

My father answered the house phone. We chatted for a while.

Then he said, 'Look after yourself, Finn. Don't take any
chances. Don't be walking on your own after dark and that kind
of thing. Be sensible. Whoever killed poor Mandy – God be
good to her – is still out there.'

'Yes, Dad – but he's not going to come near me.'

'These days you just don't know.'

I told him I'd take care. Then I rang off, and did exactly what
I'd said I wouldn't. It was well lit nearly all the way home.

•

But after I turned down the dark side-lane to my house, I felt
a presence. Afraid to look behind me, I upped my pace and
mentally raced through my options: run forward and try to get
the gate open, or bang loudly on one of the neighbours' doors
and hope they reached me in time ...

'Hey Finn, hold on.'

'Holy shit, you gave me an awful fright.'

'Didn't mean to. Sorry,' Davy said.

'What are you doing here? Why didn't you call to say you were coming?'

'I did. Look at your phone. I figured when you didn't answer that you had it on silent.'

I checked. A text and two missed calls. I looked up at him. 'Oh my God, I was so busy all evening I didn't notice.'

He followed me in the gate and up the stairs to the top floor. He looked tired but well. He didn't touch me at any point and I didn't touch him either. Back when we'd started going out together, we hadn't been able to keep our hands off each other. Now, it appeared, we were painfully polite.

'How've you been?' Davy asked. 'What a terrible thing to happen.'

'Beyond terrible. We were never friends, but I admired Mandy. I had the sense that her bark was worse than her bite; that behind it, she was decent. And her team thought very highly of her, which is always a good sign. Did I ever introduce you to her?'

'You definitely didn't,' Davy said. 'I'd have remembered.'

'Wait a minute,' I said. 'Do you remember after the Dolly Parton concert? I saw her. Or maybe I didn't say anything. She was in her car. With someone. Did I tell you?'

'You didn't say anything to me at the time.'

'You're right,' I said. 'I don't think I mentioned it.' Then I said, 'What've you been up to?' I said it quietly, like it didn't matter. But I felt nervous.

'This and that,' he said. 'Reorganising. That kind of thing.'

My anxiety flipped into anger. 'This and that' didn't qualify as any kind of answer. I didn't let myself ask him a second question, though part of me felt that he wanted me to. But, in the moment, I didn't trust myself to talk about it in a civilised way. So I let 'this and that' slide.

'You heard anything from Sadie about the murder?' Davy asked.

'What do you mean?'

'Have they any idea what she was doing in that kip of a house? Or any suspects?'

'Are you for real?'

'The husband, I suppose,' Davy said.

'Here's my phone,' I said. 'Ring her yourself.'

'Hey, what's this about?'

'If you're so interested, Davy,' I said, 'ring Sadie yourself.'

'Jesus, Finn, what's wrong? I'm only making conversation.'

'Is that what we do now? Make conversation?'

He took a deep breath. 'Okay. I know I've not been around much. But, to be fair, you've not exactly been the most available either. I've hardly heard from you all week.'

Bending his head, he let his hair fell over his eyes. He knew I liked it when he did that. His hair was shorter at the back and sides than it used to be but still long on top. I wouldn't let him cut it.

I watched him, said nothing for a time. Then I said, 'True.'

He looked up quickly, moved fast across to where I was standing and kissed me roughly on the lips. A while later, we went downstairs to my bedroom and had sex.

•

After, Davy said, 'Listen, em … I've got something to tell you.'
I felt him move away from me in the bed. He propped his head
up on his elbow and looked down at me.

'I know you've got the funeral on Saturday. Well … what I
wanted to tell you is that I'm going too.'

'Is that all? I was nearly having a stroke. I didn't have a clue
what you were going to say. Don't worry about it, though. It's
really sweet of you to offer but I'll be fine. I don't need—'

'Believe me,' Davy said. 'I know. You've made it abundantly
clear on numerous occasions that you don't need anything or
anyone.'

It was something we'd talked about. My issues with emotional
intimacy. The walls I put up. All that. All valid. And, as he freely
admitted, he had quite a few issues himself. But I wasn't going
there, not now. I didn't want him at the funeral. I didn't want
his support and I didn't want his kindness. Not after he'd dodged
my question about where he'd been and what he'd been doing
since Sunday. Three, nearly four, days ago. We lay beside each
other in silence until he spoke again.

Eventually he said, 'There's no easy way to say this.'

'Now I'm having another stroke.'

'Right,' he said. 'The reason I'm going to the funeral – that I
have to go, that I *want* to – is because I knew Mandy Breslin. At
one time in my life I knew her very well.'

41

'MANDY WASN'T ALWAYS THE WOMAN YOU knew,' Davy said. 'She used to be wild.'

'Are you telling me you went out with her? She's been dead three days and you don't tell me this till *now*?'

'Jesus Christ, no. Not that. She was a friend of my older sister, Orla – played hockey with her. They were in the same class in primary school, and again in secondary in Dundanion College. They were ahead of me, in sixth year when I was in first. I was like their little doll till I found my own friends. But later, we all hung out. Summers in Baltimore. Basically, I knew her my whole life. And I'm sad – really, really sad – that she's dead.'

My eyes filled with tears and I reached out and put my hand on his. 'It would've been nice if you'd told me. I didn't know what was going on. I—'

He interrupted me. 'We have her to thank for us meeting, you know.'

'How?'

'She was the one who told me to contact you that first time,' he said. 'Did you never wonder why I picked you rather than one of the more usual criminal solicitors?'

'I think I remember you being all mysterious when I asked who referred you.'

'Yeah,' he said. 'Mandy didn't want you to know we were acquainted.'

'But why?

He raised his eyebrows.

'Oh,' I said. 'Because of the drugs and stuff? Wanted to keep her distance?'

He nodded.

'Then why suggest me in the first place?'

'Because I went to her for advice, I suppose. And she thought it was clever for me to be represented by you rather than one of the specialists. That it would send a signal I wasn't ... I mean that a possession charge really *did* mean possession for my own stupid fucking use.' He paused. 'Is this okay? Are *we* okay?'

'Yeah,' I said.

Then he held me.

•

Later, as he slept, I lay awake in the dark for hours. What Davy had been doing during the last few days was the least of it now. The stark reality was that Mandy had asked him not to tell me that they knew each other. And that, in five years of us being friends and, since last November, lovers, he hadn't said a single word about any of it to me.

Even after her death, he hadn't. Instead, he'd been deliberately avoiding me since Monday. At least he'd denied having had a relationship with Mandy. And I was nearly sure I believed him.

Nearly. But I wondered how close they'd been, and where his true loyalties lay. And I thought about how he'd waited until after we'd had sex to tell me all of this.

And that was the worst thought of all.

THURSDAY

42

I HEARD DAVY GETTING DRESSED. I FELT HIM watching me. I felt him kiss my forehead like it was the last farewell to a corpse in a coffin. All through it, I pretended I was asleep and he said nothing. I thought that he knew I was faking. The last second before he left, I almost opened my eyes.

When he was gone, I rolled onto my back in the middle of the bed.

I felt numb.

•

Eventually, I got up. In the gloom of the early morning, I took down my yoga mat and sat cross-legged for as long as I could, trying to bring my attention to the breath. Then I did three half-hearted sun salutations. Later, after my shower, I put on a black skirt suit and white shirt and tons of make-up and red lipstick. I felt like crawling back under the covers. But I had to go.

Grabbing my briefcase and handbag, I headed down to where the taxi waited before I could change my mind.

43

THE LAST-MINUTE RETURN TICKET, PAID FOR
reluctantly by Gabriel with the office account credit card, had
cost a whopping €463. But I'd spent so long persuading him
that someone from MLC had to make the trip that I'd paid scant
attention to the detail of the arrangements. The wind went out
of me when I saw the plane – a tin can with twin propellers and
two-by-two seating that wouldn't have looked out of place on a
school bus. I'd never known that commercial aircraft could be so
puny. Sardined into place, third from the front on the aisle, and
having no other option, I watched the flight attendant give the
safety demonstration. Short and witlessly cheerful, she didn't
inspire confidence in the operation.

We took off, the engines like a pair of deafening, Sunday
morning lie-in wrecking lawnmowers. After climbing steeply,
we levelled out far too quickly and far too low for my liking.
Then, soon after the Old Head of Kinsale, as we lurched over
open water, the co-pilot produced a tartan Thermos flask and a
rectangular Tupperware lunchbox from a small gym bag nestled
on the floor between him and the pilot. It was no comfort that
his sandwiches were a sensible choice – ham and red cheddar,
nothing moist or smelly. Gripping onto both armrests, I shut my

eyes. When I opened them a while later, the pilot was handing a finger of KitKat to the co-pilot. I directed my gaze away from the disaster movie in the cockpit and peered out the window. Eventually, as petrol-blue sea gave way to moss-green land, the churning in my stomach began to subside. I fell into a shallow doze, and awoke with a jolt as the plane's little wheels hit the Cardiff tarmac with a confident thunk.

•

The taximan stopped at the end of the street.

'It's just down there, love,' he said. 'I hope you enjoy your visit. I've always wanted to go to Ireland but I've never been.'

'You should go,' I said. 'But make sure you take the ferry.'

•

I got out and stood on the corner of Cowbridge Road East and Llangollen Street. I'd told Gabriel that my report into Mandy's files would be incomplete unless we knew whether or not the McInerneys had a connection to her death and, more specifically, to the work she'd been doing. Their visit to the MLC office on Monday was bound to get into the media – but if I could find out why they'd come, we might be able to defuse or deflect any damage. I'd said that the best way of doing that was for me to meet the family, establish what had been going on and offer them the firm's support. And that we couldn't rely on the guards locating them. Based on what Sadie had told me, it might be a while before any sense of urgency would come into a simple missing persons enquiry. Meanwhile, MLC could be dragged into speculative press pieces and whispering campaigns by rival law firms. That final argument had clinched it for Gabriel, and he'd given me the go-ahead.

But I hadn't made contact with Charlene McInerney in advance, reasoning that, with a missing son and father, she would have to be at home, waiting for news. Now that calculation seemed flawed. She was more likely to be in Dublin, searching for her loved ones, handing out flyers. I hesitated, then walked up Cowbridge Road East – busy, messy, noisy, long – for a bit. Spotting a Tesco Express, I went in and wandered around, seeing nothing I wanted. But my belly had started to rumble so I bought sparkling water and a Snickers. In the queue for the checkout, I stood behind a woman speaking in Welsh to her gorgeous smiley dark-haired baby boy. I marvelled at his curls, his lashes. Was he her first, I wondered? I thought not. She had an unfrazzled poise about her. Full basket. Organic yoghurts. Blueberries. Dinky little apples. Those little cardboard snack packs of raisins. Carrots for puréeing. Not a single bottle of cheap vodka.

Back out on the street, while I gazed sightlessly at the window display in a Cancer Research charity shop, I ate the chocolate and took a few long gulps of water. Then I made my way again to Llangollen Street. If Charlene wasn't there, it was better to find out and deal with the consequences.

The Victorian terraced houses were single-fronted two-storeys, with facades of red brick and stone and a ground-floor bay window. A metre-wide garden behind cast iron railings separated the houses from the footpath and lent the street an air of gentility. I walked up and down. Having established that only one of the front doors was painted bottle-green, I knocked.

44

THE DOOR WAS OPENED BY A TALL BLACK MAN with short greying hair, a goatee beard and dark purple circles under both eyes.

'Are you from the papers?' he asked.

'No. But I'd like to speak to Charlene McInerney, if I could. I came over from Cork today. From the solicitors' office Jerry and Dean visited the day before they went missing.' I handed him my card. He took it but kept looking at me. 'We want to help in any way we can,' I said.

'I'm Ray Reid,' he said. 'Dean's dad. Charlene and I, we're, we're not together.'

He paused and squeezed his eyes shut, used both his thumbnails to scrape the tears from his cheekbones. He breathed deeply. Then he said, 'You've come a long way, haven't you?'

•

I followed him down the narrow hall through a galley kitchen to a dining area, where sliding doors gave onto a patio. Beyond that was a small greenhouse at the side and a garden that backed onto another garden and another brick-and-stone terraced house. In my mind, I saw line after line of these houses spreading out in a spider's web across the flat city.

Charlene McInerney sat at the table, hunched over an iPad, staring at the Facebook page that the family had set up to help publicise the disappearance of Jerry and Dean. I'd looked at it several times since I'd found out their identity. Apart from photographs and messages of support, it neither gave nor generated any useful information. Nevertheless, Charlene couldn't tear her eyes away from it. Maybe she was afraid to.

'Is it the police?' she asked in a flat, affectless voice.

'No,' Ray said.

He explained who I was. She looked at me then. 'Why are you here?' she asked.

Her tone was sharp, suspicious. She had thin dyed-blonde hair pulled into a messy topknot. She wore the same clothes she'd had on in the *Western Mail* photograph. She looked like she hadn't slept a wink since it was taken. On her feet was a pair of enormous red-nosed reindeer novelty slippers. I wondered if Dean had given them to her for Christmas. I guessed that she was wondering if he'd be home for this one. If he'd be home ever again.

'… They left the office before anyone spoke to them,' I said. 'And then the solicitor they came to see, Mandy Breslin, was found dead. Murdered.'

'What are you saying, that they're murdered too?'

'No – only that there might be a connection.'

'You're not suggesting they had something to do with that woman's death? If you are, you can get out of this house right now.'

'Charlene,' Ray said. 'She might be able to help.'

'That's right. It's why I'm here. You see, we don't know why Jerry and Dean came to the office. They weren't clients; they didn't have an appointment as far as we know. They didn't mention one, anyway. So we wondered – I did, really – if you knew why they were there.'

'It was about the house,' Charlene said.

45

I WANTED TO ASK, 'WHAT HOUSE?', BUT I HELD off. Anything that Charlene could tell me might be helpful and would add to what I knew about the McInerneys – which at that moment was almost nothing. I could go into specifics later, take out a notebook then too. For now, I let her go on, uninterrupted. It was the least I could do. She wanted to talk, to remember. Unless she was very lucky, remembering might be all she had left of her father and her son.

'It was Dean at first,' Charlene said. 'Because of Brexit, he applied for an Irish passport. All you need is one grandparent and he had that, so it was easy. But that started him thinking about Ireland. About going there. He kept pushing my dad to go with him. And, I won't lie, he didn't have to push too hard. After Mum died, Dad was more open to the idea of going back for a visit. As much for something to do as anything else.'

Her forehead creased and her face took on an expression of pure anguish. She wrapped her hands around the mug of milky tea that Ray had made for her before he'd left to go to the police station, to check if there'd been any developments in the search.

Charlene spoke quietly. 'Dad would never have gone if Mum was still alive. She loved him, but she didn't love that he was from Ireland. It used to be a big thing in Wales – anti-Irish prejudice. Nothing to do with the IRA: it was older than that. The Paddies came over on the boat, half-starved, and took whatever work was going, even if that meant strike-breaking. They probably didn't know what a union was, let alone a strike, but what it meant was that if you were Irish in Cardiff, for a long time – until recent years when it's all Celtic this and Celtic that – you didn't advertise it. Dad didn't. He didn't have Irish friends. He still had the accent and the name, but he blended in as much as he could. He said that was one of the reasons he became a plumber – he always said that no matter where you're from, people are glad to see you if their toilet's bunged up or their hot water's on the blink. And he was so happy that Dean followed him into the work and took over the business.'

'Do you know what brought your father over to Wales?'

'An accident. He'd planned on going to London. Sailed on the *Innisfallen* from Cork and met a truck driver on the boat, who was coming to Cardiff and said he'd give him a lift. Dad reckoned he'd save a few quid, as the train ticket would be cheaper from here. After he got dropped off, he had a walk round and saw a building site, and asked for work – labouring. Strong as an ox, eighteen years old. Got a job. Decided to stay for a while, head for the bright lights later, with money in his pocket. But he ended up hanging around. Did a night class. Started studying for his City and Guilds. Then one day he met Mum. At a bus stop. They were getting different buses and all. But she forgot her bag, see. He ran after the bus to get it back to her – so she couldn't say no when he asked her out on a date. Even though she had no

time for the Irish, her father was a miner, and … But they were
so happy. And then she got cancer and died and now …

'My daughter, Megan. She's brilliant. Such a good girl. She's
been here with me since it happened but she had to go into
college today, to sort out a few things. We're flying to Dublin
tomorrow, to make an appeal on Irish telly for information.
Megan wants to. She lives in Pontypridd now. Studies History
in the university there. She's doing an MA on Wales's links to
the slave trade. It was about the wool, she says – Welsh wool
was used to make clothes for the slaves to wear. And Swansea
copper was used on the sugar plantations. You don't think of
those things, do you?'

'No, but Cork has slavery connections too,' I said. 'I read
somewhere that the sugar islands were like oil rigs. That
everything had to be brought in. London and Bristol traders
bound for Barbados and Jamaica and so on used to load up with
farm produce – salt beef and butter – in the Irish ports on the
south coast, Cork included.'

'Megan would be interested to hear that.'

'I'm sure she knows already. A lot more than I do,' I said.

'Probably,' Charlene said.

She lapsed into silence. After a time, she spoke again. Slowly.
Quietly. 'I know they're dead. The two of them. The police say
it's too soon to give up. Ray hasn't. Not yet. And Megan's still
hopeful. But you think the same as me, I know you do.'

Actually, I wasn't sure. If the McInerneys had killed Mandy,
there would be compelling reasons for them to hide themselves
away.

I said, 'Them being missing so long, well, it …'

'Doesn't look good,' Charlene said.

After a pause I asked, 'You mentioned a house?'

'The place where Dad grew up,' Charlene said. 'His parents died. He told me that his mother died from complications after his birth and that his father died from TB, when Dad was twelve. After that, he lived with his aunt, a spinster, his mother's only sister. Sibling, come to that. He wasn't happy there – well, he was without his father, of course. But it was more than that. His aunt was hard on him. A disciplinarian. As soon as he could, he got out. That's why he stayed away so long. Never wrote or made contact with her again either. He said Cork held only bad memories, and that Cardiff and my mum had given him a life he couldn't have dreamed of if he'd stayed. But the pull of Ireland was still there, I suppose.'

'And the house?'

'It was the first place Dean and Dad went after they checked into their hotel. Got a taxi there. But it was derelict. And there was no one around who knew his aunt. All the old neighbours were gone. The street had gone to rack and ruin, he said. But he was excited. He said he was his aunt's only living relative, and that he should be entitled to the house. I thought it was unlikely – I said as much – I mean the solicitor or the police would've found him after his aunt's death, even if his aunt hadn't been able to before then. Besides, why would she leave him anything after he'd gone away and never come back?'

'It's possible that she willed him the house,' I said. 'Even if she hadn't seen him for decades. Family is still family, and she might have had regrets about the way he left. But if there was a will, there'd be an executor and a solicitor appointed to deal with the estate. And there are companies that specialise in tracing missing beneficiaries. Most likely, the solicitor would've engaged one of them to conduct a search, if normal enquiries had proved fruitless. On the other hand, if the aunt didn't leave a will, there might be no solicitor involved, no one to pursue the issue, so the whole thing might just have drifted. It's something I could look into for you now, though. Do you mind if I take a few notes?'

She nodded a reply. I jotted down a few details from what she'd told me already.

Then I asked, 'What was the aunt's name?'

'Josepha Buckley.'

'And the address of the house?'

She told it to me and I took a long time writing it down – even though I didn't need to write it at all. Because I knew it already. Because I'd been inside it with Sadie and seen the stains on the floor where Mandy Breslin had been bludgeoned to death with a hammer.

46

I'D INTENDED TO DO A TITLE SEARCH BUT I'D BEEN under so much pressure, I'd forgotten all about it. Not that it would have made much difference – I wouldn't have understood the significance of the results if I hadn't come here. After my hands had stopped shaking, I asked, 'Has anyone else spoken to you about this? About the house? The police? Here or in Ireland?'

'No,' Charlene said. 'I've been dealing with the police in Dublin. They keep asking me why the two of them went to Dublin; who they were going to meet there; where they were going to stay. Both mobiles were switched off in Dublin. The outskirts. But I haven't been able to help. I don't *know* why they went to Dublin. I haven't a clue. Why didn't they stay in Cork? Or come home?'

'Can you tell me any more about why they went to our office?'

'All I know is that it was something to do with the house. They said as much when I last spoke to them on Sunday evening. I got the text message from Dean on Tuesday, but I didn't speak to either of them after Sunday night.'

'What time was that?'

'About 7.30 p.m.'

Not long before the murder.

'Do you know where they were when they called on Sunday night?'

'I didn't ask. Dad was doing all the talking, and at that time I just didn't want to know. I regret it now, but I was only half-listening to what he was saying. I thought the whole thing was pie-in-the-sky, to be honest. But Dad went on and on, ranting that he was going to get answers. I cut him short. And talking to Dean was no better. He seemed to be even more obsessed than Dad was.'

'Had your father ever talked about the house before, about what might have happened to it? It's interesting that it was the first place they went when they got to Cork. Had finding out what happened to it been the main purpose of the trip?'

'I don't know. Possibly. Or, you know, it's more like probably, the more I think about it. Dean and Dad are close, even closer in the year since my mother died. They didn't say much to me in advance about the visit to Cork. Nothing about whether he hoped to find his aunt alive. Nothing about the house but they must have discussed it. They didn't talk to me about it. They knew I wasn't interested. That I didn't want them to go.'

'Do you know why they went to MLC?'

'No.'

'And had they ever mentioned meeting Mandy Breslin?'

'I don't remember them mentioning any names. But they probably didn't say because they knew how much against the visit to Cork I was. I thought no good would come of it. I couldn't see why now, after all this time, he wanted to go back, to reopen old wounds. And I've been proved right. They should never have gone. It isn't good for Dad, getting riled up like that. He's on tablets for his heart. Angina. And I could hear it in his voice on the phone. He was upset. Agitated.'

Agitated enough to commit murder?

47

I HAD NO TIME TO LOOK AROUND CARDIFF, AND no appetite for sightseeing but I liked the place and I had the feeling I'd be back sometime. Mostly when Cork people visited the city, it was for rugby matches. I wondered if Jerry went to see Munster play. I wondered if Dean went too, or if he was more of a Cardiff City supporter, if they both were.

But where were they now? Despite my visit, I was no closer to the answer.

At the airport, I ate a cold sausage roll and – when in Rome – a bag of Welsh rarebit flavour crisps. Then I rang Tina to find out how the day had gone. Breathlessly, she informed me that a team of detectives from Coughlan's Quay had colonised the firm's meeting rooms from early morning.

'They interviewed everyone, worked their way through every single staff member, including Dervla. And Katja, that temp who filled in for her on Monday, showed up in the afternoon – they must have arranged to meet her. Even the cleaners were called in. They were asking everyone for alibis for the time of the murder.'

'Did they actually use those words?'

'Not as such, but that's what they meant. "Where were you on Sunday night between the hours of 8 p.m. and midnight?" – that kind of thing.'

'Was Sadie there?'

'She was. I was hoping I'd get her but I got a guy called Fogarty. I had to tell him who I worked for. When he heard it was you, he was asking where you were.'

'What did you say?'

'Not a thing, girl.'

I laughed. 'Whatever you say, say nothing. And *do* you have an alibi?'

'I was with me fella, so of course I do. I presume you're in the—'

I cut off what she was going to say.

'Did they go into Mandy's room?'

'Gabriel let them look and take a few photos, but he said they weren't allowed near her files or her computer because of solicitor client privilege. I was quite proud of him. I wasn't *actually* there when it happened, but Kathleen told me he was very strong. She said he held his ground. She was proud of him too, I could tell.'

'And did the gardaí accept what he said?'

'Well they had to, didn't they?'

'What were they asking about mainly?'

'Everything. All about her clients and her work. Her mood. Any arguments. And if she was having an affair.'

'Did anyone say yes?'

'No! Everyone said no.'

So I told her what I'd seen the night of the Dolly Parton concert.

Confidentially.

And answered all her questions.

Exhaustively.

I barely made the flight.

48

ALREADY USED TO THE SMALL PLANE, OR PERHAPS sufficiently distracted by what I'd learned from Charlene and Tina – whatever the reason, the trip home seemed less strange. I regretted advising the Cardiff taxi driver to take the ferry. Cork Airport – convenient and uncrowded but permanently under pressure from the behemoth up in Dublin – needed all the flights and passengers it could get.

Back home, I went straight to my house, changed into leggings and a long sweatshirt, and tied my hair into a high ponytail. Standing at the kitchen worktop, I shovelled down a rhubarb yoghurt. Then I checked my messages. To my complete lack of surprise, there was nothing from Davy. I hadn't contacted him either. Before this week, we'd have been talking or texting three or four times a day at a minimum.

Later, as I ran to where my car was parked, I pushed him from my mind. I wouldn't think about him. I'd keep busy. I wouldn't care or feel anything. Not till I had to.

•

Pauline Doyle lived in Bishopstown. She'd told me not to dare arrive before 8.30 p.m., as she'd be dealing with bath- and bedtime until then, but if I called around 8.45, she'd be able to give me half an hour. She hadn't understood why what I had to ask couldn't wait till morning. I wasn't altogether sure myself. I told her that it had to do with confidentiality, with not wanting to involve any of the other staff in the office. That was part of it. The other part was that I didn't want there to be any record of what I was asking her to do. That was the bit I wasn't sure about. It might have been about wanting to respect Mandy's memory, and it might not.

Right fork at the Bishopstown Bar and another right and a couple of lefts after the Church of the Real Presence – I was relying on Google Maps and Pauline's hastily delivered directions. Bishopstown was a foreign land to me. Deepest suburbia. Families. Good schools. The GAA. Nothing like the mixed city-centre neighbourhood where I lived.

After a couple of wrong turns, my car, a ten-year-old black VW Golf – the replacement for my previous black Golf that had had a sudden and fiery end to its long life – found its way. It was coming up to 8.50 p.m. when I arrived. The entire front garden and driveway had been paved over in herring-bone pattern red brick, leaving no grass or vegetation of any kind. Apart from a once-a-year power wash, it was as low maintenance as it was possible to be. I could almost hear Pauline say that it was one less job for her to do. Personally, I thought it could have done with a few shrubs. Even a weed or two would have been an improvement. The house itself was just as well-kept – white-painted, pebble-dashed, with white PVC windows and a mid-brown wood-effect front door, which Pauline opened before I reached it.

'I've been watching out for you,' she whispered, her index finger to her lips. 'I was terrified you'd ring the bell and wake them again. They're like demons this evening.'

I followed her into the kitchen. She was still in her work

clothes. 'We can't keep going like this,' she said. 'Something's got to give. Cormac is on night shift tonight down in Ringaskiddy, and the pay is good but Jesus Christ, the stress when he's not here. It's the same for him when I'm out. The twins are a two-man job. Have you eaten?'

'Don't worry about me,' I said. 'I'm grand. What about you?'

'Oh I ate,' she said. 'Chicken nuggets, chips and beans. They hardly touched theirs but I'll be as fat as a fool. Do you want a glass of Pinot Grigio?'

'No, thanks. I've to drive home. You go ahead, though.'

I didn't bother telling her that I don't drink, that I never have; that, with my birth family history, I've always been afraid to. It would have been way too much information. I liked Pauline a lot and we were friendly at work, but I knew hardly anything about her, I realised. It felt strange to be here with her. She must have felt it too.

•

We moved into the conservatory. It was dark outside but for the final hints of twilight in the western sky. I sat in an armchair, wicker with floral cushions. The wicker squeaked if I moved, so I tried not to. Pauline switched on a table lamp, took off her shoes and tucked her feet beneath her on the matching two-seater. In both hands she cradled a bulbous vat of ice-cold white wine. She traced a finger through the condensation on the glass, raised it to her lips and took a sip.

'I need this,' she said. 'One every night. Sure, where's the harm?'

'No harm at all,' I said. 'Especially this week.'

'And the worst thing is that it's only been a few days, and

already what happened to Mandy is starting to feel normal. Or is that just me?'

'It's not. I know exactly what you mean. And then sometimes I get a jolt, and it's new again, the awfulness of it. I didn't know her really. I feel bad about that, now it's too late. Did you? Know her, I mean?'

'Same as you probably. Not all that well. Chatted when she was having computer trouble, or if I was installing something on her desktop. She had no patience, needless to say. She was like most of the solicitors. Allergic to IT. Just wanted it to work. Didn't care how.'

'Allergic sounds about right,' I said. 'You know I've been reviewing her files.'

'Yes.'

'She was incredibly well organised. There isn't a hair out of place anywhere.'

'Just what I'd expect,' Pauline said.

'Now, with the McInerneys gone missing, and one of the last confirmed sightings of them being at MLC—'

'What are you saying?'

'That we can expect the garda investigation to ramp up more. And likely to begin to home in on Mandy's work.'

'So …?' Pauline said.

'So, I was wondering if it would be possible for you to run a discreet check on her files, on Mandy's whole system, to see if there's anything hidden from view or deleted.'

'Wait a minute,' Pauline said. 'What brought this on?'

'A couple of things. One, the empty junk and trash folders. Almost too neat, even for her. It got me thinking that everything is so tidy and so perfect, it seemed too good to be true. I might be over-complicating things—'

'That's what this is based on? That she was too efficient?'

'No, not that. To be honest, I'm not sure what I'm looking for. Something that she might have hidden. Or removed. Is that even possible?'

'Removal?' Pauline asked.

'Yes.'

'The policy is that there must be a record kept of everything. Any files closed or not going ahead are archived, as you know, and retained – twelve years for conveyancing files, six years for everything else. No one in the office is allowed to just delete a file. It's a big no-no. Unless a client asks for that to happen. If they do, there's a process to be gone through for that.'

'So simply deleting a file – to hide a mistake, say – can't be done.'

Pauline laughed. 'Of course it can be done,' she said.

'And what about retrieval?'

'That *can* be done, unless whoever was doing the deleting did a proper job.'

'And emails? Deleted emails? Can you get those too?'

'In theory yes, but the same proviso applies.'

'How long would it take you to look into all this?'

'It depends.' Pauline went quiet. Then she said, 'You want me to search Mandy's records and to be discreet about it. Why is that, by the way?'

'Mandy's dead. Which is quite bad enough. I don't want to start rumours about anything else, especially rumours that might turn out to be completely unfounded.'

'Alright,' she said slowly. She looked doubtful.

'There's also the McInerneys,' I said. 'There's no mention of them on the system anywhere. In all honesty I don't expect to find them. But—'

'You want me to take a look.'

'Exactly,' I said. 'For them, and for anything else that you might find.'

'I'm beginning to see why you want me to keep this between us. This is the kind of thing the Garda Fraud Squad do. Are you saying that Mandy was involved in something shady? If you are, that is the most stupid thing I've ever heard.'

'I don't know what I think. But Mandy was murdered – which no one would ever have expected – and now, with the McInerneys and all … Look, I know it's a big ask. Especially the bit about asking you to say nothing to anyone about what we're doing.'

'What would you do with the information? Might I get in trouble?'

'I can't see how you would. Anything you do, you're doing it at my request.'

And Gabriel's previous strict instruction not to bother with the McInerneys had been rendered null and void by my fully authorised investigatory visit to Cardiff. Implicitly, at least.

I went on: 'The reason I'm doing this investigation – that I've been appointed by the partners to do this investigation – is because they want me to find out if there's anything they need to be worried about from the firm's point of view. They're talking about protecting people's jobs, the firm's reputation, all that. But I've also been keeping Mandy in mind. It's not like she randomly got cancer or walked out in front of a bus. She died because someone killed her. Someone deliberately, and maliciously, crushed the life out of her. And the way I've been thinking is that, if my, the firm's, investigation can do anything – anything at all, however small – that might help catch her murderer—'

'Okay, okay,' Pauline said. She stopped, looked me straight in the eye. 'I'll do it,' she said.

FRIDAY

49

GABRIEL TOOK THE NEWS ABOUT THE UN-
equivocal link between Mandy's murder and the McInerneys
with theatrical resignation.

'What can we do?' he asked. 'The fates would appear to be
aligned against us.'

Instead of his usual suit and tie, he was wearing Saturday
clothes – chinos, a rust-and-white check shirt and a green cotton
jumper, tied loosely by the arms around his neck. He plucked at
the shirt. 'I'll be leaving shortly after eleven,' he said. 'Won't be
back for the day. Georgina has me booked in for a medical MOT
out at the Mater Private.'

He added, 'She'll brook no dissent, unfortunately.'

Georgina was Gabriel's wife. From what I knew of her, she
was quietly spoken and deferred to her husband in most things.
If she was ordering him to go to the doctor, it was a cause for
concern. 'What's wrong?' I asked.

'Nothing at all. Except that my life's work is being flushed
down the toilet. And we had about a dozen guards in here
yesterday, tramping their size twelves through the office like
a herd of elephants, giving everyone the third degree. They
actually asked me for a DNA sample, would you believe? As if

I got off the plane from Nice on Sunday night and took a quick detour to Alysson Villas to commit murder. With Georgina in the car? It beggars belief.'

'What time did your flight get in?'

'Just after six. We went straight home obviously and didn't stir for the night.'

To Orchard Road. Not a million miles from Alysson Villas. Not even two.

'Tina told me the guards were in, but she didn't mention DNA tests.'

'She probably wasn't one of the chosen. All Mandy's Finance and Trusts team were done. And Dermot. A few others. Anyone whose alibi wasn't sufficiently watertight. Yes, so apart from all that, everything's dandy.'

'Did anyone object?'

'The samples were voluntary. Allegedly. But no one was brave enough to refuse.'

This was the time to ask him about the dark-haired man I'd seen with Mandy. 'Gabriel, Tina said the guards were asking if Mandy was having an affair ...'

He put up his right hand to silence me. Then he looked away and out the window. He shook his head a few times. I couldn't read his expression. Though the guards had taken a DNA sample from him, it was still too much of a stretch for me to believe that Gabriel could have killed Mandy. Nevertheless, I knew he was hiding something. I waited for him to tell me what it was.

Instead, he changed the subject. 'How are things your end? The remainder of the file review?'

I chose my words carefully. 'I've gone as far as I can go with what's there. Found nothing.'

He looked back at me again, brighter in himself all of a sudden, but he stayed quiet. It came to me that 'nothing' was exactly what I was supposed to find. I had been mulling over whether or not to tell Gabriel what I'd asked Pauline to do. Whatever my doubts about his recent odd behaviour, I'd decided that I had to inform him. Now, on impulse, I did the opposite. 'I'll be finished this evening, I think.'

'Email me when you are,' Gabriel said. 'I'll talk it over with Dermot and the rest of the partners but, if there's no more to be done, you can return to your regular work on Monday.'

'Sounds good,' I said. 'And, em ... good luck with the appointment.'

'I'll be fine,' he said.

'I know you will.'

He smiled tightly.

'I'll see you at the funeral tomorrow so,' I said.

'Yes,' he said. 'See you there.' He shook his head. 'Unbelievable ... I still can't get my head around it.'

'No,' I said. 'When you stop to think, it's ...' I stopped short of saying the platitude I was about to trot out and gave a little wave instead. I left him, small and alone behind his enormous desk, and went up to Mandy's office.

50

AT 9.45 A.M., TINA BURST IN. 'GABRIEL'S OFF TO the Mater this morning for tests. Chest pain.'

'He told me,' I said. 'Not about the chest pain, though. Mother of Jesus.'

'It's all down to stress, I'd say.'

'Hopefully it's just that.' After a silence I said, 'Hey, I think we'll be back to normal Monday. I can leave this place of detention and return to my freezing garret. If I manage to finish the review today, that is.'

We chatted for a while about what had gone down at MLC the day before and about the dark-haired man. Then I told her the big news – that Jerry McInerney's aunt had owned the house where Mandy had been found murdered.

'You must've nearly died when you heard that,' Tina said.

'I nearly did. But we need to find out for sure if Josepha Buckley is the registered owner. Will you do a search – Registry of Deeds most likely, but Land Registry as well just in case – to see? We should've done it ages ago but it slipped my mind.'

'Is that another way of telling me to feck off and leave you to your review?'

'Not yet. Tell me, what's the mood like around the office?'

'Well …' Tina said. 'It's quiet.'

'Too quiet?'

'Way too quiet. Everyone's shell-shocked after yesterday. And it's only been five days, and already nobody wants to talk about Mandy. Then the McInerneys disappearing – and your email looking for info about them – has put the complete and utter shits up everyone. They're running for cover, afraid to even express an opinion, in case they might get dragged into something. Did you get any replies to the email by the way?'

'Not a dickybird so far,' I said. 'What about Dervla? You talked to her at all?'

'She's one of the worst,' Tina said. 'Won't entertain a mention of the murder. In all fairness, she's on the frontline, answering calls from journalists and true crime eejits, day in and day out. She hangs up on them straightaway but it must be annoying. She's bound to be pig sick of the whole thing. Still.'

'Still?'

'She's not right since she came back to work on Tuesday. And she and Gabriel are definitely having some kind of an ongoing row about something but I haven't been able to find out what it's about yet.' She paused. 'I'm dreading the funeral tomorrow, are you?'

'Big time,' I said.

'But it'll be interesting to see who shows up.'

'And who doesn't.'

51

I WORKED ON THROUGH LUNCH, FINISHING shortly after 4 p.m. Then I composed and sent a long email to Gabriel – confirming that Mandy's work looked to be every bit as clean as we'd expected all along – and shut down the computer at 4.40. After that, I found a tissue in my bag and wiped it over the desk surface and the keyboard and monitor, and I slid the chair neatly back into place. I spent a few more minutes tidying the office and the bookshelves but, when I found myself straightening picture frames, I forced myself to stop. Mandy was never coming back. It didn't matter if I lit a fire in a filing cabinet or spilled bleach on the carpet. Nothing at MLC would matter to Mandy again. The only thing that did matter now was finding her killer.

On that score, progress was slow. I'd spoken to Sadie mid-morning.

'Donkey work, and good luck with the forensics,' she'd said. 'That's the hope.'

But hopeful was the last thing she sounded. The day the guards had spent at MLC had revealed nothing of significance, she said. She pressed me for news on Mandy's other man but I wasn't able to help. Then I started talking about my trip to Cardiff. I didn't get far.

'You do know that Coughlan's Quay isn't investigating the McInerneys. That it's a Dublin case. Very much so, at this stage, it seems. We're pursuing more local lines of enquiry.'

'Could you translate that for me? I'm having difficulty with the garda speak.'

'What it means is that I can tell you a lot but I can't tell you everything.'

'Well, that's put the civilian nicely in her place, thanks very much.'

'Ah come on, Finn, you know what it's like. The timing's the problem more than anything. I promise I'll tell you what's going on as soon as I can.' She ended the call, leaving me frustrated, wondering what she hadn't told me.

A little while later I remembered what I hadn't told her.

52

I WOULD'VE CALLED SADIE BACK AND TOLD HER about the 3 Alysson Villas/Jerry McInerney connection, I really would have, but I didn't bother in the end, reasoning that there was no need. Because the guards in Dublin would have found out about the McInerneys' link to MLC and to the murder house once Charlene and her daughter Megan flew to Dublin today to do their televised appeal for information.

Sadie would be back to me soon enough, pumping me for information. Either that, or she and her colleagues would arrive at the front door of the office with a warrant. If that happened, my investigation would terminate and all the firm's activities would, of necessity, be suspended. I decided that I had to push ahead with my assigned task. While I still could.

•

I'd been waiting all day to hear from Pauline Doyle. We'd agreed to keep our distance from each other while in the office, and to initiate communication via text if something materialised. No text had come. That could have meant that, like me, she'd found nothing. I reckoned it was far more likely that she hadn't even started her trawl. I needed to know which it was. Before I left work, I sent her a one-word message – '*Anything?*' – and waited five minutes. When I got no reply, I dragged on my coat. Then, head low and feet like dead weights, I crawled up the hill home.

I watched the 5.30 p.m. Virgin news straight through, and the headlines on the Six One on RTÉ but there was no mention of the McInerneys and no televised appeal by Charlene and her daughter. Something must have happened to change those plans. Maybe the two men had been found? I checked Twitter and breakingnews.ie. Nothing. I flicked off the telly and went for a long shower.

When I got out, I had a new text message from Pauline:

Insane day. Creche called. Had to collect twins and go to GP. Conor has ear infection. On antibiotic now but v sick the poor pet. Had no time but managed to check Contacts before I left work. Found this. Odd it's deleted. Will get back to search first thing Monday. Promise!

She'd also sent a link to a professional contact card – similar to a mobile phone contacts or email contacts list, but embedded in the case management system and enabled to autofill the relevant address and other necessary data on any letters and documents relating to the contact. I opened the attachment on my phone and clicked through to the website. Then, still in my towel and bathrobe, I went downstairs to my study and opened my desktop.

The contact card was for Ricky Dempsey, an estate agent. Pauline was right – the deletion was puzzling. Dempsey Auctioneers, still very much in business, was an apparently successful small property sales and letting agency, employing staff comprising a couple of junior property negotiators and an office manager/receptionist/book-keeper. Based in Blackpool on Cork's northside, Ricky Dempsey sold houses around there, and the suburbs of Gurranabraher and Farranree, many of them ex-city council properties. With a client base as far from MLC's in general – and from Mandy Breslin's in particular – as it was possible to be in Cork, it was little surprise that I'd never heard of him.

I opened the 'About Me' section on the Dempsey Auctioneers website. Ricky was in his forties, he was a good-looking man, if a little on the chunky side, and he had dark wavy hair. He'd be a candidate for the man I'd seen Mandy with – if only I could figure out how they might have met. His bio said that he'd attended the North Mon school: no connection there. He played sports that Mandy didn't favour – hurling and Gaelic football. He was involved in various community organisations and trained one of the local underage GAA teams. He was a regular guy whose path might never have crossed hers.

If by some chance it had, though, that could explain why his contact details had been deleted. She could have met him at some event – a wedding, or a party – and they could have exchanged cards. She might have saved his details initially, but if a relationship had started, she might not have wanted any link to him. There had been no incriminating messages on her phone. She wouldn't have wanted any reference to him on her work computer either.

Or maybe the deletion was more recent? If the relationship was nearing its end, as Ed had suggested, she might have wanted him gone completely: no record, not even a contact card. And if she'd tired of him, spurned him, might he have reacted violently?

I saved what I'd found about Ricky Dempsey into a file on my desktop. Then I photographed his website picture and saved it to my phone.

Now, I had three men to watch – their demeanour and their interaction with each other – at the funeral in the morning: Mandy's husband Ed, her trainee, Hugo Woulfe, and wildcard entry Ricky Dempsey. The first two – Ed and Hugo – would certainly be there. But Dempsey? I knew so little about him, I couldn't predict if he'd show. Whether he did or not, I'd have to check if his name appeared in a search of Mandy's files. I didn't recall it.

Though before this, of course, I hadn't been looking.

53

WHEN THE DOORBELL SOUNDED TWICE – ONE
short ring followed by one long – it had to be Davy. He hadn't
cancelled so I should have been expecting him. I wasn't. Even
though he came round every Friday night. Early, usually. We ate
in – I cooked – or went out to a restaurant. On summer Fridays
we swam in the sea. Rain or shine. No bother to us to zip down
to Myrtleville and on to Kinsale for something to eat. Talking,
laughing about the week gone by. Later, the slow, easy drive
back home in the bright. In the quiet. The windows down. My
hand in his. Ten o'clock, and daytime still. Then to bed. Damp
hair and salty skin. Sand in the sheets the following morning.

•

As I buzzed him in, I put on *Modern Sounds in Country and Western
Music* (Davy hates country but loves Ray Charles), low volume,
and tried to compose myself. When I heard his tread near the top
of the stairs, I glanced briefly in his direction, keeping it light.

'Hey,' I said. 'I might as well tell you upfront, we've got no
food in the house.'

'We could go out if you want. Or order pizza?'

Ray was singing, 'You Don't Know Me'. I felt Davy move close. 'I missed you,' he said.

He seemed tired, and his face looked thinner, his cheekbones sharper. But those blue eyes. I reached up and crooked my arm around the back of his neck and pulled his mouth to mine.

•

We ordered pizzas and ate them in bed. It felt decadent and seedy and deliciously normal. I pushed aside all lingering doubts. So what if Davy hadn't told me that he'd known Mandy? I remembered how she'd been with me in my office the morning after the Dolly Parton concert. People didn't cross her unless they had to. On Wednesday night he'd said she hadn't wanted me to know about her connection to him. It made sense that he hadn't told me about knowing her when we met first as solicitor and client. And that it would've been even harder for him to tell me later. If Mandy hadn't died the way she had, he might never have told me at all. I couldn't blame him too much. Though I'd always thought highly of her, of her work ethic especially, in truth, I'd been a little afraid of her. Clearly, I wasn't the only one.

But I'd had little to do with her on a day-to-day basis. Her team, who did, loved her. However tough she could be, in work she was straight. Had no agendas. I never heard her running down anyone behind their back. If she had something to say to someone, she said it directly. And yet, despite all that, she'd been having an affair, cheating on Ed for a long time.

It seemed like the more I found out about Mandy, the less I understood her.

Davy pulled on a sweatshirt and tracksuit bottoms from the stash he kept at my place – a couple of shelves of clothes and toiletries – and nipped downstairs to dump the pizza boxes in the compost bin. I went upstairs to the living room to pick something for us to watch on Netflix.

When he came up from the garden, he sat beside me on the sofa.

'I've found a few possibles,' I said. 'So first there's—'

'Listen, em … Remember what we were talking about the other night—'

'I'm not at all sure I do,' I said. 'Give me a minute to think.'

'Very funny,' he said.

He stood up, then sat down again but slightly further away. Then he moved and sat on the arm of the sofa with his bare feet on a cushion, knees bent, elbows on knees, hands clasped tightly.

'There's a small bit more to the story,' he said. He cleared his throat. 'This is the really awkward bit,' he said. He grimaced. 'I sold drugs to her. To Mandy.'

'Oh. My. God.'

'Not recently, obviously. Back in the day.'

'Once? More than once?'

'Often,' he said. 'E, coke later.'

'I don't know what to say.'

'I always thought you knew. Guessed. Not about Mandy. But, you know, in general. That I, em, you know, freelanced. Most people – most addicts, I mean – do a bit of trade.'

I shut my eyes. The truth I hadn't admitted to Sadie, had barely acknowledged to myself, was that I'd made the decision never to ask Davy the dealing question. Because if I didn't know the answer, I didn't have to think about it.

He kept talking. 'It was the nineties. Sir Henry's. Half the town was off its face every weekend, Mandy included. She was a student, or a trainee. Just qualified. I don't know exactly. Then for a while, after that scene ended, it was coke. More occasional. Parties. Dinner parties.'

'Market-fresh, ethically-sourced local produce followed by chemicals.'

'Yeah. She was going out with Ed by then but he'd always been part of the gang ...'

'You sold drugs to Ed too?'

'Ed and Mandy got the family rate. But they got tired. Got old. Got married. Had kids. It was ancient history for them.'

He gave a small, bitter laugh. 'I, well, I kept on going,' he said. 'As you know. And there's ...'

'More? More you haven't told me?'

I thought he was about to say yes. Instead, after a pause, he shook his head.

Then he said, 'I should've said all this a lot sooner. After the murder, especially. I should've told you immediately.'

'When was the last time you saw her?'

'I don't know. Ages ago. To be honest, I can't recall. We—'

'So you're being honest now, are you? That's a refreshing change.'

'Ouch. Okay. Well, I deserve that, I suppose.'

'What if she was still into drugs, though? What if that's what got her killed?'

'She left all that behind years ago. I told you. There's no way she would've been ...'

'How do you know? You said you can't remember when last you two met.'

'Yeah, that's right.'

'What about your sister? You said she and Mandy were best friends in school.'

'And?'

'Did Orla see much of Mandy in recent years?'

'They saw each other, I can't say how much.' He paused. 'If you're thinking drugs for this, you're on the wrong track. She …' He trailed off. Then he spoke again. 'Now that I think of it, I actually *do* remember the last time I met Mandy. It was at Orla's house. In February. Her birthday. She had a few of the gals around for drinks. I just happened to drop in when I was passing. Wasn't there long.'

'Did something happen? With you and Mandy? An argument or …?'

He shook his head. There were tears in his eyes. 'We hardly spoke. Just, "hi – how's it going" – that kind of thing. Though from what I saw, she wasn't off snorting coke in the jacks every five minutes. So let it go, will you? Please?' He looked tormented.

'Okay,' I said.

•

But then I remembered his questions on Wednesday night. How he'd been so interested in the garda investigation. How he'd asked if the guards had any suspects. If they knew what Mandy had been doing in the house where she was found. 'That kip of a house,' he'd called it – which made it sound like he'd seen it. Been inside it. And now, how he couldn't recall the last time he met Mandy until I pressed him and then all of a sudden he did.

But maybe he *had* genuinely forgotten and then suddenly remembered. And the media had described the property repeatedly as derelict. In other words, a kip. I told myself that I was being silly. Kept on saying it.

Until, from nowhere, a poisonous worm burrowed deep and fast inside my brain. Saying maybe I didn't have three men to watch at the funeral in the morning.

Maybe I had four.

54

WE TALKED LONG INTO THE NIGHT, OR DAVY DID,
about his cocaine habit and the things he'd done to pay for it.
Some of the stories I'd known previously, some were new to
me. As I listened, instead of being drawn closer to him, I felt
the distance between us grow, as if I was in a boat drifting with
the current, miles from shore. Not because of his addiction – he
was entitled to his past, and I knew how dark that time had been
for him, how hard he'd worked to overcome it – but because his
storytelling had a practised air. That could have been because
he'd told other people many times before, during treatment and
at NA meetings. I didn't have a monopoly on him. I got that.
But there was more to it than that. For all his apparent frankness,
his honesty rang false. Rightly or wrongly, I thought he was
hamming it up. Overdoing it, like a bad actor would.

•

As I faded into wakeful sleep it struck me that he was testing me
and my reactions, though I couldn't understand why. And that,
in baring his soul, he seemed to find no relief. I was left with the
strongest sense that he was concealing something.

Something big.

SATURDAY

55

DAVY GOT UP EARLY AND WENT INTO TOWN TO
buy fresh fruit and bread. When he came back, he made poached
eggs and we sat at the table together, the doors to the balcony
open to the morning. We ate and drank cup after cup of coffee,
talking a little every now and again about not very much – not
mentioning Mandy, not discussing who might have killed her. I
caught him watching me a few times when he thought I wasn't
looking and I didn't know what to make of that, or of how bad
I felt about what was happening with us. 'Manipulated' was the
word that kept going round and round in my head.

About the same speed as the butterflies in my belly.

•

After breakfast, I put on a mid-length black dress with long
sleeves and a high neck, and black tights and block-heeled black
shoes: high enough to look like I'd made an effort; low enough
to be comfortable on a day when there was bound to be a lot of
standing. Then I applied a gash of Mac Russian Red lipstick, and
rolled a black cardigan and a small black umbrella into my plain
black leather bucket bag.

The day was grey and muggy and unseasonably warm. The forecast was for heavy rain, the tail end of a hurricane blown across the Atlantic from the Caribbean, but it hadn't hit yet.

Davy drove the short distance between my place and his, with me in the passenger seat of his black BMW 5 Series.

'I won't be long,' he said.

'Take your time,' I said, staring straight ahead through the windscreen.

•

I watched him walk quickly along the path, his head darting nervously left and right. I had the impression that he was expecting to see something or someone, but the street was empty. He lived in a terraced artisan cottage near Shalom Park, a now sought-after location on the edge of Blackrock in the jumble of tiny streets still known as Jewtown, though the synagogue had closed. The explanations given for how four hundred Lithuanian families fleeing Tsarist pogroms had ended up here, in Cork city, varied. My favourite was that they'd misheard the destination and disembarked, expecting New York. Now, most of Cork's Jewish population had either intermarried with the local population or were long gone, in search of more sustainable Jewish communities. But some of Cork's Jews had stayed, and had played an important role in the life of the city. One of them was the eminent solicitor Gerald Goldberg, who had become lord mayor in 1977.

Davy glanced back in my direction before he went into the house. His face impassive, he seemed not to see me. I pressed the button to let down the passenger window. Nothing happened:

he had the car key. Opening the door slightly, I angled my mouth towards the gap and took in a couple of gulps of air. Just then, a small flatbed coal delivery truck laboured by, spewing fumes. My throat burned. I tugged at the neck of my dress and felt sweat pool under my arms. I opened the door wider, breathing in through my nose and out through my mouth, long and slow, counting like I'd learned. I told myself that nothing had changed.

56

WITH HALF AN HOUR TO GO BEFORE THE START
of mass, there was already a queue of mourners. We joined
them and shuffled slowly forward. In the porch was a printed
notice prohibiting begging on church grounds. Another advised
anyone in financial difficulties to make an application to the Sick
Poor Society. A third sought donations for the local branch of
the St Joseph's Young Priests Society. I hadn't known there were
any young priests left.

Once inside, we sat in silence near the back on the left. The
original St Michael's on the Blackrock Road had been consumed
by fire in 1962. The replacement had kept a traditional cruciform
plan, but it was light, bright, incongruously optimistic and
golden.

At 11.45 a.m., the bell started to toll – the signal that the hearse
had arrived. A few minutes later, the doors at the rear of the
church opened and the congregation stood. An altar boy swinging
a silver thurible filled with smoking incense went ahead of the
priest to the altar. Two of the undertakers followed, wheeling the
coffin soundlessly on a steel trolley, which surprised me – it would
normally be carried by male family members and close friends. I
wondered if the absence of the usual gesture signified conflict in
the family, or if none of them had felt able to do it.

Ed followed the coffin, head bowed, between his two girls. After a noticeable gap came Mandy's mother, elegant, ramrod straight. Her face bore an expression of pure white rage. She was flanked by Mandy's brother, Jonathan — business-like, determined-looking — and sister, Debbie, a rounder, softer version of Mandy, her cheeks red and swollen from crying. In-laws, nephews and nieces came next. They took their seats in the places reserved for them: Ed and the girls in the front, the Breslins in the pews behind. Then a hush descended and all movement ceased, as the priest began speaking into the microphone in a voice barely above a whisper.

'May the Father of mercies, the God of all consolation, be with you all.'

•

The requiem mass that followed was sombre and unhurried. There was no music, no eulogy. After the homily — from which it was abundantly clear that the parish priest had never met Mandy during her lifetime — Kathleen and Hugo Woulfe and a few of Mandy's friends, one of whom was Davy's sister Orla, filed up to the pulpit to say the bidding prayers. Woulfe's voice wavered as he said, 'Lord hear us'. Other than that he was stoic. Kathleen read with dignity, but her voice was heavy with emotion. She held herself together, just about.

The final person to speak was Orla. Super-groomed as always, freshly spray-tanned, her hair cut in an impossibly smooth jaw-length blonde bob, she looked nothing like her brother, but she moved like him and they had the same eyes.

'We pray for the Garda Síochána, that their work may bring

Mandy's murderer to justice as soon as possible. We pray that every person here with any information, no matter how seemingly insignificant, will cooperate with the investigation in full.'

She paused and, unmistakably, stared down at Ed. Beside me, I felt Davy flinch. Then she said, 'Lord hear us.'

The congregation had been left in no doubt as to who Orla blamed for Mandy's death, but it seemed that Kathleen didn't concur. She put a hand on Ed's shoulder as she returned to her place. A couple of benches had been set aside near the front for Mandy's immediate co-workers. The rest of the MLC staff were scattered around the church. I spotted Gabriel sitting with Georgina. He looked better than he had the day before: the tests must have gone well. Dermot Lyons and his long-suffering spouse – I can never remember her name – sat nearby. Tina was with a few of the other secretaries and Pauline Doyle around the middle of the church.

It looked like it was a no-show by Ricky Dempsey, but it was impossible to be sure, with every seat occupied and people – including Sadie and her work partner, Olly Fogarty – standing at the back, and in the churchyard. The doors had been propped open and a loudspeaker set up to relay the ceremony to the large crowd standing outside.

I clasped my hands together as if in prayer. All the while, I felt Davy next to me, his body tense and unyielding, his palms flat and hard on his thighs, fingers spread. I couldn't look at his face.

I didn't know who I'd find if I did.

57

A DRENCHING RAIN STARTED AS THE CORTÈGE snaked its way to St Michael's municipal cemetery – a bleak, flat place. Once we got there, Davy refused to share my umbrella.

'I'm too tall,' he said. 'It won't work.'

When Tina came, I beckoned her over. We huddled together for shelter and Davy stood some way off from us, alone and still, seemingly oblivious to the conditions. I realised that he was wearing the same navy suit he'd worn to court a couple of times. He'd always looked handsome in it, even when he was in bits. Good-looking people – provided they appear appropriately regretful and humble – often do well in front of a judge. Davy had. He'd been put off the road for drunken driving – the mandatory sanction, there was no way out of that – but by some miracle he'd been given the benefit of the Probation Act not once, but twice for Section 3 of the Misuse of Drugs Act. Cocaine. Simple possession. That's what he'd told me then. Now he was admitting to Section 15 – dealing. All in the past, he said.

Tina had met Davy when he was my client. She knew that we were together now and, though she'd never said anything to me about it directly, she'd hinted that the relationship had been the subject of office gossip for a while. I had a sense that she was less disapproving of Davy than Sadie was, but I'd never asked her; I'd shut down the topic whenever she raised it. I told myself that I was protecting our professional relationship, but it was a lot more to do with the way I was generally.

•

The large crowd stood in irregular concentric circles around the open grave, and the murmur of the Rosary prayers rose and fell with impressive, albeit temporary, piety. Most Irish people practised their religion on special occasions only – first communions and funerals mainly, now that many weddings were secular, after a change in the law had permitted marriages in locations other than a church or civil registration office.

I was too far away to see the coffin descend into the earth but I heard the sobs of Mandy's girls, and of her siblings and mother, as it did. Afterwards, as the crowd thinned, I looked out for Ricky Dempsey again, but if he'd ever been present, he was gone.

58

WHILE TINA MADE A RUN FOR IT TO HER CAR, I
made my way over to Davy. I looked up at him, his eyes
bloodshot, his hair dripping with rain, and held my umbrella
over his head.

'Hey,' I said.

'Hey.'

'You'll catch your death.'

He micro-smiled. 'I'll be alright,' he said. 'I should change,
though.'

'We can swing by your place before we go to the hotel.'

'You go with Tina,' he said. 'I don't feel ...' His voice cracked.

'I'll come home with you,' I said. 'I don't have to go.'

'You do,' he said. '*You* do.'

•

I watched him walk, head bent, shoulders slouched, to his car.
Was it grief I was witnessing, or was it regret?

59

CROSSING THE CAR PARK, I NOTICED GABRIEL DEEP in conversation with a taller man – dark hair, white shirt, tieless – in a grey suit. He glanced at me as I was passing, looked at me again more closely, and turned away quickly. I stopped. Gabriel saw me and pursed his lips.

'How are you?' I asked.

'Like everyone else,' Gabriel said. 'Getting through it.'

'It's a sad day,' I said, and waited. When no introduction came, I stuck out my right hand. 'Finn Fitzpatrick. Work colleague of Mandy's.'

'Yes,' the man said. He kept his hands in his pockets.

I bunched my outstretched hand into a loose fist and let it drop uselessly to my side. 'Have we met before?' I asked.

'No,' he said.

'I'll see you at the hotel, Finola,' Gabriel said.

•

In Tina's car – a baby-pink Fiat 500 – I asked, 'Any idea who the man in grey is?'

'He's vaguely familiar, but no.'

'Whoever he is,' I said, 'he's obnoxious.'

I told her what had happened and, before we left, snapped a blurry photo of him through the car window. Tina got the point immediately.

'You think he might be the man you saw shifting Mandy?'

'Could be.'

'If it's the same man, he's a suspect,' she said. 'You said she looked scared.'

'We need to find out who he is,' I said. 'Fast. But the answer might not come easily. Gabriel went out of his way not to introduce him to me.'

'Leave it to me,' Tina said. 'I'll ask around, see if I can find out.'

'If he's the lover, he has to be the murderer. Unless Ed did it.'

'That's a bit of a leap, isn't it?' she said. 'It might be neither. What about the McInerneys? How weird is that – coming into the office, causing a rumpus and then taking off again? It might be them.'

'It might. I still find it hard to believe that anyone murdered her. But someone did.'

•

What I didn't say was that all day and all night, I'd been replaying in my head the scenes after the Dolly Parton gig, and the following day in my office. All day and all night I'd been thinking, and trying not to think, about the look of terror I'd seen on Mandy's face.

Wondering, what if? What if it wasn't her lover Mandy was afraid of?

What if it was Davy?

60

THE MARYBOROUGH WAS A CONVERTED
Georgian mansion near the southern edge of the city. Secreted
down a steep avenue, it was surrounded by verdant gardens
and mature trees that almost but not quite masked the constant
burr of the traffic. As we arrived, a car pulled out and Tina
nipped into the space, a prime spot directly opposite the front
door. In the entrance hall, a coal fire burned convincingly – it
was fake, though it had taken me a while to twig that on a
previous visit. For a second, all I wanted was to sit in one of
the armchairs, stare into the gas flames and think.

But there was too much to do. This would provide me with
an unparalleled opportunity to observe the most important
people in Mandy's life in the one place at the one time.

Lunch was to be served in one of the extensions, a function
room used for weddings and other formal events. I'd been here
numerous times with the firm at the Southern Law Association
Dinner, an annual gathering that Mandy never missed.
Clients attended as invited guests, as did barristers and other
professionals, but the majority of the attendees were solicitors.
Mandy had told me once how important it was to make the
effort to put on the posh frock and go and mingle, but to

always stay focused on why you were there. With the kind of specialist projects that she did, her referrals often came from other solicitors. She talked about acquiring new work and fees as if it was a sacred duty. On the surface, none of it fit with what I knew about her now – the infidelity, the drugs – but I was starting to think that it might be of a piece with it; that it had to do with a desire to taste of everything that life had to offer.

I shivered. Was that why she'd died? Had someone decided to punish her for the sin of wanting too much?

61

I ENDED UP AT A LONG TABLE AT THE FAR END OF
the room with Tina and a few others from the office, along with
a random collection of Mandy's friends and relatives, clients
and business associates. For some reason – in fairness to them,
given the circumstances, it could have been privacy – the hotel
management had closed the curtains. As a result, the room was
airless and hot. I pushed my food around – a traditional silver-
service roast beef and two veg, with gravy and mash and roast
potatoes, followed by sherry trifle – and after a respectable
amount of time, got up and said I was going to the loo. I went
the long way.

While the man in grey had not come, the function room was
full, more than two hundred in attendance. People did this, gave
of their time, came and sat and talked. Funerals tend to have a
tone, an ambience. For Mandy's, it was shock mixed with a kind
of embarrassment. People like her didn't end up hacked to death
in a derelict house. And yet that's what had happened. Everyone
knew it. Like they knew – but didn't say – that the murderer
might be here among us.

Ed sat, dazed-looking, chugging a large glass of red wine.
He was with a group of men who looked like they might be

sailing buddies, Dermot Lyons among them. They were all talking loudly and telling old war stories, doing their best to distract him from noticing that half the crowd was staring in his direction.

Mandy's family sat quietly and angrily at a separate table. I spotted Ruth, Ed's younger daughter, her face blotchy and vacant, sandwiched between her grandmother and her aunt Debbie. Ruth's older sister, Ava sat palely at a table with some of her schoolfriends, her plate untouched, her expression haunted.

Gabriel was at a round table occupied by several other partners from the firm including, seated beside Gabriel, Patricia Dillane, head of the firm's Property Department. With Mandy gone, by rights she was the candidate most suited to taking over from Gabriel as the firm's Managing Partner, if she wanted the role.

But the nature of her work was a disadvantage. In most law firms, conveyancing is an unloved star that rises and falls with miserable regularity. Though a cash cow during the boom years of the Celtic Tiger, after the banking crash, no lending institution would approve a mortgage. Apart from foreign so-called 'vulture' funds, no one had bought or sold so much as a garden shed for about five years. I liked Patricia. Unlike many lawyers – who tend to complain bitterly about lawyering – Patricia loved her job. On a good day, I could understand how she felt. There was a romance to conveyancing, if you chose to see it. You were helping people to buy their first home. Or their last. The sudden beauty of an old map hidden in a dusty set of title deeds could bring the past to life on a dull Tuesday afternoon. The plans for a new estate could let you see into the future, the houses that would be built and the families who would live in them. And conveyancing files had a satisfying beginning, middle and end to them, even if the work itself was often a box-ticking and tax-collecting grind.

Seeing the various partners together reminded me again of the Southern Law Association Dinner and the non-legal guests who also attended. Estate agents came sometimes. If Ricky Dempsey had been one of them, that might have been how he met Mandy. I could ask Patricia Dillane, but if I did I'd have to explain why I was still investigating Mandy's working life – and her death – and I didn't want to do that. It would be better to ask one of the organising committee if they knew of anything.

I was on my second tour of the room, unsure what to do next, when I noticed Orla Keenan slip out quietly through one of the double doors that led to the corridor.

I followed her.

62

THOUGH DAVY WAS A FREQUENT VISITOR TO MY
parents' home, I didn't have a reciprocal deal with his family.
His relationship with his mother and father was strained. He
put it down to the bridges burned and the bonds broken during
the years of his addiction, but there was more to it. I wasn't
altogether sure that the absence of dinner invitations was all
about him. I had a feeling that his family didn't like me, though
he always denied it.

I'd met Orla several times. She had a good job, something
in IT, and was married with two children: a girl called Alice
and a boy called Shane, who was Davy's godson and whose
confirmation was next year. Davy was looking forward to it,
well up for going along and standing behind his nephew as he
renounced Satan and all his works and pomps. As of Wednesday,
I'd discovered that Orla had been Mandy's best pal at school. That
they'd remained such close friends all down the years I hadn't
known until the funeral mass. Davy hadn't been forthcoming
with the details. When I'd asked, he'd said he 'couldn't say'. It
was one more thing that didn't matter much. Or that mattered a
lot, depending on how you looked at it.

Orla was standing by the coat racks. She took her phone out

of her bag and scrolled through it to locate a contact. When she saw me, she stopped and surveyed me coolly.

'All on your ownio. Himself not with you?'

'He was soaking. Went home to change. I don't think he's coming.'

I had the feeling I was telling her something she knew already. I took in a breath. Let it go again. 'Orla, can I ask you about what you said in the church? The prayer?'

'Someone had to say something.'

'You think Ed killed Mandy?'

'I know it.'

'How …?'

'Oh, I don't have any proof. Unfortunately. But he's responsible, even if he didn't do it himself.'

'Have you spoken to the guards yet?'

'I've an appointment for Monday with a Detective Fogarty. He was at the funeral. Came up to me after the mass. He told me that up to now they've only been interviewing people who saw Mandy in the few days before she died, so that's why they hadn't contacted me yet.'

'When was the last time you did see her?'

'The awful thing is that we hadn't seen each other for a few weeks.'

'Davy said you and she were best friends at school.'

'Oh we were,' Orla said. 'And Mandy was stone-mad about Davy.'

'He said the last time he saw her was at your house, on your birthday.'

'He told you *that* night was the last time he saw her?' She seemed surprised.

'Do you think he saw her more recently than that?'

'In all fairness, Finn, how am I supposed to know when Davy last saw Mandy?' Which didn't really answer my question.

'Right. You were saying you hadn't seen her yourself for a while.'

'We were both up the walls with work. But we were in constant touch on WhatsApp. I knew things were bad between her and Ed. The marriage was kaput. Ed wasn't a bit pleased at the prospect of losing his meal ticket.'

'The cops will probably be asking if there was someone else, if she—'

'Let them ask. Mandy having an affair wasn't the reason for the break-up.'

'What was?'

'Ed. Classic street angel and house devil. Moody bastard. And his drinking was off the charts. He gave her an awful life.' What she was describing sounded like a lot of marriages. In the absence of evidence incriminating Ed that she clearly didn't possess, it didn't add up to a reason for him to be charged with murder.

'Does he know you don't like him?'

'He knows now anyway,' she said. 'But, yeah, he's known for years.'

'How come he asked you to do a bidding prayer, so?'

'He didn't. Mandy's sister, Deb was supposed to do it. I was her super sub. Though I altered the script slightly.' She laughed. 'Mandy would've loved to have seen his face when I …' Then her eyes filled with tears. 'I can't believe she's gone.'

I handed her a tissue. 'Thanks,' she said.

'Look, Orla, I know for a fact that Mandy had a lover. I saw them together. In a car, one time, though I couldn't see his face.'

'I'm not saying I agree with you. Because I don't. And so what, even if she did?'

'Do you know his name?'

'His name – if I knew it, which I don't – isn't relevant because he didn't kill her.'

'You're wrong, his name *is* relevant, even for the purposes of eliminating him from the guards' enquiries and focusing on the real killer.'

'Huh. That's another way of looking at it, I suppose.' Then she said, 'How are things with you and my brother, by the way?'

'They've been better,' I said. 'We'll work it out, I'm sure.'

'I never thought you were right for him, but it's none of my business, is it?'

We were the same height but I felt like I'd shrunk.

Her phone rang. She turned away. Not before I saw the name of the caller.

Davy.

63

THE WOMEN'S BATHROOM WAS EMPTY. I PEED
and flushed but then put down the cover and sat on it, trying
to stop trembling. When I heard the door opening, and what
sounded like two sets of footsteps, I pulled my knees up to my
chest and my feet onto the lid so that the locked cubicle would
look free to anyone checking. A young voice said, 'Anyone
here?', but I made no reply. I needed time to recover and I didn't
want to engage in conversation.

A sharp rap and a push on the door jolted me and the same
voice said, 'Hello? Is this taken?', and then, to someone else:
'Locked but vacant. Might be broken.' I was regretting my
decision to hide now but it was too late. I had to wait them out.

'You okay?' the same voice said more softly, and at first I
thought she was talking to me until she said, 'You don't look
okay.'

'I am … I'm okay.' It was Mandy's sixteen-year-old
daughter, Ava.

'It's not your fault,' the first voice said. Silence from Ava.

'It's really not,' the first voice said again.

Then Ava said, 'Sunday. If we hadn't … she might still be—'

'That's not true,' the first voice said. 'You know it's not

true. You can't beat yourself up about this. Ruth wasn't home either.'

'She was on a sleepover, for God's sake. She wasn't …' More silence until Ava said, 'Come on, we'd better get back.'

They slammed the door and I let my feet slide to the floor.

64

INTENDING TO CLEAR MY HEAD, I DECIDED TO walk from Maryborough Hill to Barrack Street. I'd never done the journey on foot before. Less than halfway home, caught in the suburban confusion of the Douglas Road, the Cross Douglas Road, the Back Douglas Road, the endlessly repeating twentieth-century suburban dwellings, and leafy park after almost indistinguishable leafy park of good addresses – and some better ones where the hedges were higher and the gravel crunchier – I realised I was wearing the wrong shoes.

I could've called a taxi but I kept on walking, even though I knew I was getting a blister. I kept on walking, even when I heard the phone ringing in my handbag, guessing it was Tina, wondering where I'd disappeared to. I kept on walking, even when the rain started to pelt down again.

I'm like that, you see. I stick at things, no matter what.

Even when I know they're bad for me.

SUNDAY

65

I DID MY BEST WITH THE BACON AND CABBAGE,
even managed a small boiled potato. It wasn't enough. In my
heart, I'd known it wouldn't be. My mother had guessed there
was something wrong the moment I'd walked in the door. Too
early, because I'd driven across town to their home on Gardiner's
Hill rather than walked. Grey in the face, because I hadn't slept.
She'd exchanged a look with my father and he'd shaken his head
almost imperceptibly, but neither of them had said anything. I
set the table and talked about the funeral, how sad it had been.
After that, responding to a signal from Mam, Dad said that he
wanted to show me some new work he'd done in the garden.
Since he'd retired from his job as an electrician with the ESB, it
was where he spent most of his time.

•

A soft mist cooled my face as I followed him down the back.

'I've taken out the Griselinia,' he said. 'Good ould shelter but
it's too vigorous and it's a full-time job, keeping it trimmed. I'm
not as young as I was.'

'You're only a boy,' I said. 'You're not a wrinklie like Mam.'

'Shh, she'll hear you,' he said and laughed. They were both over seventy and fit and well, but my mother was four months the elder and didn't like to be reminded of it.

'It's a good idea to get rid of it, though. You could put in a native flowering and fruiting hedge in the same place. You wouldn't have to cut it for ages but it would grow fast, and you'd have lovely blossom and a great home for wildlife.'

'It's what I had in mind,' he said. 'But I'll have to wait till November for the bare root stock. I've it ordered though. I was on to Future Forests during the week.' He touched my arm. 'Everything's alright, is it, Finn?'

'Everything's grand, Dad. Just tough going, with the murder and all.'

He nodded. 'Your bedroom is always there for you.'

'I know it is,' I said.

He went ahead of me into the house and I heard him tell my mother that I was fine. That reassurance had been enough to steer her, doubtfully, through the main course. But my request for a small slice of apple tart and no whipped cream gave me away irretrievably. Mam got up from her chair and came to my side of the table and put her arms around me, holding my head to her breast. 'I *knew* there was something wrong,' she said.

'It's just work. And the funeral yesterday was really hard. That's all. I swear.'

•

In the end she accepted delayed shock in the aftermath of Mandy's death as an explanation. It was almost true. I told them nothing of my problems with Davy, whom they both liked. My mam stressed enough about me already, Dad too. Always watching for signs that I might fall off the path of love and stability they'd put me on and turn into my birth mother. They'd be there to catch me if I fell, I know. But I don't want to fall. I do everything I can to avoid it.

It's just that sometimes I'm afraid I might.

66

I SWUNG PAST SADIE'S HOUSE ON THE WAY HOME.
She and Jack live in a renovated 1970s bungalow on a half-acre
plot on the hill running down into Glanmire; Jack's handcrafted
furniture-making workshop is in what used to be an ugly concrete
outbuilding that they've managed to disguise by planting lots of
ivy and jasmine and honeysuckle.

There was no one in. No matter. I'd call her later.

•

I didn't then text Davy and I didn't drive by his place. I thought
about it. And I didn't. I knew that I needed to ask again about his
relationship with Mandy – particularly about the last time he'd
met her. I'd run through my conversations with him on Friday
night, and with Orla after the funeral, a hundred times in my
head. Every time I did, I came to the same conclusion – that they
were both lying. Orla was lying about not knowing about the
affair with the dark-haired man, and who he was, and there was
something in what she'd said about Davy and Mandy that didn't
quite ring true. She'd said that Mandy was 'stone-mad' about
him. I'd believed her when she'd said that. But I'd felt something
else too. From both of them. A false note. I was going to have

to question them more vigorously, though I didn't feel strong enough right now.

•

My phone rang when I was parking up on Fort Street. No caller ID. I shoved it under my jaw as I snapped in the wing mirror with one hand and, with the other, reached across to the passenger seat to haul out the Tupperware boxes with the selection of leftovers Mam had pressed on me before I'd left.

'Who's this?' I asked.

'Where are you?'

I knew the voice. 'Why?'

'Because I'm standing outside your gate.'

'How did you get my address?'

A sigh.

'Stupid question,' I said. 'I'm two minutes' away.'

'Make it one. I fucken hate Cork and I want to get out of here as quick as I can.'

With the possible exception of Dermot Lyons with a hangover, Detective Inspector Pat Lenihan was the rudest man in Ireland. I'd met him during the Jeremy Flynn case. Dublin-based, he was an ex-Kilkenny hurler who'd been forced to retire early after one too many cruciate ligament injuries; he'd poured all his frustration and aggression into his career in the gardaí and had made DI at a ridiculously young age. I'd heard from Sadie that he'd transferred a few months ago to the National Bureau of Criminal Investigation.

All of which meant that him showing up at my door late on a Sunday afternoon could only be about one thing. Or, rather, two.

The McInerneys.

67

LENIHAN WAS BY THE MICROWAVE IN MY KITCHEN,
bent at the waist, peering in. He'd taken off his suit jacket and
loosened his tie. Late-thirties, he had tightly cropped red hair,
freckles, pale skin and a permanent sulky frown. As he breathed,
his shirt strained across the toned muscles of his back. He was fit,
no doubt about it. Still no wedding ring, though. No surprise.
No woman could put up with him.

'What d'you reckon? Two more minutes? One?'

'You realise you've appropriated my Monday *and* my Tuesday
night dinners?'

'I'd say it's done,' he said.

I handed him a knife and fork. He moved to the island and ate
standing up.

When he'd finished he said, 'She's good, your Mammy. Make
sure and thank her for me.'

I would. Whatever about feeding me, having her cooking
praised by an important man like Lenihan would please Mam no
end. Not that I had any intention of telling him that.

'Apart from taking the food out of my mouth, what do you
want?'

'To say that I put up with your interference with an operation
the last time, but—'

'An operation where, as I recall, I saved your—'

'Well, this is different.'

I raised my eyebrows.

'I'm deadly serious,' he said. He looked it. He pulled out a chair from the table and sat.

'I've spent all day at Coughlan's Quay with your pal Sadie and her colleagues. Reviewing the current murder investigation. I went up to the house at Alysson Villas as well. I suppose I should sympathise with you – I believe you worked with the victim.'

I nodded. He didn't sound sympathetic.

'And the two Welsh lads. Tell me what happened at your office on Monday.'

I told him.

'Then you went to Cardiff and found out that McInerney senior grew up in the house where Mandy Breslin died. A fact you failed to mention to your best friend, Detective O'Riordan, who was very surprised to hear you'd been holding out on her.'

'I wasn't "holding out" on her. When I was on the phone to her on Friday, I just forgot. I *was* planning to tell her. I called to see her today but she wasn't home.'

'Maybe you were, maybe you weren't – I couldn't give a shite either way, only for the fact – which I'm telling you in strictest confidence – that the McInerneys might have a different kind of connection. To an ongoing garda surveillance operation in the Clondalkin area.'

'Clondalkin? That's where their phones went off-radar.'

'That's right. Adjacent to the Green Isle Hotel.'

'Is that where your operation is? The hotel?'

'No.'

'You mentioned surveillance. Did you see them?'

'Well, I wasn't there personally but no, none of the members who were in the area saw anyone corresponding to the description of the two missing men. Nothing on CCTV either.'

'Might the McInerneys have spotted the garda presence, and legged it?'

'It's possible. If that's what happened, the question is why?'

'Could it be a coincidence, then, them disappearing just there?'

'It could,' Lenihan said. 'But we can't rule out that they *were* connected in some way; that the Clondalkin aspect was the real reason they came to Ireland and the Cork element of it was just cover. That said, neither of them is known to the Welsh police, so—'

'A criminal connection seems unlikely.'

'It does. But we can't say for sure. The more likely possibility, I think, is that they saw something they shouldn't have. Something related to the subject of our operation.'

'What kind of operation?'

'I'm not at liberty to reveal the nature of the operation.'

'It must be organised crime,' I said. Lenihan said nothing. 'If you're not going to tell me anything, then why are you here?'

He stood up. 'I'm here to tell you to back the fuck off. The last thing I want is you and your, uh, boyfriend checking in for a mini-break to the Green Isle, and you sticking your big nose in.'

Why mention Davy? What did Lenihan know?

I took a deep breath in and said, 'You're the one who mentioned the proximity to the hotel. That wasn't in the news reports and Charlene didn't say either. Why say it?'

'You went to Cardiff, didn't you? The family knew the details.

I couldn't take the chance that you didn't too. Plus, don't forget, I'm familiar with your methods from previously.'

I let that sink in. Then I said, 'Let's say for a minute that I don't back off like you want.'

'If you don't, you could wreck an operation that has taken months of work and thousands of hours to put together. Apart from that, you could destroy whatever small chance we have of finding those poor fuckers alive. Charlene McInerney and Ray Reid understood that. And their daughter. That's why they agreed to put their television appeal on the backburner. It was from talking to them that I found out about the connection to the Mandy Breslin murder locus. And about you.'

'I figured.'

'And I figured you'd be tied up with the funeral yesterday. That's why I left it till today to come down. I've better things to be doing with my Sundays, mind you.'

'Do you think they're dead, the McInerneys?'

'Dead at worst. Hiding out at best. If they *are* in hiding, anything – I mean absolutely anything – that you do could put their lives in danger. And your own. These are not nice people we're dealing with, that's all I'll say. Do you get me?'

'Yeah, I get you.'

'Are you actually listening, though?'

'I'm not a fool. I wouldn't do a thing to interfere with something like that. Especially where there's still a hope the McInerneys might come out of this alive. So, yes, Lenihan, I'm listening. I promise I won't be going anywhere near Dublin this time.' By which I meant I'd be continuing with my investigation in Cork. Uninterrupted.

'Glad to hear it,' he said. 'Now, is there any dessert? I could

do with a wedge of apple tart and a cup of strong tea before I
head away.'

•

I rang Sadie immediately after Lenihan had left. I didn't know
what to make of his visit and the glancing reference to Davy
– though he hadn't mentioned his name so it might have been
inadvertent. On the other hand, it might have been deliberate.
Apart from that, I had some repair work to do with Sadie. He'd
said she'd been 'very surprised' that I hadn't told her about the
McInerney connection to Alysson Villas.

Which turned out to be something of an understatement.

'Fuck's sake, Finn, this arrangement we have is supposed to be
a two-way street.'

'I'd intended to say it to you about the house but … I'm really
sorry.'

'Yeah? Well, do something to make up for it. It's been nearly
all one-way traffic so far.'

'Did you tell Lenihan about me going out with Davy?'

'Why would I?'

*Because Lenihan mentioned Davy. And because your partner
Detective Fogarty is going to be interviewing Davy's sister Orla on
Monday.*

'No reason,' I said.

'I was kind of surprised to see Davy at the funeral, actually.'

*An edge to her voice. But then there always is when she mentions
Davy.*

'He knew Mandy vaguely,' I said. 'Years ago.'

'Is that so?'

'Friend of his sister's.'

'Oh, I see,' Sadie said.

As if she didn't know. Though maybe she didn't. Yet.

I paused. 'Why was Lenihan really here? In Cork, I mean? Couldn't he have reviewed the murder case from Dublin? Or sent someone else?'

'It's what he's like. In that big macho head of his, no one can get a handle on a case like he can. He would have wanted to get the feel of it himself. He wouldn't have been happy doing that remotely.'

'What was his verdict? What did he say? Do you think the McInerneys are part of his case? Which I'm assuming is some kind of gangland thing? Drugs maybe?'

'You know I can't confirm anything. But you know as well as I do where Lenihan works now, so I'm not going to bother denying that it's drug-related. I don't know if the McInerneys are part of it. Or if Lenihan thinks they are. For what it's worth, my guess is not, but he's keeping his options open on a possible connection. The thing is, I've been designated as his liaison. Whatever I find on the murder, I'm supposed to feed him, pronto. Which isn't going to happen obviously because I'm not going to him with every drib and drab, and having him interfering and annoying me. I'm only bringing him hard evidence. Preferably a solve.'

'Okay,' I said.

It was all I could say, now that my brain had gone straight into overdrive. I was thinking 'drug-related'. I was thinking about Davy.

Sadie was still talking: '... Which is where you come in. My investigation is dying on its feet. These people are worse than

234

the mafia. None of them is saying anything of any use. So you
need to get me something on Mandy's lover, and it had better be
good. A name. An address. Fast.'

'Sure,' I said.

'Otherwise I'm turning off the information tap,' Sadie said.
'Do you understand?'

'Course I do.'

I ended the call.

MONDAY

MONDAY

68

6 A.M. CROSS-LEGGED ON MY YOGA MAT. NEW day. New week. #MondayMotivation. Trying not to think about the weekend from hell just gone; and the bags under my eyes; and the grinding in my gut; and the shrill, looping, circling voices that only I can hear.

The ones that say I'm sleeping with a murderer. Correction: *suspected* murderer. Correction: *used to be* sleeping with a suspected murderer.

'Cause Davy wasn't here on Saturday night. Or last night. No word from him, apart from his now-standard early morning – too-early-for-a-reply – message:

Hey, sorry I haven't been in touch. Busy busy this week but let's catch up asap x

•

I'd composed about a hundred we-need-to-talk type responses and deleted every one. Now, I considered my options. The first – officially report what I knew of his past, selling drugs to

Mandy, and let the guards deal with it – I dismissed immediately. I couldn't and wouldn't drag him into the murder investigation when I had zero evidence against him, except my own suspicious mind.

A mind which overnight had ditched all the other suspects – Hugo Woulfe, Ed, the dark-haired man in the TT, whoever he proved to be – and transformed Davy into the missing link between Mandy's murder, the McInerneys and a massive garda surveillance operation in Clondalkin.

Based on diddly-squat. Apart from an, admittedly, strange pattern of behaviour on his part and his sister Orla's – was she a little too desperate to fix the blame on Ed?

I felt hollowed out by all of it. And I couldn't tell Sadie. She'd never liked him. Even worse, she was now Lenihan's liaison in Cork. Anything I said to her about Davy, she'd gladly pass on. Even if Davy was entirely innocent – as most of me still thought he was – any report Sadie might make to Lenihan would push him deep into the kind of life-changing mud that sticks.

More than anything, I wanted my traitorous, paranoid suspicions to be wrong. But wanting wasn't enough. I had to prove it.

69

IN OTHER CITIES, BLACKPOOL WOULD HAVE BEEN
cherished – a historic village in its own right with the scenic river
Bride running through it, only minutes from the city centre.
Instead, years of neglect had been followed by a succession of
bad planning decisions – the latest idea was to bury the river in
concrete, in a crude attempt to solve a flooding problem with
its root cause upstream – that had bulldozed the heart out of
it. Nearly. What was left wasn't enough to make up for the
dereliction and the squandered potential but, with a fair wind
and the right kind of incentives – such as the big money the city
council had invested in renovating the waterfront near Mandy's
home in leafy Blackrock on the southside – it might yet turn into
something more substantial. So far, in this tale of two suburbs, it
was no surprise to anyone that working-class Blackpool, on the
northside, had pulled the short straw.

But the regulars in the Coffee Pot weren't thinking about any
of that just then, and neither was I, much. I was drinking black
tea and paging blindly through the *Echo*, waiting for Ricky
Dempsey to arrive and take me to view a house near Patrick's
Hill ('an ideal investment opportunity', his website called it).
I'd opted for that rather than one of the ones he'd dubbed 'a

builder's project'. I didn't think I'd make a convincing builder. I'd suggested meeting in the cafe rather than at his office or the property, hoping that I might persuade him to sit and talk for a few minutes, allowing me to cultivate a casual relationship with him from the start, thereby making it easier for me to introduce the topic of Mandy later, so as to gauge his reaction. I had a whole scene of dialogue rehearsed in my head, and I was confident that I could handle him.

My phone pinged. A message from Ricky Dempsey: *Outside*. I peered through the window and saw him waving at me from his car; he'd stopped temporarily in the middle of the road, and was grinning and pointing at the traffic behind him. So much for the cosy chat I'd envisaged. I gathered up my coat and bag, and hurried onto the street, sitting quickly into the silver grey Toyota Avensis. He took off like a jet before I could shut the door properly.

About forty, Dempsey was a powerfully built man with broad shoulders and biceps that stretched the sleeves of his blue shirt skintight. He'd made a good start on what gave every indication of turning into an impressive beer belly. The broken veins on his nose told me that he had a fondness for whiskey too. He looked like what he was – a jock gone to seed. In fifteen years, if he wasn't careful, Hugo Woulfe would look exactly like him.

'I'm on my way back from an appointment,' he said. 'It was easier to collect you on the go rather than trying to find parking.'

'No problem,' I said. 'I … the traffic is dire, isn't it?'

But my tongue was in knots. This wasn't playing out as I'd planned.

70

AT SHANDON VIEW, THERE WAS A TIGHT TERRACE
of two-storey homes perched a few metres from the edge of a
cliff. Ricky Dempsey edged his car expertly backwards into one
of the driveways and switched off the engine.

'Often the name can deceive, but is that a view of Shandon
or what?' he said, pointing both his index fingers, like twin gun
barrels, at the iconic tower that rose up out of the slope opposite.
Two of its sides were faced in white limestone, the other two
in red sandstone: the colours of the city of Cork. Blackpool
rested below us, softened by rain. Sometimes, the landscape in
this town can take your breath away, the half-hidden drama that
slams up against the ordinary.

Inside the house, it was fifty shades of beige: magnolia-
painted woodchip wallpaper; brown-and-white vinyl in the hall
and kitchen; tan carpet on the stairs – and pale wood laminate
flooring everywhere else. The rooms were sparsely furnished
– a two-seater sofa; a square wood-composite table with four
chairs; upstairs, a bed and a cheap MDF chest of drawers in
each room. The place must have been cleaned after the previous
tenants had moved out and before it was put on the market, but
not since. I smelled the stale odour of vacancy but no dampness.
There would be a queue of people wanting to rent it. With the

chronic, seemingly never-ending housing crisis, and the grossly inadequate response of successive governments, there were queues for every kind of property these days. This was one of the better ones.

'Everything's included,' Dempsey said. 'White goods, the lot.'

'Right,' I said.

'It's a case of get-the-keys-and-start-raking-in-the-money,' he added.

'Yes,' I said.

'Or were you thinking of owner-occupying?'

'No,' I said.

'Okay …' he said.

I sensed that he had me tagged as a time-waster and that he was tiring of my monosyllabic responses, but I wanted to let his patter play out and see what happened next.

'The owner's looking for a quick sale.'

'Sure,' I said.

'I've a few cash buyers interested. You've your finance organised, I presume?'

I made no reply.

'You'll need to give me proof of funds before I can accept a bid.'

'Naturally,' I said.

'Well, then,' he said. 'We seem to be done here and I've a new client to see, so …'

He ushered me back downstairs and nearly pushed me out the front door.

'Which way are you going?' I asked as we stood at the front of the house.

'Out by the Commons Inn,' he said.

'I'll go with you, if that's alright?'

Dempsey's eyes narrowed. 'Is your car out there or something?'

'No,' I said. 'I walked from my office.'

He didn't ask where that was, and it occurred to me that maybe he didn't have to.

'I work at MLC,' I said. 'I'm a solicitor.'

'Yeah?'

'We're all a bit shell-shocked still, like,' I said. 'Because of the murder.'

He couldn't pretend that he didn't know what I was talking about. The story had been headline news on every media outlet for an entire week. 'I'm sure ye are,' he said.

Most people wouldn't have left it there – they'd have been after the inside story, some juicy snippet that hadn't been made public – but Dempsey did. Which caught my attention.

'You knew Mandy,' I said with enough of an uplift at the end to turn it from a statement to a question.

'No, no I didn't,' he said. 'I didn't know her at all.'

'Are you saying you never met her?'

'Why would I have met her?'

'Maybe at the Southern Law Association Dinner, she went every year …'

'I'm a hundred per cent sure I've never met her or seen her. Not there or anywhere else.'

'I thought you—'

'Why would you think that? Why would you think anything about me and her?' His tone was feather-light and he was smiling, and his teeth were big and white.

'I suppose I didn't think it,' I said. 'It was more that I wondered, that's all.'

'Why would you wonder?' he asked.

'I just did,' I said.

He took two steps towards me and grabbed a loose hold of my right wrist. I shook his hand away.

'I told you I didn't know her,' he said, but he stayed where he was. Too close.

'She had your contact details on her computer,' I said.

'So what?'

'So I thought maybe she knew you,' I said.

'What the fuck is this?' he asked. 'You're not interested in the house at all, are you?'

'It's a great buy,' I said, and I felt his hot wet breath on my face as he caught my wrist again, tightly this time. 'But no, I'm not going to be purchasing.'

'You came here to check up on me,' he said.

'Not really,' I said.

'"Not really"?' he mimicked. 'Except I know who you are. Finn Fitz-fucking-patrick. I know all about you and your amateur detective bullshit.'

I felt my throat constrict. There was no one about and the cliff edge was very near. 'Let go of my wrist,' I said. 'You're hurting me.'

'I'm not touching your wrist,' he said as he gripped it harder. Then I stamped on his instep and he let go after all and stumbled backwards. I took in a gulp of air. 'You bitch,' he said.

'I didn't touch you,' I said. 'Just like you didn't touch me.' I was all too aware that I'd told no one where I was going. But I was here now, and I had no intention of wasting my journey. 'Tell me how you knew Mandy Breslin.'

'You're a fucking troublemaker,' he said. 'So what if she had my contact details? It's not a crime, is it? I didn't know she had them and I didn't fucking know her and I sure as hell didn't kill her, if that's what you're suggesting.'

'I'm not,' I said. 'You are.'

He opened his mouth to bark out a response but caught himself. Instead, he threw back his head and laughed. Then he said, 'I'm only messing with you, Finn. That was a great job you did before, the way you got that pervert locked up. Fair dues, like.' He turned and double-locked the front door. 'Where will I drop you?'

'On reflection, I'd prefer to walk,' I said.

'Suit yourself,' he said. 'And, whatever you do, take care. Cork isn't what it was. I won't let my kids out on their own after dark. Daytime is as bad. Too many druggies and too much anti-social behaviour. Wait and see, the guards'll find out eventually that it was one of them weirdos killed that poor woman. Until they do, God only knows who'll be next.'

71

PAUSING FOR BREATH ON PATRICK'S BRIDGE, I looked around. No silver grey Toyota Avensis. No Dempsey. I hadn't really expected him to be following me – and he had no need to, given that he knew where I worked. I took the safest way back to the office anyway, keeping to Patrick Street, closed to private cars at this time of day as a result of a widely despised traffic-calming measure known as the 'Pana Ban'. The ban didn't bother me much either way but I was grateful for it now, reckoning that however angry Dempsey was, he was unlikely to drive down Patrick Street after me, risking garda attention and a fine, even for intimidatory purposes.

I relaxed a little. As I walked, I turned the meeting over and over in my mind. Dempsey was rough and unsophisticated and not too bright. He didn't seem like someone Mandy would bother with. But sexual attraction doesn't conform to rules. He was strong and dark-haired. He could have been the man I saw in the car, her lover. He had scared me. In a public place. In broad daylight. If she had rejected or challenged him, how might he have reacted? It was all too easy to imagine Ricky Dempsey shattering Mandy's skull with a hammer.

•

When I got back to the office, I did a full attendance note, describing him as, 'a possible associate of Mandy's', transcribing his vehicle registration number and car make and model from a photograph snapped on my phone as he drove away, and listing his denials in order – that he didn't know Mandy; that he had never met her; that he hadn't seen her at the Southern Law Association Dinner; that he hadn't killed her. I sent a text message to Sadie, telling her to check her Gmail for information on Ricky Dempsey, a possible candidate for the dark-haired man, and emailed the attendance note to her. She texted back with two thumbs up.

•

I reread my memo. His final denial – that he hadn't killed Mandy – I could do little about for now, but I could make a stab at picking holes in the others. I pinged an email to Mary Bulman, a solicitor in Muldoon & Co – who had been a member of the Southern Law Association Dinner committee for as long as I could remember – and asked her to give me a call when she got a chance. Then I ran downstairs and stuck my head around the door of Kathleen's office. There were too many people there to talk privately so I mouthed, 'Tea room' at her, and hoped she'd follow.

She did. 'What's going on?' she asked.

'Quick question – Ricky Dempsey. Did he know Mandy?'

'Who's Ricky Dempsey? Though the name is familiar somehow ...'

'Estate agent in Blackpool. Not commercial property. Residential.'

'I don't think we ever had anything to do with him, or at least Mandy didn't …'

'Think, please Kathleen, it might be important. It might help find the murderer.'

Kathleen's eyes filled with tears. 'I'll do a search for his name on the system,' she said.

'I've tried that,' I said. 'He's not listed. He showed up as a deleted contact, that's all.'

She bit her lip and thought for a while. Then she asked, 'What about telephone call logs?'

'I didn't think of that,' I said. 'I'll ask Dervla on reception to have a look for me.'

'No good,' Kathleen said. 'That's not how Mandy worked. Any calls for her came through to me directly. I screened them. I have all the records. I save – I mean, I used to save – the individual call records to the relevant file if there was one opened, otherwise they would go into Miscellaneous.' She paused. 'Finn, the more I think of it, that name is ringing a bell. I could be wrong, but I'd nearly swear he rang at some stage in the last few weeks.'

'How long will it take you to check?'

'Come with me now,' she said. 'I'll look and keep looking till I find it.'

I stood beside Kathleen as she checked the phone records. Mandy got a lot of calls every day but Kathleen had been right. Dempsey had phoned for Mandy two days before she died – twice, on the preceding Friday afternoon – leaving no phone number and a simple message on both occasions: 'Ask Mandy to get back to me', and, 'Tell Mandy I rang again'. Both calls were marked as having been returned.

'If Mandy was able to call him back,' I said, 'she had his phone number.'

'Which means she knew him,' Kathleen said. 'I didn't. But that wasn't unusual. She got so many enquiries from prospective clients – she wouldn't take on all of them, or even half, she was good at weeding out the wheat from the chaff, as good as she was at everything else – that they wouldn't register fully with me until they came across my desk as new file matters—'

She gasped. 'Is he a suspect in her murder?'

'I don't know,' I said. 'It could be nothing. I have to do some more digging.'

'Is that your role, Finn? Think about it. You'll get no thanks from the powers-that-be in this place, whatever you do – they're only bothered about keeping a lid on any scandal that might hurt the firm. Honestly, I don't think they care about finding Mandy's murderer at all. And I know you want to help, but please promise me you'll be careful. Whoever it was that killed Mandy has killed once already, and—'

'Don't worry,' I said. 'I'm good at minding myself. But thanks.'

•

As I climbed the stairs to my office, I texted Sadie with the update about the phone messages. Despite the grimness of the situation, I couldn't stop smiling and I knew the reason why.

If Dempsey was the murderer, Davy was off the hook.

72

I SPENT THE REST OF THE AFTERNOON CATCHING up on my regular work. Tina had done a great job of deflecting and diverting while I'd been tied up with the review, but there were limits. Besides which, it wasn't fair on her. I ploughed on and barely thought about Mandy and Ricky Dempsey and, when I thought about Davy, I resolved to, for once, deal head-on with what had turned out to be merely a relationship issue, instead of avoiding it – or catastrophising with ridiculous gothic scenarios that cast him as Mandy's murderer, when in reality I hadn't a scintilla of evidence linking him to the crime. It's good to talk, I told myself. If I said it often enough, maybe I'd actually do it.

Then, just before 5.30 p.m., Mary Bulman rang back in response to my email and I asked her to confirm what I was sure I knew already: that Ricky Dempsey had attended the Southern Law Association Dinner. I expected her to say yes. Once she did, I was ready to ask her if she remembered him talking to Mandy and if she'd noticed anything else.

But instead the conversation went like this:

'Ricky Dempsey? From Blackpool?' Mary asked.

'Em, yeah,' I said. 'Estate agent. Auctioneer. Big burly guy.'

'He's never been to the SLA Dinner.'

'Are you sure?' I asked.

'Have you met him?'

'Earlier on today.'

'And you have to ask?'

'Well, yes, that's what I'm doing.'

'I've been a conveyancing solicitor for more than twenty-five years,' she said. 'And I've never met an auctioneer like him. He is the greatest I-don't-know-what-you-may-call-it on the planet. Not a nice man. I wouldn't give him a shoebox to sell, but he does a fair few mortgage valuations and the odd bank sale, repossessions – that kind of thing. What work he gets is through his football and hurling connections. As far as I know, that's how he keeps going. I could be wrong, but I don't think a solicitor has ever invited him to the SLA Dinner. Jesus Christ, you're not thinking of bringing him, are you?'

'God, no, I only met him for the first time today and I wasn't impressed,' I said. 'I got the sense from him though that he knew Mandy quite well.'

'Hah! Doubt it. He was only trying to get news of the murder out of you, Finn.'

I let Mary talk on for a few minutes while I collected my thoughts. After the call ended, I put my head in my hands. I had really wanted Ricky Dempsey to be the man. The man who'd been Mandy's lover. The man who'd killed her. They had to have known each other. After all, there was the deleted contact card, and Kathleen had found proof that he'd phoned Mandy two days before she died. There was still a good chance that I was right about him.

On the other hand, I had to accept, there was an equally good chance that I was wrong.

73

AFTER ALL THE WORK I'D DONE ON THE CASE
that day, I was back where I'd started. At the centre of the
whirlpool. Struggling to stay afloat. My doubts about Davy
pulling me under.

So I checked his fitness classes schedule on Facebook. Once
I'd established that he'd be busy for the next while, I drove to
his house – I had a key. In theory, I might have left something
behind. A book. A coat. But the trouble was that it had been so
long since I'd spent the night there that I'd have found it hard
to fabricate a plausible excuse. Better to pop in when he wasn't
home. No questions to be asked or answered. Find nothing to
link him to Mandy's murder. Resume normal service.

I parked up and got out of the car, my keys in my right
hand. There was no one but me on the street. The only sound
was the rain battering on the roofs and rushing in the gullies.
Davy's house was in darkness. I'd have been in and out unseen in
minutes. If the locks hadn't been changed.

74

I COULDN'T CONFRONT DAVY. IF I DID, I'D HAVE TO admit that I'd been trying to get into his house when I knew he wasn't there. Not a problem, usually. But we were way past usual, in a silent limbo that was driving me crazy. In the end, I decided that the *only* thing I could do was have it out with him.

I messaged him: *In car. I'll collect you from work and drop you home. 8 okay?*

He replied: *Too awkward. Faster for me to walk.*

I responded immediately: *Either I collect or I go to your house and wait for you there.*

The second was the easier option as I was already there, though he didn't know that. After a few minutes he replied: *Collect. 8.15.*

•

The gym was in an old stone building on Keeffe Street on Morrison's Island – a triangular projection into the south channel that forces the river into a radical change of direction. I'd only walked and never driven to Davy's workplace before and I realised now how hard a task that was. One-way streets,

and heavy traffic coming and going from the night classes in the
College of Commerce, made arriving outside the door on time
nearly impossible. Too early I managed, and had to go around
the block again. Which made me too late. Luckily, so was he.
As I rolled into place, he was coming out the door, smiling and
waving at someone I couldn't see. The smile left his face the
moment he spotted my car. He got in and I drove off.

At first, neither of us said a word.

Then he asked, 'What's wrong?'

'There's something going on with you,' I said. 'Something's
changed.'

'Something's changed alright,' he said. 'An old friend died.
Was murdered. I'm upset. You're upset. A lot of people are
upset.'

'That's it?'

'I'm busy at work. I told you.'

'There's more to it,' I said.

'You can think that if you want.'

'Why did you change the locks?'

'*What?*'

'I went to your house earlier to … em … I'd forgotten, ah—'

'I don't buy that,' Davy said. 'I reckon you were planning
to poke around, conduct a search. The guards would need a
warrant, but not you, right?'

I blushed, but didn't concede. 'I had every right to enter your
premises,' I said. 'Seeing as you'd granted me licence to do so by
giving me a key.' It wasn't a point I'd fancy arguing in court.

'What did you think you'd find?'

'I didn't know.'

'You think I'm using again, is that it?'

'No, well … maybe. To be honest, I'd hadn't really thought of that, until just now you said it. Christ. Are you?'

'I'm not.'

'Because it would explain a lot if you were.'

'I told you I'm not.'

'That's what you *would* say, I guess. You'd deny it.'

'I wouldn't be able to. If I was using again, you'd fucking know.'

'Is it someone new? Is that it, have you found someone new?'

Silence. Then he said, 'There's no one new. I—'

'There's *something*, I know there is. Tell me. Please.'

'Jesus, Finn, would you let me talk? First of all, you know how I feel about you.'

'That's not an answer.'

'It *is*. I love you. That hasn't changed.'

'Don't make this about love,' I said. 'You. Changed. The. Locks.'

'Finn,' Davy said. 'Locks break.'

'So the lock broke and you never said anything? Didn't give me a new key?'

A sigh. 'There's been a lot going on.'

'I don't think I'd forget to tell you,' I said.

'I don't think I'd be searching your house.'

'When was the last time you saw Mandy? You told me first you couldn't remember. Then you said it was at Orla's house when you accidentally called in one Friday. But Orla didn't seem sure about that at all. In fact, she seemed really surprised you'd said it was that night.'

'That *was* the last time I saw Mandy, I swear. How would Orla know anyway?'

'Funny. That's what she said too. She's very protective of her little baby brother.'

Silence. We were stopped at the Anglesea Street lights.

Then I asked, 'Did you have something to do with Mandy's death?'

A look of horror crossed Davy's face. But I kept talking. 'Where were you that night? The night of the murder. Sunday. You're always at my house on Sunday nights. But not *that* Sunday night. Why?'

'Y—you would think that of me?' He opened the car door. 'I can't do this,' he said. 'I'm going before we both say something we'll regret.'

He got out and walked ahead of the stationary cars, in the direction of his house. When the light changed to green, I drove off and didn't look back.

TUESDAY

75

ED WAS WEARING THE SAME ANCIENT PINK POLO shirt he'd had on the first morning he'd shown up at the office. He hadn't washed it in the meantime. His hair looked dirty too. He ran his hands through it and gave his head a scratch. I waited for him to speak. He was the one who'd asked me to visit the house again. I'd been happy with the invitation, reckoning I might learn something about where Ava had been on the night of Mandy's disappearance. I was even happier to be handed an excuse to ask Ed a few more questions without having to conjure up one myself. But I'd been sitting at the kitchen table for a while now, and I still had no idea what he wanted.

'It's been tough,' he said, at last. 'Trying to get to grips with everything and look out for the girls as well. You were kind to me last week. That's why I thought of contacting you.'

'I'm glad you did,' I said. 'How can I help?'

'It's practical advice I … em … need. I've never done this before, as you can imagine.'

•

I explained that a full death certificate wouldn't be issued until after the inquest, but that an interim, fact-of-death certificate could be obtained from the coroner which would allow him to begin the process of administering Mandy's estate. I talked him through a list of the tasks he could accomplish himself and another of those he'd be better off leaving to a solicitor. It was basic common sense but Ed took ridiculously detailed notes, as if he expected me to set him a test at the end and he was determined to snag a gold star. I was starting to find it unsettling.

Then he said, 'You're so good.'

'It's nothing.'

'It's not nothing. It's important to me. Especially when you're so busy.'

I made a stab at a gracious smile. I've never been good with compliments.

'That report you're compiling must be taking up a lot of time, though.'

'Report?'

'That's what you're doing, isn't it? Analysing Mandy's work, reporting to Gabriel?'

'I don't remember mentioning any report.'

'I thought you did?'

'I can't think why I would have,' I said.

'I'm sure it's going fine anyway.'

I made no response.

Ed went on: 'You'd let me know if it wasn't, I'm sure.'

'What?'

'If there was something I should know?'

'I don't know what you're saying,' I said. 'Or what you expect me to say.'

'I mean,' Ed said. 'Like you did when you told me about what you saw, Mandy with ... that man. I really did appreciate you giving me the heads-up on that. And there's the garda investigation. They're telling me nothing, which I think is ... They've allocated a young liaison guy for the family but he doesn't seem to know much.'

'I understand.' I was beginning to, at least. Ed hadn't wanted legal advice from me: *this* was the reason he'd asked me to visit, to sound me out on what I knew. 'Mandy was an excellent solicitor,' I said. 'You know that.'

'I'm sure there isn't anything to worry about. But we all make mistakes. And for the girls especially it would be good to have advance warning if—'

'Have you something you want to tell me, Ed – something she talked to you about?'

'God, no! Not at all. There's nothing. Nothing whatsoever. It's just—'

'Ed, who told you I was writing a report about Mandy?' He had been sitting with Dermot Lyons at the funeral lunch. It could've been Lyons or any one of twenty other MLC staff members.

'Didn't *you* tell me?'

I was certain that I hadn't. But if Ed remembered who had, he wasn't saying.

76

I DIDN'T KNOW WHY ED SUDDENLY CARED SO
much about what Mandy had been doing at MLC. He'd never
intimated that he had the slightest interest in her job while she
was alive. I couldn't recall seeing him in the office even once –
and he'd been vehement in his denials of having any particular
concerns. But I'd never believed his story about not knowing
the identity of Mandy's lover. It occurred to me that his novel
interest might be connected to that. And that I might be able
to use the situation to my advantage if I could give him the
impression that any sharing of information on his part might be
reciprocated by me.

'I'm not sure what I can do. Like I said, Mandy's work was
beyond reproach.'

Ed's face was impassive, but I noticed that he looked away as
I said that last piece. Was I missing something? I thought about
asking him more but decided to stick with Plan A.

'Anything that I do or discover within the walls of MLC has
to remain there,' I said.

'What happens in Vegas stays in Vegas?'

I laughed. For the first time, I glimpsed what Mandy might

have seen in Ed, a frivolity to balance her intensity, and how she might have thought for a while that that would be enough.

'I'll do my best for you,' I said. He smiled. 'I never said that, of course.'

'Of course,' Ed said. He did a zipping motion with his thumb and index finger across his lips.

'I've been thinking,' I went on. 'About the affair. The other man. It's going to come up when the guards talk to you.'

'They haven't interviewed me yet,' Ed said. 'Not formally.'

'It's only a matter of time,' I said. 'You remember that solicitor I told you about?'

'I do.'

'Did you call him?'

'No. Not yet.'

'You should. The gloves will be coming off, now that the funeral's over. They're going to be looking at you. They'll want a quick result.'

'They'll find nothing on me because there's nothing to find.'

'That's as may be,' I said. 'But they could make your life difficult all the same.'

'Jesus,' he said. 'As if it's not difficult enough already.'

'If they had a name for the other man, it would take the heat off you.'

'I've been racking my brains,' Ed said. 'I know it seems weird that I don't know.'

'I have to admit that the guards might think that. They *might* not believe you.'

'The only thing I know for absolute sure is that she met him through work.'

'Do you think he was someone from MLC?'

'Possibly. Or connected somehow.'

'An estate agent maybe?'

'Maybe. Or maybe a client. I just don't know.'

I hid my disappointment. He hadn't given me anything I hadn't guessed at already. But I had one question left. 'Alright …' I said. 'Oh, by the way, I never realised you knew Davy Keenan.'

'Davy? Yeah, he came to the funeral. He was more Mandy's buddy than mine. She and his sister Orla were besties from way back. How do you know him?'

'I thought Mandy might've told you. I've been going out with him.'

Ed had been drinking a glass of water. He nearly choked. Then he said, 'I wouldn't have put you two together in a million years. You've got hidden depths, Finn. I had you down as a goody-two-shoes. Though I did hear Davy turned over a new leaf. Mind you, it would need to be an entire tree. He was a lunatic. We all were. He turned it up to eleven, though. I always liked him. But we lost touch. Give him my regards, will you?'

'Sure,' I said. 'Next time I see him.' Whenever that would be. 'Before I go, is it okay if I take a look around Mandy's study, just in case there's anything there that should be in her office at work?'

'I'd be delighted if you did,' Ed said. 'It'd save me a job.'

•

Mandy's home study occupied a small room to the front of the house. Her desk was to one side of the window, looking out on the water. On the other side, an armchair patterned with pale pink roses was angled towards the view. A mauve soft wool rug hung on the back of the chair. On the back wall, an old doorway had been blocked up and turned into bookshelves. Otherwise, apart from the paintings on the walls and another bookcase, the room was empty.

'It used to be connected to the old master bedroom next door,' Ed said. 'We think it was a dressing room. But that's the guest room now. We're on the next floor up – we were – and the girls are in the attic.'

'A dressing room? What a waste of the view that would have been.'

'It's north-facing, that's probably why. It can get chilly in here, though she never minded.'

The writing desk – slim, walnut, with a low raised ledge at the back – was bare apart from a notebook, a Post-it pad, a few pens and pencils, a tangle of disconnected wires and a gaping space where the computer had been.

'The guards have it,' Ed said. 'They took her desktop and her laptop. I don't know if they'll be able to access any of the information, though they have IT experts so maybe …' He smiled ruefully. 'I'll leave you to it,' he said.

He'd told me that Mandy had loved the kitchen but this place felt more like her place of retreat, her safe haven. There was a key on the inside of the door.

I wondered how often she locked it.

77

WITH ED GONE, I MADE STRAIGHT FOR THE
bookshelves. I hadn't pegged Mandy as a reader, but apparently
she was. She had good taste, too: P.D. James, Ruth Rendell, a
fine selection of Tartan Noir and, it seemed, all the Irish crime
writers. On the flyleaf of each book, she'd written where and
when she read it – 'July 2011, Marbella', 'Christmas 2015, home'.
On the front of one of the shelves, there was a stack of her most
recent purchases, still unread. I ran my finger along their pristine
spines and swallowed the lump that came to my throat.

There were a few law books – old texts from her college days,
drafting guides and a couple of folders of loose precedents and
blank client instruction forms. I flicked through them but there
was nothing of any consequence. If there was anything to be
found, it was at the office.

Which reminded me. I sent another '*Any news?*' message to
Pauline Doyle. Her son, Conor had recovered finally from his
long-lasting ear infection and both twins were back in crèche.
She'd returned to work. But all day she'd been telling me she was
'super busy' and 'catching up'. Unless she started delivering, I'd
have to find someone else to do the IT search.

I took a last look around Mandy's study. There was no

excuse for me to linger any longer and I didn't. But I didn't go downstairs either.

•

The back room didn't feel like a guest room, as Ed had said. It felt lived in. The bed was rumpled, and there was a half-drunk glass of water and an open pack of soluble Solpadeine on the night table. I opened a drawer and the door of the wardrobe. I walked to the window to look out over the garden. I was trying to decide what to do next, when I heard a voice behind me.

'Finn, what are you doing in here?'

I spun a circle on my heel. 'Ruth! How are you?'

There was no need to ask. She looked wan and thin and inconsolably sad. Like the last time I was in the house, she was in pyjamas and if I were to hazard a guess, she hadn't worn anything else, or left the house, since the funeral on Saturday.

'What are you doing?' she asked again.

'I was looking for the loo. But this door was open. The garden is so lovely.'

No reply.

'I've been helping your dad sort out your mum's study, checking for anything that might relate to her work at the firm.'

Still no reply but she relaxed a little and came towards me. 'Whose room is this?' I asked.

'Dad's. The last few months it's been his anyway. Since the summer.'

'Before that he slept upstairs?'

'Yeah, but his snoring got too bad and Mum said she couldn't sleep.'

'I hate snoring too,' I said.

'Ava said that wasn't the real reason though.'

'Oh?'

'She said it was because Mum and Dad were going to be getting a divorce.'

78

RUTH'S STORY CORROBORATED WHAT DAVY'S
sister Orla had said, that the marriage was well and truly over.
That meant that Ed had been less than honest about his and
Mandy's sleeping arrangements and, crucially, about the state
of their relationship. He'd told me that he thought she was
coming back to him, that the affair with the dark-haired man
was nearing its end. And he was the one who'd brought up
the topic of the bedrooms – I hadn't asked – but I'd accepted
what he'd said. Though he'd used the word 'were', I'd filled in
the gaps myself. But he wasn't under any obligation to tell me
anything about his marriage. Maybe it was understandable that
he'd lied?

I had to talk to Ava. I needed to ask her about the divorce –
technically a separation at this stage as under Irish law, a divorce
can only be granted after the couple have been living apart for
two years. I also needed to ask about what I'd overheard her say
in the bathroom at the hotel. But it was tricky. Ava was only
sixteen, two years away from becoming an adult in the eyes of
the law. Also, her responses to any questions I might put to her
could be incriminating of her father and possibly of herself. On
the other hand, I had no official role in the murder investigation.

There was no prohibition on a family friend asking questions of a teenager – other than that it felt all wrong to me.

Wrong to take advantage of a young person for my own ends. Wrong because I was biased. Identifying Ricky Dempsey, or Ed, or whoever else it might be as Mandy's killer would all mean one thing: that Davy wasn't guilty. I wondered how far I'd go to find out the truth – or the version of the truth that I wanted. I'd bent rules before, but I'd never been so close to a case. I couldn't trust my judgement. Until I figured things out, I had to take a step back.

I went out to the hallway. Ruth followed in silence. At the door to Mandy's study I said, 'I'd better go. I just want to double-check there's nothing left to take into the office. Take care of yourself, Ruth. If I can – if you need – well …' She nodded. Then, suddenly, she gave me a hug and, seconds later, disappeared up the stairs. I felt like a waste of space. In the midst of my own drama, I had become horribly selfish. The poor child had lost her mother. She was in pain. And I hadn't done a single thing to help.

•

I hadn't the heart or the mind to question Ed any more that day. I left the house and got into my car. I'd just turned the key when the passenger door opened and Ava sat in. She looked old and young at the same time. Mostly, she looked frightened.

'I need to talk to you.'

'What's wrong?' I asked.

'Please drive,' Ava said. 'Anywhere.'

79

THERE USED TO BE TWO BLACK SWANS ON THE
Lough. One day there wasn't. Next time I saw him, I asked the
park ranger what had happened.

'They're very aggressive,' the ranger said. 'Don't couple up
well. We think this one might have killed its mate. Though he
looks all innocent now, doesn't he?'

I considered his sleek feathers and his orange eyes. I thought
innocent was the last thing he looked. 'Did you ever find the
other black swan's body?'

'Nope,' he said.

•

I was thinking of that conversation now. We'd driven from
Blackrock and I'd stopped at the Lough, a place beloved of
Corkonians – either a big pond or a small lake, depending on
your point of view. It's undeniably urban in feel, the water
rimmed with concrete, the hum of passing cars – but it's a natural
feature, not an artificial one, and it has enough wild birds and
trees and grass to blur the edges of the city. People walk and
run here at all times of the day and night, strangers and locals.
Coming here had seemed like a good idea – until I remembered
that Alysson Villas, the place Ava's mother had been murdered,
was nearby, a five- or ten-minute walk away.

'We can go somewhere else, if you like,' I said.

'Here's fine,' Ava said. 'Or it's not fine. Nowhere's fine anymore. But it'll do.'

'You're not dressed for a walk,' I said. 'I've got a jacket in the boot, if you want?'

'Okay,' she said.

•

We strolled in silence but, when we got to the playground, Ava stopped. The swings and climbing frames were empty. It was close to 7 p.m. It would be dark soon. The birds would sleep and bats would swoop between the trees.

'Ruth said she told you about the divorce,' Ava said.

'She didn't mean to. It slipped out.'

'I'm glad it did,' Ava said. 'I didn't want to say anything at first, though I suppose I knew I'd have to tell someone sometime. Dad doesn't know we know. But I overheard them talking.'

'Who?'

'Mum and Dad.'

'When was that?'

'Summer. Middle of July. They were out the back on the terrace, but the windows were open. They couldn't see me but I was listening.'

'What did they say?'

'Mum said the marriage was finished and Dad asked her to give it another chance.'

'What did your mother say to that?'

'She said no. She said she wanted to tell us during the school holidays, so that we'd have time to get used to it. He asked her to wait three months. They argued. That was nothing unusual but this was a bad one. Eventually she said she'd wait for a while on the condition that he'd look for a new place to live. He said he needed time for that. She said she'd give him two months.'

'Two months would take them to the middle of September. Did they tell you?'

'No. Mum got … died before she had a chance to.'

'Maybe she changed her mind?'

'It's possible she did. I think that's what Dad hoped would happen. But she sounded so sure. And normally once she decided something, she stuck to it.'

I said nothing for a time. She was right about Mandy. But I knew there was more to be said. There was what I'd overheard in the bathroom at the Maryborough Hotel. Ava had volunteered the information about the divorce and I hadn't chased or pressured her for it. Now that we'd got this far, I hoped she'd tell me the rest without me having to ask. Without the humiliating revelation that I'd heard part of the story already, because I was hiding in the loo.

'Is there something else you want to tell me?' I asked.

She started to cry. I put my arm on her shoulder but she shrugged it off. 'I blame myself,' she said.

I held her gaze and listened to what she said next.

'I wasn't at home that Sunday night. Dad told the guards I was, that we both were. But I was out. With friends. I went out in the afternoon. I was supposed to be home by 8 p.m. but I didn't … I-I stayed out until, I don't know exactly, sometime after midnight. Dad was up when I got home. He saw me.'

'That's important information,' I said. 'You know what it means.'

'It means that my father has no alibi for the time of the murder,' Ava said.

80

I DROPPED AVA HOME AND WHILE SHE WENT upstairs, with her permission, I confronted Ed. He was lying on a sofa in the drawing room – all Farrow & Ball and soft sheen, wide-plank hardwood floors and Persian rugs – watching *Escape to the Chateau*. He sat up when I walked in and muted the volume. I stood in front of the television and said my piece.

In response, he shilly-shallied. 'She's only sixteen. I knew she'd been drinking. I could smell it off her. Not just alcohol. Weed too. I didn't want her to have to explain where she'd been and what she'd been doing. It was easier to say we were together.' He paused. 'Finn, I was protecting my child. That's all I was doing.'

'I have no doubt that that's what you *thought* you were doing,' I said. It wasn't true. I had plenty of doubts about Ed. But it's hard to call a man a liar on his own patch. Besides, it wouldn't help Ava if I did. And it wouldn't help me. 'It's not fair on her. The thought of having lied to the guards on top of everything else. It's eating her up.'

'Are you advising me to tell the truth?' Ed asked.

'I'm not advising you at all,' I said. 'Other than to tell you to make an appointment with that solicitor. He'll advise you what to say. Or if you'd be better off staying silent.'

'Oh my God. You'll be reading me my rights next.' I let that comment go without reply. 'Or the guards will,' he said.

'The thing is, Ed. If they catch you in one lie, they'll start to think that you're lying about other stuff too.'

'They won't,' he said. 'I …' He stopped, stared at me. 'Is that what you think? That I've been lying?'

'I have to wonder,' I said, 'if you've been completely honest.'

'About anything in particular?' I stayed quiet. In the silence, the old house creaked.

'You don't believe me about *him*,' he said. 'About me not knowing who he is.'

'No,' I said.

'Why would I lie?'

'You tell me.'

'It makes no sense.'

'Except I think you told the gardaí that everything was rosy in your marriage. That was the impression you tried to give me first too. You only said there was another man in the picture after I told you that I'd seen Mandy with someone else.'

'I had no alibi,' Ed said. 'If the guards found out that Mandy was having an affair and that she'd wanted a separation, suspicion would fall on me. They wouldn't even bother their arses looking for someone else. Spurned husband kills wife. It's a cliché.'

'It's a cliché,' I said, 'because it's so often true.'

'Not this time,' Ed said.

'Help me to believe you.'

'How can I do that?'

'Tell me the name of the other man.'

'I don't know it.'

He'd left me with no choice but to call it like it was. 'For God's sake, stop lying,' I said. 'You've done quite enough of that already.'

81

'WE WERE FRIENDS, THAT'S WHAT WE WERE,' ED said. 'Me and Mandy. Buddies. Always. Our families knew each other. We were at the same school. Spent every summer together. The good old days, all hanging out in a gang, and then gradually it became more than that. We got closer, ended up on our own more of the time, just us two and—'

'Ed,' I said. 'The name.'

'We were grown-ups. We knew what was important. Mandy had occasional outside interests. I did too. Variety is the spice of life and all that. Just physical. Didn't matter. We were happy, I want you to understand that – really, really, happy. Our daughters were the centre of our lives. Then, everything changed.

'I knew she'd been having a fling with someone, that it had been going on for a while. But that had happened before. It didn't affect … This was different. He wanted all of her. And she wanted him too. She told me in July that the marriage was over. I … I found it hard to accept. She gave me a reprieve. Two months. I hoped against hope that she'd give him up. But once she set a course, she didn't alter. I knew in my heart—'

'But who was he?' I asked.

'I told you, she met him through work. That was true. I thought you'd find out. I'm surprised you haven't.'

'Did other people at the firm know?'

'I'm sure they did. Woulfe surely did?'

'Hugo Woulfe, her trainee?'

'Lapdog, more like. He knew all her secrets, knew about *him*, had to.'

'And the name, Ed, the other man's name?'

'It was Owen McCormack.'

82

AFTER LEAVING THE HOUSE, I DROVE OFF QUICKLY but stopped at the end of Castle Road. Because I was in a grey area as regards my duty of client confidentiality – where Ed had been seeking quasi-legal advice from me – I couldn't tell Sadie straight out what Ed had told me. But I reckoned I was on safe ethical ground in directing her where to look. I'd warned Ed that he had to tell the investigating gardaí voluntarily about his fake alibi for the night of the murder. Otherwise, he'd put his daughter Ava in the invidious position of having to grass up her own father. He was a pathetic excuse for a man, but he seemed to take my point about that. I was nearly sure he'd tell.

I was less sure if Ed would reveal Owen McCormack – an MLC client – to the gardaí as Mandy's alleged lover. And I didn't know if Ed was telling the truth about McCormack. He might give the guards a different name. Or he might not tell them at all.

As confidentiality rules applied not just to the individual solicitor–client relationship, but to the whole firm, I couldn't simply tell Sadie what Ed had said about McCormack, or that he had been a client of Mandy's. I had to find another way to make him a person of interest to the investigation. All of which meant that I was going to have to do a lot more digging.

I sent Sadie a text message: *Ask Ed again about Sunday night. Can't say anymore.*

Sadie replied: *I'll call you in two mins.*

I sent another message: *Can't tell you what he said. Rules of the job. Just ask him again.*

She replied: *You can tell me. Just come down off that windy high moral ground.*

I didn't respond.

OK. Fine. Anyway we interviewing him formally tomorrow.

I don't think he knows that, I replied.

He doesn't yet. Might we get a different answer re Sunday to what he said before?

You never know :-) I sent another text:

Another thing – news on DNA semen test? Why so long?

FFS Finn it's not like on TV. Have you any idea how long the delays in Forensics are? 10 days is v fast. Should have it tomorrow.

What about the computers you took from Mandy's home office? Anything?

Sadie replied: *Laptop was for work. Passworded. Desktop open access but zero on it except online shopping and net browsing. Before you ask, nothing significant.*

Thanks.

Still mostly one way traffic with the info Finn. You need to bring me more than this.

I will. Promise.

•

I googled Owen McCormack on my phone. His company, Finertech, owned and occupied one of the giant glass boxes that were springing up around the city as the economy limped out of recession. I wasn't sure what Finertech did – something incomprehensible related to data synergies and analytics – but it was a great place to work, according to the shiny-toothed millennials beaming from every page of the Finertech website.

Owen himself smiled not at all. He didn't have to. He was worth over €400 million. Tall and thin and fit from the running that, according to an *Irish Independent* business pages profile, was his main hobby. He was extremely handsome. And he had dark brown hair. He was the man I'd seen at Mandy's funeral.

The man in grey.

83

IF I'D KNOWN THEN WHAT I FOUND OUT LATER,
I wouldn't have done what I did. But my blood was up, and
though I knew that Ed was still holding back information, at last
I had something to work with – something that couldn't wait
till morning.

Hugo Woulfe lived with his parents in a crumbling period
mansion near the top of Wellington Road. After the Irish War
of Independence, the residents there had been given the option
of changing the name of the street from that of the hero of
Waterloo to something more fitting to the new Irish Free State.
They voted to keep the Duke in situ. Arthur Wellesley was an
Irishman, after all, even if he didn't like to admit it.

I pushed open the heavy cast-iron gate, and rang the doorbell.
Mrs Woulfe, older than I'd expected – Hugo must have been an
afterthought – eyed me nervously. 'Will you come in? Though
it's a little late and Hugo …'

'I'll be across in Henchy's,' I said. 'Ask him to follow me over.
Please.'

•

Though he didn't drink much, or often, Henchy's pub on St
Luke's Cross – Tea and Wine Merchants, according to the black

and gilt sign on the front – was my dad's local. Even on a Tuesday night, empty seats were a rarity but I secured a lone high stool by the bar, and ordered two bottles of fizzy Ballygowan. I drank the first in two or three gulps, and nursed the second.

After twenty minutes, there was no sign of Hugo Woulfe. I'd wearied of counting the gleaming spirit bottles behind the counter and was berating myself for my foolishness in coming here, when the door behind me swung open with a crash and every eye swivelled to see who was on the way in.

Hugo Woulfe nodded a perfunctory greeting to the barman, then, looking in my direction, tipped his head to the right. I followed him outside. He was standing, legs apart, arms folded across his chest. He was all in black: black trainers, black tracksuit bottoms, black T-shirt.

'You upset Mummy,' he said. 'For that, *inter alia*, you will not be forgiven.'

'Tell me about Mandy Breslin and Owen McCormack.'

'She was his solicitor. He was her client. It's no secret.'

'I have reliable information that they were having an affair.'

'Like I told you before, Mandy wouldn't do anything like that.'

'I know what you told me,' I said.

'If she was having an affair, which I consider to be highly unlikely, by the way, I knew nothing about it.'

'I don't—'

'No, *I* don't,' Woulfe said. 'I don't know who you think you are, or what your role is. Calling to my home at 10.30 at night? Intimidating me? And my mother? This is highly inappropriate behaviour. I fervently hope that it isn't repeated. For your sake.'

Then he disappeared around the corner and into the night.

WEDNESDAY

84

TEN ENDLESS DAYS SINCE THE MURDER. I WENT
into work at 8 a.m. The door to Mandy's office was shut but
unlocked. I pushed it open and loitered on the threshold. The
place looked untouched since I'd last been there the previous
Friday. Inside the room, the air was heavy and stale.

I logged into the case management system to check when
Owen McCormack had become a client of MLC. Nearly
three years ago. Timewise, according to what Ed had told me,
he fit. I did a search for Mandy's emails to him. Most of the
communications had been via his assistant and the Finertech in-
house legal department. McCormack was cc'd on everything.
He interjected only occasionally with a query or a clarification
that Mandy responded to efficiently and succinctly. Their tone
was polite and friendly but unfailingly businesslike. If it was all
an act, intended to disguise a torrid affair, it was a good one.

But after Hugo Woulfe's denials, I no longer knew whether
to believe Ed. If what he'd said was true, why didn't Woulfe
acknowledge that Mandy was having an affair? Was it because,
like Kathleen, he genuinely hadn't known? Or did he have
something to hide? Had he loved her? And had she rejected
him? He'd been heavily involved in most of Mandy's Owen

McCormack files. If McCormack and Mandy had been carrying on an affair, it was scarcely conceivable that Woulfe hadn't picked up on it. Was he loyal to Mandy even in death – or had he become so overwhelmed with jealousy that he'd killed her in a fit of rage?

Then came the McInerneys – what had they to do with any of it? How did they connect with the murder or with Lenihan's surveillance operation? And where exactly did Ricky Dempsey fit into the picture?

I circled back. Whether Ed was lying about Owen McCormack being Mandy's lover, or telling the truth, Ava's testimony would ensure that he no longer had an alibi to protect him. He and McCormack, as soon as the guards found out his name, would move straight to the top of the suspect list. Not mine. I couldn't get away from Davy. He hadn't been honest with me since the murder, and maybe long before it. He'd only admitted to knowing Mandy – and provided me with a highly edited version of their murky history and their friendship, if that's all it had been – so that he could go to her funeral. If he hadn't gone, no one, least of all me, would have questioned his absence.

But he'd wanted to go. To mourn Mandy.

Or to work out if he was a suspect?

85

UPSTAIRS IN MY OFFICE, TINA ARRIVED WITH THE post at 9.45 a.m. On the top of the pile was the title search I'd requested. 'It's definitely Josepha Buckley's house,' she said.

'So Charlene McInerney was telling the truth. Not that I ever truly doubted her.'

'And what does it mean?'

I hadn't told Tina about DI Lenihan's visit to my house, or about the McInerneys' possible link to his operation. I'd promised him confidentiality and I'd promised to keep away from the missing persons investigation in Dublin. I'd kept both promises. For now.

'What we knew already. That the McInerneys had a connection to the place where Mandy was killed and that they visited the house that same night. As to what it really means, your guess is as good as mine.'

'You look pale.'

'Just tired. Not getting enough sleep.'

'You sure that's all?'

'Maybe I'll give up coffee,' I said.

'You should take up wine. I never have any problem sleeping.'

I laughed. 'I have a small bit of mega top secret news,' I said.

'Tell me this minute. Immediately. Now.'

'I think I know who Mandy's lover might have been,' I said.

•

After Tina left, I sent Sadie a message: *DNA result on semen yet? You said it would be today?*

She replied: *YES! DNA is def not Ed's. Also no match with anyone on PULSE. Source unknown. Now your turn. Who is M's Other Man??*

Finally, an objective fact: Mandy Breslin had had sexual intercourse with a man other than her husband on the day of her death. Sadie had said they'd be interviewing Ed formally today. He could no longer escape disclosing to the gardaí that he had no alibi for Sunday night. But would he give them Owen McCormack's name? The man Ed claimed was Mandy's lover. The man Hugo Woulfe said wasn't.

I replied to Sadie with: *Ask Ed for M's lover's name when you see him today.* In reply, she called me. I didn't answer. I put my phone on silent, let it ring, shoved it in a drawer.

•

The Met Office had issued an orange alert, but I barely registered the rain beating against the windowpane and, above me, the roof slates rattling. I was more aware of the wind – the intermittent, irregular pattern of it: uneven gusts of nothingness blowing in from nowhere.

All that I'd learned about the case told me that there were plenty of suspects in Mandy's murder, that any of them could have done it. All that I felt told me that, unless I could prove otherwise, Davy was still among them.

86

PAULINE DOYLE BREEZED IN THE DOOR. 'SORRY it's taken so long but he's only just this morning—' She stopped and the look on her face made me resolve to check the mirror the second she was gone.

'You're exhausted, so you are.'

'I didn't sleep well,' I said. 'Thinking about things, over and over.'

'I can come back another time if you like.'

'No, no. How are you? And how's little Conor?'

'He was really sick, howling with the pain in his ear and the antibiotics took forever to kick in – but he's better now. And the two of them are gone back to crèche, thank God.'

'That's great news,' I said.

'I've even better news for you. I found something. Well, quite a few things, actually.'

'Well, don't just stand there,' I said. 'Talk to me.'

'I have to explain first. When files are deleted from the desktop, from your computer – even if you go as far as deleting them from your trash folder too – they still remain on the server. Only when you do a permanent delete from the recycle bin on the server are they gone forever. Even then, it's possible to get them back if they're not overwritten. But we can leave that aside for now. Also, you need to know that file data and client names and contact details are stored in different places on the server. That's why I spotted the deleted contact first, before I left on Friday. It jumped out at me when I looked at the SQL database. I only got to the rest now.'

'Let's pretend I understand what you're talking about, and move on. What did you find?'

'Five files – what look like five complete matters – and those same five clients, along with three more client data cards and the Ricky Dempsey auctioneer contact card. All deleted.'

'What kind of files?'

'It'll be easier if I can talk you through it.' She handed me a memory stick.

•

During the six months prior to her death, according to what Pauline had found, it looked like Mandy had processed a number of residential mortgage applications. Once these had been completed, the file information and client names had been deleted from the case management system but the associated transactions remained on the accounts system. Funds had come in to MLC from the bank and been paid out to the client, less a sum for costs and necessary expenses, called outlays – such as Land Registry fees. The mortgages appeared to have been registered and the title deeds sent on to the bank in the usual way. Though Mandy didn't do that kind of work usually – residential conveyancing was done in a different department, Patricia Dillane's – on the face of it, there was nothing unethical or untoward about any of the files.

I thanked Pauline for her work and asked her to keep digging. She said that she would. Then she asked, 'What do you think this is about?'

'I'll read the files properly later,' I said. 'See what questions they raise and what answers they give. Though, actually, there's only one that's worth anything.'

'What's that?'

'Why did Mandy delete them?'

87

THE NORMAL WORLD CONTINUED TO TURN.
People were seeking me out – clients, other solicitors – and I
had an Inbox full of unanswered emails. With Tina's help, I did
what I could to service my workaday duties, dashing off a pile
of 'I'll-be-back-to-you-ASAP' messages before I left the office.
But I wasn't thinking about Tina, or my job or any of that, now.
I was in my alternate reality, the one where the only thing that
mattered was finding out who'd killed Mandy. And proving that
it wasn't Davy.

Which is why I was in the lobby of the Finertech building,
standing in front of the reception desk. 'Finn Fitzpatrick solicitor
from MLC,' I said. 'I'm here to see Owen McCormack.'

'Do you have an appointment?'

'I met him on Saturday at Mandy Breslin's funeral,' I said.
'He'll want to talk to me.'

'So does that mean that you have an appointment? Because if
you haven't I'm afraid—'

'Hmm. You're afraid? Interesting.'

The receptionist was gratifyingly flustered by my response.
'Well, what I'm saying is that the rule is, no one gets into the
Finertech building without an appointment. No one *ever* gets

to see the chief without an appointment. We have a very strict access policy. I'm going to have to ask you to leave. Besides, Mr McCormack is a very busy—'

'Just tell him I'm here,' I said. 'Trust me. When he hears my name, he'll see me.'

•

I had no idea if that was true. There was a ninety-five per cent chance it wasn't. My other idea was that I'd phone McCormack on his personal mobile – I'd copied the number from his records on the case management system – and ask him if he'd been having an affair with Mandy.

But this current approach, if it worked, was better. I'd both hear and see his response to my question. The receptionist looked me up and down a few times, and thought for a while. I stayed where I was and tried to project non-aggressive assertiveness and confidence. In the end, he concluded that there was a tiny chance that kicking me out would be the wrong thing to do.

'I'll tell his office you're here, Miss, em …?'

'Fitzpatrick,' I said. 'Finn Fitzpatrick. Solicitor. From MLC.'

He picked up the desk phone, simultaneously gesturing for me to move back from the desk and take a seat.

•

I waited. And waited. And waited some more. I thought about the McInerneys, about how they'd waited for Mandy on the same morning that she'd been found dead, and how, though I knew it had something to do with the house at Alysson Villas, I was no closer to finding out what they'd wanted of her or why they'd gone to Dublin. I checked my phone. Their story had slipped down the news websites, perhaps at Lenihan's behest. It was something I could ask Sadie about, but I didn't want to talk to her until after I'd met McCormack. She might know about him by now – Ed might have told her his name. If she knew, there was no reason for me to be here except I had to see him for myself. Locate a speck of truth in a sea of lies.

After forty minutes, my bluff was looking like it hadn't paid off. Another ten minutes later, when a uniformed security guard emerged from the lift, I reckoned that things could go either way. I stood and readied myself to sprint for the door in case they went badly. Instead, the uniform said, 'Come with me.'

88

THE ONLY UNUSUAL THING ABOUT OWEN McCormack's office was its size. It had all the accoutrements you'd expect with a successful tech entrepreneur – a fancy desk; a boardroom table; a selection of expensive-looking chairs; a couple of designer sofas; a beanbag or three; digital screens in various sizes – but it was ridiculously large, taking up most of the top floor of the Finertech building. The walls were floor-to-ceiling glass and, on a clear day, would have allowed an uninterrupted panorama over the river, and on further, towards the harbour. The items of furniture were gathered together loosely at one end. The door through which I'd entered was at the other. At a push, the carpeted space in between could have accommodated a game of tennis.

Standing beside his desk, McCormack wore an open-necked blue shirt, tucked in, and charcoal slim-fitting trousers with polished black leather shoes. He radiated energy and power. Ed hadn't been lying, I decided instantly. This was the other man. It had to be.

'We met briefly on Saturday,' I said.

'Say what you have to say,' he said.

'I saw you together,' I said. I couldn't be fully sure, but

I reckoned now wasn't the time for nuanced discussion. McCormack made no response. 'It was a Thursday night in June,' I went on. 'You were in her TT, in the passenger seat.'

He turned away and gazed out the window into the grey beyond. The city lay below us and I knew that there were other tall buildings in the vicinity – the Elysian Tower, One Albert Quay – but so thick was the mist that nothing else was visible. We might have been the last two people in the world.

'Get out,' he said.

I held my ground and, after a time, he turned to face me. He was in tears. 'I asked you to leave,' he said.

'I don't think you want me to go,' I said.

McCormack said nothing.

I said, 'For now this is between us. Though it won't be for long. Even if the guards don't know about you quite yet, it's a matter of hours at most.'

'Apart from what you think you saw, what do you think you know?'

'That it was serious,' I said. 'And that you loved her very much.'

'Who told you that?' McCormack asked.

'You did.'

89

WE MOVED TO THE SEATING AREA AND TOOK A
sofa each. McCormack put his left hand over his eyes briefly.
Then he took it away and looked straight at me. 'I know I'm
going to be a suspect.'

'You can take it that you will be. Though if you have an alibi
for that Sunday night …?' If he had, he wasn't saying. Which
made me think he didn't. 'Tell about you and Mandy,' I said.

'Why should I tell you anything?'

'How did you two meet?' I asked. I hadn't answered his
question, but it was a fair one. None of this was my business. By
rights, he should have thrown me out, or never agreed to see me
in the first place. But there's something I've noticed about the
bereaved – mostly, they want to talk about the dead person. It
turned out McCormack did too.

'We didn't meet in person,' he said. 'Not at first. Not for a
long time. She was recommended by a valued senior employee
of mine. Orla Keenan. I believe you know her?'

Davy's sister. *This* was where she worked? Small wonder that
she hadn't been keen to give up the name of Mandy's lover. And
that she was so down on Ed.

'I do,' I said.

'I was taking some personal funds out of the company. I needed some place to put them that would be tax efficient and at the same time easy to manage, with minimum input and time from me. My focus is on the company always, not on the money I make from it. Money matters if you don't have it. It's less important when you have a lot. The trick is to keep as much of it as you can. And to make it your servant, not your master.'

He paused. I reckoned he was used to having people hanging on his every pronouncement but I let the mini TED talk go unacknowledged and waited for him to start talking again.

After a time, he did: 'I emailed Mandy initially. After that we talked on the phone. I liked working with her. After a few months, things got more personal, we became something like friends — not real friends, we still hadn't met — but friendly, I guess. I was travelling a lot. I looked forward to talking to her from whatever hotel room I was in. Facetime mostly, if she had documents to go through with me. It was easier. Sometimes I'd show her the view from my window on my phone, that kind of thing. When we finally did meet, a very long time later, we knew each other so well that …' He paused, smiled ruefully. 'The rest is history,' he said. He sat back on the sofa with a finality that suggested that, as far as he was concerned, the conversation was over.

As far as I was concerned, he wasn't getting away with that. 'When did your relationship with Mandy become sexual?'

'Jesus Christ,' he said.

'Think of it as practice,' I said. 'The guards aren't going to let you off with drawing a tasteful veil over what came next.'

'That doesn't mean I have to tell you.'

I shrugged, let the silence do its thing.

'She was reluctant to take it further,' he said.

'Because you were her client.'

'Yes, that was big for her,' he said.

'The ethics of it and all that,' I said.

'Right,' he said. 'And she'd never been unfaithful before …'

Ed had told a different story. 'Did Mandy tell you that?'

'She did, but she didn't have to,' he said. 'It was obvious.'

'Obvious how?'

'The way she was,' he said. 'We did a lot of talking first – months and months, years of it actually – and Mandy was … shy, I guess. In the beginning.'

Shy and Mandy were two words I'd never expected to hear in the same sentence.

'Once she said yes, though, when we moved our relationship onto that level, there was no going back for either of us. We knew. We both just knew.'

'When was that?'

'She wanted to wait until after Christmas.'

'So we're talking about January of this year?' Ed had told me that the affair had been going on for much longer, a couple of years at least. From what Owen McCormack was saying, it had been – emotionally at least.

'Yes.'

'Where did you—'

'My house, usually,' he said. 'And I have a small studio apartment in this building, on the floor below this – there's a separate access route from here down to it. Very private. Occasionally, we used hotels. Not often. She didn't like … well, you know how small Cork is.'

'When did Ed find out?'

'He didn't know a thing until she told him they were done as a couple.'

'When was that?'

'July,' McCormack said. 'She wanted to wait until the kids were on school holidays. They went away as a family to the south of France for two weeks at the start of the month.'

'How did you feel about that? Her going away for all that time with another man?'

'Not great,' he said. 'But she hadn't had sex with him for years, so—'

'You sure about that?' I asked.

'One hundred per cent,' he said. His voice was hard and too loud.

'So it's July. They're back from holidays,' I said. 'Does she tell Ed and the kids?'

He looked away. 'Just Ed,' he said. 'He, em ... persuaded her to give him time. Until September.'

'Not good,' I said.

'No,' he said. 'But it was okay. We had the rest of our lives.'

'You weren't afraid she'd change her mind?'

'No!' he said. 'Not in the slightest. Ed was a womaniser and a drinker. He didn't love her, and he sure as hell didn't respect her. The way we saw it, we had another eight weeks to plan our future. This ...' He stood and spread his arms wide. 'This football pitch of an office was going to be for the two of us. Partitioned, of course, Mandy would have needed her own space. She was joining the company as my chief counsel. Joining the board of Finertech too. Leaving MLC. They never appreciated her anyway – Gabriel, Dermot Lyons, none of them. And then ...'

'The unthinkable happened.'

'Unthinkable, yes,' he said. 'Unimaginable.'

'Tell me about your contact with Mandy on the day of the murder.'

'What are you asking?'

'Did you see her? Talk to her?'

'Both,' he said. 'She called to my place, as was her habit on a Sunday morning, on her way to Douglas to do the grocery shopping. I live just off the Douglas Road. Down a lane. Detached. Secure. Completely private.'

'What happened?'

'What do you think? We did what we usually did when we hadn't seen each other for a day or two. Except neither of us knew that it would be the last time we made love. I keep thinking about that. If only I could've done something to change what came later.'

'What time did Mandy leave?'

'Around noon – 12.15 or so.'

'You said she often visited on Sunday mornings. Was anything different this time?'

'Not really,' McCormack said. 'She was a little worried about something. A work thing. It didn't seem like it was major. She was going to be leaving the firm soon anyway, so—'

'Had she told anyone at MLC, do you know?'

'No. She was definite about that. She said the shit was going to hit the fan when she did, and she needed to have her own ducks in a row first. Her priority was the kids, making sure they were okay. She was amazingly protective of them, she wanted no one at MLC to know before they did. And she was working hard on getting Ed on board with the separation too. Getting him to face up to it. Engage his own solicitor. Money wasn't going to be an issue. She was going to pay him off, whatever it took.'

'What did you do for the rest of Sunday?'

'Went for a run. Did some work. Nothing much.'

'So you were alone on Sunday night?'

'Yes, I was.'

'When was the last time you talked to her?'

'Early afternoon – she rang me as she was driving home; I called her again later, around nine, or a little after it, but I couldn't reach her. I know now why. She was probably ...' He welled up again, but we both knew that the later call could have been insurance. McCormack had been Mandy's lover and he had no alibi. His tears, real or fake, meant nothing.

'Did Mandy use her regular mobile to talk to you?'

'She had a second. Just since January. Before that, we talked on Facetime. At work sometimes. Late at night, mostly, after the kids were in bed. Her from her home study. It was only when things got physical, when we needed to arrange meetings, that she got the other phone.'

'You know the guards are going to need that number.'

'I imagine they will.'

'Have they talked to you yet?'

'No.'

'You need a solicitor,' I said. 'It's not up to me to say but in my opinion, he or she may well advise you that it'll go better for you if you're the one who informs them of your involvement. And you shouldn't delay, if that's the way you want to go.'

'So I understand. When I got the message that you were waiting to see me, I knew any hope I had of remaining out of this was gone. I've already put the wheels in motion. As we speak, my lawyer is arranging a discreet disclosure of … whatever – all of this that I've told you. Including Mandy's second phone number. He's warned me that when the cops find out – which will be any minute now – they're going to be all over me like a nasty blue rash.'

'He's not wrong,' I said.

•

Everything McCormack had told me was plausible. I believed that he loved Mandy, and that he wanted to spend the rest of his life with her. But I remembered the look of terror on her face. What might he have done to her if she'd changed her mind about him? About all of it?

90

IN THE TWILIGHT, I HEADED WEST. THE RAIN AND storm had passed. In the aftershock, a ghostly stillness had fallen on the city. All was quiet but for the light buzz of late-evening traffic, and the irregular plash of the river against the stone quays and the wooden buffers that were used to prevent ships being battered at their moorings in the days when they sailed this far upstream.

On reaching Izz Cafe on George's Quay, I went inside and ordered – warm flatbread, fresh from the oven, a portion of their silky home-made hummus and a Palestinian coffee, fragrant with cardamom. Then, on a sheet of paper, I set down the differences between what Ed had told me – about the length of the relationship and Mandy's alleged previous affairs – and what McCormack had, which included the bombshell about Mandy's plans to leave MLC and become Finertech's chief counsel. Ed was a proven liar – most significantly, he had lied about having an alibi. His credibility was in tatters and as a result, I was inclined to believe much, even all, of what McCormack had told me.

But that didn't mean that McCormack hadn't killed Mandy, or that Ed had, or hadn't. Ed's lies could be explained away as a misguided, scattergun attempt to direct the finger of blame away from himself. He was trying to be too clever, and his tactics wouldn't work. As I say to clients all the time, you tell the truth for two reasons: the first because it's the right thing to do; the second because it's easy to remember. Besides which, if you get caught out in one lie, it casts everything else you've said into doubt.

The focus of the garda investigation would narrow for now onto the two men in Mandy's life – her husband Ed and her lover Owen McCormack. It occurred to me that I needed to doublecheck that Ed had told Sadie about McCormack. And that I only had McCormack's word that his solicitor would contact Coughlan's Quay. If he had, Sadie would be pursuing that lead right now.

Just in case, I texted her: *Has Ed told you the lover's name? Has a solicitor been in touch?*

She replied: *Yes + yes. Also WTF is going on? Why are you not returning my calls?*

Been busy. Sorry. I'll call you when I can, I replied.

•

I knew who the dark-haired man was now, but I still had so many unanswered questions. What Davy's involvement was. What he was hiding from me. The Ricky Dempsey connection. The deleted computer files. The McInerneys. And, most puzzling of all, perhaps – what Mandy was doing in the house where she was found. If I could figure that out, maybe other parts of the mystery might fall into place.

I leaned my head against the wall and shut my eyes. For a few minutes, I breathed deeply and let the music fly me far, far away. Then I threw back the rest of my coffee and left.

91

A PALL OF GLOOM HUNG OVER 3 ALYSSON Villas. Tails of blue and white plastic tape dangled limply from the tall steel barriers that had been erected as a temporary fence, blocking access to the front garden and the public footpath in front. Any prospect of getting a closer look was quashed by the sight of a single uniformed male garda, cold-looking in his 'GARDA' emblazoned bomber jacket, stationed on the road outside.

'I thought ye'd be finished with the house by now,' I said to him.

'Would be except for the students. There's a worry some of them might gain access and start posting sensitive photographs on social media.'

'They'd never, would they?'

'You've no idea, girl,' he said. 'When you think how many of them were around in the area the night of the murder, and not one of them saw or heard anything. So much for Neighbourhood Watch.'

'That's students for you,' I said. 'No danger of them doing any actual study, mind you.'

He laughed. 'You from around here?'

'From over along,' I said. Looking around, I noticed the lights were on in the upper storey of the big house at the end. I remembered what Sadie had told me. 'Is the old man home from hospital?'

'I don't know,' the young garda said. 'I saw a woman earlier on, is all.'

'The daughter must be home from England,' I said. 'She was due.' I dredged the name Sadie had given me from the cloudy depths of my brain. 'Polly ...'

'Do you know her?'

'Her dad, the old man, was a ... GP,' I said. 'That's right. Doctor ... Keyes. Retired. Sick in hospital. I'll call into Polly now and see if I can do anything to help.'

92

THERE WAS A DOOR-SIZED WOODEN PEDESTRIAN
gate, black paint peeling from it in strips, set into the eight-
foot wall. Pushing it open, I went up the short slanting path
to what, though unlit, was clearly the rear entrance. I felt
for a doorbell or a knocker. Finding none, I switched on my
phone light and made my way around the side to the front,
past overgrown shrubs and ivy, the twiggy remnants of a
clematis clawing at me. A half-hearted security light flickered
on belatedly as I approached the front door. A white Ford
Ka sat in the driveway, where the gravel was weedy and
untended. 'Alysson' was large, a half-timbered, arts and crafts
style Edwardian, which would once have sat grandly amidst
spacious gardens, before the houses of Alysson Villas had been
built. The remaining outside space would still have been ample
for most modern families' needs, but it had been decades since
any child had played on the neglected lawn.

'I live round the corner and down a bit,' I said, which was
true, though a fifteen- or twenty-minute walk away would have
been more accurate. 'Finn's the name. You're Polly, aren't you?'

'Yes, but—'

'Just wondering if I could lend a hand,' I said. 'Looks like you're busy.'

She glanced behind her at an array of cardboard boxes. 'Oh, I am,' she said. 'Swamped. But I'm not going to do any more tonight … em …' She was in her mid-fifties and had acquired a slight English accent. She looked like London was right for her in a way that Cork had never been. Over there, she would have had no hesitation in sending me away. Back home, she was less socially sure.

'You look like you could do with a sit down,' I said. 'Why don't I make us a cup of tea?'

•

I rinsed the pot and mugs several times with boiling water and used two spoons of loose leaves that smelled fresh enough. The tea drawn, I joined Polly at the oil-cloth-covered kitchen table.

'When did you get back?'

'Sunday afternoon,' she said. 'I've been coming once every month or six weeks for the last year-and-a-half, at the weekends, but I had to sort out a few things at work before I came this time. I knew it'd be a longer visit, and that I'd need to be around on weekdays. Everything shuts here at the weekend. I'm on my own, you know, no brothers or sisters to help.'

'Is he …?'

'No immediate danger. But he's never coming back here,' she said. 'Needs residential care. That's what they say. Even the agency we've been using up to now.'

'What were they like?'

'Reliable. Good. It worked well for a long time. He always

hated the idea of a nursing home. But I'll be around to settle him in at least. I'm trying to pick out some familiar objects for his room at Mount Desert. He's out in the Regional at the moment but he's ready for discharge.'

'Have you got an Enduring Power of Attorney done? Sorry, should've mentioned: I'm a solicitor, so—'

'He did one years ago but he's fine mentally. Which is a blessing, I suppose – except that he knows where he's going; that he can't come home. That he can't manage anymore.' She paused, 'And you're a solicitor? How interesting.'

'It can be,' I said.

'Anyway, the next step is to sell the house. I got it valued earlier in the week.'

'Who did you use?'

'Random,' she said. 'I found an estate agent's flyer in the hall. Rang him and he came out the same day. I nearly had a canary when he told me that he'd done a valuation of no. 3 – the murder house – recently. Said he'd dropped cards in all the surrounding houses too. It put me off, to be honest. That link.'

'Do you know anything about no. 3?'

'No – I'm gone thirty-five years now. A single lady lived there – elderly – when I was young. Miss Buckley. Josephine? Joanna? Something like that. Dead twenty-plus years. Vacant since.'

'Did the estate agent say how he came to do the valuation on no. 3?'

'I didn't ask. I didn't warm to him. And I don't know if he's the best choice. He doesn't sell much in this area. I might get a second valuer to take a look. Or it might be wiser to wait until all this dies down before selling. I don't know, though. The main entrance is from Magazine Road, and that's the postal address. If we changed the name of the house from "Alysson", or used a street number, people mightn't clock that we're so close to Alysson Villas, where the murder … That's what the estate agent suggested, but it's hard to know what's best.'

'The estate agent. What was his name?'

'Ricky Dempsey.'

93

TINA'S TITLE SEARCH HAD ALREADY ESTABLISHED
as a certainty what Charlene McInerney had told me in Cardiff:
that the owner of 3 Alysson Villas was Josepha Buckley, Jerry
McInerney's aunt with whom he'd lived when he was left an
orphan, and that she was still registered as owner. Now Polly
Keyes had told me that she'd been dead for twenty years. All of
which went some way towards explaining why the house was
almost derelict, but brought me no closer to understanding why
Mandy had died there.

It was after 10 p.m. Realistically, there was no more to be
done until morning. But I was over-caffeinated and wound up.
If I went to bed, I wouldn't sleep. And what good was it having
Ricky Dempsey's mobile phone number if I wasn't prepared to
use it?

•

He picked up immediately, before the phone had a chance to
ring. I heard chattering voices and the thump-thump of a sound
system.

'Hah,' he said. 'I thought I'd heard the last of you.'

'You can't get rid of me that easily.'

Dempsey laughed. 'What I can I do you for?' he asked. He was slurring his words.

'We need to talk about 3 Alysson Villas,' I said. No reply came, but the background noise lessened. He'd moved to a quieter place. He was interested. 'You did a valuation there recently,' I said.

'Even if I did, there's nothing illegal in that,' Dempsey said. 'It's what I do for a crust, in case you hadn't noticed. Value houses. Sell 'em. Make money. Ka-ching!'

'Was that the plan for 3 Alysson Villas?'

'I know nothing about the plans for that house,' he said. He laughed again. He was definitely drunk.

'I have a witness who says you do.'

'Witness? What? Who? I don't know a fucking thing about …' He lapsed into silence.

'Who asked you to value it?'

'A solicitor,' he said. He seemed more confident.

'What was the solicitor's name?'

'I'm surprised that you of all people have to ask.'

'What do you mean?'

'Considering you work with her. *Worked*, I mean. Before she—'

'You're saying it was Mandy Breslin.'

'That's what I'm saying.'

'Can I call out to see you in the morning? To talk about this?'

'By all means,' he said. 'Though I'm in Marbella on a golfing trip so—'

'You left the country?'

'I'll have you know this was planned for fucking ages. I can't help it if I'm not there when the guards from Coughlan's Quay call for a visit.'

'Did they?'

'Indeed and they did. I know you're the stupid bitch that gave them my name. Except I wasn't there, was I? So that'll teach you.'

'When are you back?'

'The weekend, I'd say. Definitely. Back in the office bright 'n' early Monday morning.' He giggled. Then he said, 'Listen to me, pet, would you ever get it into your thick head that I know fuck-all about that poor woman and fuck-all about that house, other than having the misfortune to be in it a few days before she got killed. I got an email from Mandy. She asked me to do the valuation on 3 Alysson Villas. I did it. All in a day's work. Normal. If it wasn't, why would I paper the rest of the area with flyers, advertising that I'd been around?'

It was a fair point. 'You worked for her before?'

'Loads o' times.'

'But you told me you never met her.'

'I didn't.'

'How is that possible?'

'I hardly ever meet solicitors. She was like the rest of ye. She communicated by post or email. Email mostly. Phone sometimes.'

Dempsey was right. Everything was done remotely. Other than accidentally, I couldn't recall the last time I'd met an estate agent in person. 'You rang her last week. What was that about?'

'I don't remember. I make a lot of calls. Em, not about this, though, I don't think. Maybe one of the other valuations.'

'What other valuations?'

'Nothing really. Easy drive-bys. Remortgages. For banks. You know. Loan-to-value ratios. Convince the fucking bank that a house is worth "x", so that it's okay for Joe and Josephine Soap to mortgage themselves up to the hilt so that they can pretend to convert their attic or put on an extension, and that the house will be worth "y" when they do.'

'Pretend?'

'Oops! Well, o' course, some of them do what they say they're doing, but a lot of the time they're using some of the money for other things. The son or daughter's drug habit. Paying off the car loan. Credit card. The big wedding. Or maybe gambling.' He laughed. 'I s'pose those last two are the same thing. What I'm saying is that there's no harm in it, like.'

'No harm at all. Except that for some reason Mandy ended up dead. What do you know about her murder?'

Dempsey's reply was swift and unambiguous. He hung up.

THURSDAY

THURSDAY

94

FOR THE SECOND MORNING IN A ROW, I WENT
to Mandy's office. This time I left the door ajar and switched
on the computer. It huffed and puffed into life and I typed in
the password, and waited for the email programme to open.
When it did, I typed Dempsey's name into the search box. I
found nothing. The same thing happened when I put in the
email address that I'd hurriedly located on his website. There
were no emails from Ricky Dempsey to Mandy Breslin. Either
Dempsey had lied or Mandy had gone through her Inbox and
Sent items and laboriously deleted every communication that
she had with him.

There was no mention of Dempsey on the case management
system – I'd checked that previously. But there was a chance that
the emails from Dempsey to Mandy hadn't come to her directly.
I buzzed Kathleen.

'Strange thing happened,' I said. 'I was talking to Ricky
Dempsey, the auctioneer who phoned for Mandy in the days
before she died. He says he did a few property valuations for her,
that he emailed them to her. But I can't find anything. Might he
have sent them to you?'

'I'm nearly sure not … No, hang on. Let me see.' I could hear
her keyboard clacking. Then she said, 'You're in her room.'

'Yes.'

'I got such a shock when I saw her name come up on my phone. For a second I forgot she was—'

'Oh Kathleen I'm so sorry. I didn't think.'

'It's not your fault. I'm in a fog. Barely know what day it is.' Then she said, 'There's no email to or from Ricky Dempsey. I knew there wasn't – I was only double-checking.'

'It's weird,' I said. 'He sounded so certain.'

'Well if he *is* so sure, why don't you ask him to send them through again?'

'He's in Marbella,' I said.

'Oh dear.'

'I could ask his secretary.'

'You could,' Kathleen said. 'And what are you hoping to find?'

'I don't know,' I said. 'Maybe something. Maybe.'

'This Dempsey, what's he like?'

'Unpleasant is putting it mildly. There's not a jury in the land would acquit him.'

'Of what?'

I laughed. 'Take your pick,' I said.

'Hmmm. Finn, you know what I'm going to say next.'

'I do,' I said. 'You're a bigger worrier than my mother.'

•

After managing to escape Kathleen's ministrations as politely as I could, I rang Dempsey's office. The secretary sounded cross. She asked why I couldn't wait till Monday, like everyone else was going to have to.

'It's just with Mandy gone, we're trying to make sure that we follow up on her work properly. And I was talking to Ricky last night. He didn't seem to think there'd be a problem …' He hadn't said a word either way, because I hadn't told him I'd be calling his office. Though, to be fair, I hadn't known myself that I would be, not then.

'I'll see what I can do,' she said. 'If I get a chance. Which at this moment in time is a big "if". What email address do you want me to forward them to?'

I gave her mine. 'I'm grateful for your help,' I said. 'Especially as you're so busy.'

'September is always mad,' she said. 'He never normally goes away this month. Why he decided to fly off on a last-minute trip is beyond me.'

'When did he go?'

'Tuesday.'

Dempsey had told me that the trip was planned well in advance. I'd had my doubts about that. This confirmed it. Though I couldn't yet see the full picture, his links to the murder scene, and the fact that he'd skipped the country the day after he met me at the Shandon View house, meant that, logically, he'd moved to the top of my suspect list.

It was Dempsey after all. Not Davy. I should have been happy. But my gut was paying no heed to logic. And so I wasn't either.

95

I HANDED €20 IN CASH TO THE WOMAN BEHIND the glass partition and got a receipt in return. I gave her the details I had – a name and address; an approximate date, give or take five years. Then I took a seat. Ten minutes later the same woman gave me a copy of Josepha Buckley's death certificate. She had died twenty-two years ago. I wrote the date of death on the back of my hand, and placed the envelope and the receipt in my handbag.

It was shortly after noon as I walked back up Adelaide Street across the part of the city that's known as 'the Marsh'. It's as if Corkonians are saying, 'We know Cork is marshy, like – but this bit is *really* marshy.' True to its name, in the great flood of 2009, all around here was under deep water, as was most of the city. By some kind of miracle, no one had died. Since then, the population of the city had been convulsed by the stalled humongous urban wall-building and water-pumping plan that the Office of Public Works claimed would ensure it wouldn't happen again. Building a tidal barrier was too expensive, they said. Until sea levels rose, presumably – they'd have to build one then. Either that, or call in King Canute.

I passed the small green rectangular park, its benches empty as usual – I could never understand why – and arrived, ultimately, at the courthouse on Washington Street. I made my way to the basement via the door underneath the grand limestone steps. In the Probate Office, at the end of the corridor, I completed a PAS1 form and parted with another €20.

But there could be no instant results this time: the information I was seeking would take a day or two to come through. I left the Probate Office and went back to work, oblivious as yet to the fact that what I would eventually discover would change my view of everything I thought I knew about Mandy Breslin.

96

I'D SUCCESSFULLY MANAGED TO AVOID RUNNING into Hugo Woulfe since my ill-advised visit to his house on Tuesday night. I'd been going through the motions: doing the necessary to move my work on; hardly talking to Tina; barely keeping in touch with Sadie. I'd been hiding inside my investigation. Mostly, I'd been hiding from myself, from how I truly felt.

I hadn't spoken to Davy for days, and I was lonelier than I'd ever been. But I kept seeing Mandy's terror, the time after the Dolly Parton concert when she'd seen me with him and the morning after in my office. Clicking onto his Facebook page, I saw that he'd cancelled more classes. He was running out of road. Vague apologies and 'something came up at the last minute' excuses would cut it for only so long. He'd been upset and shocked when I'd asked him about his whereabouts on the night of Mandy's murder. But he'd known that I was frantic – he could have said where he was that Sunday night, set my mind at rest. Instead, he'd walked off without giving me an answer. Our relationship had been built on not asking too many questions of each other. He'd always claimed that he wanted more openness. Yet the one time I tested him, cracks appeared.

Thinking, overthinking, about Davy was doing me no good. I slotted the memory stick that Pauline Doyle had given me into my desktop. I made a list of the properties that Mandy had mortgaged for clients in the six months prior to her death and then deleted from the case management system. All were on the northside. One by one, I clicked into the 'Documents' section of each file and opened every valuation. All of them had been done by Ricky Dempsey.

It made some sense that Mandy had used Dempsey to value the houses for mortgage purposes. As a bank-approved valuer, that was his job. But it wasn't hers – it made no sense whatsoever that she had been doing that kind of work; even less, that she'd deleted the files as soon as she'd finished them.

Concentrating on the five files that were fully readable, I went through the procedure followed on each of them. Everything looked completely standard, from compliance with anti-money-laundering obligations – full sets of scanned identity documents for five different clients and proofs of address – down to the payment out of the funds and the filing of the title deeds with the bank once the mortgages were registered. I didn't know what any of it had to do with Mandy's murder, but there had to be some kind of a thread binding everything together.

I went back to the list of properties and mapped out a route.

97

BEFORE I LEFT THE BUILDING, I DROPPED INTO Tina's office. She was at her desk. Her smile on seeing me turned to a frown when she noticed my coat on my arm. She looked over meaningfully at Kathleen, a few desks away. I could tell that they'd been talking about me, and that Kathleen had told Tina of her concerns. Kathleen nodded and returned to her work, leaving Tina to say whatever it was they'd agreed on. I handed her a yellow Post-it.

'I'm waiting for the result of a Probate Office search on this,' I said. 'Could you phone in an hour please? See if you can hurry it along?'

Tina took the note and stuck it on the corner of her screen. She spoke quietly. 'Should you be doing this? Isn't it the guards' job to—'

'I'll explain later,' I said. I paused. 'Em, I have to go out for a while.'

A sigh and another look exchanged with Kathleen. I wanted to tell the two of them that what I did with my time was none of their business but that wasn't strictly true, especially in Tina's case. 'I'll talk to you tomorrow,' I said. 'I promise.'

'I'm holding you to that,' Tina said. 'Tomorrow we talk.'

98

IT WAS AT LEAST FIFTY YEARS OLD AND IN NEED of repair. Moss dotted the faded roof tiles. Grey net curtains sagged behind grimy windows. An anti-water charges poster clung tenaciously to the inside of the downstairs bay, even though that campaign had long since ended in success for the protesters. This was the fourth house I'd seen on my trip around the northside, and I was sensing a pattern that added up to: 'long-term rental, uninvolved landlord'.

I'd received no response when I'd rung and knocked at the first three properties. I wasn't surprised. It was the middle of the working day. I'd shoved a note and my phone number through each of the letterboxes. If I was lucky, one of the tenants might call. Most likely, nobody would. Curiously, even though the mortgages had been for property improvements – two attic conversions and a rear extension, according to the forms that Pauline had managed to retrieve from the files – there was no sign of any recent building work.

This house was like the others, except for two important details. A waste skip, half-full, stood in the driveway. And the front door was wide open.

'Anyone home?'

A woman who looked to be in her early sixties, strong and fit-looking in dirty blue jeans and an old wine-coloured, round-necked jumper emerged from the back of the house. She ran her hand through her cropped silver hair.

'I'm looking for the owner,' I said. 'I—'

'I'll stop you before you go any further,' she said. 'They're gone.'

'Who are?'

'The tenants, who do you think? I got rid of them finally. That last shower cured me of being a landlord, I can tell you. This place is going on the market as soon as it's cleared out.'

'You're not going ahead with the extension, so?'

'What extension?'

'The new kitchen and utility room. The reason you got the mortgage.'

'You've got the wrong woman,' she said.

'This is 13 Moy Place, isn't it?'

'Yeah but—'

'Are you Sheila Miller?'

'Yes …' she said slowly. Then she said, 'You never gave me your name.'

I handed her a business card. 'I'm Finn Fitzpatrick, from MLC Solicitors,' I said.

'MLC? I normally deal with Dermot Lyons. Did he send you?'

'Let me show you something,' I said.

•

I took her through the remortgage and valuation forms.

'This house is mortgage-free,' Sheila Miller said. 'It was supposed to be my pension.'

But the paperwork showed that she'd recently obtained a loan for €85,000.

'That wasn't me,' she said.

'Isn't that your signature?'

'It looks like it, but no, I don't think it is.'

'And that's your PPS number? Your date of birth?'

'Yes, yes, both,' Sheila Miller said.

'Did you use MLC when you bought this house?'

'Of course, Dermot's been my solicitor for years but he passed me on to someone else for this. Patricia Dillane – I only saw her once or twice. To sign contracts and then again for about five minutes to sign the deed after I got the keys. She had an assistant, some young girl who was in contact with me as well, but …' She paused. 'What does all this mean?'

'I can't be sure yet,' I said.

'But what do you think?'

I thought carefully about what to say next. I was still concerned about damage limitation for the firm at that stage. I had no clue then how irrelevant that would seem later.

'In my opinion, Sheila, it would be a good idea if you came into the office as soon as possible to talk this through.'

'Talk what through?'

'That's what I'm trying to figure out. Why don't I take your number, and someone from the office will ring you tomorrow to arrange a time?'

She called it out to me and I put it into my phone. Then she said, 'Maybe it's the guards I should be talking to.'

'If you want,' I said.

She thought for a while. 'No,' she said. 'I'll wait.'

She'd grown frail in the short time I'd spent with her. I wanted to reassure her; to tell her that it was all a big misunderstanding. But the more I'd learned, the more certain I was. This was no misunderstanding, no mistake.

This was fraud.

99

IT WAS AFTER 5 P.M. ON THE WAY BACK TO THE
office, I rang Ricky Dempsey's secretary and asked her again to
forward me the emails between him and Mandy. 'Absolutely
not,' she said. 'I'm way too busy for that.' I did a U-turn and
swung my car in the direction of Blackpool. When I got there, I
threw my car on the footpath, inches from the front door.

Dempsey's secretary had her coat on and her keys in her
hand. She didn't greet me. She knew who I was and why I was
there.

'If I were you, I'd send me those emails and I'd send them
now,' I said. 'You seem to have forgotten that a woman has
been murdered. And the guards are going to want to interview
Ricky when he comes back from Marbella on Monday. He
can't dodge them a second time.' She looked shifty.

'He *is* coming back, isn't he?' I asked.

'He said today he might stay a bit longer. And he warned me
to—'

'What?'

'He said that when he was talking to you on the phone, he
was after a few drinks and that he might have given you the
wrong impression about a few things. He said that if you called,

I shouldn't talk to you; that I was to give you nothing. He said to delete everything to do with Mandy Breslin as well.'

'Did you?'

'Not yet,' she said. 'It didn't seem right. Like you said, it's a murder investigation.'

'And you want to be on the right side.'

'Yeah,' she said. 'I know Ricky had nothing to do with it, he wouldn't, but …'

'Forward me the emails. As you're at it, print them as well. All of them. Now.'

She took off her coat.

•

On the way back to MLC, I rang Tina. What I'd learned about Mandy was too big for a phone conversation, but I asked about the probate search. She said that she'd phoned the office and that they'd said it would be ready at 9.15 in the morning.

'You're a miracle worker,' I said. 'I thought it'd be another couple of days.' I added: 'One more thing, Tina – could you put me through to Gabriel, please?'

•

'Don't go home, Gabriel,' I said. 'Wait for me.'

'Why?' he asked.

'I've got news. About Mandy.'

'What kind of news?'

'The bad kind.'

100

GABRIEL'S DOOR WAS AJAR. I HELD BACK AND observed him through the gap. Uncharacteristically still, he stood in the middle of the room, hands in his pockets, shoulders rounded. With his suit jacket undone and his tie loosened, he might have been the accused in a criminal trial, awaiting the jury's verdict. Behind me, I heard someone coming up the stairs. It was Dervla. She touched me on the elbow and said, 'It's time to get this over with, at long last.'

•

'I know what you're going to say,' Gabriel said. 'We both do.' He nodded in the direction of Dervla, now standing to his left. I stood facing them. After what I'd just heard from the two of them, I badly needed to sit down but I stayed where I was.

'I wanted to tell you sooner,' Dervla said. 'To tell the guards too. You probably guessed there was something we weren't saying.'

'I had,' I said. 'But not this. And not that you knew about it all along.'

'No,' Gabriel said. 'It must be something of a shock.'

'It surely is,' I said.

'Yes. So unlike her to get involved in something like this. But the human heart—'

That was too much for me. 'The human heart? For fuck sake, this is dishonesty on a grand scale.'

'Well, really,' Gabriel said. 'You do family law – I would have thought that this kind of thing is quite common.'

'What is?'

'Adultery.'

'Oh,' I said.

'My sister lives in Ballincurrig Park, just off the Douglas Road,' Dervla said. 'On her way home from mass every Sunday, she used to see Mandy driving into Owen McCormack's house. She never had to wait for the electric gates to open, so either she had her own remote control or he was watching out for her. It didn't take a genius to figure out what was going on. I told no one, apart from Gabriel. But after Mandy went missing, was found murdered, I said that we should tell the guards.'

I turned to Gabriel. 'You didn't want to?'

'Not unless it was relevant to her death,' he replied. 'That's why I tasked you with the report. You hardly knew Mandy, didn't work with her. You had the distance that was needed. And that's why I didn't sign off on the report. Why I kept my distance from the entire process.'

'I wanted to tell you,' Dervla said. 'I thought you deserved to know. That's why I was so unhappy that you were sending the report to the Law Society. That you'd been kept in the dark.'

'I do apologise,' Gabriel said. 'I have no excuse. Other than that I was trying to avoid scandal for the firm. And that I didn't want to lose McCormack as a client, obviously.' He paused. 'It sounds petty, I know.'

'It does, Gabriel, it does,' I said. 'But that's not why I called you.'

'You mean there's something else?' Dervla asked.

'There is,' I said. 'Something much, much worse.'

101

WE'D MOVED TO THE BOARDROOM, THE THREE OF us, and had been joined by Dermot Lyons and Patricia Dillane, the partner in charge of conveyancing. I gave them a summary of what I knew.

'All the houses were unmortgaged,' I said. 'Bought by existing clients of the office as rental investments. Mortgaging them was easy – the banks wouldn't have looked too closely at the security because of the loan-to-value ratio. Mandy was borrowing a relatively small percentage of the market value for legitimate home improvements, like extensions and attic conversions. She used faked estimates and invoices, I reckon, but she had the rest of the information she needed – title documents, copy passports and proofs of address, tax numbers – already on the purchase files here in the office. After that, all she needed was a good printer, a scanner, a few tweaks to out-of-date documents or addresses, a couple of rubber stamps and a compliant estate agent in the person of Ricky Dempsey. He handled the property valuations and quite possibly processed the mortgage applications on her behalf – though I haven't had time to confirm that last part yet.'

'You think he knew what was going on?' Patricia Dillane asked.

'I've read the emails between him and Mandy. He's definitely involved to some extent. And he would have been an ideal partner in the enterprise. As well as being an estate agent and a valuer, he's a mortgage broker too. Even if he wasn't getting a share of the fraud monies, he would've been paid for the valuations and received a commission from the bank on the mortgages he sold. Also, from talking to him, I believe that he's someone who's prepared to turn a blind eye. He made it quite clear to me that it wouldn't bother him if the borrowed money was used for something other than its stated purpose. So whether he knew, or whether Mandy was just using him and his amoral approach – his general fecklessness – I don't know.

'I haven't been able to ask him about any of these latest developments, because good old Ricky's currently playing golf in Marbella. He left the country the day after I confronted him about knowing Mandy. His secretary doesn't know when he'll be back. All of which points to him knowing that something wasn't kosher in his dealings with Mandy. Then again, the murder was a bit of a giveaway on that front too, so it's hard to say ...'

'Who else knows?' Lyons asked.

'Full details, only the people in this room. But Pauline Doyle knows a bit, she's been running IT searches for me, and Tina knows a few of the pieces, though not the big picture.'

'What about Kathleen?' Dervla asked.

'She told me that Dempsey rang the office looking for Mandy a couple of times, the Friday before her death. She logged the calls, as normal, thinking he was a new client. He probably contacted Mandy directly on her mobile most of the time. Kathleen says that she knows nothing about him other than those recent contacts.'

'How can that be?' Patricia Dillane asked. 'She would have to know. The loan papers, the valuations, any of the documents coming in would pass Kathleen's desk – wouldn't they?'

'In the normal way, yes,' I said. 'But the mortgage documents weren't processed via this firm. Mandy was using a different email address – mandy.breslin.mlc@gmail.com – so it only *looked* like an MLC transaction. She requested that all the bank paperwork, the mortgage packs and so on, went to that Gmail, as well as by post. The rental property addresses were used for the borrower's loan details and she set up fake emails for them too. The solicitor's address on all of the loan approvals that I've seen was this firm's name, followed by a post office box. Whether she ever collected the envelopes, I don't know. But she wouldn't have needed to if she had it all digitally.'

'So there's a chance that no one else knew about the … f-fraud?' Gabriel asked.

'I can't say,' I said. 'There's Dempsey, of course. His phone is switched off now, by the way, so I'm only assuming he's still in Spain. He's got to know the game is up. It was pure luck that I ran across his connection to 3 Alysson Villas. When I was talking to him on the phone about that, he mentioned other valuations that Mandy had requested for him. From those, and the deleted files that Pauline found on the system, and meeting Sheila Miller when I visited one of the property scam houses at 13 Moy Place, I was able to tie Mandy to the fraudulent mortgages. As for others knowing, there's Kelly Tobin, his secretary. She cooperated with me in the end, though I couldn't get her to say much. She says she knows nothing, but she might be trying to save her own skin.'

'Anyone else?' Lyons asked.

'Maybe someone on Mandy's team saw something, and didn't know what it was they were seeing. Or maybe someone in the Accounts department here? But according to the account records on the system, the mortgage funds were paid directly by online transfers from MLC's account to the client by Mandy herself – her reference is on the transfer anyway. I assume that she did it from her desktop, which wouldn't be that unusual?'

Patricia Dillane shook her head and said, 'It's a normal part of conveyancing practice. I do it every day of the week. It's fast and it's technological progress, of course, but the old days of cheques and bank drafts were a lot safer, in my opinion. Though they weren't fail-safe either, I suppose. You know, I was aware that Mandy was worried about something. She spoke to me a few weeks before her death. I couldn't in my wildest dreams have guessed what she was hiding.'

'People go to their solicitor,' I said. 'They trust us with huge amounts of personal information. The vast majority of the profession wouldn't dream of transgressing but, if a solicitor decides to abuse a client's trust, the reality is that he or she can. It's a criminal's dream and, in the short-to-medium term, they can hide what they've been doing. In Mandy's case, she used the insider knowledge she had about the clients.' I paused.

'But she went way beyond insider knowledge. The bank accounts she transferred the mortgage proceeds to were in the name of the house owner clients. The one owner I've spoken to directly – Sheila Miller – was adamant that she got no payment. Therefore, my working assumption is that, without the clients' knowledge, Mandy opened new bank accounts in their names, using their ID documents, and then accessed and operated those accounts herself.'

'Oh for Christ's sake,' Lyons said. 'That takes the biscuit. She's dead, at least. Was she working with someone else in the firm or not – that's the question we need to ask ourselves now.'

'I don't know, but it's at least possible that no one else in the firm saw or knew anything. If Ricky Dempsey's name hadn't cropped up accidentally, and if I hadn't followed that lead, I don't know when this whole thing would've been spotted.'

Patricia Dillane said, 'The missed mortgage payments might have raised the alarm but only if the property owner received a letter or letters from the bank. That may not have happened for quite some time, unless the tenants were assiduous in forwarding post, as presumably the mortgage address was also the property address. Worst case, the issue mightn't have emerged until someone went to sell one of the houses, and the dodgy charge showed up on the title.'

She went on, 'Property fraud is a growing problem, both here and across the water. The Property Registration Authority have set up an alert service, but very few house owners know about it or use it, as far as I can see. Criminals target vacant properties, or places that are rented longterm and that have no debt registered. They impersonate the owner, fake ID and tax numbers, and use the clear unburdened title to raise a mortgage, even to buy and sell.

'That's right,' I said. 'Mandy didn't have to invent all that much – she had the existing client information, along with scans and photocopies of their signatures to draw on; everything she needed was held on file because anti-money laundering legislation and Law Society regulations require them to be. A few certified copies and forgeries later, and the property owner has applied for a mortgage they know nothing about.'

'And is that what Mandy was doing?' Gabriel asked. 'Conspiring with organised crime figures? How would she even know those kinds of people?'

The cold unvarnished truth was that she knew at least one of those kinds of people. She'd known him most of her life because he was her best friend's younger brother. I shook my head, disguised my silence by taking a slug of water.

'The bigger question is, *why* would she do this?' Patricia asked. 'Risk everything? Going to jail? Getting struck off the roll of solicitors? She was one of the best lawyers I've ever known. I don't understand it. I just can't see it.'

After a silence I said, 'I can't understand it either. Though it does seem that she was planning to leave her husband – had more or less left him. And that she was leaving here too.'

'What?' Gabriel asked. His head swivelled towards Dervla. She met his gaze with a look of defiance. I didn't know what that was about, but Gabriel's shock reminded me forcefully that I'd forgotten to tell them what Owen McCormack had said about Mandy's intention of joining Finertech as chief counsel. I told them what I knew now.

Then, though I didn't know if I believed it, I said, 'Maybe all this was supposed to be temporary. Maybe Mandy borrowed the money to pay off Ed's divorce settlement. She might have planned to pay everyone back later. But at some stage, on a sale, as Patricia said – but equally in a fees review, or the annual audit, even just by chance – there was a risk that she'd have been found out. She had to have known that. Or perhaps she was flirting with the dark side and it went too far. There's a slim possibility that she was playing some sort of game.'

'With whom?' Patricia Dillane asked.

'Herself?' I suggested.

'Maybe she was being blackmailed,' Patricia said. 'Have you thought of that?'

I had. I'd thought of who might be blackmailing her too. I'd even thought that that same person might have been the one in control of the payee bank accounts. But I said nothing.

'I think you're being excessively charitable, Patricia,' Gabriel said.

'The woman was a thieving bitch,' Lyons said. 'I never liked her. Most people didn't. She was ambitious. Didn't suffer fools. And, no offence, ladies, but like a lot of female solicitors – present company excepted, of course – she could be very abrasive.'

Patricia Dillane's expression darkened, and she rubbed her cheek like she'd been slapped, but she said nothing. Like me, she'd heard this kind of comment too often to bother engaging, knowing that if she did, she'd be told not to be so touchy, or that she was very 'emotional'.

For once, I couldn't let it pass. 'I'm not excusing anything that Mandy did,' I said. 'And far be it from me to defend her, especially in these circumstances. But last time I checked, abrasiveness and ambition aren't considered faults in people with penises. No matter how small.'

Lyons glared. Gabriel blushed. Dervla raised her eyebrows. Patricia Dillane snorted. 'Now, now, Finn,' she said. 'Let's move on. I'd say we'll never know the half of what Mandy was doing. But whatever it was, and for whatever reason, it got her killed.'

'Lie down with dogs and, in my experience, you stay down,' Lyons said.

'Succinctly put, Dermot,' Patricia Dillane said. 'So now what?'

Gabriel said, 'Finn, I want you to—'

'Make first contact with the guards on the firm's behalf?' I asked.

'Eventually,' Gabriel said. 'Once we know where we stand. But for now, we have to keep it tight. Get a handle on what she was doing. Keep control of this.'

Maybe this is what it'll be like at the end of the world, I thought. We'll be cleaning the guttering as the roof falls in, painting the garden fence as the asteroid strikes.

'It's too late for that,' I said flatly. 'We need to contact the clients in question, tell them, and then tell the guards. Immediately. Well, as it's night-time now, it can wait until tomorrow, I guess. Though it can't go beyond that. There's a perfectly valid argument to be made that tomorrow is the soonest we could have told the guards. The file deletions that Pauline found were strange. But we couldn't have known their significance until today when I went to the various houses and met Sheila Miller, and the penny well and truly dropped.'

There was no response from Gabriel. Then Dervla, who had been silent throughout the meeting, spoke. 'Gabriel, please, can you understand what Finn is saying? That the guards must be told.'

Patricia Dillane said, 'I agree one hundred per cent. This is clearly a garda matter. After all, this is first and foremost about finding and catching a murderer.'

She was right. But I was still the only one in the room who knew about Mandy's connection to Davy. And until I knew for sure what his involvement was, I wasn't saying anything about him.

FRIDAY

FRIDAY

102

WE'D SPENT ANOTHER HOUR, PLANNING THE disclosure of Mandy's wrongdoing to the guards and then to the relevant clients. We'd also discussed the radically amended report that the firm would have to prepare for the Law Society, and how best to inform the rest of the staff. Gabriel, decisive again after his worst fears had in fact come to pass, had said he'd call everyone to a meeting at 10 a.m. and, on his instructions too, Dermot had rung around and arranged a partners-only meeting for two hours before that, at 8 a.m. Finally, we'd agreed that after those meetings – which might throw up some additional information – I would make the initial interface with the gardaí via Sadie in Coughlan's Quay garda station.

Sometime around 11 p.m. I'd got home and turned on the heating and made myself a cup of camomile tea. I'd pulled a blanket over me on the sofa and listened to Patsy Cline, and wondered what the hell had happened to my life. Patsy didn't have the answer – and neither did Willie, or Merle, or George Jones and Tammy Wynette – but a little after 2 a.m., Kris Kristofferson told me to let the devil take tomorrow and that seemed like as good an idea as anything else. I'd gone downstairs, had a bath and crawled into bed and slept for five or ten minutes every now and again until it was time to get up.

Now it was 9.15 on Friday morning and, instead of being at work, I was at the courthouse. I had on a navy pinstripe skirt suit with a cheery blue shirt and make-up an inch thick, and even though I knew I looked – and felt – like death underneath, I didn't look too bad on the surface.

Tina had told me that my search results would be ready at the Probate Office first thing, so that's where I was headed. The search was important, because I hoped it would give me more information about the house where Mandy had been found dead. None of the deleted mortgage files found by Pauline had related to 3 Alysson Villas, the former home of Josepha Buckley, Jerry McInerney's deceased aunt. Neither of them had been clients of MLC. But if a grant of probate or administration had issued in relation to Josepha's estate, it might give me some crumbs to follow. On the other hand, if no grant had been extracted, the trail would go cold again.

I entered the probate office with faint hope rather than any real expectation. I leaned on the blonde wood counter and rang the bell. Then I sat and waited for someone to come. Today of all days, I was in no rush to get to MLC and this was a pleasant space – a basement, but bright and airy thanks to a renovation that had conserved the distinguished historic building and given it a contemporary twist. I planned to arrive at MLC just as Gabriel's 10 a.m. staff meeting started, so that I wouldn't have to talk to him or anyone else in advance. I was all out of talk about Mandy.

For now.

103

'I THOUGHT IT MIGHT BE YOU,' EDNA, TINA'S contact at the Probate Office, said. 'I heard it was urgent.'

'It is,' I said. 'Thanks for doing the search so fast.'

'It was no bother. And it was easier because of you not being the first.'

'How do you mean?'

'When I inputted the name of the deceased, I remembered. It was a telephone inquiry, you see. I'm not sure when, but it could have been about two or three weeks ago. Asking how you'd find out if someone, a dead person – this very one, the late Josepha Buckley – had made a will. I explained to him that we wouldn't necessarily know anything about a will.'

'Well, no. Unless the will was probated, it could just sit on a file or in a drawer, and it might never come near you. Um, who *was* this person who called you?'

'I can't say, sorry. Not to you, anyway, Finn. GDPR and confidentiality and that.'

I thought about arguing but decided to wait and see if she said anything else. 'I understand,' I said. 'I'll take a look at what you have for me anyway.'

Edna laid an A4 brown envelope on the counter, her right-hand palm down across it.

'Interesting reading,' she said. 'Very.'

I realised that she was trying to give me a message without saying anything. 'Any particular bits?'

'The executrix,' she said. 'The beneficiary, even more so. And the only asset. That's interesting too. Newsworthy, in fact.'

I slipped the papers out of the envelope and scanned them quickly. 'You're right, Edna,' I said. 'It's a real page-turner.' I flicked back to the first page of the Inland Revenue Affidavit, where the filing party's contact details were. The name, I recognised. The box number too. 'Do you recall meeting the person who filed this application?'

Edna shook her head. 'It came in by post,' she said. 'None of us noticed anything at the time. The documents were perfect. No queries. Very straightforward. Just took their place in the queue for the grant of probate to issue.'

'I'm not asking you to do anything against the rules,' I said softly. 'Absolutely not. But if I was to get it into my head that the person who made the telephone inquiry might be a visitor from overseas – from Wales maybe – might I be heading in the right direction?'

Edna made a single downward motion with her head that, to anyone watching, might, or might not, have been a reply. Then she turned and went back to her desk.

104

'GABRIEL WASN'T VERY CLEAR ON WHAT MANDY was doing,' Tina said. 'He said it was something to do with mortgage irregularities. Which I took to mean – I think everyone did – sticky fingers.'

She was crumpled in the chair opposite, elbows on my desk, chin in her hands. The staff meeting – standing room only with everyone crowded into the boardroom, the long table shoved up against the windows, and the overflow on the landing outside – had ended forty minutes previously. Twenty minutes was all it had taken for Gabriel to destroy Mandy's reputation and the firm's. It was hard to see how MLC could recover from this. The murder on its own was survivable, just about. The property scam was significantly more damaging – Gabriel knew it, and so did everyone else. All around the building I felt the unmistakable buzz of CVs being dusted off and LinkedIn profiles being burnished.

I said, 'He doesn't want to say much because of the ongoing murder investigation. He's afraid of making things worse. Though he obviously had to say something. As far as I know, he had a private word with Mandy's team as well. Asked them for their cooperation.'

'Do you think he'll get it?'

'Maybe,' I said. 'But maybe there's nothing to get. It looks to me like she was running her own show. She and Ricky Dempsey.'

'What makes you think he was involved?'

'Apart from the flit to Marbella?'

'Apart from that, yeah.'

I walked her through what I'd learned.

'So he did the property valuations,' Tina said. 'And without them, Mandy couldn't have organised the mortgages. That's it?'

'Don't forget, he's a financial consultant as well. I'm willing to bet he had a hand in getting the mortgages – a variety of them – approved by the different banks. That was cute: not putting all their eggs in one basket. And once the broker has a copy passport and proof of address and pay slips, a real PPS number and a completed application form, all certified by a reputable solicitor, do they even have to meet the client? By rights, they should – but they mightn't.'

'Did Dempsey know they were fraudulent at the time, though?'

'Whether he did or not, he knows now,' I said. 'He was negligent or incompetent or he was in it up to his neck – it doesn't matter much which. What really matters is, did he kill Mandy?'

'Do you think he did?'

'I don't know,' I said. 'He's a nasty man but I don't know if he's a murderer.'

'And where do the McInerneys come in?'

'For some reason, that's what shocked me the most,' I said.

'How do you mean?'

'Okay. So, as you know the woman who owned 3 Alysson Villas was one Josepha Buckley, dead twenty-two years, according to her death certificate. After I got the result of the probate search, I went back down to the Births, Marriages and Deaths Registry, and got a copy of Jerry McInerney's birth certificate. Annie Buckley was given as his mother's maiden name. Then I searched for Annie Buckley's marriage certificate to Thomas McInerney, Jerry's father according to his birth certificate. That confirmed it – Josepha Buckley was Annie's bridesmaid, her sister. She was Jerry's aunt, the woman he lived with after his parents died. She never married. Her closest relative was her nephew Jerry, but it seems that they had a falling out or whatever and, like his daughter told me, he went to Cardiff and didn't come back.'

'Until he did.'

'Until he did. But before he did, he rang Edna in the Probate Office, enquiring about his aunt's will. She had it because Mandy had lodged a probate application. Edna didn't tell Jerry the contents of the will – the probate application was still pending – but she gave him Mandy's name and the name of the firm. Edna knew it was Mandy's file because she was named as the filing solicitor. The thing is, Mandy was also the executrix in the estate of the late Josepha Buckley, according to a will that could have been genuine but might be – no, in reality, was – forged.'

'How can you be sure?'

'I'm not. But I'm taking a calculated guess.'

'Why?'

I opened a copy of the will and pointed at the relevant clause. 'As you can see, Mandy named herself as sole beneficiary.'

Tina blew out a breath. 'You're right,' she said. 'That *is* even worse than the fraudulent mortgages.'

'She didn't prepare the probate application on the MLC system,' I said. 'There was no digital record of the file, even a deleted one. She didn't have to because the way a probate application is done, it can all be concluded on paper – as you know, the Revenue Commissioners are changing to an online process, but it hasn't happened yet. The grant of probate would never have come to MLC, because she used the same box number she used for the mortgages as the return address for the probate. The same mobile phone number too. But her own name and home address was in the body of the form as executrix and beneficiary. It was all quite calculated. She probably planned to use a different firm to sell the house, maybe one not from Cork, to conceal the trick further.

'And she *was* planning on selling the house. Ricky Dempsey said he was doing a valuation when he was up at 3 Alysson Villas recently. But this wasn't for a mortgage application. He went up there to take photographs and measurements for his website. I noticed some foliage around the front gate had been cut back. Nothing major, but enough to permit access for viewings. I think that was him. He lied to me, said he didn't know what the plans for the house were. But he did. He knew that the house was going on the market – executor's sale. Then the long-lost relatives showed up, and ruined things.'

'I can't figure that out,' Tina said. 'The McInerneys came to MLC to see Mandy because the Probate Office had given them her name as the person who had filed the probate documents.'

'They gave them her name and mobile phone number, but not the contents of the will, because a will only becomes a document of public record after probate. They must have tried to contact Mandy on the fraudulent mortgage mobile. Maybe they spoke to her, maybe she arranged to meet them here. If not, they must have googled her, found out where she worked.

'Either way,' Tina said, 'they had good reasons for wanting to see Mandy. They showed up here first thing Monday and went to the waiting room to wait. But why did they go?'

'After all this time, that's still the question,' I said. 'They came to MLC. Demanded to see Mandy because they knew she was handling Jerry's aunt's estate. Then, inexplicably, they left again. But why? Why leave the place that has all the information they need?'

105

'I'VE GOT SOMETHING,' I SAID. 'AN IMPORTANT new development in the investigation. I've been authorised by the firm to make a disclosure to An Garda Síochána. I'm interpreting that as you. Come to my house, I'll make you lunch and a cup of coffee – or three – and tell you all about it.'

I wanted to steer her away from Coughlan's Quay, and away from my office, figuring that the distance might help me and Sadie work through why Mandy had done what she did, and why she died. Also, if I saw her on her own rather than at the station, she might throw me a few extra nuggets of information, both about the murder and the McInerney missing persons case.

'Proper lunch?' Sadie asked. 'Not just cheese and oatcakes?'

'Toasted beer-mash sourdough from ABC in the market, chicken liver and brandy pâté from—'

'You had me at the sourdough toast,' Sadie said.

•

I gave her the dossier I'd compiled, and talked her through what I'd learned. She flicked through the pages while she ate, and said nothing until she reached the end. Then she leaned back in the chair and interlaced her fingers behind her head. 'So as well as the adultery, Mandy was a crook.'

'You sound disappointed,' I said.

'No.'

'You do,' I said.

'No,' Sadie said again. 'Are you, though?'

'Disappointed? Yeah, I am. I admired her, her work, you know. This is, well, it's a shock.'

'Are you saying you don't believe she did this, the fraud?' Sadie asked.

'Ah, of course I believe it. It's all there. The full trail. It's the why of it I can't grasp.'

We discussed Mandy's possible motivations from every angle except one – I held back what I knew about her connection to Davy. His name never came up, even though Sadie knew now that Davy's sister Orla worked for Owen McCormack.

'Look, Mandy was a woman with a lot going on,' Sadie said. 'But she's dead. We can't prosecute a dead woman for fraud. Unfortunately. So the fraud is only relevant to my current investigation if it's the reason she got killed. By an accomplice, perhaps.'

'By Ricky Dempsey, for example.'

'Yeah, but the way you're telling it, Dempsey may not have even known what Mandy had going on. You're also telling me that the McInerneys didn't already know when they came to the office that she'd stolen the house from them. So, where do you say they fit with the murder?'

'Well the house, the scene of the crime,' I said. 'That's got to be important. Vital. The McInerneys were there – the location Mandy was murdered – close to or at the time she died. Have you an update on them? There seems to be a total news blackout.'

'That's because Lenihan has made sure there is. And because Charlene and the rest of the family have bought into it for now. In the background, there has been a serious search going on, but no joy – there hasn't been sight nor sound of the McInerneys since they went to Dublin. On the other hand, we *have* found out more about what they did while they were still in Cork.'

'What was that?'

'They visited Blarney Castle.'

'That might fit with one of Lenihan's theories,' I said. 'That the McInerneys' visit to Cork might have been cover, that their Dublin visit was the real purpose. So tell me more.'

'The Monday after Jerry and Dean left MLC, they checked out of their hotel, got on the hop on, hop off tourist bus down at the bus station. They kissed the Stone. Went for a walk in the gardens. Turned off both phones. And never got back on the bus. They must have got a taxi, or had access to a car, but we have no fix on that yet. Blarney Castle is the last trace we have of them, until that text message Dean sent the next day telling Charlene they were in Dublin. Then he switched his phone off again and they disappeared.'

'What's your take on their link to Mandy's murder?'

'That's the thing. I'm no longer convinced that the McInerneys are linked to the murder.'

'You're saying there's no connection? But there must be.'

'I'm not saying there's *no* connection,' Sadie said. 'I'm saying Mandy went to 3 Alysson Villas to check up on the house she was in the process of stealing from Jerry McInerney. I think her lover, Owen McCormack followed her there or arranged to meet her there for some reason. He's admitted that, as well as seeing her in the morning, he talked to her on the phone – her affair phone that we've been unable to find – on Sunday evening while she was out on her walk. He didn't have much choice but to admit it because of his phone records.'

'And you think he killed her?'

'I do. He has no alibi. As to his motive, the stuff you've brought me today makes me think that, if she was defrauding other clients, maybe she was defrauding him too. And that he found out. And that's why he killed her.'

'She wasn't doing any kind of mortgage work for him,' I said.

'No, but he told us she set up offshore trusts to manage his money. Maybe she funnelled some of his money into a trust for herself?'

'That's a possibility. Hard to prove – you'd need a whole team of forensic accountants – but, yes, it's certainly a possibility.'

'The other thing I've been thinking is that maybe Mandy and McCormack were in on the mortgage fraud together, thrill-seeking to spice things up?'

'I can't see it,' I said. 'It's too low-rent. McCormack is super rich. He seems careful with money and even more careful with his company. I can't see him risking everything for a few hundred thousand. Even a million would be small change to him.'

'Okay, try this on for size instead,' Sadie said. 'We know that Mandy was planning to leave MLC and join him. If he discovered she had criminal tendencies, maybe he wouldn't have wanted her on his board?'

'It could be something like that,' I said. 'That he felt betrayed by her.'

'Or, what if it was way more basic, more traditional?' Sadie said. 'What if there was another man? A third man?'

'Apart from her husband?'

'Yeah. Apart from Ed.'

'I don't like that idea so much, somehow. It doesn't seem—'

'Owen McCormack didn't like that idea either. He got rather irate at my suggestion. Turns out he has quite the temper.'

'Why are you focusing so much on him? You seem to have completely discounted the McInerneys and their disappearance.'

'I haven't. Though I don't think they have any link to Lenihan's investigation either. I think they deliberately disappeared themselves because they found out about Mandy's murder.'

'Before anyone else did? Before the news was out? How did they find out?'

'I don't know that yet,' Sadie said. 'But I know McCormack killed her.'

'Not Ricky Dempsey.'

'No.'

'Even though he fled to Spain to avoid being taken in for questioning?'

'No. Well, fair point. Ricky is still on my suspect list, I'll grant you that.'

'And Hugo Woulfe,' I said. 'Very odd behaviour right through this.'

'Remind me, who's Woulfe again?'

'Mandy's trainee.'

'Oh yes,' she said. 'So his mother has him at home the night of the murder. All night. I checked it out myself.'

'Hugo's mother's not enough to rule him out. And then there's Ed. What about him?'

'That's why I like McCormack so much all of a sudden. Because Ed's in the clear.'

'Even though he has no alibi?'

'Oh, but he does,' Sadie said. 'Alibi number one didn't stack up – his young daughter inconveniently being out at the time getting pissed. But alibi number two did. While Mandy was being killed, aging toy boy Ed was frolicking in bed with Carla Boyd, who, at a sprightly fifty-eight, is his very married, very embarrassed, next-door neighbour.'

106

BACK AT THE OFFICE, I TOOK OUT THE PROBATE papers that Mandy had lodged for the estate of Josepha Buckley, Jerry McInerney's long-deceased aunt, and read them again. It was still hard for me to accept that she had forged the will and made herself the sole beneficiary. Audacious and daring, it was the act of an amoral desperado with nothing to lose. I remembered how careful she had been with her children's welfare, in picking the right time to tell them about the separation; and how meticulous her work was. That Mandy didn't square with this one but she was complicated, and the proof of what she had done was in front of me in black and white.

Despite what Sadie had said, Ed's alibi had made me think that the murder had little to do with either Mandy's marriage or her affair. The alibi made it inconceivable to me that Mandy wouldn't have followed through on her intention to leave Ed. As a result, though Owen McCormack had no alibi for Mandy's murder, he had no motive that I could discern to kill the woman he loved either. I didn't know if Mandy was stealing his money and diverting it into a trust for her own benefit, but I didn't think she was. And I didn't buy Sadie's theory of a third man, a second lover, either.

All of which meant that Mandy's murder had to be closely

related to the property scam and that whoever she'd been in cahoots with had probably killed her. Ricky Dempsey was the obvious candidate – he was stupid and violent, and he'd skipped the country as soon as he'd found out that I knew about his business relationship with Mandy. But the complex nature of the scheme also meant that the involvement of another person in addition to Dempsey was likely. Someone with criminal connections. Someone like Davy.

And yet, why kill Mandy and why then? Had she, however belatedly, tried to pull out of the fraud or threatened to report it? Possibly. Because the timing of the murder raised questions. Just before the property scam's biggest payoff – the sale of 3 Alysson Villas – a valuable house despite its lamentable condition.

Most valuable of all to Jerry McInerney and his grandson Dean. The guards had speculated about a gangland connection from the beginning, because the two men had disappeared in west Dublin, near the location of Lenihan's surveillance operation. Did they keep their phones off because they'd been told to by the people they'd arranged to meet? And if there was a meeting, what was its purpose?

Meanwhile Davy had been missing during all that time. He hadn't stayed with me on the Sunday night, and had cancelled his clients and fitness classes on the Monday, the day the McInerneys went to Blarney Castle. Was he the one who'd driven them from there to Dublin? And if he had, where were they now? Dead? Or in hiding? How deep in was Davy? Was he living a double life that I knew nothing about? Still involved in crime? Blackmailing Mandy about her past cocaine and ecstasy use? And if she'd wanted it all to stop, to start her new life with Owen McCormack, to leave behind her practice as a solicitor and work in-house for Finertech, had Davy killed her? Had he killed the McInerneys too?

The thought horrified me. And yet, I was the one who'd come up with it.

•

I leafed through Josepha Buckley's probate papers again, picking up the death certificate and holding it in both my hands. 3 Alysson Villas had been both Josepha Buckley's home and the place where she had died. The one-page official document held the bare, ordinary facts of the extinguishing of a life. The certificate would have issued within a few days and without the need for an inquest because the cause of death was given as, 'myocardial infarction: heart disease ten-plus years'. Unlike Mandy, Josepha Buckley had died a natural death, certified by her GP.

Whose name, I noticed, was Dr Seamus Keyes.

The man who until recently had lived in 'Alysson', the big house at the end of the street. He'd been in hospital on the night of Mandy's murder, and for a few weeks before it. His daughter Polly had told me that he was ready to leave hospital and move to Mount Desert Nursing Home on the Lee Road. He'd be there by now. Apart from Jerry McInerney, he might be the only person left who'd known Josepha Buckley.

It struck me that Dr Keyes might have known Jerry McInerney too, and that he might be able to corroborate – or contradict – the reason Jerry had left Cork. Charlene McInerney had said that Josepha Buckley had been a disciplinarian; that her father had left home as soon as he could. But was any of that true? And, after so many years, did it matter?

I decided that it did.

107

I'D BEEN HERE BEFORE, MANY TIMES, TO CONSULT with clients and to make wills. Visiting some nursing homes could be upsetting – the cramped accommodation, the mean dimensions of the public areas, the nearly overwhelming pong of cabbage and wee. Mount Desert was different. Its spectacular hillside location would have been enough to set it apart, but there were the beautifully planted gardens as well and the high ceilings, wide hallways and generous room sizes. Everything was tastefully designed and there was a charming café too. All of which came, naturally, with a hefty price tag.

I went to the reception desk and asked for Dr Seamus Keyes's room number. I didn't anticipate a problem gaining access, but I'd brought a briefcase with me for cover and held my business card, slightly damp from hand sanitiser, in my right hand just in case.

The attendant, a red-haired, pink-skinned woman in a blue tunic, said, 'Oh dear, you didn't hear the bad news.' She told me that Dr Keyes had died suddenly, only hours after arriving at Mount Desert. 'Are you a friend of the family?'

'How sad. I only met his daughter Polly a few days ago at the house.'

'But Polly's here now!' the attendant said. 'Packing up his things. Will I take you down to her? This must be an awful shock.'

'I'll go myself,' I said. 'If you could let me know the room number, please.'

•

The door to Room 24 was open. I knocked and went inside. A large packed suitcase lay open on the bed. There were two half-full black bin bags and a box with photographs and pictures on the floor in front of the locker; another smaller box of books and trinkets sat on the armchair.

'I'm almost done here,' Polly said without looking up. 'Nearly ready for the next guest. I wonder is there anyone around to help me out to the car?'

'I can help you,' I said.

'Thank you.' She glanced up. 'I'll be … em … do I know you from somewhere?'

I reminded her who I was, and told her more of the truth this time: that I'd worked with Mandy Breslin and that I'd been appointed to investigate on behalf of the firm.

'So you were snooping when you visited me at "Alysson"? And you're snooping again now? Or are you looking for work from me? With my father hardly cold?'

'Not at all,' I said. 'Though I know how it looks.' I told her about the McInerneys, my visit to Cardiff and the McInerney/Buckley family's link to her father, that as well as being Josepha Buckley's neighbour, his name had been on her death certificate as the attending doctor. 'I wanted to ask him if he remembered anything about Josepha Buckley or her nephew, about the family – the circumstances of Jerry's leaving, or the deaths of his parents.'

'Why? Isn't that what the police are for?'

'Well, yes, but the McInerneys went missing in Dublin. The Dublin guards don't seem to be too interested in the Cork family tree aspect. It's probably nothing to do with their disappearance anyway. I just thought it was worth asking your father. I thought he might have been interested in the story too.'

She softened. 'He would've been. He had an amazing memory. And he loved talking about all his old patients. His surgery was on Magazine Road. He could have named every occupant of every house before the area changed. Still did, anytime I took him out for a spin in the wheelchair. Before he got too weak for that. Being so incapacitated was hard on him. He was such an active man. It's a blessing he went quickly in the end.'

'I'm sure it doesn't feel like much of a blessing today. I'm sure you'll miss him.' She blinked away tears, nodded. After a pause, and feeling like a complete heel, I asked, 'Do you remember him saying anything about 3 Alysson Villas and the people who lived there?'

She shook her head. 'I've been off in London so long. When I came home, it was all in-one-ear-and-out-the-other with me. But one of his carers might have listened more closely. He had three regulars for daytime and two regulars at night. They shared out the week between them. In recent years, they knew him better than I did. If you like, I'll give you their names and mobile numbers? All I have are first names but you could talk to the agency? I'm sure they'd be glad to help.'

I thanked her and wrote them in my notebook. Later, outside in the car, I inputted the numbers into my phone contacts.

Which was when I discovered that one of the carers was in my phone already.

108

I DROVE ALONG THE NARROW BYROAD, ABOUT two miles off the Cork–Limerick dual carriageway, through high hedges of hawthorn marked blood-red with their autumn hoard. With the windows down, I could hear the traffic behind and above me, like white water over rocks. Too late I realised that I'd gone well past the entrance, so I pulled into an open gateway to the barren stubble of a harvested cornfield, where a lone scald crow pecked and scraped at the dark earth. Aside from the crow, there was no one about, no animals or people; no life of any kind. Below, the land fell away in a wide empty slope to a wooded valley, before rising again. Beyond that hill, to the south, lay the city, but there was no hint of it here.

After my phone call to the homecare agency – and after they'd confirmed the identity of the carer – I'd made another call and arranged to meet here at 6 p.m., but I'd driven straight from Mount Desert and was too early. I got out of the car and began walking. On my left, I passed an old dwelling that had been modernised and extended to double its previous size, with an expansive cobblelock driveway and a parking area large enough to accommodate several cars. There were almost none of these homes left in their original condition but at one time the two- and three-roomed cottages on an acre of land were much sought after, a major improvement on the mud-walled hovels, known as botháns, which were inhabited by large swathes of the population here and all over Ireland until the early twentieth century.

A few fields further along, I turned into the rutted lane, lined on both sides with fieldstone ditches and tall lime trees whose top branches met in the middle. The leaves had turned and a bad wind would bring most of them down soon, but for now they clung to their branches. The avenue was longer than it had seemed and the thought of feeling my way back along here after dark made my impulsive idea of arriving on foot seem fanciful and unwise. I thought about going back for the car but I didn't and, after a couple of minutes more, stepped out of the shade into a three-sided farm courtyard floored in rough concrete and neatly swept. The house stood on one side and on the other two was an L of antique stone out-buildings. A dusty olive-green Land Rover Defender with a cream roof was beached in the far corner, though it looked like it had been ten years or more since anyone had moved it. Of Kathleen's blue Fiat Punto, there was no sign.

●

Mid-nineteenth century or older, the farmhouse was built in the typical style, with three sash windows on the first floor, six panes over six, and two on the ground floor, the door in the middle. The woodwork was done in thick layers of white gloss that contrasted with the original unpainted plaster, free of ivy and other creepers save for a gnarled wisteria, its leaves almost gone for the year, its tendrils drooping over the fanlight. It looked for all the world like a prosperous farmer's residence, but I knew that it was no such thing. Not anymore. The land had been sold off in parcels over decades by Kathleen's father, a bare three acres remaining. After he'd died, Kathleen and her mother had stayed on. Then the mother had died too, leaving Kathleen the house.

I went up to the nearest window and peered in, but the shutters were fully closed. I rang the doorbell and got no reply. Then I walked around the edge of the yard. To my surprise, the Land Rover was still taxed and insured, and looked in better nick than it had appeared from a distance. I opened a couple of the creosoted stout wooden doors and checked inside the outhouses furtively. Everywhere was as tidy as I might have expected it to be: a winter's worth of firewood chopped and stacked against a wall; a spade; a small axe; a few shovels and rakes leaned against another. The handle of a thick-bristle yard brush stuck out of a wheelbarrow in one of the barns. The last door I came to was locked with a shiny new padlock. A yellow extension lead snaked in from the building next door. There was no window and I speculated that the more expensive tools and equipment might be stored in there – a lawnmower or a chainsaw and maybe a better axe than the one I'd seen, but I didn't know. I looked back at the house and noticed the PhoneWatch alarm box on the top right-hand corner of the facade. With Kathleen gone five days a week, it made sense that she would take precautions, though I wondered if it was connected, or just for show.

Rambling back to the other side of the yard, I sat on a windowsill and went to take out my phone but, in rushing, I'd left it behind in the side pocket of the car. Just then, Kathleen's car turned in the gate. I stood quickly, waving as she approached. She hooted and flashed the headlights in reply. I walked to the gable end and glanced across the garden. More trees edged the lawn: younger plantings, beech, and a tightly spaced mixed hedge with enough evergreen – holly and Scots pine – to block the view, rendering the house entirely private.

•

We hugged briefly. 'You made it!' she said. 'I'm so glad you came. But how did you …?'

'Missed the gate,' I said. 'I'm parked in a gap below on the road.'

'Ah,' she said. Did I sense a prickle of irritation?

'It's beautiful here,' I said.

'Sure I couldn't imagine living anywhere else.' She reached into the back seat of the car, and took out a cake box. 'It's why I'm late,' she said. 'Or am I?' Again, that sharpness.

'Not at all, I'm early,' I said. 'And there was no need to—'

'There was every need,' Kathleen said. She gave my upper arm a squeeze. 'I get few enough visitors. Besides, it was an excuse for me to get one of these. Wait till you taste it.'

She directed me to a room off the front hall. 'Step into the parlour there,' she said. 'I'll be back in two shakes.'

She flicked a switch. A pair of red tasselled wall lamps either side of the fine marble fireplace came on, but did little to dispel the gloom. Faded black-and-white family photographs and a couple of fly-specked hunting prints decorated the walls. Some of the paper had peeled and been restuck. I went to the window and opened back the shutters to let in the dregs of the evening light. I ran my hand on the thinning gold silk of a chaise longue and rubbed off the dust between my palms. After a quick survey of the rest of the furniture, I sat into a high mahogany armchair with a worn black seat, but regretted it the second I felt the horse-hair stuffing scratch the backs of my knees. I opted for the sagging sofa instead and shoved a damp scatter cushion under my left thigh to stop me falling into the middle.

This might have been the good room once, but wherever Kathleen spent most of her time now, it wasn't here. She hadn't invited me there, or into the kitchen. I thought I knew why; and it saddened me that she was still clinging so desperately to the vestiges of her family's past. It was no accident that the outside areas were much better kept than the interior. I was willing to bet that most people from the locality didn't get past the front door, and that they had no idea how far Kathleen's fortunes had fallen. Her entire salary probably went on heating this place and repairing the leaks in the roof. Mandy's home was a similar age and size to this one, but the contrast couldn't have been greater.

Kathleen rattled back in with a tray which held a crocheted tea-cosied pot, bone china cups and saucers, and two generous slices of coffee and walnut cake on a delicate, though chipped, footed platter. She served one of the slices to me with a mountain of whipped cream.

'Now,' she said. 'Didn't I promise you a treat? The woman in the village shop does them. I've told her loads of times that if she went to the farmers' market, she'd sell out.'

I oohed appropriately, though the cake was too dry and the buttercream strangely chalky. We ate and drank and chit-chatted for a while. Then I said, 'I suppose you're wondering why I wanted to see you like this, away from the office.'

She looked down at me from the high mahogany chair. Though she still wore the floaty cream pussy-bowed blouse she'd had on at work, she'd pulled her hair into a small ponytail, tight and low, and changed from her pleated skirt into tan corduroy trousers and a chocolate-brown lambswool V-neck jumper. She looked surprisingly robust and, unlike me, didn't seem remotely affected by the horse-hair. 'I was rather,' she said.

'It's just that ...' I said. 'Well, the truth is, something's been bothering me.'

109

KATHLEEN REMAINED COMPLETELY STILL. AFTER A long silence, she spoke. 'You think I knew what Mandy was up to with the mortgages. That I helped her.'

'Did you?'

She tipped her head to one side. 'But you *know* I didn't.'

I grimaced. 'It's just that I keep thinking you must have seen something, spotted some sort of—'

'I told you. I told Gabriel. I saw nothing. I was as shocked as everyone else. More. We were so close. That's what I thought. And in the end, it turned out I didn't know her at all. Maybe no one did.'

I nodded. 'What you're saying … It's all …' I searched for the right word. 'Believable' wasn't it. Because I didn't. Not anymore. 'It's understandable,' I said. 'It was a clever scheme.'

'That's what she was. Clever. She needed no accomplice to do what she did.'

'Who killed her, so?'

'If I was a betting woman, I'd put my money on the McInerneys. The young one was a tough nut, a real thug.'

'You *met* them?'

'I-I saw them on the video,' she said. 'Same as you. What …?'

'Oh, of course,' I said. 'Sorry.'

She flapped her hand to indicate 'no problem' and then said, 'Or I've been thinking that it could have been random. One of the students?'

'The guards think it was planned,' I said.

'The murder might have had nothing to do with the, em, fraud, you know.'

'That's very possible,' I said. 'But I still can't get my head around how she was able to hide it all from you. The affair? The mortgages? The forged will? The probate application?'

She brought her hand up to cover her mouth. A tear trickled from her right eye and she wiped it away absently. After a long moment she said, 'I didn't want to say this. Ever. But she didn't keep everything secret from me. Not quite everything.'

110

'I KNEW ABOUT THE AFFAIR WITH MCCORMACK.
I don't know why I told you I didn't. Or maybe I do.' She
clamped her eyes shut, opened them again, fixed me with a
mournful stare. 'I didn't want to admit to myself that it was
happening,' Kathleen said. 'I couldn't bear the thought of the
children being hurt. I've known them since before they were
born, shared every milestone. Christening. First communion.
And Ed … I know he's not everyone's cup of tea, but we were
a team. Managing her. Mandy. Making sure she, I don't know,
remembered birthdays, that kind of thing.'

'Mandy didn't seem like the birthday-forgetting type,' I said.

'Other things, so,' she snapped. I must have looked sceptical
because she said, 'It's hard to describe. But I was part of the
family. One of the gang.'

'And the affair?'

'I found out about it gradually.'

'How?'

'I saw that she had a second phone. That was the start.'

'Do you know the number?'

'Not offhand. I have it written on a Post-it in my desk. Just in
case. I don't need it anymore obviously. She …'

'She?'

'Well, I think she had a third phone as well. Maybe. But I only knew for sure about the one I saw. The affair one. I don't know what she would have needed a third phone for. At least I didn't. I assume now that it had something to do with her fraudulent financial activities.'

'Going back to the affair,' I said. 'You had some suspicions, and then?'

'She told me. Confided.'

'Was that usual?'

'There was nothing usual about it. She hadn't had any previous affairs.'

That conflicted with what Ed had said, but tallied with Owen McCormack's story. 'Are you certain of that?' I asked.

'Completely.'

'What did she tell you about it? And when?'

'January or February this year. She was smitten. It was love, she said.'

'Owen McCormack told me that she'd told no one at MLC.'

'No one except me.'

I believed Kathleen when she said that she knew about the affair. I was less convinced by the way she'd said that Mandy had confided in her, but didn't challenge her on it.

'After she told you, how did you feel?' I asked.

'I was disappointed. Sad, too. For the girls. For poor Ed.'

'Did you say that to her?'

'I said some of it. I mainly said that I didn't want to know more. That if I did, it'd be awkward for me when the kids or Ed called looking for her, wondering where she was.'

'Yes,' I said. 'I can see that it would be.'

'So she stopped giving me the nitty-gritty.'

'And that was better?'

'It was better. It was worse too. We were drifting apart. I kept my distance as much as I could. Did my work, 8 a.m. to 4 p.m., in and out, but didn't, em, didn't love it anymore.' She paused. 'In the old days, I'd have known what she was up to. At least I think I would have. But because of the affair, I'd pulled back. I regret that now. Maybe if I'd noticed what she was doing with the mortgages, I could have done something sooner. Nipped it in the bud.' I said nothing, waited for her to continue. 'Mind you, inaction can have as many consequences as action. I'm feeling them now. More than most.'

'What do you mean?'

'I'm tainted,' she said. 'Guilty by association. You thought it.'

'I—'

She interrupted me. 'Gabriel's offered me redundancy. I'm going to take it.'

'Oh dear,' I said. 'I'm so sorry.'

'Yes,' she said. Then, unexpectedly, the atmosphere lightened. 'Don't worry,' she said. 'I'll be fine.'

She smiled and for a second I wondered how I could have doubted her. But I had. And I still did. Then, from outside, came the sound of an engine. Kathleen got to her feet and peered through the gap in the shutters.

'It's Billy Manning from a few fields over. You'd have passed his cottage on the way, I'd say. He's the big man around here now. Wasn't always. He bought a lot of our land. Has his eye on the house too, I'll bet, but hell will freeze over before I'll sell. To him especially. I'd better go out to him, though. His precious border collie went missing a few weeks ago, and he's been searching for all the hours ever since. I won't be long.'

She slipped out the front door and went to the driver's window of the massive silver double-cab pickup truck. I got up from the sofa and watched and listened for a moment or two, and heard Kathleen say, 'Any news of poor Bess?', but I stepped back when Billy glanced in my direction. He couldn't have seen me – I was hidden by the fold of the shutter – but I moved from the window all the same. Then I put the tea things back on the tray and made my way towards the kitchen.

111

KNOWING I HADN'T MUCH TIME, I MOVED AS FAST as I could down the badly lit hallway. I ended up tripping on the carpet – loose and wrinkled, a 1970s swirling brown-and-gold pattern that had probably been expensive when new – and nearly dropping the tray. I kicked at the door on my left. It fell open to reveal the shabby remnants of a formal dining room with dull, naked floorboards. A large rolled-up rug against one wall. Wallpaper stripped and removed. A rectangular mahogany table and eight chairs stacked higgledy-piggledy in the far corner. At the centre of the room, a stepladder and a few unopened paint cans. Windows bare of curtains and gaps around the walls, where a sideboard should have stood and an over-mantle mirror should have hung. I wondered if Kathleen's father had sold them off, or if she had had to.

I left the room, taking care not to trip again. At the end of the hallway, a small door opened into the kitchen, a dismal chamber with a Belfast sink, a faded gingham curtain underneath instead of cupboard doors, a 1950s larder cupboard, an open ironing board with a cheap plastic linen basket underneath, a very old fridge and a well-scrubbed deal table and two hard chairs. One of the chairs had a pile of papers on it, and a closed laptop sat on the table in front of the other.

I slid the tea tray onto the draining board and turned to examine the laptop. Off. On hearing the sound of an engine – Billy Manning leaving, I assumed – I went immediately to the sink and began rinsing out the teacups, giving silent thanks that however bad things were for Kathleen, at least she seemed to have plenty of hot water. I heard her come in behind me but stayed where I was, my back to the door.

'What are you doing?'

'I wanted to help,' I said.

'You wanted to have a nose, you mean.'

I made no reply but gingerly placed the final saucer on the draining board and wiped my hands on the tea towel. After a moment I turned and said, 'I'm sorry.'

'If you've seen enough, I think it's time for you to be going.'

I moved quickly, too quickly, and collided with the chair, watching helplessly as the stack of papers collapsed in an avalanche onto the floor. 'Oh my God,' I said.

At the same time Kathleen shrieked, 'Leave them, leave them, for pity's sake!'

But I'd already dropped to my knees and started gathering them up – brochures for every conceivable home improvement. And the bank brochures for the mortgage applications that would fund them. Too late, everything became clear to me. I looked up in time to see the steam iron in Kathleen's right hand.

Then it all went black.

112

'WHERE'S YOUR PHONE?'

On my back.

Kathleen standing over me.

White latex gloves.

Clear plastic disposable apron.

Both barrels of a side-by-side shotgun pressed to my throat.

'H – h – hand … bag,' I said.

'Not there.'

'Du … dunno, so.'

'You'll have to do better than that.' She struck the end of the shotgun hard against my chin. I gasped.

'Office. Must have. Left. In the office.'

'Hmm. That's actually quite handy if it's true. Don't worry, I'll check.' She put her weight on the gun, almost choking me. 'Now get up,' she said. 'And behave.'

I didn't move at first. Wasn't able. She kicked me hard in the thigh. She'd changed her shoes and was wearing black wellies. New-looking. 'Come on!' she said.

I scrambled to my feet somehow. She had tied my wrists together with a length of orange clothesline that dug into my skin, cutting off the circulation. My hands had already started turning blue. How long had I been out cold?

She pushed me across the yard, the shotgun jabbing at my back all the way. It was fully dark outside but the automatic security light illuminated our destination – the padlocked outbuilding I'd noticed earlier. She shoved me in the door.

'On your knees. Now!'

I knelt, turning around in a quarter-circle towards the entrance as I did, trying to identify an escape route. There wasn't any, not with that huge gun blocking the way. Then Kathleen let go of the shotgun barrel and took something out of her pocket and held it to me with her free hand. 'Put that in your mouth,' she said.

I lifted my bound wrists and took the cloth – a sock, grey and smelly – and placed a little of it in my mouth. 'All of it,' she said. I complied and vomit rose in my throat. I swallowed it back and breathed short and fast through my nose. 'Face down on the floor.' Not easy when both hands are tied in front. 'I haven't got all night,' she said. 'Thanks to you, I'll be hours and hours sorting out the mess you've made. As if I haven't enough to do.'

She prodded me in the back. Already unbalanced, I toppled to the ground, turning as I fell, landing on the right side of my face. A deafening crack and a searing pain around my eye. Kathleen sat heavily on top of me, crushing my lower back, and raised my head roughly and tied a gag – a pair of opaque tights – around my mouth. I wriggled, tried to unseat her. She thumped the side of my head: the left side this time, mercifully.

'More of that and you're dead,' she said. 'You'd be dead already except …' I stopped struggling. Wondered what she meant by 'except'. Next, she tied a blindfold – a scarf, I thought – around my eyes. I groaned. The pain was excruciating. I felt her lift off me and a lightish swipe – relatively – of the shotgun butt to my head. 'I'm warning you,' she said.

After she tied my ankles together with what felt like more clothesline, I heard her get to her feet. 'I didn't want to have to do this,' she said. 'I always liked you. But you couldn't let it go. You had to keep digging. You stupid, stupid ...'

The slide and click of the padlock.

The tap-tap-tap-tap of my gaoler's footsteps.

It was Friday night. Davy wouldn't be calling round to my house as usual. Not after what I'd said. After I'd accused him of being a murderer. *Falsely* accused him.

I was alone.

Without him to miss me.

With nowhere I needed to be till 9 a.m. on Monday.

And completely trapped.

113

TWO, THREE, FIVE MINUTES LATER WHAT SOUNDED
like the front door of the main house opened and slammed
shut immediately afterwards. Kathleen was in the yard again,
coming back. I made myself as small as I could, my body tensed
in terror.

But she didn't come in. She spoke. Quietly. Loud enough for
me to get the message.

'By now you're probably planning on escaping. Don't bother.
You'll fail. And, if you try, it will go worse for you in the end.
Your death will be slower. A lot more painful.'

Her walking away.

Not into the house.

Going somewhere else.

To get my car?

Maybe.

Definitely.

And if she finds the phone in the side pocket, she'll know.

She'll know I lied.

The car – and the phone accidentally left in it – had been my
one hope. That someone would notice me gone. My parents.
Tina. Maybe even Davy. Realistically, maybe not him. But

someone. Surely someone would miss me; would notice I wasn't answering my calls. Sadie would. And she'd track me with my phone. Find me. Save me.

Now that wouldn't happen. And the only person who could save me was me.

114

I STARTED COUNTING – ONE MISSISSIPPI, TWO
Mississippi, three Mississippi, four Mississippi … When I got
to what I thought was fifteen minutes, I stopped. If Kathleen
was bringing my car back here, she'd have done it by now. She
couldn't take the risk that someone – Billy Manning, for one
– had seen it parked on the road. So she had to be taking it
somewhere else, hiding it, or parking it in plain sight near my
home. She'd have those keys too. She could go there. Have a
snooze, if she felt like it. Pack a bag for me. Make it look like I'd
left town. If that was her plan, it was almost foolproof. The one
thing it gave me was time.

Rolling onto my back, I started at the blindfold, raising my
bound hands and using my thumbs to push it up like a headband
onto my forehead. Easy. But no change. It was so dark in the
shed, I might have been blind. Maybe I was. Maybe the head
injury had caused me to lose my sight?

I dismissed the thought and went for the gag next, tighter
than the blindfold, my mouth stretched wide in a rictus grin. I
tugged and tugged until it gave enough for me to yank it down
over my chin to my neck. I vomited out the sock and spat and
gulped in the musty barn air like it was mountain fresh. Then,
I shimmied and shifted on my back to where I was pretty sure –

though I was getting less certain with every second that passed – the entrance was. When the top of my head hit wood, I did a full sit-up, lifting my bound arms to give me upward and forward momentum, and then I back and forthed with my bottom to bring me into a seated posture, my shoulder blades pressed against the door. Exhausted, I leaned my burning right cheek gently against the cool stone wall to rest for a minute before moving on to phase two.

But, eyelids heavy, breathing shallow, I slept.

•

I awoke with a start and a foul taste in my mouth – and no clue how long I'd been asleep. It might have been a concussion that had put me out. Or it might have been the chalky buttercream icing, if Kathleen had crushed sleeping pills and fed them to me? Maybe she'd thought that I knew; that that was why I'd come?

But she couldn't have known that I'd find the brochures and realise that she'd been the one responsible for the property scam; that she'd blamed Mandy and presumably killed her when she'd found out. Both Ed and Owen McCormack had said that Mandy had been worried about something to do with work. I hadn't listened. Hadn't looked closely enough. Instead, I'd become obsessed with Davy's involvement. Had hurt him. Had ruined everything between us.

I had to get on. If Kathleen wasn't back already, she could come at any second. Bending forward, I felt for the corner angle of the cut stone doorway. I started a sawing motion with my bound wrists, up and down, up and down, on the rope that I'd thought was a clothesline when I'd seen it earlier. Now I reasoned that, if she'd planned to attack me and keep me captive, she'd have had something better to tie me up with, and she'd have used the gun to subdue me rather than a steam iron. It seemed that I'd forced her to improvise and, for a time, that gave me hope that she might have made more mistakes.

Nevertheless, the clothesline was proving to be a formidable foe. Then I recalled the forensically-aware latex gloves, wellies and disposable apron. She'd probably used them, or something like them, when she killed Mandy. But why had she kept them?

I was making slow progress but I kept up the sawing motion. I told myself that Clint Eastwood had escaped from Alcatraz in that movie. He'd been patient. Digging a tunnel with a spoon. But he'd had a plan. I didn't have any, apart from playing dead, overpowering Kathleen and getting the gun from her. Vague, it depended on my limbs being free. Which didn't look like it was ever going to happen. My hands and wrists were grazed and raw. Even worse, I felt no movement in the rope binding my wrists.

Then, suddenly, one of the strands snapped. I got loose and I massaged my hands and wrists as best I could to bring the life back into them before starting on my feet. But the knots binding my ankles were impossible to open, for my dead fingers anyway. I lay on my back and raised my feet to ninety degrees and started sawing again. Perversely, the legs were easier, resembling some of the yoga poses I knew.

Only at first. It wasn't long before every muscle and sinew in my thighs and calves was screaming. I had to take longer and more frequent breaks and had almost lost all hope when, finally, I felt one of the strands loosen. I went at the bonds with my hands and after an eternity managed to untie them. At last I was free. As free as a woman confined to a locked windowless room with stone walls two feet thick could be.

115

MY FEET ON THE EARTH FOR THE FIRST TIME IN many hours, I pressed my ear to the door. Not a whisper did I hear but for my own laboured breath and the drumming of my heart. I had no way of knowing for sure. but I had to assume that Kathleen had not returned. I began with the wood. Kicked it. Shouldered it. Stopped when I realised that I was only hurting myself. Then I searched for a weak point, went over every millimetre with my fingertips, probing for a loose knot or a crack, anything. It was packed tight as a ship's timbers. But on bending, I felt a tiny space at ground level and, at its edge, the smooth coating of an electric lead. I remembered the yellow one I'd noticed earlier.

And when I brought it up close to my eyes, I thought I could see it too, a paler shade of darkness. I dropped to my knees and followed it, hand over hand on the wire, along the floor, the lower edge of the wall, ever faster, ever deeper into the barn, my tights holed, my knees chafed and bleeding.

Then I heard it, the faint, muffled but unmistakable sound that I'd missed. The reason for the yellow lead.

116

THE ELECTRIC LEAD ENDED IN A FOUR-WAY MOBILE
plug point, two of them in use. The appliances they served were
covered with a sound-proofing combination of old curtains,
the wooden rings still attached, bedsheets and hessian sacks.
Efficient, too: the hum of the motor was a lot louder once I'd
dragged the coverings onto the floor. Now I could hear the noise
perfectly. And there was no way of unhearing it.

Small exterior lights indicated that both freezers were
switched to their highest settings. I opened the first. The interior
light revealed it to be brand new and clear of ice. Apart from the
plastic wrapped body of Dean McInerney, it was empty.

His torso lay towards the top, slightly sideways, and tilted
downwards, the 'Jack Wills' lettering on his hoodie legible
through the plastic. His hands and arms were tied by his sides
with two sections of rope, one encircling his upper arms and
chest, the other about his hips.

He had been shot. What was left of his head was wedged
in the bottom right-hand corner of the freezer. His legs now
ended at the knees – probably the only way a big man like Dean
could have fitted. Probably the only way Kathleen could have
transported him from the house too. She must have placed his

severed lower legs in the freezer first, then slid his bound torso in after that and pressed it down hard before rigor mortis set in.

I shut the lid on the horror. While I still had the strength, I forced myself to open the second freezer. An older model, it had a basket – containing a bag of Tesco Value frozen sweetcorn and a clear bag with a few lamb chops – hanging askew at one end. At the other slumped the body of Jerry McInerney, much smaller and lighter than that of his grandson Dean, in a hunched seated position. Easier for Kathleen to handle. A black-and-white border collie, its fur crisped and frosted, lay arched across his lap. The dog had had its throat cut. Jerry had a huge hole in the centre of his chest, where his heart had been. The heavy plastic Kathleen had wrapped him in was engorged with dark globules of his frozen blood.

Now I knew what had happened to the McInerneys. And I knew what Kathleen had meant when she'd told me that I'd be dead already, 'except'. She'd meant that she had nowhere to store my dead body. That I would remain alive only until she bought a third chest freezer. The way I saw it, I faced a stark choice. Get free. Or end up dead.

117

EVERY HUMAN INSTINCT I HAD WAS TELLING ME TO keep the freezers shut. To afford the McInerneys some dignity in their terrible deaths. To put the fact that I was sharing my enforced living room with two human corpses and a dead dog as far from my mind as I could. But I needed the light.

The barn wasn't quite as windowless as it had first appeared. Two ventilation slits about a foot long and a few inches wide had been left high in the rear wall. I wasted precious time conjecturing if I could expand them to my size but they were too narrow and too solidly constructed for that to be of any use. I dragged out the freezers slightly and created a crawl space for myself behind them that left me feeling more trapped and, crucially, too far from the exit. I rehearsed various versions of my initial 'play dead and overpower Kathleen' plan, but any scenario I constructed left me in too much danger of again ending up on the flat of my back with the shotgun at my throat. Only this time she wouldn't hesitate to pull the trigger.

In the final analysis, flight seemed like a better option than fight. I needed to get Kathleen away from the door to give me the space to run out behind her and escape. And maybe, if I was lucky, lock her in with her own padlock. I had barely decided on the plan when I heard the sound of an engine in the distance and, some minutes later, the sound of quiet footsteps and the click of the security light in the yard. Kathleen was back. I could expect a visit at any moment.

Quickly, I took off my shoes and placed them carefully, so that they were poking out from the end of the body-shaped pile of sheets and sacks, covered with the old curtains, that I'd made, positioned in front and to the side of the two freezers and visible – but not too visible – in the dim light. Then I hid myself, squatting, under two of the remaining hessian sacks in the corner to the right of the front door. Waiting. Hardly daring to breathe. Watching and listening. For any sound of movement from the house; for the security light to flick on again.

For a long time, nothing happened. Too long. I bitterly regretted my choice of position when both of my legs fell asleep. I sat onto the floor properly, knees bent, and massaged my calves and bare feet. Then I was overcome with a desperate need to pee. The only thing I could do about that was not a good idea in the current circumstances. I held it in and fantasised about my bathroom at home, about clean white ceramic tiles and stainless steel taps.

•

When Kathleen came, she came silently. She must have turned off the security light at the mains before leaving the house. I might not have heard the lock opening, had I not been listening for it. She slid the bolt back and, flinging open the door, switched on a powerful flashlight. Over her left arm, the shotgun hung, broken. When she saw the open chest freezers, she dropped the flashlight and took the shotgun in both hands, readied it for firing.

'What have you done?' she roared. She advanced towards the rear of the barn and, as she did, I crept out behind her. Turning, I saw her kick at the pile of fabric. I pushed the door shut but, before I had a chance to bolt and padlock it, the first shot rang out, splintering the wood. I ran.

As I rounded the gable end of the house, the second shot came.

118

I FELT THE EXPLOSION, FALTERED, NEARLY FELL. Kept running. On the grass now. Easier. Except for the burning in my left upper arm. Kept running. If she wanted to shoot me again, she'd have to reload. I didn't doubt that she had plenty of ammunition – Kathleen was always extremely well-organised – but I had to hope that the spare cartridges were in the house rather than on her.

At the far side of the lawn, I grappled with the thorny boundary hedge. If I could get through it, I'd be able to make it cross-country to Billy Manning's cottage. On the other side, my face and hands torn, my feet bleeding, I started running again, in the direction of the road. If I followed the roadside ditch on the inside, it would lead me to Manning's. I could see the orange glow of the city in the sky. My lungs bursting, I kept running. Running for my life.

Then I heard the sound of the Land Rover. Tearing through the hedge, like it was made of matchsticks. I changed direction. Headed away from the road. Threw myself into a drainage channel. Pulled a few branches over me.

Hid. Hoped. Prayed.

119

SHE STAYED IN THE FIELD ALL NIGHT, THE ENGINE turning over, idling, revving; walking; driving, forward and back, making frenzied circles every now and again. Her headlights shone like prison camp beacons, swiping intermittently across my watery refuge, making it impossible for me to move in any direction. She must have known that she'd injured me. That even if she couldn't find and capture me, the longer I was left without medical attention, the more likely I was to die. At times, I felt dead already, below ground, the earth encasing me.

The pain reminded me that I was alive. I was glad of it, though I could have done without the cold, the chill autumn air and the shallow muddy stream in which I lay. Shivering. On my belly. At some stage, I realised that I'd wet myself. It wasn't as big of a humiliation as I would have expected. All I felt was relief.

•

Abruptly, as the first pink speckles of dawn emerged in the east, Kathleen drove off. Back through the hedge. It must have been close to 7 a.m. I thought that perhaps she intended to make her escape. Or that she might have been seeking to dispose of the

McInerneys' bodies. More likely, she was trying to lull me into giving up my hiding place. So that she could come after me again.

Even so, I reasoned, I had a brief window while she was driving away. I started crawling on my belly along the drainage channel, stopping every now and again to listen for the Land Rover. Calculating that, as long as the engine was running, she was in it and I could escape.

I was wrong. Up ahead, I saw the channel narrowing into a pipe that I assumed was needed for the stream to run under the road, or connect with the roadside drain. Above it was the hawthorn hedgerow I'd seen a lifetime ago, the evening before. A more open hedgerow ran beside the drainage channel on my right. It seemed impossibly high to climb from where I was, but Billy Manning's house was somewhere at the other side of it. Kathleen would expect me to make for there. For all I knew, she had the Land Rover faced in my direction, ready to move when I did.

On my knees, I moved with my forehead raised barely above the edge of the drainage trench. My bruised right eye now fully closed, with my left I spotted a flash of blue passing, heard the car driving at speed – Kathleen's Fiat Punto, heading towards Billy Manning's house, waiting for me to emerge. She'd only left the engine running in the Land Rover to fool me.

Daunted, I couldn't think. Then I connected with the most important part of that last sentence. She'd left the engine of the Land Rover running. More fool her.

120

Crouching.

Limping.

Leaning.

Sick.

Shoulder. So much pain.

Now my other arm keeping it steady. Better.

Holding on.

And I get there.

Climb in.

No time to close the door.

Fall on the handbrake. Tearing gears.

Bare feet sore on the steel pedals. So much pain.

But I'm moving. Driving.

Safe.

121

ALMOST.

At the end of the lane, before I could pull out and head for the main road, Kathleen slammed the Punto sideways across my path and blocked my exit. Dipped her head and shoulders. Popped back up again. The shotgun out the passenger window.

Pointing straight at me.

Flooring the accelerator, I drove at her. So low in the seat I couldn't see where I was going. A shot. A hit. Windscreen smashed.

Pushing. Pushing. Pushing.

The crunch and screech of metal.

Silence.

Seconds later the acrid smell of smoke in my nostrils. I jostled open the door of the Defender and collapsed out onto the roadway. Then stood. Then saw.

The passenger side crushed.

Kathleen in the driver's seat.

Against the stone ditch. No way out.

Still. Quiet.

But no sign of the gun.

And she still had one cartridge left.

I circled back around the Land Rover to approach the Punto from the other angle.

Shouted. 'Kathleen?'

No reply.

Stuck my head out for a look.

Saw her. Moving. Eyes open wide. Wider …

Then I felt it.

The arm round my neck.

122

'I SAW WHAT YOU DID,' A MALE VOICE SAID. 'YOU'RE a madwoman.'

'It's not what it seems. She—'

'Kill her, Billy,' Kathleen said. 'She's a murderer – killed my boss Mandy. Tried to kill me too. You saw her.'

'Call the guards,' I said. '*She's* the murderer. Serial killer.'

She bent forward. Knocked out the shattered windscreen with the butt of the gun. 'Help me out of here, Billy,' she said.

'Don't go near her, she's got a gun. Call the fucking guards!'

'Help me. Billy. Please.'

'She killed Bess,' I said. 'Your dog.'

'She's lying, Billy,' Kathleen said.

'I saw her. Black-and-white border collie. Throat cut. In a freezer up in the barn.'

'Jesus,' Billy said.

'Come on,' Kathleen said. 'You know me.'

'Yeah, I do,' he said. 'That's the trouble.'

He loosened the chokehold on my neck and grabbed my shoulder. I cried out in pain. 'Sorry, sorry,' he said. 'Look, I don't know what the fuck's going on here, but the guards are on their way and if either of ye moves so much as a muscle I-I'll …' He ran out of words. Then, from someplace beyond the trees, we heard a siren.

And Kathleen took aim to fire her final shot.

123

HER MOUTH WAS WRAPPED AROUND THE END OF the shotgun barrel, both hands out of sight but on the trigger. I didn't want her to die. She needed to be brought to trial, to be convicted and serve three life sentences for the three lives she'd taken.

'Don't do it,' I said. 'Please, Kathleen. It wasn't supposed to end like this. This isn't you. I know that. You needed money. For the house. You were entitled to it. But things got out of hand. You didn't want anyone to die. Events forced you to change your plans.'

The burning smell was growing stronger with every second. Black smoke and jaunty orange flames burst free of the metal and danced across the bonnet of the Land Rover.

'Get back!' Billy Manning shouted. 'It's going to blow.'

'*Kathleen!*' I screamed. 'You need to get out now!'

She shook her head. Then she took the gun from her mouth and coughed. 'I'm very sorry about the McInerneys. Them coming into it was … unfortunate.' She looked defeated and I thought in that moment that there might be a chance.

'Give me the gun,' I said. 'Throw it out onto the ground.'

'I'm sorry for shooting you as well, Finn. But it's your own fault.'

'Kathleen. The gun. Please.'

'I'm not sorry about Mandy. She deserved it. Had to die. That was the plan. Good plan, too. All for nothing in the end.'

'I'll help you, Kathleen,' I said. 'Come on.' I stepped forward. Knelt up onto the bonnet. Stretched out my hand. But Kathleen put the gun in her mouth again.

I cried, 'No! No! No! No!' Then Billy Manning was beside me. Dragging me away as the fatal shot rang out.

We were nowhere near a safe distance away when both vehicles exploded.

SIX
DAYS
LATER

124

THE AMBULANCE PARAMEDIC WHO TENDED ME AS
I lapsed in and out of seasick consciousness on the helter-skelter
ride to Cork University Hospital; the junior A & E doctor who
spent what felt like hours tweezing what he informed me were
5 shotgun pellets from my left shoulder and upper arm,
clanging them one by one into a steel kidney bowl; the nurse
who sluiced my wounds clean of dirt and leaves and thorns and
twigs and dried blood; the radiographer who X-rayed my eye
socket and cheekbone … All of them said the same thing: 'You
were lucky.'

Confined to bed in Cork University Hospital, under
observation – which as far as I could see meant being prodded
and re-prodded every five seconds, when all I wanted was to be
left alone – I didn't feel one little bit lucky. And when my parents
came to visit, all I felt was shame. Their matching expressions
imparted everything I needed to know about how upset they
were. If I'd told someone – anyone – where I was going when
I'd gone to visit Kathleen, and why, none of this would have
happened. At the very least, it wouldn't have happened in the
same way.

The way that had left Billy Manning – the stranger who'd

pulled me off Kathleen's car and thrown himself on top of me, bearing the worst of the explosion – nearly dead, down the hall in ICU in an induced coma. And me, lying uselessly on top of the covers in this hospital bed, wearing loose white cotton pyjama bottoms with the legs cut to mid-thigh; and on top, on the left, a fetching T-shirt with the shoulder and sleeve removed entirely; on the right, the sleeve torn off at the bicep. Apart from the bruises all over every part of my body, and an array of wrenched muscles, and a spectacular knife-sharp pain in my right hip – an injury I must have sustained when I dropped into the drain to hide, though I hadn't been aware of it at the time – I'd suffered head and facial wounds, an injury to my eye socket, deep scrapes down my arms and legs, both knees rubbed raw, and ugly cuts to my hands and feet.

'Superficial,' the A & E junior doctor had said. 'No major bones or arteries or vital organs hit. Amazing, really. You were—'

'I was lucky,' I'd said, before he could say it again. 'I get you.'

•

'Oh Finn,' my mother said now from the discomfort of the single bedside chair, as fat tears rolled down both her cheeks. 'Oh Finn,' she said again.

My father stood, shifting from foot to foot. 'When you're released from here, you'll have to move home for a while,' he said. 'I don't want any argument out of you.'

I'd never been in worse shape. The consultant had told me she'd have to wait for the swelling to go down before making a decision about what to do with my eye socket and cheekbone.

Surgery looked likely but not until some as yet unspecified future date. My left shoulder was strapped and bandaged as much as it could be, and I had a drip in my arm replenishing the fluids I'd lost.

•

But, sore as I was, and bad as I felt about what I was putting them through, I had no intention of recuperating at my parents' house. I'd refused all pain relief apart from paracetamol and I'd opted to switch to oral rather than the intravenous antibiotics I'd been on since my admission. I'd pestered the nurse mercilessly until she'd said that the drip could be removed sometime during the next few hours.

Because five nights in this place was enough. I needed to get out of the hospital. And I needed a clear head when I did.

125

'I'M BUSY,' SADIE SAID. 'I'VE GOT MULTIPLE MURDER investigations to complete.' She added, 'And you shouldn't be doing this. You should stay in and get better.'

'I need you to come between 7 and 7.30 a.m. Before the disgusting breakfast. Before the consultant's ward round.'

'Not a chance.'

'I'll never get better if I stay here,' I said.

I meant it. I was desperate to escape. I'd gone so far as to borrow another patient's phone to ring Sadie because I didn't have mine. Being under the same roof as the man who'd rambled into the story and suffered grievously for my heedlessness had something to do with it; but the hospital made everything smell, taste, feel worse. And there was the noise. The beeps of the machines and the squeaks of the trolley wheels, and the unidentifiable bangs and jolts and moans had my already frayed nerves as taut as an overwound guitar string, ready to snap. I didn't say any of that to Sadie. I didn't have to.

It was after eight when she arrived.

'Um, I got delayed,' she said.

'You okay?'

'You're asking *me* if I'm okay? Have you looked in the mirror lately?'

She dumped the contents of a SuperValu bag-for-life on the bed – oversized white cotton T-shirt and grey hoodie, loose dark grey linen drawstring trousers, white tube socks and a pair of well-worn blue-and-white Nike pool slides for my feet.

'You found everything easily enough?' I said. She gave me a look and I laughed. It hurt. 'Fucking ouch!' I said.

'Fucking ridiculous, is what this is,' she said. Then, 'You need help with these?'

'I'll manage, no bother. Pull the curtains, will you?'

I did need help getting dressed, though, and she gave it without another word of complaint. We both knew I'd lasted longer here than she would have.

'Can you walk?'

'Definitely.' I didn't know if that was true.

'Hang on a minute,' Sadie said. She came back with a wheelchair and a nurse I hadn't met before, who looked like she'd just come on duty. She was tanned, like she was just back from holidays.

'She knows you're leaving. I told her.'

I was thinking, *What the fuck?* but said, 'That's, ah, that's good.'

'Not,' the nurse said. 'You're not getting out of here without a formal discharge.'

'I'm nearly sure the consultant said it was okay,' I said. 'Maybe give her a call?'

She pursed her lips and said, 'Wait here,' and left the ward at a good clip.

'*Go*, Sadie!' I said. 'Right instead of left and we won't pass the nurses' station. We'll get to the lift the long way around.'

But I made her stop for a moment outside the ICU, where the lights were dimmed and the curtains drawn, and the ventilator keeping Billy Manning alive pumped and sucked and wheezed and rasped and groaned.

126

'SO I DIDN'T TELL YOU SOONER,' SADIE SAID. 'Because, you know, you're supposed to be working on getting better, but we found your car more or less where you said it would be.'

'And this,' she added. 'After I cleared the mountain of empty Tayto bags out of the side pocket.'

'Don't knock the Taytos. Or the mess. If the car was cleaner, Kathleen would've found my phone and dumped it.'

'True.' She tossed the phone to me. We were in my living room, me lying full-length on the sofa, wrecked after the climb upstairs, her standing by the kitchen island. I caught the phone, glanced at it for a few moments, then slipped it under a cushion.

'Forty-two missed calls,' I said. 'Forty-one from my mother, probably.'

'One or two from Davy maybe?' Sadie asked innocently.

'I don't … I didn't look,' I said. 'I'm sure—'

'Did he visit you in the hospital?'

'He didn't. He may not even know …'

'Oh he knows alright,' Sadie said. 'You're front-page news. Again. Making a habit of it at this stage, girl.'

'Didn't realise,' I said. 'No phone, so—'

'Did you break up with him?'

'I'm not sure. Probably did.'

'Who started it?'

'No one really started it,' I said. 'We had a fight. Which I suppose I might have "started". I think. I was in the wrong. Completely. Totally. I see that now. I'll … Now that I'm out, I'm going to call him. See if he ever wants to talk to me again. Though I wouldn't blame him if he didn't.'

'Maybe you should leave it for a while. See how you feel later. Concentrate on the recovery for now.'

'You never liked him.'

'It's not that,' Sadie said. 'Not anymore.'

'What, then?'

'Em, I suppose you've been through a lot, just. A trauma.'

'Yeah,' I said. 'And?'

'I got you milk and brown soda bread. And those disgusting oatcakes you like.'

'Sure, I've tons of them already,' I said.

'So I see,' Sadie said. 'Now. And Tina says she'll call up and bring you stuff from the market as well, if you want. She's going to ring you later on.'

'Thanks.'

'I could hang on here for another while if you want, hold off on going into work. I could ask Olly Fogarty to come up? The two of us could take your formal statement. Get it out of the way. If you're up for talking in that level of detail, like. About what happened?'

She'd done a short preliminary interview at the hospital. I'd known there was more to come. I didn't know if I was ready for it, but there was only one way to find out. 'I think that'd be okay,' I said. 'But you've got to make me a proper coffee first. I don't care if the caffeine makes the pain worse, I'm gasping. And you have to bring me up to date on what's been happening with the case.'

127

'SO IT LOOKS LIKE IT WAS ALL KATHLEEN. NINETY-nine per cent anyway,' Sadie said. 'The estate agent – Ricky Dempsey – was peripheral. He's saying he never met Kathleen. He thought all the time that he was dealing with Mandy. He admits that he pushed the valuations; massaged the figures; accepted the copy identity documents she gave him; told the various banks he'd seen the originals when he hadn't. But he's saying he knows nothing about the murders, and I'm inclined to believe him.'

'He's back from Marbella?'

'Flew home. Presented himself at Coughlan's Quay voluntarily, by arrangement. Gave a statement prepared in advance by his solicitor.'

'Who's he got?'

'Conleth Young.'

'I recommended him to Ed at one stage. He won't need him now, I guess.'

'No,' Sadie said. 'Y'know, I don't think Kathleen ever expected to be caught.'

'She had it all set up to look like it was Mandy's property scam. It was perfect.'

'And then she murdered her.'

'It didn't go how she intended. The McInerneys meant she had to improvise.'

'Rotten luck for them,' Sadie said. 'Jerry hadn't been back in Cork for fifty years and the poor guy, his first visit home gets him and his grandson killed. His daughter, Dean's mother, is devastated, as you can imagine.'

'The unfortunate woman, I can't even think about her. Or Dean's dad and his sister,' I said. 'I've thought about making contact with them. To express my sympathies. But …'

'Best not,' Sadie said. 'Let them contact you if they want.'

'You're right,' I said. What happened was so … And so random. Anytime, over so many years, Jerry could have travelled to Cork but by the time he did so, Kathleen had her paws on the house. She'd chosen well. Knew the place from when she was working Saturdays as a carer for Dr Keyes in the big house. Did all her research on the ownership. Realised it was a sitting duck. It would've been her biggest payoff. A whole house sold.'

I paused. 'I've been wondering why no one at your end followed up with Dr Keyes' carers. If they had, Kathleen might have been caught a lot sooner.'

Sadie looked embarrassed. 'Actually,' she said, 'someone did. Someone even spoke to "Kate" on the phone. But the member in question never thought to ask about Kate's background, if she had another job. If he had—'

'Who was it?' I asked. 'Who fucked up?'

'It wouldn't be fair to say. Especially as I can't guarantee I wouldn't have made exactly the same mistake myself.'

'Okay,' I said. 'So the McInerneys found out Mandy's name via the Probate Office. Rang her from Wales on the Friday, and arranged to meet her on the Monday of their visit. Except it wasn't Mandy they were talking to on the phone.'

'It was Kathleen,' Sadie said.

'She had to act fast,' I said. 'Delete everything to do with the property scam from the case management system, or her house of cards would come tumbling down. The only thing left were those call logs from Ricky Dempsey. Whether that was an accident I can't be sure, but I think it was probably deliberate misdirection.'

'Makes sense,' Sadie said.

'And she fixed the Monday morning meeting for the McInerneys with Mandy to fob them off for a while, to keep them under control. Spun them a line about some kind of misunderstanding; told them she'd sort everything out. Like Dempsey, they thought they'd spoken to Mandy.'

'One thing I don't understand, Finn – wouldn't some of the others in the office, Tina, say, have heard what Kathleen was doing?'

'They probably did hear but didn't take any notice. They wouldn't have suspected anything from her talking to Mandy's clients and making arrangements. Just that she was doing her job like she did every day.'

'And when the McInerneys came to the office on the Monday morning ...'

'Kathleen intercepted them while they were in the waiting room. She'd been talking to Gabriel. Knew they were downstairs. I'm fairly sure she told him to let them stew for a while, and that she was the one who suggested he send me down to them. That never made any sense to me. In retrospect, I see that she was keeping her distance from them, so that it would look like she hadn't had any contact with them. But she did. Do you know how?'

'It wasn't by phone, anyway,' Sadie said. 'She must have slipped into the waiting room and met them unseen.'

'It's possible,' I said. 'The CCTV doesn't cover that door.'

'That was the riskiest element. If she'd been seen by anyone at that point—'

'But she wasn't,' I said. 'She talked to them and arranged to see them in Blarney later. Promised to tell them everything but not in the office. Told them her job would be in danger if she got caught, or some such rubbish, and that they had to leave straightaway without saying a word to anyone.'

'She'd left the door of the murder house open so that the body would be discovered early.'

'But not too early. There was still time for the McInerneys to come for their appointment and leave none the wiser, but they were now nicely in the frame as suspects for Mandy's murder. That's why she had them come into the office. To muddy the waters. Which it did. Kind of.'

'So the McInerneys leave MLC in a rush,' Sadie said. 'They check out of their hotel and take the bus to Blarney Castle to kiss the Blarney Stone, but never get back on the bus. They go for a walk instead, disappear off the radar.'

'Meanwhile, Kathleen appears to be devastated by Mandy's death – I made her a cup of tea, for fuck's sake. Has to leave the office. When she does, she goes to meet the McInerneys in Blarney.'

'Then she drove them to her house and murdered them, like she'd been planning since their call on Friday.'

'Have you got the full post-mortem results?'

'We've to wait a little longer for all the tests,' Sadie said. 'The – em – bodies, they, em, took a while to thaw.'

I felt my stomach leap. 'Go on,' I said.

'You sure you're able?'

'Tell me about the McInerneys' phones. They never went anywhere near Dublin. How did she manage that?'

'It was the jeep,' Sadie said, 'the Land Rover Defender, that led us to that solution. It's hard to find a vehicle if you don't know what you're looking for. Once we saw that one, we started looking for it on CCTV and traffic cams.'

'And?'

'Like I said, she lured them to her house, killed them. The following morning, she drove the Land Rover into town and parked in Kent Station car park. Got on the Aircoach to Dublin Airport. Kept the phones off but made sure to send a message from Dean's phone to his "Mum", Charlene, as the bus approached Dublin. She must have noticed that he didn't have a password on his phone, that he used his—'

'Oh please, no,' I said.

'Yes. His fingerprint. Which she was able to use because she cut it—'

'Stop,' I said. 'What happened after Clondalkin?'

'She turned off his phone again but stayed on the bus, obviously, and went on to the airport. There she disposed of both the phones – broken up – in a bin or three. She's caught on CCTV but would never have been spotted, except we were looking for her. We haven't found the phones. Might never. She had fish and chips and a small bottle of Chardonnay in the Gate Clock bar in Terminal 1, then turned around, got on the next Aircoach and came back to Cork. Put poor Dean's thumb back in the freezer with the rest of him. Don't know what to make of that, really.'

'Most likely, she was just being careful.'

'Busy woman,' Sadie said.

'Found time to buy a new freezer though. And get it delivered.'

'She'd already bought it in Harvey Norman on the Saturday. It was delivered on the Monday afternoon,' Sadie said. 'She even got the delivery guy to set it up for her in the barn. He came forward after the news broke. She bought the other tools on the Saturday as well. In B&Q in Mahon Point. Used cash for all purchases.'

'A good bit of cash,' I said. 'She must have used some of her mortgage fraud haul.'

'Doesn't look like it,' Sadie said. 'None of the mortgage fraud funds were touched.'

'Oh,' I said. 'That sort of makes sense.'

'Does it?'

'I'll explain in a minute,' I said. 'First, tell me, where did she do the killing?'

'The dining room. She must have directed them in there. She'd moved the furniture and the rug. She must have pre-covered the floor in plastic before they arrived, because there was very little blood on it. She shot Dean in the head from behind. He probably never knew what hit him. Poor Jerry did. She got him in the chest.' Sadie swallowed. 'That's kind of the bit I found the hardest. That Jerry saw his grandson like that. Kathleen had to kill Dean first, because of his size.'

I stretched out my hand towards her. She gave it a squeeze. Then she let it go, blew out a breath, and started talking again. 'The blood spray was massive. That's why she had to strip the wallpaper. She washed down all the surfaces – did a pretty good job. But the whole place lit up like an ultra-violet Christmas tree all the same after the Bureau sprayed it with luminol.

'She wrapped their corpses in the heavy plastic,' Sadie went on. 'Transferred them across to the barn by wheelbarrow. Jerry was small and thin, so he stayed intact. Dean was too big, so she had to do a job on him to make him portable.' She paused. 'It's completely mad when you think about it.'

'In the end, it was, yeah.'

'What do you mean?'

'I think it started small. Office politics. Bog standard resentment. Nasty, admittedly. But it festered. Grew toxic. Revenge fantasies that then became all too real. And Mandy never suspected a thing. Maybe even at the very end she didn't know what – or who – had killed her.'

'The affair seems to have been a tipping point,' I went on. 'As far as Kathleen was concerned, Mandy had it all. The affair showed that she was careless with her good fortune, didn't appreciate it. So Kathleen decided to destroy her.'

'With the fraud.'

'Yes,' I said. 'But the *type* of fraud was important. Mandy's work was fundamental to who she was. The idea of Queen Mandy being dethroned as a cheap swindler, her memory besmirched, must have given Kathleen enormous satisfaction. It was ready to go, and it was due to happen soon. But it wasn't supposed to happen when it did, and I don't think it was supposed to happen the way it did either. The McInerneys ruined everything. Kathleen had to pivot suddenly. Delete everything about the mortgage fraud and leave no trail. It didn't quite come off, because Pauline Doyle found the deleted files.

Kathleen remembered to empty the Trash folder on Mandy's desktop but forgot about the one on the main server. The fraud could've taken months or years to show up otherwise, long after the trail had gone cold. Kathleen very nearly got away with it.'

'So Kathleen always intended to kill Mandy, you think?' Sadie asked.

'Yes. She told me she did. But not like this. My guess is that she would've staged a suicide just before the big fraud reveal, with a faked note or email setting out Mandy's sins, blaming stress or the marriage breakup. Maybe Kathleen never intended to spend the money. I'm sure she didn't consider herself dishonest. Maybe in her own mind, spending the money would have been beneath her. Or it could simply be that she didn't have the time to spend it. That the whole thing got away from her.

'No one would've looked behind the suicide, if that's how it had gone,' I went on. 'A convenient written confession from Mandy. Just another crooked solicitor – a nine-day wonder for everyone except her family and close friends.'

'There's one thing I still can't figure out,' Sadie said. 'How did Kathleen get her to go to that house in Glasheen? Mandy didn't know anything about the McInerneys, or the scam. There was no reason for her to be there. I don't understand why she went. It was Sunday night. She drove there herself, for no apparent reason, like a lamb to the slaughter. Why?'

'It can only be because she'd arranged to meet Kathleen there. Mandy was worried about something to do with work. I thought she'd had some contact with the McInerneys and found out something about the fraud but—'

'Doesn't look like it,' Sadie said. 'And we haven't been able to find any phone contact between Mandy and Kathleen on the Sunday of the murder. Not on the phones we have, anyway.'

'Kathleen knew that Mandy had an affair phone,' I said.

'We never found it. But we got the number from Owen McCormack, so we were able to source those records that way. There was no contact with Kathleen on that, or between Mandy and the burner Kathleen used for the mortgage fraud.'

'If there's no phone record of contact,' I said, 'the visit to Alysson Villas must have been arranged face-to-face.' I sighed. 'Poor Mandy. Going about her life, oblivious. With no idea how much she was hated. No idea how far she was going to fall.'

'And how fast,' Sadie said.

'Her future, her life, all snatched away.'

'Jerry and Dean McInerney too.'

'But for Kathleen, it was all about Mandy,' I said. 'The McInerneys were collateral damage – in the wrong place at the wrong time, in possession of the wrong information.'

•

And now Billy Manning was clinging to life by his fingernails. If he ended up dying, it wouldn't be Kathleen's fault.

It would be mine.

128

WHEN THE DOORBELL RANG, WHILE SADIE WENT downstairs to let in her work partner, Detective Garda Olly Fogarty, I checked my phone. I'd been right. Most of the missed calls were from my mother, but there were two from my dad, and one each from Sadie and Tina – and four were from Davy, along with three text messages from him, the first from before the news had broken:

> *Hey Finn can we talk? Meet? Soon? Call me x*

The second came after:

> *Heard the news. Can hardly believe it. Hope you're as well as you can be. Worried. Can I come visit u in CUH? Won't come unless you say it's OK. Let me know. Lots of love xxx*

That was followed a day later by:

> *I guess you're not ready for visitors. Sorry if that last message was the wrong thing to say. I shoulda just gone to hospital and not waited for permission. Too late now xxxx*

'It's not too late,' I said aloud. But before I had a chance to reply, I heard Sadie and Fogarty on the stairs. Sadie introduced us.

'We've met,' I said. 'That day at the station with Ed. And I saw you at the funeral.'

'You've been in the wars since then,' Fogarty said.

In response, I tipped my chin upwards. I had no words. Then Fogarty said, 'Some gaff. I'd say she cost you a fair oul' bit o' twine to build.'

I laughed.

'Jesus, Olly,' Sadie said. 'Now is not, repeat, *not* the time.'

'I'm only admiring it. It's nice, like.'

'Don't mind him, Finn, he's a fucking ignoramus. Even out at Kathleen's, he was on about how much the place was worth and wondering if it had much road frontage for sites.'

'Stop,' I said. 'Every time you make me laugh, it hurts like hell.'

'Now look what you've done, Sadie. Now who's the fucking ignoramus, who?'

I laughed more.

But the double act got serious after a while, and – they must have agreed the format between them – Fogarty took the lead on the questions with Sadie chiming in occasionally. It worked well. He didn't know me like she did. He let me tell my story and asked short, basic questions that got me thinking about the facts of what had happened more clinically, and he prised the details out of me, piece by agonising piece.

At the end, I signed the final page of his handwritten notes, initialled each of the others and handed them back to him. 'You mentioned the dog,' he said. 'There was a big bloodstain inside on the left of the front door, on the way into the front parlour.

Away from the main kill area. The Bureau reckon she cut the misfortunate sheepdog's throat there.'

'I think Bess was dead for a while. Before the McInerneys. I got the impression she'd been missing for a few weeks.'

'Her first victim?' Sadie said. 'Even before Mandy?'

'I think so,' I said. 'Practice, maybe.'

''Tis the least of it, I suppose,' Fogarty said. 'But sure when Billy Manning wakes up he'll be able to tell us.'

I said nothing but tears pooled in my eyes. 'He *is* going to wake up,' Sadie said. 'And he's going to be okay.'

'I don't know if he will and—'

'Well I do,' Fogarty said. 'I phoned CUH a short while ago. He's on the mend, they reckon. Well, that's what that lovely blonde nurse from Killorglin told me anyways.'

I started to cry. 'Thank God,' I said. 'And you too, Olly. I'm so grateful to you.'

Sadie put her arm around me. 'Don't be too grateful,' she said. 'Bear in mind that the nurse is the only reason he phoned. Pity, I was almost impressed with your initiative for about five seconds there, Fogarty.'

He said, 'So, em, Finn, I'll type up that statement for you and—'

'Trying to change the subject now,' Sadie said.

Ignoring her, he continued, 'And you can check through it and make any additions or alterations you want. But the hard job is done now and you should have a rest for yourself. I'd say you could do with one.'

He wasn't lying. On top of which, I was nearly sure my period had just started.

'I might go down to the bedroom for a while.'

'I'll help you,' Sadie said. 'You head off, Fogarty, see you back at the ranch.'

•

She waited while I went to the loo and got me comfortable in the bed after.

'After I'm gone, you should probably call your parents before you fall asleep.'

'I will,' I said. 'I'm going to call Davy too.'

Sadie said nothing but disapproval hung around her like a cloud of hairspray.

'He did phone me,' I went on. 'Several times. And texted. And I miss him.'

'Okay,' Sadie said. 'I'll slip away, so. And you take care of yourself.'

I watched her walk to the door of the room but she didn't leave. She stood with her back to me, her left hand on the doorframe, her head bent, not moving.

I thought she was overwhelmed by it all, or upset, so I said, 'I'll be fine.'

She turned. 'It's not that,' she said. 'It's not your injuries. It's something else. And I don't know if I'm doing the right thing by telling you.'

'Just tell me,' I said. 'Whatever it is.'

'The thing is, it might be nothing,' Sadie said. 'That's why I didn't want to say …'

'It's obviously not nothing,' I said. 'What is it?'

'It's about Davy.'

129

LATER THAT DAY, WITH TINA'S HELP, I MOVED TO the spare room. I told her that the shower on the ground floor was easier for me to get in and out of — and it was — but that wasn't my reason.

After that, I went upstairs only as a last resort. The washing machine and tumble dryer were downstairs, and I dressed in rotating sets of pyjamas and hoodies that I washed less often than I should have. I did what I could by way of yoga and physio, and streamed *Sex and the City* on my laptop. For sustenance, I set up a kettle in my study and drank green tea instead of coffee. In the bottom drawer of my desk, I kept a tin with oatcakes in it in case I got hungry. Mostly I didn't; though I ate the plated dinners my parents brought me. I had no choice — they watched until every molecule was gone.

Tina rang most days. She tried to keep me updated on how things were going in the office, until she realised I didn't want to hear. After that, she rang and talked instead about everything but the office. Sadie called by often and brought me occasional sweet treats. One day she told me that Lenihan had made a series of arrests in his Clondalkin operation; that there'd be a big report about it on *Six One*. I told her I'd tune in, but when it came to the time, I didn't bother. There *had* been no connection between the McInerneys and his case.

And what Davy had been doing was entirely Cork-based too. Nothing at all to do with Lenihan, whose mention of my 'boyfriend' seemed to have been as random as the text message he sent me – *Heard from Sadie u out of hospital. Get well soon.*

•

The days drifted by in a fog, broken only by the pathetically ineffectual attempts I made to work from home. Even after the operation on my face, I forewent the relief and the temporary bliss offered by the Tramadol I'd been prescribed for the pain. Every so often, when the gnawing torment got too bad, I took the pills out of the cardboard pack and ran my fingers over the foil and the blisters but I'd put them away again and take a couple more paracetamol instead. I knew I'd get past the physical injury but, with my family history, didn't want to be left with a more permanent legacy.

The one bright spot in the wreckage was that Billy Manning had made a remarkable recovery. He called to see me a few times, and sent me pictures and videos of his new puppy. He'd told me that none of what he'd gone through was down to me; that it was all Kathleen. After a while, I let him think I believed him.

I ignored Davy's messages – they'd grown shorter and fewer and ultimately petered out – until the middle of November. I was due to go back to the office part-time the following Tuesday for the few weeks before Christmas, and full-time once January came. But I wanted to clean house before the New Year, and I couldn't do it right without talking to him.

So I took a chance and booked an early-evening table in Isaacs on MacCurtain Street. On the other side of town, we'd been there together a few times but it wasn't one of our places. Then I texted him and told him where I'd be and when. He didn't reply, but he was waiting by the entrance when my taxi pulled up. He came to the door of the cab to help me out.

'Don't,' I said.

He stepped back from me and followed without a word, as I fumbled with my bag and coat and limped my way to the table. My wool scarf was nice, but other than that I wasn't fit to be seen. I was wearing black leggings – tights weren't an option due to the tender scabs on my legs – underneath a loose black cotton dress and, on my still-sore feet, to my eternal shame, black cotton men's socks and black crocs. Davy, on the other hand, even after everything that had happened, looked as sickeningly gorgeous as ever in a navy cashmere jumper that I'd bought for him in Brown Thomas. He was charmingly tired and pale around the eyes. As you'd expect.

The beautiful Isaacs dining room had high ceilings and tall plate-glass windows that looked out on the street named for Tomás MacCurtain, the lord mayor of Cork who was assassinated by the Royal Irish Constabulary in 1920. A recent marketing initiative by local businesses had re-christened the entire area 'The Victorian Quarter', though because of the age of the buildings rather than in honour of her deceased Britannic majesty, the self-styled empress of India. Even so, I reckoned poor Tomás must be spinning in his grave.

The restaurant was decorated for Christmas with fragrant arrangements of holly and ivy, and fronds of fir, all trimmed with red ribbons. It was as full and buzzy as ever. While I caught my breath, we sat in silence till the waitress came with the menu. I didn't need to look. Comfortingly, apart from the specials, it never changes. I ordered the salmon and potato cakes and a large bottle of sparkling water; Davy, the lamb curry with poppadoms.

•

'How are you?' Davy asked.

'What did you call him?'

'Straight in,' he said.

'What. Did. You. Call. Him.'

'Ah, we called him Tom, after Maura's father.'

'"We". Lovely.'

'Finn, I wanted to tell you. I did try. Not hard enough. Obviously.'

'How long was it going on, you and her?'

'It wasn't,' he said. 'It didn't. It was a one-night stand.'

'Just the once. Really? Please.'

'It was a weekend.'

'Oh sure, if that's all—'

'That's all it was, I swear.'

'You went out with her for two fucking years.'

'I did. In the past. I'm not denying that. You knew that already. But it was over. Before that weekend, I hadn't seen or talked to her in years. I was with you. She was with someone else as well. But then she broke up with the guy she was with, and it was around the time we had that break. February. You'd said you wanted to press pause for a while.'

'Pause. Not stop.'

'I know,' he said. 'I know.'

'Had you been in contact with her all along? All the time we were together?'

'No. Not at all. I met her by accident. That Friday night at Orla's birthday.'

'The night you told me was the last time you saw Mandy.'

'It *was* the last time. I'd wanted to avoid saying it because of what happened after the party. I got chatting to Maura there – she and Orla had always stayed in touch – and she came back with me to my house after and—'

'And Orla knew about the pregnancy?'

'Yeah, that's why she was so surprised I'd mentioned that night to you. She knew I hadn't told you. She was putting me under pressure to tell you everything.'

'And to break up with me.'

'Not exactly. But she always liked Maura. She said I had to give a relationship with her a chance. For the baby's sake.'

I clenched my fists. Folded my arms. Let the rage that I felt curdle inside me.

•

The waitress came with the food. Neither of us picked up a fork but I took a sip of water.

'I don't know why I ordered this,' I said.

'You like it normally,' he said.

'I'm not feeling very normal,' I said.

'You know, em, what happened isn't as simple as … Do you want to hear it or …?'

Did I? The truth was, I did. I needed to hear it from him. It was the reason I'd arranged the meeting. 'I'll shut up and listen,' I said.

'Okay,' Davy said. He continued, 'Like I said, I hadn't been within miles of her for years. Four. Five. I associated her with the bad times. She was never in my league with the coke, and she cleaned up her act a lot more easily than I did. Still drinks … Drank. Until the pregnancy. But no drugs. None.

And she'd had that breakup, like I said. It wasn't like I went out looking for her … I didn't intend anything to happen, but I take full responsibility for what did.'

'So you're admitting she didn't force you to spend the whole weekend fucking her?'

'I thought you said you were going to shut up and listen?'

'Go on, so,' I said.

'That was it. One weekend. I told her about you … about us … I … And then you and I got back together shortly afterwards. Middle of February. And happy days, I thought – until … Until she contacted me again – like *months* later, to say she was pregnant. She didn't know for sure at that stage whose it was. I wasn't the only possibility. It could have been her ex. Or me. And she was totally finished with the ex by then. But she said she wanted to tell me cause—'

'She wanted you back.'

'She never said that.'

'She meant it.'

'Maybe. Probably.'

'Definitely.'

He shrugged. 'I told her I was with you and that we were serious and that I'd support her during the pregnancy and that I'd be fully involved with the baby. If it was mine. But I made it clear that I wasn't getting back with her and if you still wanted me after all this I was still going to be with you. I told her I was going to tell you immediately. The same night I found out.'

'Which night was that?'

'The night of the Dolly Parton concert. Afterwards.'

'How very thoughtful of you,' I said. 'You wanted me to enjoy the gig, before you ruined the memory forever.'

'That's one of the reasons I didn't say it then. We'd had such a good time. I said to myself that it would be better to leave it for a few days.'

'What was the other reason?'

'What?'

'You said that was one of the reasons. What was the other?'

'I saw Mandy. You did too. With that guy. Not Ed. Her cheating. It shook me. And you didn't even know that I knew her. It was all too close to home so I—'

'Put it off.'

'Yeah,' Davy said.

'She looked afraid when she saw you. That look of terror.'

'It wasn't me she was afraid of, it was *you*; she was terrified that you'd tell people. That Ed would find out before she had a chance to tell him herself.'

'How do you know that?'

'She rang me the next day. Said it.'

'But Ed knew all along,' I said. 'That's what he told me.'

'She didn't know that. She really didn't. That was my impression, anyway. No one at MLC did.'

'Except Kathleen, obviously. She told me that Mandy told her.'

'I'll take your word for that, but it'd surprise me if Mandy actually did,' Davy said.

'She knew everything else about Mandy. Her computer password. The MLC bank codes. You name it. That's how she was able to pass her own fraud off as Mandy's.'

'That's work stuff. It's different. Mandy wouldn't have told anyone before she'd sorted things with Ed. It was a big deal for her. She told me she was expecting him to react badly and she wanted to protect the kids.'

'Kathleen *did* know about the affair, though. That's what precipitated the fraud.'

'She must've found out about it by herself so. Anyway, bottom line, whatever about Mandy, I shouldn't have waited. I should've told you.'

'Yeah,' I said. 'You should've.'

'And then the days turned into weeks and months, and there was always a chance that it wasn't mine and that there'd be no need to say anything at all … Which was completely gutless of me obviously, I do know that. And then Mandy got killed and then – fucking hell, Finn – you actually thought I'd killed her.'

'You were behaving so weirdly. Like you were hiding something.'

'I was. But not that.'

'Where were you that Monday, the day Mandy was found murdered? With Maura?'

'We were at the maternity hospital. She had some spotting on the Sunday. We were due a scan on the Monday anyway. I'd cancelled some classes so that I could be there but she had to go in the night before. It ended up being a false alarm.' He went on, 'I was building up to tell you but then Mandy died and you got kidnapped or whatever, and I couldn't get in touch with you, and the baby came early—'

'A series of unfortunate events,' I said.

'I'm not making excuses. It's just how it went.'

'Mother and baby are doing well?'

'Yeah.'

'And you've had the DNA test.'

He nodded. 'Tom's my son.'

I swallowed. It wasn't news to me. But it was hard to hear. After a silence I said, 'Congratulations.'

'Thanks,' Davy said. 'I'm so, so sorry.'

'You can't be,' I said. 'You're not sorry about Tom, are you?'

'I wasn't talking about—'

'But you don't regret him, do you?'

'I can't, can I?'

'No,' I said. 'You can't.'

'I still love you, you know,' he said.

'Oh, fuck off.'

'I mean it,' he said. 'I do.'

'But you're with her now. Maura. I know you are. Sadie saw you and her going into the Maternity section in CUH the day she came to collect me from hospital. Your arm around her. Carrying her little suitcase. I know everything. People think I want to know this shit, and they tell me. They even tell me she's living in your fucking house now, for fuck's sake.'

'She is. But we're not together. We tried for a bit after the birth. For Tom's sake. We broke up again. We don't get on. Without alcohol and cocaine, we *really* don't get on.'

'Oh my God, was that who I was for you? Because I don't drink? And I don't take drugs? Was that it? Was I your fucking minder?'

He waited a little too long before he said, 'No, Finn. No. You can't believe that.'

I shook my head. After a long silence, I said, 'You claim you're not with her, but you're still in the same house.'

'She's going to be getting a place of her own. Soon. Till then, I'm sleeping in the box room and she's in my bedroom with Tom and the cot. And he's great. He's the best. But I don't want to be with Maura. I want to be with you. And I know that's probably too much to ask of you right now but—'

I said, 'It's too much to ask of me ever.'

130

I DIDN'T STAGE A DRAMATIC WALKOUT. I FORCED myself to stay. I made myself listen to every bullshit line. I wanted to finish it, to draw a clear line that I'd never cross again. A little after 10 p.m., I walked home, dry-eyed and alone. It was the longest walk I'd taken since I'd been shot. And it was a mistake. The pain in my body, my muscles, every part of me shrieking and tearing, was bone-deep. But the pain in my heart was worse.

At 4.07 a.m., I took my first Tramadol. At 4.08 a.m., I swallowed two more. At 4.09 a.m., I crouched over the toilet bowl, index and middle fingers down my throat. After the three pills came back up, I popped the blisters on the rest and flushed them away. Later, I crawled upstairs and into my own bed for the first time in weeks. It was my bed. Not ours. Not his. I'd had it before him. I'd paid for it. And for my house. Every cent. His absence couldn't control how I lived. I would get through this, I told myself. I would get over him.

Then I cried for eighteen hours.

131

'ARE YOU SURE YOU'RE ABLE?' GABRIEL ASKED.

He looked better than he had in a long time, a man saved from the gallows, determined to wring every last gift from a life he'd never expected to get back. Mandy hadn't been guilty of anything. It had been Kathleen, a rogue actor, but she was support staff only, not a solicitor; not a partner. Also, as she hadn't spent the proceeds of the mortgages, and as MLC had agreed to pay all interest and charges due, the banks would be repaid in full and the property owners wouldn't be out of pocket either. MLC would get a rap on the knuckles from the Law Society – the firm would be required to pay a fine and a sum of money both for inconvenience and by way of apology to each of the fraud victims – but it would survive.

'I've spent enough time on my own,' I said. 'I need to come back full-time.' My need wasn't financial – I'd been on full pay. Though that was one of the reasons I was sure he'd agree to my request. After a token protest. 'And it'll be the Christmas break in a few weeks,' I added.

He shrugged. 'Give it a go, so,' he said.

'Thanks,' I said.

'Yes,' he said. 'Well, em, I suppose thanks can go both ways.'

'Ah now Gabriel, don't go all touchy-feely on me.'

'Hmmm, no danger,' he said. He smiled.

'Where's Dervla?' I asked. 'She wasn't on reception.'

'She's gone. Left.'

'Because of the murder? Or the fraud?'

'Neither,' Gabriel said. 'She told me she wanted a change. The day Mandy went missing, Dervla was at an interview. I arrived back from my weekend in Nice to a temp on reception that she'd arranged without so much as a by-your-leave, and a note in an envelope on my desk saying where she was. I wasn't pleased, I can tell you.'

'I'd noticed there was tension between you. Later on, I figured it was to do with Owen McCormack, with the affair, and all that – but there did seem to be something else as well.'

'Well, there you have it. I tried to persuade her to stay. Offered her more money but she'd made up her mind. After all these years, I couldn't believe it.'

'I'm sure you miss her,' I said.

'I don't have time for that, I'm afraid. There's a lot of mopping up to be done, and Ed wants us to handle Mandy's probate.'

'Really? I advised him to get separate representation.'

'He has a tax advisor, but decided to stay with us for the legal side. He's probably expecting a good deal on the fees. Which he'll get, of course.' Gabriel paused. 'I thought you might handle it, actually. There hasn't exactly been a queue of people wanting to deal with it. And unfortunately we need all the fees we can get. We've lost clients. Not too many: most have been very loyal. But some, including Mr McCormack, Mandy's former, em, paramour, well, he's decided to take his business elsewhere. There's quite a bit to be done on transferring those files, so again I thought maybe you might assist ...'

Straightaway, I said I'd do it. I was glad to be entrusted with the probate, to be able to finish things out and get closure. I was curious to see Ed too.

For the same reason. Obviously.

132

MANDY'S OFFICE WAS SHUT AS I WENT PAST, WITH a white rectangle on the cream-painted door where her nameplate had been. Tina had told me there was talk that it might be reconfigured as a communal workspace but no decision had been made yet. She was waiting for me in my room. She'd put flowers in a jam jar on a filing cabinet, cleared the surfaces of detritus, and straightened and wiped everything. She'd also placed a fresh barrister's notebook dead centre on the desk, topped by a new black Bic biro, lid on and unchewed.

My eyes blurred. Unable to speak, I brought the back of my hand to my mouth. She hugged me and said, 'I'll bring you a coffee with the post. About 10 a.m.?'

'Perfect,' I said, my eyes blurring again.

•

I pressed the button to start my computer and, while it booted up, opened the notebook and folded the cardboard cover back and underneath. Running my hand over the paper, crisp and smooth, I drew a test line with the black biro to check that it worked. It did. I took a deep breath and, without allowing myself to think too much about what I was going to say, picked up the desk phone and rang Ed to arrange an appointment for him to come into the office the following week. Then I went downstairs. Before I started work, there was someone I needed to apologise to. And I wasn't looking forward to it one teeny-tiny little bit.

133

HUGO WOULFE SHARED AN OFFICE WITH TWO
other junior solicitors – he'd received his parchment at the Law
Society's autumn ceremony – in an annex to the rear of the
second floor. He was on his own when I entered his room. His
hair was longer than it had been. Otherwise he looked the same.
He smiled broadly when he saw me. 'Welcome back,' he said.

Startled at the warmth of the greeting, it took me a while to
mutter, 'Thanks.' Then I said, 'I came here to apologise. For that
night. For calling up to your house. I shouldn't have, and—'

'Stop,' he said. 'You were right to ask those questions. Though
maybe not then, or in that way, admittedly. And you were right
about Mandy. She was having an affair, I just didn't know. What
matters is that you found her murderer. For that, I'll be forever
grateful.'

'That's very gracious of you. I appreciate the kind words.'

'I feel a "but" coming on,' Hugo Woulfe said.

I laughed. 'Not so much a "but" as a, do you mind telling
me what was the nature of the relationship between you and
Mandy?'

'She was my boss. She became my dear friend. I had a lot
of … family problems. My father didn't … doesn't approve

of me, and Mandy helped me understand that it didn't matter. Now that I'm qualified, I'm moving out of home to my own place and ...'

'That's good news,' I said.

'I'm gay, you see – that's the reason, one of the reasons, my dad doesn't like me.'

'I didn't know,' I said. 'I'm so sorry your dad isn't supportive.'

'It's okay. It really is. For a while, only Mandy knew. Now everyone does and no one gives a shit. Which is the best thing of all.'

'I'm sure it is,' I said. 'It's so sad about Mandy, though.'

'Yes. I'm glad she had some happiness before she died. With Owen, I mean. I never liked Ed.'

'No?'

'No. Actually I had him picked out as the murderer.'

'But he had the perfect alibi,' I said.

He laughed, 'So I heard.' He added, 'Ed and Kathleen were tight.'

'She told me they were a team,' I said.

'He was forever on the phone to her.'

'Was he?'

'It kind of annoyed me, but it wasn't as if there could've been anything going on between them.'

•

Back upstairs in my office, my mind drifted over everything – Mandy and Kathleen and Ed and the girls, and Owen McCormack, and the McInerneys and the family they'd left behind, and Billy Manning and Davy and me. The one person left in an incontestably better position after it all was Ed. Mandy had been about to leave him, and he would have received a good settlement in the divorce, but now he had everything. He still had the best motive for murdering Mandy, though he didn't do it of course. Kathleen did.

It came to me that I might have been wrong about her. That she hadn't done it out of hatred for Mandy, but out of love for Ed. I wondered if he'd had an inkling. If, perhaps, he'd suspected all along. But, whether it was for love or for hate, it didn't matter. The end result was the same and there was nothing more to be done. Unless there was.

EIGHT
DAYS
LATER

134

EVERYTHING I DID REMINDED ME OF THAT morning in September. The fast run downstairs. The glance round the door of the client waiting area. The sight of Ed. Though this time he was dressed differently, in a chunky knit cream wool polo and faded denim jeans. There was one other change – he looked happy.

I took him into one of the small meeting rooms off reception, and we went through the usual dance of sociability and mutual sympathy. Briefly. Because Ed wanted to get down to business. More specifically, he wanted my help in figuring out exactly how rich he was. The short answer? Very. The long answer involved me taking him through the Schedule of Assets line by line, pointing to the approximate policy and share valuations, and the date-of-death account balances I'd managed to obtain from the various institutions during the week or so since my return to work.

But it had been the other information – the details Sadie had provided – that had interested me the most.

Towards the end of the consultation, I got Ed to sign the client contract and a number of forms and authorisations, watching as he scribbled illegibly on the documents I passed to him.

'It's a good job you weren't the one forging all those signatures,' I said.

His hand stalled for a second, then started again. After signing the final document, he looked up at me with studied confusion. 'What?'

'Bad joke,' I said. 'I was referring to Kathleen – the mortgage fraud. Sorry.'

'I forgive you,' he said. 'Thousands wouldn't.' There was a steely sharpness to his voice. I smiled as if I hadn't noticed. 'So, are we done?' he asked.

'For today. I've a few more things to get, and then I'll get you back in to sign the probate papers before I lodge them.'

'Will that be before Christmas?'

'All going well, it will,' I said.

'Good. I'm taking the girls to the Caribbean for the holidays. Do a bit of sailing. None of us wanted to be at home. You know the way.'

'How are they doing?'

'They're sad for now, but they'll bounce back,' Ed said. I let that comment hang. 'Not for ages, obviously,' he said quickly. 'But time heals.'

'So they say,' I said.

'All we can do is hope.'

'Yes. For sure. You know, Ed, there's one thing that's been bothering me.'

'Really?'

'It's the house where Mandy died.'

'I've never been there,' he said. 'I don't think I ever—'

'I have. It's horrible.'

'I'm sure it is,' Ed said.

'How did Mandy end up going there?'

'*That's* what's been bothering you?'

'That's the thing,' I said.

'I suppose we'll never know, but I assume she must have arranged it with Kathleen.'

'How?'

'By phone? Or maybe in person? They did work together, after all.'

The landline rang and I answered it. Then I hung up. 'It's funny,' I said. 'Everything today has been reminding me of the morning Mandy went missing. And that's another thing, there now.'

'What are you talking about?'

'Did you ever contact Conleth Young, that criminal solicitor I recommended?'

'Of course not,' Ed said. 'Why would I?'

'It's what I was just saying. Everything's so like that Monday morning.'

'What are you telling me?'

'Because that was Detective Garda Sadie O'Riordan. She's at reception. It seems that she'd like you to present yourself at Coughlan's Quay garda station. Just like the Monday when Mandy was found dead. Only this time, if you don't go voluntarily, she and her colleagues will be arresting you.'

Ed leapt to his feet. 'This is disgusting. I'll be complaining about this at the very highest level.'

I scrawled a phone number on a piece of paper and held it out to him. 'You tell 'em, Ed. But be sure and call that solicitor before you say anything at all.'

He tore the note from my hand and left the room in a squall of outrage, slamming the door behind him.

135

IT'S THE SMALL THINGS THAT TRIP YOU UP; THE things you don't realise are things until it's too late and the future you've planned is in ruins. Things like the phone records I'd asked Sadie to check.

Ed and Kathleen had been careful all along. And they were extra careful after the McInerneys appeared on the scene. Stopped using their own phones. There would be no record of contact between them after that fateful phone call from Wales on the Friday afternoon. They'd had three, four, five calls a day up to that point. One short call from Kathleen's mobile to Ed's in the immediate aftermath. Then nothing. Zip. Zero.

They switched to burners straightaway. Which was a good idea.

Except the phone Kathleen was using – needs must – was the one she used for the property scam. The number Ricky Dempsey rang about valuations; the one the banks used to talk to 'Mandy' about mortgage drawdowns. During business hours. Monday to Friday. Never used at the weekends. At all. Switched off. Untraceable.

Until that weekend. Then it showed up in all kinds of places. B&Q. Harvey Norman. Kathleen's house. And Glasheen. Not a surprise. Because that's where Kathleen was too. For an hour or so before she killed Mandy, and made her escape via the back gate of 'Alysson' onto an unsurveilled section of Magazine Road, where she'd parked her Land Rover, still taxed and insured if anyone cared to check. And after her suicide, the guards did.

Not that it mattered. They weren't looking for anyone else in connection with the murder. Not initially. Once they started looking, they found Ed. Or, rather, an unrecognised number that Kathleen's mortgage phone rang fifty-seven times that weekend, having never called it before. A burner phone, located for the entirety of that weekend in the vicinity of Blackrock Village and Castle Road and Mahon Point Shopping Centre, across the road from B&Q, and the surrounding area.

Then nothing. Both phones went dead, along with Mandy's affair phone, which Ed had surreptitiously removed from her rucksack before she'd gone to meet Kathleen in Glasheen. Gone because she'd been asked to go. By Ed. Who'd said that Kathleen had phoned, looking for her. That she needed to meet Mandy near where she had her Saturday carer job. That it was important. And that she didn't have her mobile with her. That it had been stolen. That she'd been mugged. Or something worse. Something serious. A ruse that ensured Mandy went without attempting to call Kathleen first or along the way.

Owen McCormack had mentioned that Mandy had been worried, though he'd known only that it was related to a work issue. The work issue was Kathleen: Mandy had spoken to Patricia Dillane about her some weeks before the murder, about the drop-off in the quality of Kathleen's performance; the forgetfulness; the financial pressure that had forced her to take a weekend job – though Patricia hadn't known where that was, and maybe Mandy hadn't known exactly either until the final night of her life. All of which ensured that Mandy went to her death in Glasheen without a second thought.

It's the small things that trip you up.

Like Ed's satnav records from the night he'd driven Kathleen home from Cork after she'd dropped my Golf back near my house while I was locked in the barn. Ed had been so clever. To get there, he drove his Volvo along winding back roads, far away from prying eyes and cameras. Didn't drive up to Kathleen's house. Dropped her near the end of the lane. The car engine I'd heard in the distance before her return. He'd forgotten all about the satnav he'd used to find his way there. But the satnav had remembered, and it was damning.

•

There'd be other small things too in the months to come that would copperfasten Ed's conviction. Because the McInerneys, in forcing the last-minute change of plan, had ruined everything.

Though not as much as Ed had. In giving himself that cast-iron sexual alibi, he'd upset Kathleen. Oh, he'd make it up to her, he'd promised, and it was all for them, she knew that. But she started making mistakes. Didn't burn quite everything, like they'd discussed. Like the pile of papers on the chair in the kitchen that I'd knocked over.

Or the Valentine's card – still in its envelope, a message written in block capitals on the inside: 'WITH LOVE FROM YOUR VERY OWN E' – in the drawer of Kathleen's nightstand, which wasn't incriminating in any way. Except that it had been touched by Ed's very own fingers – a little sweaty always – and licked with Ed's very own saliva.

She'd kept the list too. The one Ed had written for her of the equipment she needed to buy, neatly rolled up with the elastic-bound wad of notes he'd given her. The money she'd used for the industrial-quality plastic packaging. And the large wheelbarrow she'd used to transport the McInerneys from the house to the barn. And the new chest freezer. And the tins of paint. And the latex gloves. And the cutting equipment ('just in case', Ed had written). And all the rest. So generous Ed had been in stumping up for supplies, that Kathleen had had nearly €1,000 left over. Safe in the inside pocket of her sensible M&S handbag.

I didn't know all of that then, when Ed came into the office. Most of it I found out gradually from Sadie over the next while, the full details only at the trial. After my meeting with Ed that day, I returned to my room and sat with my thoughts in the slow, quiet afternoon.

I thought about Ava and Ruth. With Ed having caused Mandy's death, he could no longer inherit from her and so, under their mother's will, their aunt Debbie and uncle Jonathan would become their trustees and guardians, and the girls would inherit the vast majority of Mandy's assets. But only half of the house – under the law as it currently stood, as the surviving joint tenant, Ed would keep his share. What would happen to the house, whether it would be sold or rented out, or boarded up until his release, or whether the girls would pursue a civil case for the wrongful death of their mother against him, was unclear as yet. It wasn't right – and the girls would have to move in with Debbie at her home in Ballinlough – but maybe getting away from Castle Road and Blackrock was the least worst option for them for now.

I thought about all the other things too; the small and ordinary things and the terrible things that had happened in the long months since that warm summer night. And all the while, outside my attic window, the grey gulls wheeled and cried against the pewter sky.

ACKNOWLEDGEMENTS

Cruel Deeds is out in the world as a result of the wisdom and kindness of a lot of people. I'd especially like to thank everyone at LBA Books, in particular my agent Luigi Bonomi, and Alison Bonomi, Amanda Preston and Hannah Schofield; and all at Hachette Ireland (and Hodder and Stoughton) in particular Joanna Smyth, my copy-editor Susan Feldstein, proofreader Aonghus Meaney and, most of all, my editor Ciara Doorley; and Alan Kirwan (banker and cousin), Catherine Ryan Howard (bestselling author/crime-writing savant), Casey King (star consultant on garda procedure), Chris Evans (whose brilliant research I stole and gave to Megan), Claire Connolly, Dave McCarthy (Practice Evolve case management guru), Fin Flynn, Marguerite Phillips, Miriam O'Brien, Nick Daly, Paul O'Donovan, Rachel O'Toole, Siobhan Lankford, and Tadhg Coakley who advised or assisted or corrected or read or soothed or suggested at crucial moments. All and any errors remaining in the text are my own and may have been put there to serve the story, which is, of course, entirely fictional.

I ask my friends and relatives and everyone who has helped me in my writing life thus far, including Kieran O'Connor who took my author photograph and designed beautiful book-related paraphernalia for me, to please accept this as a full repeat of the acknowledgments and thank yous in *Darkest Truth* — since it was published in 2019, the love and support you've given me has been even more extraordinary. Thanks especially to you, dear reader, and extra thanks if you take the time to write an online review; to feature-writers and radio folk; to reviewers and book bloggers; to book club members, many of whom I've had the pleasure of meeting; to libraries and librarians especially Cork County Library and Arts Service and branches (including Midleton, Newmarket, Clonakilty and Bandon) and Cork City Library and branches (including Ballyphehane), and in particular to Patricia Looney and Ann Riordan, and all the One City One Book team; to my friends and colleagues in Finbarr Murphy Solicitors and throughout the legal community in Cork and beyond; to booksellers and bookshops (a special mention for Waterstones Cork, for their endless support and for giving me my own window!); to literary festivals and event organisers – including Murder One, Fiction at the Friary, Cork World Book Festival, West Cork Literary Festival, Kinsale 'Words by Water', Waterford Writers Weekend, UCC School of English, and Dromineer Nenagh Literary Festival – who've invited me to read; and to the wonderful and inspiring company of writers who have been so welcoming and generous to me: I look forward to meeting and thanking each and every one of you in real life.

Last but not least, there's my family, and these acknowledgements have been extra hard to write because Daddy – Michael Kirwan, who couldn't be kept away from the launch of *Darkest Truth* despite being very unwell at the time – isn't with us for the publication of *Cruel Deeds*. We miss him so much. My eternal gratitude and love, as ever, go to him, to my mother Breda, to my nieces and nephew, Elizabeth, Molly and Michael, to Nicola and Rob; and to my sister and brother, Marcia and Neil, to whom the book is dedicated.